NO LONGER PROPERTY OF SEATTLE PUBLIC LIBRARY

RECEIVED

AUG 26 2021

BROADVIEW LIBRARY

Praise for *An Uncommon Woman*

"Intense, evocative, and laced with intricate historical details that bring the past to life, *An Uncommon Woman* will transport you to the picturesque and dangerous western Virginia mountains of 1770."

Interviews and Reviews

"Frantz captures the challenges of life on the frontier in this skillful inspirational romance."

Publishers Weekly

"Frantz shows why she is one of the elite authors of historical fiction during the pre–Revolutionary War time period!"

Write-Read-Life

"Laura Frantz writes in a way that intoxicates her readers and leaves them with a desire for more."

Urban Lit Magazine

"In *An Uncommon Woman*, author Laura Frantz transports readers to a setting she has mastered, the eighteenth-century mountain frontier. Sensory-rich descriptions bring the landscape to life. Traverse perilous forest trails, shelter with raw relief in the rough but welcoming environs of a fort, experience the tension of an isolated homestead that might stand peaceful today but lie in smoking ruins tomorrow. Peopled with characters as resilient and compelling as the terrain they inhabit, *An Uncommon Woman* is an engaging story that had me up late turning pages."

Lori Benton, Christy Award–winning author

NO LONGER PROPERTY OF
SEATTLE PUBLIC LIBRARY

AUG 20 2021

Books by Laura Frantz

The Frontiersman's Daughter

Courting Morrow Little

The Colonel's Lady

The Mistress of Tall Acre

A Moonbow Night

The Lacemaker

A Bound Heart

An Uncommon Woman

Tidewater Bride

THE BALLANTYNE LEGACY

Love's Reckoning

Love's Awakening

Love's Fortune

TIDEWATER BRIDE

LAURA FRANTZ

Revell

a division of Baker Publishing Group
Grand Rapids, Michigan

© 2021 by Laura Frantz

Published by Revell
a division of Baker Publishing Group
PO Box 6287, Grand Rapids, MI 49516-6287
www.revellbooks.com

Printed in the United States of America

All rights reserved. No part of this publication may be reproduced, stored in a retrieval system, or transmitted in any form or by any means—for example, electronic, photocopy, recording—without the prior written permission of the publisher. The only exception is brief quotations in printed reviews.

Library of Congress Cataloging-in-Publication Data
Names: Frantz, Laura, author.
Title: Tidewater bride / Laura Frantz.
Description: Grand Rapids, Michigan: Revell, a division of Baker Publishing Group, [2021]
Identifiers: LCCN 2020018355 | ISBN 9780800734961 (paperback) | ISBN 9780800739669 (hardcover)
Subjects: GSAFD: Love stories.
Classification: LCC PS3606.R4226 T53 2021 | DDC 813/.6—dc23
LC record available at https://lccn.loc.gov/2020018355

Published in association with Books & Such Literary Agency, 52 Mission Circle, Suite 122, PMB 170, Santa Rosa CA 94509-7953, www.booksandsuch.com.

Scripture used in this book, whether quoted or paraphrased by the characters, is taken from the King James Version of the Bible.

This book is a work of fiction. Names, characters, places, and incidents are the product of the author's imagination or are used fictitiously. Any resemblance to actual events, locales, or persons, living or dead, is coincidental.

21 22 23 24 25 26 27   7 6 5 4 3 2 1

To the true Pocahontas and her people

1

James Towne, Virginia Colony
Spring 1634

Alas, she was not a tobacco bride, but she had been given charge of them. A daunting task for a young woman of six and twenty, even if she was the cape merchant's daughter. All winter, reams of glowing recommendations for these fair English maids had piled like a snowdrift atop her father's burgeoning desk, their names sifting through her conscience like icy flakes.

Jane Rickard. Mary Gibbs. Jane Harmer. Audrey Hoare. Jane MacIntosh. Margaret Boardman. Jane Jackson. Abigail Downing . . .

A shame there were so few Janes!

She smiled wryly as she stood near the crowded wharf, the list of tobacco brides clutched to her bodice to hold in whatever warmth could be had in Virginia's incessant coastal wind. Glad she was to be named Selah. Surely no other woman aboard the coming *Seaflower* could claim that.

All around her swirled the reek of salt water and fish, tobacco and tar. Noisy gulls flew overhead, screeching as if they, too, were welcoming the long-awaited ship. At first sighting a quarter of an hour before, the men of James Towne had been the first to gather, those long suffering souls enflamed through the wants of the comforts of marriage. Each groom would pay one hundred fifty pounds in good leaf tobacco for a bride, an extravagance denied many.

But first, the colony's officials assembled at the forefront of the welcome. Dressed in their Sabbath best, hair and beards freshly trimmed, some almost beyond recognition save Alexander Renick.

Xander, his intimate circle called him. Broad of shoulder. Terribly tall. Strikingly bearded. With the wrist of an able swordsman to boot. One of Virginia's "ancient planters" who was not so ancient but among the surviving few who'd landed first and defied death since the settlement's founding nearly thirty years before.

And now he was looking her way, amusement—or was it disdain?—in his gaze. A flush she tried to tamp down warmed her winter-pale face. She hadn't expected to see him today as the brides came in, widower though he was.

He gave a slightly mocking sweep of his hat. The sun played off his dark hair, worn loose about wide-set shoulders. "So, Mistress Hopewell, all is in good order, aye?"

"We shall see, Master Renick. Have you come for a bride?"

This time, he turned swarthy. At her boldness?

"If ever a fair maid deserved an industrious husband, 'twould be Alexander Renick, esquire." Her tone was as mocking as his exaggerated bow. "I can add you to the roll of eligible men . . ."

"Which no doubt exceeds the number of king's daughters aboard."

8

"True. There are never enough women here."

He ran a hand over his jaw. "Tell me, as I've been upriver, what will happen once they dock?"

Selah looked to her papers, though she knew the details by heart. "The women will be churched first, then lodged in married households and looked after till their choices of husbands are made."

"So, all of Virginia will go a-courting." He adjusted his hat in the rising wind. "In the hopes of keeping our men from forsaking the colony or taking heathen brides."

"Something like that," she murmured, stung by the poignant truth of his words. "Mattachanna is missed."

A pause. His eyes bore the intensity of a summer storm. Silvery as a newly minted coin one minute, then brilliantly blue as the Chesapeake Bay the next. They'd not spoken of the tragedy that befell him till now. In fact, they rarely spoke at all. "You call her by her Indian name. Not Lady Rebecca."

"An English name does not make one an Englishwoman," Selah replied. "Mattachanna was a Powhatan princess, and I can call her nothing else."

He cast her a last, piercing look. She expected no reply. That telltale hardness of his bearded jaw, the dare-not-trespass edge that defined him, was full blown now, hedging her out, marking a line she dared not cross.

With a low farewell, he took a step back. "I'm off to Rose-n-Vale."

"You won't stay for the—" Flummoxed, Selah left off. What *was* she to call the tobacco brides' arrival?

"The coming carnival?" With a shake of his head, Xander turned away, the edges of his dark cloak furling and unfurling like a sail in the wind.

Carnival, indeed. But truly, that was what the occasion felt like amid so many merry masculine voices and rollicking laughter. More men were amassing, gazes riveted to the tall-masted ship that had been home to the coming brides for three months or more.

"My best to Widow Brodie and those noble hounds of yours," she called after him, trying to dismiss the topsy-turvy feelings his scarce appearances always wrought. Regret foremost. Fascination a close second. Disdain a distant third.

Thankfully, the *Seaflower* proved a worthy distraction with so many women at the railing. A rumble went through the gawking men as they pressed forward like the tide with a great swell of anticipation. Pity lanced her. The New World had gone hard on them. They craved company. A comely apron. A full plate. Something beyond their narrow world of drudgery and hardship. She'd seen these men at their worst, knew their rare merits and many faults like the wares of the colony's storehouses, and, sadly, wouldn't give a farthing for most.

"Sister!" On the upraised deck, carrying over the ruffled water, came a familiar shout. Shay?

Her nettled spirits soared. How long her younger brother had been away, all because their father believed him bored with merchanting and in need of a different venture. He stood by Captain Kendall, looking cheerful if a tad thinner than when he'd left James Towne six months before. Salt pork and ship's biscuits did not suit him. How she'd missed his company.

He was first off the ship, running full tilt down the gangplank on unsteady sea legs through the crush of men. He finally reached her and nearly knocked her down, more from his rank smell than his embrace.

"Selah, at last!"

She held her breath as she clasped him, joy bubbling inside her. "You look none the worse for the voyage, Brother."

"Eight dead and twelve landed sick," he told her sorrowfully, looking about. "Where's Father?"

"On his way."

"And Mother? Is she well?"

"In her garden, aye." Where else would she be in spring?

"I'm ravenous and needs be off." With a gap-toothed grin he bolted, reminding her of Xander's departure in the same direction a quarter of an hour before. With a last look over his shoulder he shouted, "The stories I shall tell you!"

Smile fading, she returned to her list. Which poor women had perished, and which would be taken to the infirmary? Their own charge, a faceless if not nameless lass—Cecily Ward—might be among them. Already she felt she knew these women. So rigorous were the Virginia Colony requirements, only those young, handsome, and honestly educated need apply. The youngest was but sixteen, the eldest eight and twenty. As for their Cecily . . .

> *The daughter of a deceased gentleman, knows how to spin, sew, brew, bake, make cheese and butter, general huswifery, as well as being skilled in making bone lace.*

Selah returned her gaze to the women now turning away from the ship's rail to disembark. The trials and tribulations of being shipbound was telling, their expressions guarded, even grave as they faced whatever James Towne offered them. And James Towne, recently christened James

Cittie in a laughable bid to appear other than it was, boasted aplenty. Each bride would receive a parcel of land, something unheard of in England and that surely helped hasten them here. On the voyage they'd been given new clothes and white lambskin gloves. For those who craved sweets, prunes were purchased. All funded by English investors.

On this side of the Atlantic, Selah and her father were to oversee disbursing other promised goods now shelved in the James Towne store. Petticoats, aprons, two pairs of shoes, six pairs of sheets, and white caps, or coifs, that married women wore as a mark of distinction.

But first, the brides themselves.

Rose-n-Vale was part two-storied frame timber house, part Flemish bond brick, an odd melding of the old and the new, the rustic and genteel, but it was his and it was home. Several miles upriver from James Towne, Xander's "castle in the air," as Rose-n-Vale was called, was a haven for no other reason than it was away from the petty politics and ongoing squabbles of Virginia's largest settlement.

Surrounded by tobacco fields in various stages of cultivation, the sprawling, hard-won estate was a testament to how he spent his time. Beyond his far-flung borders his neighbor's fields lay fallow. Xander still felt the lack of his fellow planter and friend felled by the violence of 1632. On the other side of him lay Hopewell Hundred, equally idle, but owned by Ustis Hopewell, the cape merchant, another trusted friend. 'Twas rumored some of it was Selah Hopewell's dowry. But till she tamed her tongue and her temper, he doubted any man would claim it, or her.

Xander entered through the riverfront door and removed his hat. He sent it sailing toward a table near the stairwell, where it landed with a soft thud, nearly toppling the vase of flowers his housekeeping aunt had placed there. With a wince, he righted the skewed arrangement before entering his study, easily the most used room in the house.

"Alexander?" A feminine voice carried from a side door.

"Aunt, are you well?" She'd had a headache when he'd left for James Towne. The Virginia climate did not suit her Scottish sensibilities.

"Fully restored, Nephew." She smiled, drying her hands on her apron. A touch of flour whitened her wrinkled cheek. "I've just finished the sennight's bread baking. But I'm hungrier for news of the tobacco brides."

Starved for feminine company, likely. He rounded his desk, eyeing the tardy ledgers and mounting correspondence. "The *Seaflower* was almost in when I left town."

Her eyes rounded. "You did not stay to see all the maids land?"

"Nay." Clearly this was a trespass of the highest order. "If I'd known you were interested, I would have delayed my leaving. I spoke first with Mistress Hopewell—"

"Selah?"

"Aye. She told me the women were to be put up in married households, and then the courting would commence." He cast about for more details, the disappointment in his aunt's expression making him dig deeper when he'd all but forgotten the matter. "There were a good many eager fellows on hand to greet these would-be brides."

"But not you, sadly."

"My mind is more on plantation matters."

"Understandably, after so long a winter. Will we be dining alone again this evening?"

Again. The simple question sagged with dismay. Alone. Adrift. With no bridal prospects in sight. "Aye, but tomorrow we're invited to the Hopewells', in fact." He turned toward the mantel, where his pipe collection rested, a far more attractive sight than desk work. "I had business with Ustis Hopewell at the last, and he extended the invitation. How about you accompany me? Rest from your labors."

"Oh, a splendid plan! When shall we leave?"

He paused, picking up an English clay pipe with a pinwheel maker's mark on the heel. "Half past five, mayhap? By shallop, not overland, if the river's becalmed."

"I'll be ready. Perhaps a bowl of early strawberries would be welcome. Selah spoke of deer ravaging theirs last I saw her."

"Strawberries, aye. I believe the Hopewells are to host a tobacco bride. You'll be among the first to meet her, whoever she is."

This had the intended effect. She clasped her hands together with childish delight. With that, she left him, returning to the kitchen to do whatever aging aunts did, leaving him to pinpoint exactly why he hadn't stayed longer at the docks.

Because he was a widower of two years.

Nay, most men remarried within weeks.

Because the wind was cold.

Nay, the wind was the warmest he'd felt since last autumn.

Because he disliked James Towne.

True enough, aye. But more so because the one woman who unsettled him so oft of late had such mesmerizing eyes . . .

2

"Daughter, we are to have company, your father tells me. Can you pick some posies from the garden?" Candace Hopewell's gaze swung from Selah to their housemaid. "Izella, set two more places at table, please."

As Izella disappeared into the dining room, Selah turned toward her mother, pulled from her preoccupation with the tobacco brides. "Two, you say?"

"Master Renick and his aunt, Widow Brodie, likely. You know how fond she is of company. 'Tis been hard on her leaving Scotland for a more rusticated life here."

"Why this unusual supper invitation?"

"Business." Candace opened the bake oven and released the aroma of wheaten bread.

Business. What else could it be? Selah's orderly train of thought took a tumble as she passed out a side door to do her mother's bidding. Xander Renick's preoccupation—*obsession*—with business trumped everything and made him guilty in her eyes of more than one mercenary charge. Yet her father favored him. And Xander oft sought her father's counsel, an honor bestowed to precious few in fractious James Towne.

As always, the garden's earthy scent cleared her kitchen-sated senses. Sadly, the soil was not fully awake and there would be no armful of summer's best. Walking the crushed shell paths, she perused April's timid offerings. Golden ragwort and fleabane and dwarf irises alongside an abundance of greenery. June's bounty only beckoned.

Yet her mind was not on blooms but on the fine points of Master Renick's company. Did this mean he had come out of mourning at long last? Selah picked several shooting stars fit for their table and buried her face in the mostly scentless blooms.

Perhaps he'd reconsidered taking a tobacco bride. Or her father had persuaded him. Lord knew Rose-n-Vale needed a mistress. Raising her gaze, Selah focused on the bedchamber window of Cecily Ward. Might Cecily suit? For all she knew, matrimony might be the matter her mother had mentioned.

An interesting assemblage graced their supper table. Ustis presided with his usual good humor and candor, thus talk was never dull. Even though he'd been a bit wan of late, slowly recovering from a severe winter's cold, the malady hadn't dimmed his spirits. And with so many hands in the kitchen, the table boasted early English peas and new potatoes, mounded into their best stoneware bowls. Shay, also in fine fettle, regaled them with tales of whale sightings and the *Seaflower* being pursued by a Spanish galleon till they'd outrun the enemy on a favorable wind.

If not for company, Selah would have stayed riveted,

rooted to her place in their oak-paneled dining room amid the gentle flicker of candlelight. But tonight, with the click of utensils scraping pewter plates and the men's tankards being refilled with ale, she and her mother and Izella wove in and out, finally serving dessert, a custard sweetened with West Indies cane sugar and crowned with candied lemon peel and the strawberries Xander's aunt had brought. Such a delicacy raised Cecily's russet brows.

"For our guests." Candace smiled as Izella served them. "Especially for Cecily Ward as we welcome her to Virginia."

Clearly enjoying being the center of attention, Cecily sampled a spoonful and pronounced it sublime. "I'd never thought to taste such a wonder in the New World."

Her pretty speech only added to her comely appearance. Red-haired and jade-eyed, she looked more Scots than English, a mystery soon solved.

"My mother, God rest her, was from the Highlands. She never lost her Scots speech even after marrying my father and making her home in England." Her gaze traveled round the table in turn as if assessing each of them before resting on Xander. "I heard there were Scotsmen aplenty among the colonists here."

"Mostly indentures. A few poor gentlemen, tradesmen, serving men, libertines . . ." Ustis sent a droll look Xander's way. "Ten times more fit to spoil a commonwealth than begin one, so said our infamous founder, John Smith."

All laughed, and Xander leaned back in his chair. He smiled in that maddening, almost apologetic way, which Selah noted with a beat of exasperation. "I am but a humble Scot, Miss Ward. The son of a silversmith from Culross in the kingdom of Fife."

Humble Scot, indeed. Most men would boast of being a burgess and council member, tribal negotiator and foremost landowner in Tidewater Virginia . . . if not ruthless tobacco lord.

Cecily already seemed smitten as she slid another coquettish glance Xander's way. Selah tensed. Should she warn her? Xander looked down at his tankard, his neatly trimmed beard hardly masking his swarthy hue.

"The Scots part is true, but don't believe the 'humble' part." Shay grinned, spoon aloft. "He'll own all of Virginia one day, some say. Makes the gentry of James Towne squirm."

Reaching out, Xander rubbed his knuckles across Shay's sunburnt scalp affectionately, earning a wince and a chuckle.

"Harrow!" Shay exclaimed, asking for seconds in the same breath.

"Shush, Shay," Candace scolded gently. "Your tongue is too loose!"

Smiling, Izella served him the last of the custard as talk turned to settlement matters.

"What's this I hear about you burgesses wanting to carve all of Virginia into pieces?" Ustis questioned. "And appoint a sheriff of James Towne?"

"There's truth to it, aye." Xander set down his tankard. "Virginia is to be divided into eight shires."

"*Shires?*" Ustis lay his napkin aside. "Betimes I regret stepping down from the governor's council. Sorting fact from fiction is quite tiring but for your confirmation."

"I advocate for counties, not shires, as do most settlers coming into Virginia who want to handle matters differently than England. Five thousand strong to date, most at odds with English custom." Xander looked to Selah, brow raised. "Rather, five thousand fifty-seven, aye?"

She smiled, surprised he'd kept tally. "And once the brides marry and the begats begin, a great many more."

"Daughter!" Candace flushed like a schoolgirl as Xander gave a low, roguish laugh. "No such talk in the presence of company."

"She is only speaking truth, God be praised. 'Tis no secret these brides were sent for to increase the populace." Ustis sent a nod Selah's way. "A far cry from the hundred or so poor fools who first set foot on our shore, most of them men."

"I've had many a fear we'd become like the lost souls of Roanoke Island." Widow Brodie gave a noticeable shudder. "God rest them."

A sorrowful hush descended till Xander said, "We still hear secondhand reports of Roanoke survivors living among the interior tribes."

"One can only hope." Candace raised a Delft blue cup to her lips. "A great many people vanished without a trace. How can that be?"

Selah looked at Cecily, wanting to protect her from such dire talk. But truly, much of life in Virginia was still an ongoing fight for survival, thus anything other than the utmost honesty seemed misleading.

"We've made it through the terrible starving time, the lengthy droughts, and all sorts of Indian unrest. For that we can be thankful." Ustis stood, praising the meal before withdrawing to his study with Xander.

When Shay excused himself to reunite with friends down the lane, the four women remained at table, sipping their beverages and talking of daintier matters as the candles sank lower in their holders. Now and then Selah's attention strayed to the study, where wisps of pipe smoke surrounded the conversing men like Scottish wraiths.

Raising a hand, Cecily suppressed a yawn, which didn't escape Candace's attention. "You must be exhausted, my dear."

"On the contrary." Cecily looked considerably fresher than she did upon her arrival. "The hot bath you insisted upon and a nap this afternoon has quite revived me, not to mention this fine elderberry tonic."

"I suppose the courting commences as soon as you've rested." Widow Brodie's eyes lit with interest. "We all await to see which gentleman you fondly bestow yourself upon."

Selah smiled, her prayers for felicitous matches unending. "Tomorrow shall prove interesting once formalities are finished and matchmaking begins in earnest."

"Indeed. But why is it with so few women here"—Cecily all but pointed a finger at Selah—"*you* remain unwed?"

"Why, indeed," Selah replied, draining her cup only to have it refilled by Izella. "I am too preoccupied with storekeeping to settle by some hearth with bantlings about me."

"Bantlings are needed more than merchanting," Candace said quickly. "'Tis not for the want of offers our daughter remains cloistered behind the counter."

Feeling the start of a scold, Selah made light of such. "Never mind me. Any woman on two stumps is considered a catch and has offers aplenty."

"You are a modest miss," Cecily replied. "Tell me, for I fear a false start, who is the settlement's foremost bachelor?"

A sudden hush.

Widow Brodie smiled a tad smugly. "You need only look to the study for your answer."

Cecily's expression turned conspiratorial as her voice faded to a whisper. "No man I've seen since making landfall I deem your nephew's equal. But tell me, why was Master Renick not amongst the throng of eager men at the docks? Is he above taking a tobacco bride?"

Widow Brodie pursed her lips as if pondering her reply. As blood kin and housekeeper and aware of his many habits, she knew best. "Alexander is a man of singular intentions. His days are a blur of tobacco cultivation, and his horribly ill-bred greyhounds—"

"I adore dogs!" Cecily replied with equal vehemence. "The fawn-colored greyhounds especially."

"His are but red and black, though he jests about sending to England for the coloring you describe." Her aging face collapsed into fiercer wrinkles. "I do not share your fondness for canines, but a finer man you'll not find on Virginia soil."

Cecily leaned forward. "Tell me more."

Candace eyed the study as Ustis and Xander passed into the adjoining parlor. "You see, when our men first came to James Towne, most were genteel English, unaccustomed to laboring and hardship. That sort soon foundered. But Master Renick is cut of a different cloth. He simply rolled up his sleeves and got to work, fearing no Indian or wild animal or anything else. After many trials, he cultivated seed from the West Indies, a milder, sweeter tobacco than what had come before. We carry it in our store, though most is shipped to England to fetch the best price."

"Surely there is more to the man than his tobacco."

Precious little, Selah thought, breathing in the fragrant pipe smoke.

Widow Brodie sighed as a burst of masculine laughter issued from the adjoining chamber. "He has a young son—"

"A son?" Cecily's countenance clouded.

"He is a widower like so many." Widow Brodie's tone turned mournful. "We all grieve the loss of Mattachanna—"

"Matta—an *Indian*?" Cecily's eyes narrowed. "How is it that a man of his supposed standing took such a bride? Are not these natives as the newspapers describe? A rude, barbarous, naked people who worship the devil?"

At that very moment Xander's gaze pivoted to them from where he stood by the hearth. Had Cecily's voice carried?

Candace put a finger to her lips. "Lady Rebecca was her Christian name, God rest her. She was a believing Anglican, baptized in the faith, second to none with her catechism, schooled by Reverend Criswel himself before her marriage."

This passionate defense was met with scandalized silence.

Stemming a sigh, Selah steered the conversation to safer shores. "Master Renick is but one of many eligible men. But in truth, our recommendations may not dovetail with your affections."

Curling her nose, Cecily took a fan from her pocket and stirred the smoky air. "I shall proceed with due caution. Glad I am we brides may court at our leisure, though I shan't impose on your hospitality overlong."

"Marry in haste, repent at leisure," Widow Brodie cautioned. "I've often pondered marrying again, but at my advanced age . . ."

"You've not one foot in the grave," Candace told her. "Though Rose-n-Vale would be loath to lose you."

"Alexander is in need of a wife more than a housekeeper,"

Widow Brodie said. "Perhaps then he could remedy that sad situation of his in Scotland . . ."

Cecily nearly pounced on that slip, opening her mouth to inquire further, when Selah intervened. "Please, let us speak of other things."

Candace nodded. "Tomorrow Shay will give a tour of our humble town to all the tobacco brides, starting at the fort, or what is left of it, then the old church and current marketplace."

"What of the plantations so talked about outside of town? I should like to live inland or upriver, away from the coastal swamps and miasmas the ship's captain warned about. Be mistress of my own plantation." Cecily snapped her fan shut. "Besides, we brides were led to believe James *Cittie* was quite populous. A bit more refined than we have found it to be."

"There are some lovely vistas east of here that might suit your fancy," Selah said. 'Twas her dream, too, to flee town. She couldn't fault Cecily for that, yet she did not care for the ambitious glint in her eye. Was she a schemer? A shrew? Looking to her aproned lap, Selah put down the ungracious thought. "There's many a man in need of a wife at Bermuda Hundred, the plantation at the falls of the James upriver. A picturesque spot."

"Nearer the Naturals?"

"Aye, but we have come through a second war and are trying to keep peace."

A very tenuous peace, Selah did not add. Many of their friends and neighbors had been killed in the Indian wars. How they themselves had survived the last conflict was nothing short of a miracle. The Powhatans were a powerful people, unwilling to be a conquered nation or be Christianized. If not for Xander and the few men like him whose continual over-tures to honor and keep peace . . .

"I feel a bit wilted." Cecily yawned again, this time more openly.

But the men showed no signs of weariness as the conversation continued robustly. Selah stifled her own yawn and helped Izella clear away the empty cups and dishes.

"To bed with you." Candace spoke briskly when Cecily drifted toward the parlor. "In the morning we'll have mush and mulberry syrup at first light."

3

Of all the seasons in this New World, spring was Xander's favorite. Virginia even trumped Scotland in his recollections. He recalled his childhood with dimming clarity. The mists and woodland bluebells, the stretches of light as the land embraced the sun after a long winter, the deep lochs and windswept coasts. He closed his eyes, grasping for details denied him. So much had slipped in and muddied the memories since he'd landed on Virginia shores as a lad. His own Scots speech seemed muted too.

This day, as he stood on his own ground, his thoughts were pressed full as a hogshead of tobacco with a great many unsavory things. Tobacco flea beetles. A barn roof riddled with hailstones from the latest tempest. Spoiled seedbeds. Ailing indentures down with the seasoning. Recently appointed, unscrupulous tobacco inspectors.

"True Word!"

His eyes opened at the sound of a youthful voice hailing him by his Powhatan name.

"Wingapo!" Xander called out the customary greeting as the lad emerged over the brow of the hill scored with green fronds of transplanted tobacco and the noonday sun. He'd not seen Meihtawk in a month or more. But whenever he did, he was struck by Meihtawk's similarity to Mattachanna. Same bone structure and wide-set eyes. Same handsome Mattaponi bearing and warmth of expression. Though they were cousins, the resemblance was remarkable.

"I bring news," Meihtawk said in English, clearly coming in his role as tribal courier.

At once came the clutch of concern. It seemed all of Virginia braced for another onslaught of terror after a recent tentative peace. Xander leaned his hoe against a stump and gave Meihtawk his full attention, including his leather flask.

Swallowing a drink of well water, Meihtawk looked him in the eye. "Chief Opechancanough asks that you come and kindle a council fire at Menmend, where he hardly has room enough to spread his blanket."

So, the invitation came with a complaint. Yet the complaint was a valid one. The Powhatan Confederacy, made up of many tribes including the Mattaponi, continued to lose beloved ground, their villages thrust farther west year by year, their once vast territory shrinking before their very eyes. Frustration formed a tight knot in Xander's chest, eased only slightly by Meihtawk's obliging manner. It was he who had saved so many colonists in the latest hostilities, warning them of the last planned attack.

Xander nodded. "Tell Opechancanough that I have heard his request and will come. But I will need time to prepare. If all goes well, I will meet you in six sleeps at Monacan Fields when the sun is three fingers high."

At this, Meihtawk's face lit with undisguised gratitude. His was a hard task as emissary. Yet surely he knew Xander

26

would not refuse the invitation. Though Xander was continually torn between his loyalties to the English and his ties to the Naturals, the Naturals oft gained his allegiance and the upper hand.

With a farewell, Meihtawk disappeared over the hill, a few indentures watching his going.

Xander drew a linen sleeve across his sweat-spackled upper lip, returning to his hoeing. Field hands spread out on all sides of him as far as the eye could see. His goal at first light had been five hundred tobacco hills by dusk. Orinoco was a laborious crop, robbing the soil and depleting the workers along with it. His attempts to be versatile, to cultivate other exportable crops, were unending.

At suppertime, he sat down at his own table, heaping his plate full of pickled herring and bread. He ate slowly, thoughts full of another table, the fine feast they'd had at the Hopewells' a sennight before. Tomorrow he'd return, not to dine but to buy. And he'd go early to avoid the usual bustle.

Supper done, he made a move to retire to his study and the quiet to be had beyond the clatter of his aunt cleaning up. Her question caught him at the door.

"Did I hear you say you were going to James Towne on the morrow, Alexander?"

He turned around. "Aye. Are you in need of something?"

A decisive bob of her capped head. "A Border ware jug, if you please. I tripped over Ruby and broke one. And any gossip that can be had about the tobacco brides and their courting."

"Thankfully, the latter is as easily gotten," he replied. "Consider it done."

"Thank you, Nephew," she said over her shoulder as they went their separate ways.

Once ensconced in his study, his greyhounds near the hearth, he pondered a pipe. Ruby looked up at him moodily as his gaze swept the planked floor where she lay in all her gangling splendor.

"You're a beauty, girl. Don't let Aunt Henrietta tell you differently." He stooped to scratch her velvety head, her reddish coat agleam in the fading light. "As for you, Sir Jett, as noble a creature that ever lived, I believe you shall accompany me to visit Chief Opechancanough. His continued awe of you may serve me well."

Ruby's black companion gave a deep, resounding bark, eyes alive with the excitement of hearing his master's voice. Only with difficulty did Jett finally lay his sleek head on an outstretched paw.

"And let us not forget Selah Hopewell's kind regard of you both. Surely that speaks to your canine character."

At once, Selah's comely liveliness at their shared supper leapt to mind. 'Twas usually Mattachanna's dusky face that stared back at him. Reaching for an elaborate brass tobacco tamper, Xander pressed last year's leaf into the pipe's bowl, tamping down the old, festering ache along with it. Once lit, he inhaled, wanting to banish the vision.

His latest leaf smoked pleasant, strong, and sweet. Consignment agents in England told him buyers were paying thrice what other crop masters made. Even the lowly outpost merchants were clamoring for more Rose-n-Vale hogsheads. 'Twas even rumored a thoroughfare in the town of his birth had been named after him. He shrugged off such ridiculousness as more fancy than fact.

He, a Scottish silversmith's son.

While Shay removed the merchant scales from their box to begin the day's business, Selah unpacked newly arrived crates from England holding coveted Chinese porcelain. These fragile goods she displayed in a front window to entice passersby. Such fine wares never lasted long. Obsessed with appearances, James Towne gentry were the first to storm in when a supply ship arrived. Since the tobacco brides' coming, the brass bell at their door seemed to jingle sunup to sundown.

Glad she was her father as cape merchant took care of accounts while she and Shay handled anything from axes and adzes to linen thread and glass buttons. Goods were arriving regularly now, her favorites from the exotic Indies. With each passing year their inventory grew. Once, James Towne was clad in rags but now boasted the finest imported cloth. Nor were there shelves enough for the wealth of fragrant spices from far ports alongside sweetmeats and culinary delicacies. Though life continued uncertain, at least they faced the future with their bellies full.

Humming a song learned at sea, Shay passed through an adjoining door to a side room where transactions were once made with visiting tribes. A new trading post had been established north of them along the Chickahominy Path, but the latest treaty forbade any cloth, cotton, or other goods be supplied to the Naturals. Though the walls of old James Fort had come down—literally fallen into disrepair and used for firewood in years past—the invisible barriers between Naturals and English still stood stalwart and unsettling.

Some dared to bridge the distance. Those with the mettle of Xander Renick.

As she thought it, the front door's bell sang out. Though it was early, with light barely peeping over the eastern horizon and illuminating their counter, he was their first customer. Beyond the open door stood his saddle horse, a handsome black. She wondered its name. She knew its reputation. Gotten from Massachusetts, this hardy breed was said to pace a mile in under two minutes, oft traveling upwards of eighty miles in a single day.

"Good day to you, Mistress Hopewell." He removed his dark felt hat, his gaze canted toward her. Or was it the wares she'd recently shelved behind her?

For a second he hovered on the threshold, sunlight framing him. Though he'd come through their door countless times, he still managed to make a lasting impression. Blame it on his unusual mode of dress, she guessed. A long linen shirt absent of the ruffles so popular with more foppish men draped his upper body, his lower clad in buckskin breeches, his long legs encased in black leather boots. He'd discarded his doublet, a style of dress she'd never liked, in favor of a looser weskit. Not the common dress of field hands but hardly that of a gentleman. His beard was trimmed, shadowing his jaw in neat angles, a hint of Scots red within.

"Good morning, Master Renick." She looked to the fragile item she held, nearly forgetting about it. "Are you in fine fettle this Wednesday morn?"

"Aye," he returned brusquely. "I've need of a quantity of trade goods. The better sort."

"I doubt you've come for these porcelain cups." She returned the last to the shelf as he recited what was needed.

"A large quantity of Venetian glass and Cádiz beads, enough to fill two knapsacks. Nine dozen copper pendants.

Small tools. As many brass thimbles as you have. An assortment of buttons. Sewing needles and linen thread. Some glass play-pretties."

"For the children?" she asked, reaching for an assortment of tiny angels and animals. She began assembling the requested items, counting and miscounting, glad to have something to do other than stand mindlessly before him and fix him further in her thoughts.

He signed for the goods to be paid in tobacco, his signet ring glinting on his right hand. His signature was as striking as all the rest of him, the *X* boldest of all. She wondered that he never signed *Alexander*, his given name. *Renick* was an illegible blot of swirling ink save the *R*.

"So, Mistress Hopewell, how goes the courting in town?" He gave her that unsettling half smile as he was so wont to do.

A peculiar warmth drenched her as she continued gathering his goods beneath his scrutiny. "Wise you are to be in the country, sir. James Towne's air positively throbs with the heartfelt palpitations of men and women hurtling toward matrimony."

His robust laugh ended abruptly with the opening of the belled door. All levity vanished as Helion Laurent's gaze landed on the goods atop the broad counter. Selah resisted the urge to sweep them all into the waiting knapsacks. If she'd been but a few seconds faster . . .

"Monsieur Renick, I have seen you little about James Towne of late."

Laurent's voice, as richly layered as a French patisserie, resounded in the still room. 'Twas the only thing Selah liked about him. That and his sonorous name, seemingly pulled from the pages of a French fairy tale. His attire, from his

31

silver-threaded doublet to the large rosettes on his boots, bespoke his genteel standing in James Towne and his last journey to France.

He drew closer, subtle accusation in his tone. "Going over to the Indians? And Mademoiselle Hopewell is aiding you, I see."

"My business is none of yours," Xander replied evenly, gaze never lifting from the purchased goods. "And Mistress Hopewell is simply doing my bidding."

With a dismissive snort, Laurent sauntered about, examining the merchandise, occasionally reaching out to touch some new or novel item. Eventually he stilled before the apothecary jars along a far wall, the tools of his trade as colony physic. But what he dispensed Selah wanted nothing of.

Quickly, she packed up what Xander bought, taking care not to damage his wares.

The sudden, protracted silence brought her father out of his accounting room at the back of the store. "Well, Xander. You are about your business early."

"A fine ride to town on a May morn," he replied. "This wind makes water travel chancy."

"Indeed." Ustis's gaze took in the burgeoning knapsacks. "Though your purchases might fare better by shallop."

Selah reached out a discreet hand and pressed her father's arm in warning. Realizing Laurent was in their midst, Ustis recovered quickly, taking up a knapsack and accompanying Xander out the door. Selah followed.

Standing out on the dusty street, well beyond overhearing, Ustis spoke his mind. "Tobacco is not your only business, aye? You are journeying to the Powhatans. But not in your official role of emissary since I see no pearl chain about your neck." Spying a pendant on the ground, a favorite of the tribes, he stooped to return it to its sack. "Need I remind you that no man shall purposely go to any Indian towns, habitation, or places of resort without leave from the governor or commander of that place where he lives . . ."

Xander finished reciting colony law. ". . . upon pain of paying forty shillings to public uses as aforesaid."

Ustis stood and adjusted his spectacles. "Granted, forty shillings is a pittance to a tobacco lord."

"I would rather pay thrice that than ask high-minded Governor Harvey's permission."

Selah drew nearer, the scent of horseflesh strong. "Father, you forget yourself." At his blank stare she said quietly, "You are speaking to the recently appointed commander of his shire."

"Ah, of course." Ustis looked to Xander as if seeing him in a new light. "And as such you are free to go and do as you please. With certain limitations."

Selah gestured to Helion Laurent's tethered horse. "Such an endeavor is fraught with risk."

"Risk?" Xander looked down at her, amusement in his tone. "Going over to the Naturals or wrangling with the governor and his councilors?"

She nearly rolled her eyes in exasperation at his teasing. "Both."

Yet this bewhiskered English warrior would go unflinchingly into hostile territory, come what may.

She tried a tone of supplication. "You cannot dismiss what happened to those hapless settlers who agreed to Chief Opechancanough's last summons."

"Tomahawked to the last man, despite being armed to the

teeth," he returned matter-of-factly. "That I cannot deny. Pray for me, aye?"

The earnest plea tumbled forth, and Selah's hand shot out to touch his sleeve. "I *will* pray for you." *That God has mercy on your stubborn, mercenary soul.*

His gaze fastened on her hand, and she released him, the burn of embarrassment following.

But Ustis was not finished. "What brings you to their camp?"

"I know not."

The terse reply did not allay Selah's alarm.

"Might I beg you to reconsider?" Ustis asked him. "Take adequate weapons? A guard?"

"And give the appearance of an invading army?" Xander shook his head. "Meihtawk brought the summons from the Powhatans' principal stronghold of Menmend. I trust him with my life."

"Aye, he has not failed us in friendship yet. But I would not turn my back on the wily chief, no matter what treaty was recently struck. As for our own government, beware of Harvey and Laurent and their minions lest they get word of what you are about and accuse you of spy."

With that, her father returned to the store while Selah tarried outside. All around them James Towne was slowly awakening, the saltwater air heavy with the scent of hot cross buns from the bake shop across the shell-strewn street. Gulls careened overhead, screeching and scavenging, further raking her nerves.

"Let us return to more amusing matters." Xander tied a bulging saddlebag shut. "Has Cecily Ward made her choice?"

Selah looked hard at him, surprised at so personal a mention. Was he partial to Cecily at first meeting? "Nay, not yet. No bride should be pressured, the council has said."

Xander swung himself into the saddle. "Tell that to a great many overeager men."

"Truly, several matches have been made already." She smiled, or tried to, still uneasy at his going. "How long will you be away from Rose-n-Vale?"

"Not overlong. Plantation work doesn't allow for extended leave." He winked as he looked down at her. "Don't look so downcast, Mistress Hopewell."

He that winketh with the eye causeth sorrow.

The timely proverb did nothing to weaken Xander Renick's spell.

She looked to her feet rather than dwell on him. "I cannot make peace with your dangerous mission."

"What does it matter to you?"

"It matters to all of Virginia, Master Renick." *Especially your young son.* "You are . . . irreplaceable."

"And you, fair lady, are generous with your praise." He reined west. "Your prayers go with me and are a far more formidable weapon than any rusted matchlock or rapier."

Their eyes met a final time. Throat knotted, she watched him go up the street between rowhouses till he was out of sight. Another gull swept down, pecking at some garbage. Its frantic scavenging sent her back into the store, smack into Laurent. She looked about in vain. Shay and her father were occupied elsewhere.

"I'm in need of your assistance in deciding a feminine matter."

Oh, how he provoked her simply by the overtaxed patience in his oiled tone.

Taking her by the elbow, he led her toward a shelf of fripperies, his cologne overpowering. "What is your personal recommendation for a woman of exceptional taste?"

Shrinking from his touch, Selah led him to more coveted items. "These lambskin gloves here? Or perhaps this blue vial of toilet water?" She refused to lift her eyes to his. "Why not purchase both and let the lady herself decide?"

He laughed. "Well played by the cape merchant's daughter. Are you always so pecuniary, Mistress Hopewell?"

"If you mean am I trying to pick your pocket, sir, nay." She moved away from him, relief flooding her when the shop door opened with a jingle and another customer entered in.

To her disdain, Laurent went out without so much as an adieu and bought nothing. Nothing at all.

4

"Father, I must go to Mother for a spell." Selah fled through the store's back door toward the outskirts of town, seeking their timbered house with its well-laid garden of four acres. Mulberry trees, planted when the colony was first founded, offered shade on all sides.

Candace was already at her labors, uprooting stones and thistles. She raised a hand to shade her eyes when Selah hurried through the low gate attached to the paling fence. She straightened. "Is something the matter, Daughter?"

Winded, Selah sank onto a low bench. "I've just sold a bill of goods to Xander, who's en route to Menmend."

Candace's brow furrowed as she sat down beside her daughter, hoe forgotten. "Well, that is certainly news. Whether good or ill, I do not know."

"Father questioned him about the wisdom of such a journey, but he seems intent."

"Such is Xander's way. Determined. Resolute. But let us consider facts over feelings. He lived with them as a lad in a peace exchange, speaks their language, even married into their tribe. Chief Opechancanough is Mattachanna's kin.

And Xander is held in high esteem by the Powhatans when few white men are."

"Glad I am of that, but since Mattachanna's death, the peace their marriage brought has been repeatedly broken. No colonist seems safe."

"Not all the treachery can be laid at the Powhatans' door. The colonists' hands are also stained with blood."

"Will it never end?" Selah looked west, past newly leafed trees that rustled in the coastal wind. "I pray for peace, but peace does not come."

"What stake have you personally in this?" Candace asked. "Rarely are you so flustered."

Selah lifted her shoulders in a shrug. "A great many brave men have perished. I pray he is not among them."

"I agree. But my motherly instincts tell me your concern is of special note."

Withholding a sigh, Selah pondered her reply, trying to make sense of her tangled feelings. "'Tis for little Oceanus, I fear. He should not lose both father and mother."

"Oceanus may well have forgotten his father by now, being raised by his Scots kin so far from our shores. Though I do recall your father saying Xander recently spoke of returning him to Rose-n-Vale now that Widow Brodie is there."

At once hope took wing, only to be tempered by truth. "I wonder if his dear aunt, aging as she is, would have any more patience with a child than with those hounds of his."

"If he were to remarry, his aunt wouldn't be so taxed," Candace said, plucking a burr from her apron. "I might ask your father to speak with him about a tobacco bride. Cecily is certainly smitten. Then Oceanus would have a stepmother and could come home for good."

"Cecily? I fear she is . . ." Selah groped for the right words yet couldn't deny Xander asking about her. "Unsuited to him."

"Is she? Why not let Xander and Cecily make that determination?"

"Oh, aye," Selah murmured, trying to quiet herself as something green and vile gripped her belly. "Father warned me not to become personally involved in the brides' choices, nor let my prejudices or partialities show."

"Wise, aye." Candace studied her daughter more intently. "What else has transpired to leave you on shaky ground?"

There was no escaping her mother's scrutiny. "The physic, Laurent, came to the store, probing into Xander's business. The ill will betwixt them fairly crackled."

Candace took a breath. "They have ever been at odds for reasons unknown to us. Helion Laurent is not highly favored in the colony, though he is powerfully placed."

"I do wonder at their animosity. Mayhap—"

A door slammed. The rising wind snatched Selah's words away.

Cecily appeared all a-fluster at the back of the house. "I am sorry I have overslept—"

"Nonsense!" Candace waved a hand, her voice carrying across greening patches of ground. "Come join us. A lovely spring morn awaits."

Cecily came down the path, linen skirts swirling. "I asked your maidservant your whereabouts, but she could not answer. Why does she not speak?"

"Izella is mute, injured by a slave trader coming here years ago." The lament in Candace's tone never faded when speaking of their faithful maid. "We took her in, helped her heal, and employed her, though we do not own her. She communicates in hand gestures."

"Aye, she pointed to the garden. A shame she is deprived of her tongue. I told her to expect a suitor."

"And who is it today?" Selah voiced the question they asked every morn. Of the half-dozen suitors Cecily had entertained since arriving, none had found favor.

"Richard Peacock of Indigo Hundred." Cecily took the seat Selah offered her. "I must say, becoming Goodwife Peacock sounds quite colorful if nothing else. But I know so little about him. Please enlighten me."

What could she say about a man she'd always found rather . . . ordinary? "Being a gentleman of the first fashion, he is well named." Selah dwelt upon the good. "A man of his word who settles his debts in a timely manner at our store. Prefers rum to port and is fond of candied ginger. A faithful churchgoer."

"He comes well recommended then," Cecily mused. "A fine prospect. The others, nay."

Selah and her mother exchanged glances. Courtship was fraught with complications. Ustis had already chased away one suitor who'd played his lute beneath Cecily's window one moonlit night. But 'twas the Sabbath, after all, and since 1618 music had been banned on that holy day. Outlandish tales about lovestruck swains and unsure maidens abounded. One man was reputed to have even swum across the James River to reach the lady of his choice at a distant plantation.

Leaving them to their chatter, Candace rose and resumed her weeding as the sun spread more light across the garden's colorful enclosure.

"Why are you not storekeeping?" Cecily asked, picking a yellow crocus to tuck into her bodice.

"I needed to speak to Mother a moment but best hasten back," Selah answered as she turned out of the garden gate. "I shall be home eventually, anxious to hear more of Goodman Peacock's pursuit."

Cecily's low laugh followed her down the lane. "Don't forget the brides' meeting at church this afternoon."

"Three o'clock, aye."

Selah returned to a store brimming with men perusing trinkets to aid their courting. Her father raised a concerned brow over her sudden departure, but she simply smiled, and he returned to his ledgers.

All morning she kept busy, glad for the distraction, amused and touched by turns with the men's choices. Shoe buckles in satin-lined shagreen cases. Deep red and pale pink coral necklaces. Toilet water with hints of orange flower and musk. Small gifts that bespoke good intentions and the social standing of the giver.

If Master Renick was bride seeking, she doubted he would need any additional enticements. Rose-n-Vale was fetching enough. As for his personal merits . . . Those quicksilver eyes. That elusive half smile. The dark mane of hair that couldn't decide whether to curl or lie straight. Or was it more his character? Stubborn Scot that he was, he was as remarkable as Mattachanna in many ways.

What was it that turned her thoughts to him? Her desire to see him reunited with his son? Selah knew her old friend would be unhappy with their separation. She missed Mattachanna as she missed Oceanus. Her fondness defied the grave. Once she and Mattachanna had been no bigger than minnows, turning cartwheels across James Towne's common, picking fruits and flowers in her mother's garden, admiring trinkets at the store. Often present when her kinsmen came to trade or make a treaty, Mattachanna was a ready, willing playmate. Though other folk shunned the Naturals, even their children, Selah's parents made no uncharitable distinctions. Miss Mischief, her father called Mattachanna affectionately. She was ever merry and given to pranks.

Two years it had been since her passing. Oceanus would now be four. Selah's mind spun back to that day at the dock when the woods began to fill with autumn color. Xander and his family had embarked on the *Pleasure*, a handsome, forty-ton pinnace, Mattachanna's hope to visit his homeland a reality. Waving till her arm ached, Selah watched them depart till their ship was no more than a speck of wood riding the azure horizon.

And then long months later her joy turned to gall when Xander returned and came down the gangplank alone. Where was her beloved friend? Their delightful son? Selah scoured the deck to catch sight of Mattachanna trailing behind or preoccupied with baggage. Xander seemed a bit dull-witted after so many weeks at sea, his muscled frame gaunt. The long voyage had gone hard on him. Had he fallen ill? Selah's heart seemed to stop as her father spoke the words she could not, so thick was the lump in her throat.

"Welcome back, Xander. You have been sorely missed." Ustis embraced him heartily while Selah stood apart. "But what of Mattachanna and your son?"

Xander answered with a terse, sorrowful stab to the heart.

"Mattachanna is no more. Felled by a fever and buried in England at Gravesend."

Ustis's joyful expression turned slack with astonishment. Speechless, her father was.

Xander stepped aside as unsteady, sea-legged passengers moved past them. His features were tight with pain, his eyes more bloodshot than blue. "Oceanus remains in Culross with my kin."

Another blow straight to the heart. Nary a word could Selah speak, neither in shock nor solace. She stepped back, swallowed the hot words thickening her tight throat, and ran home. After fumbling at the latch of their back door, she entered the kitchen, tears spotting her hands and coursing in warm rivulets down her flushed face. At her sudden appearance, Izella nearly dropped a copper pot. Brows arched, Candace set down the herbs she fisted and walked toward her distraught daughter.

Selah choked on the hateful words. "Mattachanna is dead."

As her mother's arms went around her, Candace's own frame shook from grief. Together they stood locked in a stunned embrace.

When they drew apart, Candace took out a handkerchief and dried Selah's tears and her own. "So Xander returns a widower."

"That is not all. Xander has left Oceanus in the care of his kin." Selah took a breath, voice rising, her heart rent by more than sorrow. "How dare he deprive his son of a father at such a time? Oceanus adores him. This is their home. He's even robbed him of his Indian relations. 'Tis a cruel mind and heart he has to leave the lad amongst strangers in Scotland while—"

43

Too late did Selah realize the extent of her outburst. Only when a door shut soundly behind her did she cast a look over her shoulder. Xander stood with her father, hat in hands. Oh, how his piercing eyes haunted. Her ire seemed to kindle his own anguish like sparks from a forge fire.

Her father's stern voice cut through her mortification. "I have asked Xander to share a meal with us before he returns to Rose-n-Vale, to not only partake of sustenance but be comforted in his trouble by the comfort wherewith we ourselves are comforted of God."

Oh, how the timely Scripture smote her. Shattered, she fled upstairs to nurse her disgrace and heartache in the privacy of her bedchamber. Let them sup without her. How could she ever look Xander Renick in the face again?

Ever since, the shame of her hasty, heated words felt like a branded *S* upon her forehead. Often she had avoided him. Mourning kept him cloistered for a time. But now he was oft in James Towne . . .

Later, her mother had confided his reasons for doing what he did. But Selah felt she did not deserve to hear them. "Oceanus fell ill with the same fever that took his mother's life. Once he'd recovered, Xander decided he could not subject a child to a long voyage, nor conscience returning the lad to Rose-n-Vale without a mother amid the ongoing perils of life in the colony."

Further humbled, Selah didn't dare mention Oceanus again. She simply prayed for him an ocean away. That he would be well and good and soon return to them. That he would, even at a young age, not forget his James Towne roots and his extraordinary mother.

Even now as she stood behind the store counter, another

prayer lifted from her empty, contrite heart. *Father, can Thou not mend this frightful feeling? Of wishing sore words unsaid?*

How she longed to rewind time and set foot again on the docks, greet Xander with the solace and understanding he deserved in time of grief. But nay, 'twas too late. The bitter memory struck another lick.

Ask his forgiveness.

What? She was alone in the store, yet the voice was as clear to her as if spoken by her earthly father. But before she had time to ponder it . . .

"Ah, Mistress Hopewell, how glad I am to see you this morn. You've been so preoccupied with all this bride business that I'm oft left to the devices of your rascal brother!"

"What is it you buy?" Selah inquired with a smile as Goody Wyatt approached the counter.

"I'm desirous of some of your Aztec chocolate." The aging matron leaned heavily on her cane. "But only the freshest, newly imported will do. My dear sister desires mustard powder and horseradish."

Selah nodded. "None of your usual hartshorn or vinegars?"

"Of course, how could I have forgotten? All of them, please."

She paid for her purchases once Selah had bundled them, and the door shut at the stroke of three. With a word to Shay in the anteroom, Selah let herself out again, this time for the timber-framed church where the remaining unwed maids were assembling. The parish rector greeted her as she entered. She paused to admire the flowers her mother had brought to sweeten the place ahead of their meeting.

Cecily appeared, tardy yet smiling. "I have a private matter to discuss with you as soon as possible. Your father said you shall do everything within your power to assist me."

Curiosity soaring, Selah took her place before the seated tobacco brides, some who looked downcast, others smiling. Her heart turned over. These were extraordinary women who'd bravely come, many orphaned, all seeking a better life. How she wanted the best for them. Kind husbands. Rewarding toil. Healthy children. Manifold friends.

A prayer was said. Selah listened as a few women stated grievances that she and Reverend Midwinter sought to mend. One was heartbroken her husband-to-be had died the morn of their wedding. Another was in a fury her choice had been stolen by another maid. Two women wanted to return to England.

At meeting's end, Selah took a fresh tally. Two maids remained abed with maladies while the rest were settling into their hosts' homes and pondering their prospects. Sixteen brides were already wed, and four more marriages were to occur on the morrow.

"Well done," the reverend said at the close with a glint in his eye. "'Hear my soul speak, the very instant that I saw you, did my heart fly to your service.'"

Selah smiled at his wit. "Shakespeare. *The Tempest*."

Her gaze wandered to a near window. At almost every hour, strolling couples could be seen about town. All were adjusting to new faces, new names. These fair maids had a gentling effect on the masculine town and somehow created a wistful tug to Selah's carefully hedged heart.

As she exited the church, Cecily caught up with her. "'Tis such a lovely spring day. I've a mind to go beyond James

Towne. What say you?" At Selah's hesitation, she clutched her arm. "At home in Yorkshire, we often took an afternoon stroll in the country."

"If you don't mind carrying a weapon, aye," Selah said. "Danger might be lurking. A boat is sometimes more easily managed and allows one to go farther at greater speed. And in better weather, 'tis safer."

"Do you have one?"

"Shay has a small canoe that will suit. Are you willing?"

"Of course. Let's be away!"

5

On a cloudless, mid-May morn, Xander left Rose-n-Vale when the dew lay heavy on field and forest. More than two and a half years had passed since he'd traveled to the Powhatans. Not since Mattachanna died had he ventured there of his own accord, nor been invited. Much had changed. Thrust back as they were by the English, the Powhatans' principal village was no longer in the same place.

And he was no longer the same man.

Pondering this, he took his time. His horse, Lancelot, was content to simply canter. Saddlebags stuffed with gifts from the Hopewells' store, Jett loping alongside him, he made good time, crossing streambeds and traversing great stretches of forest cleansed by a recent rain. Meihtawk would meet him just ahead, where the recent treaty laid the boundary line between English and Powhatan land. Glad for company, he never liked to be too much alone with his thoughts. Of late they'd taken him in a direction he was unwilling to go.

The troublesome matter had begun with his aunt, when he had asked her to join him at the Hopewells'. A simple shared supper it was not. Somehow the courtesy of her coming had turned into a hope he might take a bride.

But not Cecily Ward.

"Nephew, pardon my temerity . . ." She paused long enough to cough at his pipe smoke. That noxious weed, she called tobacco. "Have you ever understood the reason Selah Hopewell is not yet wed?"

He stretched out his legs and managed to say despite his discomfiture, "I have not given it much thought, Aunt."

"Perhaps it begs considering." Her powdered face assumed a rare excitement. "That night at supper I was struck by her winsome manner. She moves and speaks so becomingly. Once I thought she possessed more of her father's merits, but she has grown into her mother's graces. And there's no denying she is lovely with her corn-silk hair and those intelligent green eyes, even if she is a tad befreckled."

He didn't respond, nor did he need to, as she kept up a steady volley of adulation.

"'Tis a wonder no man has claimed her. I once heard something about a smitten sea captain, but I cannot recall the details, which were precious few, only that her wise father thought a seafaring husband little better than no husband at all." She took a breath. "With all this fuss over tobacco brides, I feel Selah Hopewell is being overlooked. Tell me, Alexander, do you find her the least comely?"

He nearly choked on his pipe. "I would have to be in the ground to say nay."

A raised brow. "How thankful I am you are above ground *and* aware of her charms."

Smoky rings spiraled to the ceiling as he weighed his reply. "Mistress Hopewell shows no inclination to marry."

"Well, have you asked her?"

"I have not." How to best put it? "She is a tad too independent minded for me. Too . . . spicy."

She chuckled, then sighed and studied the dogs lounging at his feet. "I daresay a woman's company would exceed these baneful creatures'. In honor of your mother, my dear sister, please give remarrying some thought."

She left him then to retire to her bedchamber. But the questions she had raised refused to be quelled. They followed him now into the howling wilderness, where he'd best be concerned about watchful eyes and launched arrows. Still, the thought of Selah Hopewell would not budge.

Even recollecting her passionate rebuke of him when he'd returned from England alone failed to hold its usual sting. And she had, at last meeting, called him . . . what?

Irreplaceable.

If ever one word had the power to go to a man's head, if not his heart . . .

Jett growled, a low, throaty foreboding. Xander slowed, Lancelot showing no sign of disquiet. Meihtawk? In seconds the lad appeared between a break in the trees ahead, a feather aflutter in his loosened hair.

"Wingapo!"

The familiar greeting dissolved Xander's tenseness. He reached into his pocket and tossed Meihtawk a quantity of candied lemon peel. Meihtawk promptly popped a piece into his mouth and stroked Jett's black head. Dismounting, glad to stretch his legs, Xander fell into step beside him.

"You smile today, True Word. You are glad of your visit after so long?"

"I am remembering that first time."

"When you came to the People with the spinning circle?"

The reference to his compass stole Xander's smile. "I nearly lost my life that first foray into the woods."

God rest the three colonists who'd gone hunting with him but were soon bristling with arrows. He'd been but a boy, no serious threat to the tall, painted warriors surrounding him. When they'd taken him back to their village, he'd stayed quick witted enough to remain alive, surrendering his coveted compass without being told to.

With a flash of his dark eyes, Meihtawk said, "Do not forget the talking bark."

Xander's smile resurfaced. "When I charcoaled a message to my mother?"

Though the incident had occurred long ago, the harrowing if amusing story still warmed countless ears.

He had taken care to send a message to Rose-n-Vale on a piece of bark he'd etched with coal. The reply penned on paper by his fretful mother and delivered by a Powhatan courier left the Naturals in varying degrees of astonishment over the talking wood. Rather than feeling superior, it led him to be thankful for the basic things he took for granted that made the Naturals marvel.

Later, after wedding Mattachanna, he'd been caught by surprise when she'd dragged out a quantity of gunpowder from his stores and attempted to sow it as if it were seed. Exasperated with powder being in short supply, he'd explained such a substance could not produce what she hoped, that the precious commodity could only be had a more laborious way.

Such artless unpretentiousness made the arrogance and guile of James Towne beyond enduring.

He took a deep, untainted breath and drank in the lushness

of late spring. Beyond settlement borders there seemed an uncanny stillness, free of the ring of anvils and axes and gunshots, the relentless cacophony of settlement life. There was danger here, aye, but the wonder of the undisturbed natural world was uppermost.

"I miss your summer residence near the falls of the Powhatan River," Xander told him in the Powhatan dialect. "And your winter camp on the Pamunkey."

"The old days are gone." Meihtawk entered a fragrant pine barren. "That land is now scarred and broken by land stealers."

Of which Xander was foremost. He'd earned his own land by venturing to James Towne, inherited his father's, and been awarded a vast tract by Chief Opechancanough upon wedding Mattachanna.

"Do you know why I have been asked to come to Menmend?"

"You are the father of the chief's grandson, the husband of his favored daughter."

True. Yet Xander sensed this did not safeguard him. "What are the chief's current thoughts about the English? I would be prepared."

Meihtawk batted away an insect. "He and his warriors are still united in their desire to subdue the English, to make use of their trade goods. The men of James Towne are regarded as much an enemy as the Monacans and other warring tribes."

And in turn, the English would stop at nothing less than all Naturals becoming subjects of the English king.

He heaved a rare, unguarded sigh. Why the previous all-powerful chief, Powhatan, had not wiped the fragile settlement of James Towne off the map in 1607 remained a mystery.

They reached Menmend in the noonday heat, famished and sweating heavily. The vast village contained a great many *yi-hakan*, those round huts made of reeds and bent saplings. A great stir rose up at their appearance, a few of Mattachanna's kin rushing toward them. The women especially were gracious, their features carrying such an echo of Mattachanna that his eyes smarted. Amid much fanfare, they led him to Opechancanough, who stood with favored wives and esteemed werowances beneath a large arbor.

Tall and lithe, the powerful chief looked first at Jett, then at Xander, his pleasure in their coming apparent, though the werowances stayed stoic. Rife with superstitions and spirit worship, all but a few of them regarded him with equal wariness, even hostility. He was reminded of the outcry that arose at Mattachanna's heartfelt plea to be instructed in Christianity, to learn more about the talking book and the living God of the Bible. Because of her openness to his faith, their own relationship had flowered.

Facing Opechancanough, he stored the sweet memory away as his lengthy absence settled over him. Opechancanough bore a slight limp, and a jagged scar marred his naked side. From the English or a warring tribe?

Standing before such an assembly, Xander felt the weight of the Powhatans' grim regard of the Tassantassas, the English. Though they feared the colonists' guns and weapons, they found the settlers a helpless bunch, unclean and equally foul of temper, blindingly arrogant and greedy for gain, unable to provide for themselves and nearly starved out of existence early on. From an early age he'd purposed to be guilty of none of those things.

Hand straying to the precautionary pistol hidden in his

pocket, he was unsure if he'd even survive this unexpected summons. Though he was able to speak with a certain freedom of expression, knowing their tongue, he was by no means fluent in all their ways. But to the headman's every query, Xander had, in the past, given a truthful reply. He did not flatter or deal in deceit. Nor did he take sides. He had earned his name among them.

To his relief, he was seated as a guest and offered a pipe of tobacco, which was shared with the chief and his attendants. Only after the ritual smoking could any discussion ensue. Grateful to be off his feet and collect his thoughts, he found their leaf bitter, a far cry from Rose-n-Vale's smooth sweetness.

Gradually the awkwardness of first arriving in camp abated. Opechancanough's eyes narrowed with humor as he observed Jett sitting obediently at his master's side. Powhatan curs were small hunting dogs, not pets, and were an unruly lot oft eaten during starving times. To see a sleek, well-fed English dog, obedient to his owner, was a startling sight. Even now most were warily regarding the giant greyhound, no doubt sensing he would defend his master at all costs. Or perhaps transform into a more frightening apparition at will.

"I bring gifts." Xander gestured to his horse, which patiently bore his load beneath a willow oak. "I can provide more at your bidding, the best to be had from Tassantassas ships that come over the great water from the land of the English king."

At the chief's nod, he and Meihtawk began unpacking saddlebags, displaying the wares on corn-husk mats spread upon the ground for that purpose. A whisper of excitement stirred among the wives at the bright ribbons and sewing notions.

Opechancanough lingered with pleasure on the copper, though he seemed pleased enough at the variety and abundance of offerings. Yet all knew these were but a pittance, mere trinkets, meant to mollify at worst, promote peace at best. An expected gesture of goodwill.

"My desire is to reopen a path between our people." Xander could state his aim no more simply than that. He could not help it if the men of James Towne had different motives, would mock his being here as a fool's errand. He purposed to do what he could, the Lord guard his life. Never did he forget he had farmed Powhatan land, or what once had been.

"You speak and act from the heart and make me strong, True Word. And you will not be against what it is I have to tell you." The chief stood and motioned for the proceedings to continue. "But first, we will feast."

Heaping trays of roasted bear meat and venison, smoked fish, oysters and crab, birds of every feather, dried maize, and *powcohiscara*, a delicacy made from walnuts and other nut meats, soon surrounded him. Finally, a full two hours later, Xander tossed a bone Jett's way. Sated, he could not help but feel he was being fattened for slaughter. At best, he needed fortifying ahead of the private, intense meeting to come.

Alone with the chief, Xander stifled a yawn. He'd long schooled himself to the Naturals' unhurried rhythms and ponderous silences. In his youth while part of an English delegation, he'd witnessed one of the chief's attendants slain on the spot for an untimely interruption, after which

Opechancanough resumed speaking where he had left off. 'Twas a lesson not soon forgotten.

As usual, Opechancanough began with a recitation of the misdeeds done them by the Tassantassas since Mattachanna had died and the old alliance between them had again eroded. But even this trailed off into more personal matters. It seemed the chief's grief for his favored daughter had given way to his interest in Oceanus, whom he had seen but once since his birth.

"And how is my daughter's son, my grandson, who lives across the great water?"

The question struck an increasingly raw nerve. How could he honestly answer with so many leagues and lost time between them? "Last I heard, Oceanus is well and old enough to travel. I have written to his guardian to tell him the time has come to return him home."

"Such is well and good." A slight smile eased the chief's weather-beaten features. "A boy should not be so far from the land of his birth lest he forget the old ways and the faces and customs of his people."

On this they agreed. Overcome by a twist of pathos, Xander fixed his attention on the elaborately carved corner post of the chief's dwelling. Yet it was Oceanus's face he saw. A baby, not a boy. "Once he returns, I will bring him to see you here. Surely he has the look of his mother about him and perhaps you yourself."

With a nod, Opechancanough's warmth vanished. "Let us now speak again of other, more serious matters. My spies bring a bad report. Of late, we learn that the white chief, Harvey, attempts to sway the Susquehannock and lesser tribes to serve as guides in expeditions to make war on us."

Spirits leaden, Xander listened, unsurprised at news of further scheming. "I keep no company with Harvey as I have decided to step down from the governor's council. I know nothing firsthand."

A long pause, filled with purling tobacco smoke and displeasure. "Yet surely you hear secondhand of the mischief the governor and his men make? Though you are not among them, their treachery knows no end."

"I do know this . . ." Xander exhaled a wisp of smoke. "Beware of armed slavers sent to harm or capture any Naturals on the borders of English settlements, the tributaries foremost."

Another nod. "It is as you say. There was harm done recently to the Nanticoke."

Xander longed to dissolve the ill will at play. "In the pursuit of peace, I recently came before the council to ask that two or more royal commissioners investigate and handle any and all disputes between Indians and English. To establish accountability and rectify wrongs done."

"How was this proposal received?"

Badly. Harvey's arrogance had been contemptible. Xander cast about for an answer, hesitating till the tightness in his throat eased. "I am still awaiting action."

Passing Xander the pipe, Opechancanough lifted his eyes heavenward. "Then what I am about to propose to you might help smooth the way."

6

The May day was balmy, the sandy beach occupied by children at play. One old man was roasting oysters over a fire, shells strewn at his bare feet, gray smoke billowing with the unmistakable tang of the sea. He held up a pearl with a toothless grin as Selah and Cecily passed by in search of Shay's canoe hidden in the reeds.

"'Tis my first foray up this river." Cecily put a tentative foot in the boat, trying to be graceful while Selah prepared to push off. "What do you Virginians call it?"

Selah handed her an oar. "The Naturals named it the Powhatan, the English the James." Thrusting the canoe into the water with unladylike strength, Selah jumped in and seated herself in the stern.

"My, such a rustic mode of transport." Cecily looked askance at her own oar once they were under way. "How do you navigate without getting all wet?"

"Practice," Selah said simply, buoyed by her many childhood jaunts upriver, an expertise born of coastal life. "If the wind holds, we'll be pushed along as much as we paddle."

"Though you are adept with the oar, it seems quite a masculine pursuit. I'm afraid I'm little help." With awkward strokes, Cecily fixed her attention on the shore. "What if we overturn?"

"I pray not. Can you swim?"

"Nay, but I'm sure you can."

"I'll keep to the shallows. You enjoy the shoreline from the bow. Soon you'll see plantations, tobacco fields, wharves, and all manner of watercraft."

"I do believe upriver is best."

For a time, they glided along in silence, taken with the vast blueness that made Virginia's largest river so memorable. Selah felt remarkably free and unencumbered, the sunlight warm upon her back. On such a sublime spring day, she wouldn't ponder Xander's journey toward the western mountains that marked the river's beginning. Or her father's persistent aches and pains. Or Helion Laurent's increased visits to the store. Or—

"Look over there near that pretty cove," Cecily called over her shoulder. "A house appears to be abandoned."

"'Tis my father's property, Hopewell Hundred, meant for my brother in time."

"Why does it sit empty?"

"The tenant died last year." She'd not confess he'd been felled by a tomahawk while hunting on disputed territory. Steering the canoe away from the sight, Selah said, "Keep your eyes open and prepare to be delighted."

They traversed another winsome blue bend in the river, and Cecily's paddling ceased. "Who owns that comely hill just ahead?"

Truly, Rose-n-Vale was perfectly placed. "'Tis home to

Alexander Renick, whom you've met." Always, that wistful twinge followed, the beauty shot through with the bittersweet.

"A commanding house, fairer than any I've seen in James Towne." Cecily gave a sigh more of delight than exertion. "And bricked more than timbered. Fit for a handsome master. Shall we land the canoe and rest?"

"I suppose." Selah aimed for the sandy shore and a widespread oak, which offered both shade and privacy. Well out of sight of any at Rose-n-Vale.

Cecily stood when the canoe stilled, then stepped from its rocking bottom onto the shore with far more grace than when they'd launched. "'Tis ironic that we're on Renick land and 'tis Renick I wish to discuss."

Despite her misgivings, Selah spread a blanket on the sand. She offered Cecily a flask of cider, a sense of foreboding building. Cecily's interest in Xander was no secret, so her next words hardly came as a surprise.

"I should like you to go to Rose-n-Vale"—Cecily handed back the flask with the hauteur of a queen giving orders—"and ask the master if he is of a courting mind."

Forthright, she was. Straight to the point as any man. Still . . . "For so delicate a matter, perhaps you should send my father instead."

"On the contrary. I think you may be more persuasive. Your mother tells me you were a friend of Master Renick's former wife. Matto . . . ?"

"Mattachanna."

"Ah. I've yet to see an Indian. What was she like?"

"Beautiful. Gracious. Astute."

"A pity she died young." Cecily made a contrary face.

"The only fly in the ointment is this. I shan't want charge of a half-breed boy."

Cecily's distaste was commonplace yet unpalatable. Selah bit her tongue, her thoughts veering in a new, nettlesome direction. Was that yet another reason Oceanus was left behind? So Xander's remarrying might have no obstacles?

Cecily reached for a twig in the sand. "He hardly seems the devoted father, leaving his son behind in Scotland."

Selah chafed at both the slight and the truth behind it. Their separation tore the heart out of her. Did Xander not feel it too? Why had he not heeded Mattachanna's dying plea to not part? True, the latter was just rumored, but . . .

"You are a friend of his aunt, are you not?" Cecily fixed her with a near glare. "Visiting Rose-n-Vale wouldn't be amiss."

"Under pretense of speaking with Widow Brodie?" Selah shook her head. "I would not go in deceit."

"Ha! We must be coy in these affairs of the heart. Play it sly." Cecily smiled as if the matter was settled. "Your father said you would do everything in your power to assist me."

"My assistance is hardly needed. A man like Alexander Renick knows his own mind. The very thought of appearing in his study about any bride business makes me shudder."

"Well, *I* cannot do it. The council gave you charge of these fair maids, of which I am one."

Selah schooled her temper. "Truth be told, I cannot see you at Rose-n-Vale." There, she had said it. The resulting offense on Cecily's face was plain. "I don't see him remarrying, is what I'm saying. He is ever preoccupied with his crops, his many indentures, the affairs of Virginia. Even now he has gone over to the Naturals. He has little time for courting and less for a bride."

"The right maid might change that. He strikes me as a shrewd, perceptive Scotsman well deserving of a wife equally so." Cecily's confidence remained undimmed. "Say you'll go to him when he returns and plead my case."

"You realize that living on a plantation—one of the Hundreds, as they're called—places you at greater risk for Indian attack?"

"I suppose so." Cecily shrugged her slender shoulders. "But James Towne holds no charms for me. Already I feel hemmed in by all the fences and rowhouses there, few and crude as they are. I belong in the country."

Selah sighed. She'd oft felt the lure of open fields and unfenced lands herself. Yet the danger remained. "Perhaps one day Rose-n-Vale will be as safe and lovely as it sounds."

Cecily began drawing in the sand with her twig. Selah made out the initials *A* and *C*. "Mistress of Rose-n-Vale. How I warm to the title." Tossing aside the twig, Cecily stood. "Let's go nearer the house, shall we? 'Tis scandalously large, I hear."

"Trespass, you mean?"

Already Cecily had started up the bank, skirts raised above her scarlet garters. Selah trailed her uphill, relieved Xander was away and would never know they'd encroached on his territory. Winded, they came to the place that gave them a territorial view, the James River at their backs. Up here where the wind blew free, the air smelled sweet in any season.

Wildflowers spread before them like a floral carpet, a few mighty oaks casting shadows and breaking up the cleared landscape. A sizeable arbor stood at the back of the main house, a showy display of red blooms not yet ablaze on leggy stems. The expanding mansion so talked about in town was now before them, its newest windows large and sashed with crystal glass, the roof crowned with diamond-turned chimney stacks.

Surrounding the house stood orchards, all young, mostly of stone fruit, some trees thriving, some struggling. Timbered dependencies fronted a lane to the west beyond the summer kitchen.

Cecily came to a stop. "Why, even Governor Harvey cannot boast of such a dwelling! And fences as far as the eye can see. But all wood rails, not stone like in the Old World."

Selah felt a grudging admiration. Truly, Xander had accomplished much and come by it honestly given the sweat of his brow and his agile mind. No one had handed him anything with a velvet glove.

"What's that curious structure in the far field?"

Selah followed Cecily's finger. "'Tis a drying barn to cure tobacco. One of them. His indentures work year-round building, not just toiling in the fields."

Even as she said it she heard the ring of a hammer and voices. Labor was in force all around them, the very pulse of the growing plantation. And then came a deep, resounding bark, carried on the warm wind.

Selah's attention narrowed to the dog sprinting at full speed toward them, a streak of deep red amid so much spring green. Cecily stepped behind her, peering over Selah's shoulder in alarm. "What on earth . . . ?"

"'Tis Ruby Renick," Selah said as the hound stopped at her bidding, tongue lolling and tail wagging wildly. "But where is your constant companion, Jett?"

Cecily extended a careful hand to stroke Ruby's sleek coat. "What an odd-looking breed. All legs. And such a small head! One would think there's not a brain in it."

"Don't be fooled. They're quite clever. Devoted, even gentle. Oceanus adored them. He'd sometimes ride on their backs." 'Twas Oceanus's laugh she most remembered, and his delight in the natural world. She'd come visiting whenever she could. But not nearly enough.

Cecily raised a hand to shade her eyes. "I believe I spy his aunt coming out of the house."

Had Widow Brodie seen them gawking?

"We'd best hie home." Selah scoured the darkening horizon, mindful of the last hailstorm. "Those coming clouds cry rain."

They bade Ruby farewell and hastened down the hill toward shore. Their return downriver was swifter, Cecily's attempts at paddling surer. Once they landed, the wind shifted, their skirts along with it. They returned the canoe to its hiding place among the reeds as raindrops began falling, dimpling the water.

The *Bountiful Ann*, newly arrived from the West Indies, now shadowed the James Towne wharf, its sailors roaming free of the vessel. Some drank openly from flagons of ale. A dash of ribaldry rode the air amid coarse conversation and laughter. The tawdry tavern near the waterfront, a favorite haunt of seamen, would not sleep tonight. Eyes down, Selah paid the sailors no mind, but Cecily returned their brazen stares.

"Who was it said these Virginia wenches are toad ugly?" roared one, to drunken laughter. "I beg to differ!"

Passing the sheriff making his rounds, Selah hurried down a

safer street arm in arm with Cecily. Home was but a few minutes outside town, and never had she been gladder to arrive.

As they entered the kitchen, Candace turned around from the bake oven, hands full of a golden loaf of wheaten bread. "There you are! I was beginning to fret." She set the bread on the table to Cecily's admiring exclamations, voice fading to a whisper. "There's a visitor in the parlor."

"A visitor?" Cecily said.

"One who desires your company. Goodman Wentz. You can invite him to sup with us if you wish."

"I shall see." Cecily returned to the door. She removed a shoe and shook it free of sand, then did the same with the other before venturing toward the parlor.

"I'm sorry we're tardy." Washing up at a near basin, Selah began telling her mother and Izella of their adventure upriver.

"You saw naught of the master?" Candace asked.

"None but Ruby, though his aunt appeared at the last. I believe Xander is still away."

Candace's brow furrowed. "God protect him."

Shay and Ustis came in, having closed and locked the store. "A great many rowdies out tonight, though I'm glad enough of these West Indies goods." Ustis hung his hat on a peg. "Tomorrow we'll take inventory as the warehouses fill. Tonight I must give the annual accounting as cape merchant so shall be away in the governor's chambers."

Laughter floated from the parlor, and Candace met Ustis's inquiring glance. "Cecily has another suitor."

"From the sounds of it, aye," he replied, taking a seat. "Wentz, is it? I thought Peacock was still in the running. And what of you, Daughter?"

Selah began slicing bread. "I am no tobacco bride, mind you."

"A father can wish, aye?" 'Twas his eternal lament. "Today Master Jacoby came in with all nine of his grandchildren, buying them this and that. I thought how fine a thing it would be to have some descendants."

Selah withheld a sigh. "There is always Shay."

"Much too young for an attachment," Ustis said over the drone of rain on the slate roof. "You, on the other hand . . ."

"Ustis," Candace chided, setting a crock of butter and cheese on the table. "Such tiresome talk hardly helps Selah go groom hunting."

Ustis continued undaunted. "The best men will soon be taken once all this matrimony dies down."

A lengthy prayer was said, matrimony duly mentioned, in which Ustis all but named the suitor he favored.

"Amen," he said reverently before reaching for a slice of warm bread. "'Tis my duty as your father to pursue the subject, Daughter. Pray to that end."

Across the table, Shay winked at Selah as if to ease her.

"I should rather marry for love than the price of tobacco," Selah returned quietly.

"Love hardly fills the larder. Marriage is first and foremost a business matter. Affection may come in time, but 'tis clearly secondary to prudence."

They'd gone around and around like this ever since Selah had come of age. Oddly, she didn't take offense. She understood his reasoning, his practical nature, his fervent desire to see her happily settled well past his own lifetime. Even as her own hopes for a love match dwindled.

Oh, there'd been a few fleeting glances, some passing consideration of men to appease her father, mostly gentlemen who frequented their business and church. Even the gallant Captain Rycroft, who came in and out of port. But nothing lasting. Nothing that stayed with her, made her want to don a coif like the married women of James Towne.

Candace eyed her sympathetically. "Our prayers for the right man shall be answered in time, perhaps. For now, let us celebrate Cecily's new beginning, shall we?"

7

Market day always resembled a fair. Nearly everyone in the colony seemed to turn out to either parade their wares or purchase them. Booths and tents arrayed James Towne's streets made muddy by a night's rain. On her feet at first light, Selah listened to the din of people coming and going past their house on the main thoroughfare into town.

Yawning, she tied her braids beneath her cap and put on a new apron edged with Brussels lace. Having lain awake the night before in her curtained bed, her ears tuned to any rustle in the bushes heralding another of Cecily's love-struck suitors, Selah felt unfit for any task. Across from her the would-be bride had slept fitfully, her courting slowed by a fever. Nearly everyone new to Virginia succumbed to some malady upon arrival.

But this morning, Cecily had risen early, the fever finally broken. She sat at the kitchen table drinking the boneset tonic Candace had brewed her while Ustis muttered about Spaniards as he ate his breakfast, a recent ship's sighting a concern. Between Indians inland and the Spanish by sea, they were constantly on alert.

"I've a mind to move upriver to Hopewell Hundred," Ustis declared between bites. "James Towne is in a dismal strategic position. Not only that, there's a growing need for supplies inland. Those prosperous planters require a cape merchant nearer them. Trade would be brisk. I've reason to believe we might fare better all the way around."

"You've been in James Towne since its founding. You might well miss it." Candace regarded her husband thoughtfully. "I'm partial to Middle Plantation, just seven miles distant and so well situated between the James and York Rivers."

"We'd be better protected there with the new palisade stretching for leagues and leagues between us and the tribes," Shay said. "And Xander says the land is better for tobacco and wheat."

"Ah, wheat." Ustis's head bobbed above his plate. "Former tobacco fields make fine ground for grain. And now, with Governor Harvey crowing Virginia has at last become the granary of all His Majesty's colonies, we might try our hand at it."

Candace looked toward Selah as if awaiting her thoughts on the matter. But 'twas Cecily who spoke, her interest plain. "I've not seen Master Renick of late. Is he still away?"

"Perhaps today we shall find out, if Widow Brodie comes to market," Candace said. "But what of Goodman Wentz?"

"'Tis no crime to have two suitors, surely." Cecily smiled her pleasure and looked at Selah as if reminding her of her mission. "At least for now."

Pushing his plate away, Ustis burst into verse. "'There is a lady sweet and kind, was never a face so pleased my mind; I did but see her passing by, and yet I'll love her till I die.'"

At their mirth, he rose and put on both jacket and hat,

ready for business. Shay did the same. "We shall see you ladies later today, aye?"

"If Cecily feels well enough," Candace returned as they went out.

"Oh, I am in need of fresh air, perhaps an afternoon jaunt." Cecily was already on her feet and moving toward the window to judge the weather. "Another sunny day! But quite warm for June. Such a contrast from England."

"Are you homesick, my dear?" Candace asked.

"Only when the weather makes me perspire unbecomingly. I must remember to carry a fan and stay shy of the unrelenting sun . . ."

Selah slipped out the door behind her father and Shay, a headache pulsing between her temples.

Selah moved among the many booths set up in the market, making a mental list of wares that were missing from their own store shelves. Just offshore the latest supply ship lay becalmed in deep waters, having brought a great quantity of Kill Devil, as her father called the West Indies rum. Selah suspected it would be used primarily to ply the Naturals with, to fool them into forsaking more territory.

Her thoughts swung to Xander again, unwillingly yet persistently. In moments, as if sensing her musings, Widow Brodie made straight for her and touched her sleeve.

"Good day, Mistress Hopewell."

Selah smiled a greeting. Was Xander near? She looked past his aunt, searching for his familiar figure in the melee. How much easier it would be to simply plead Cecily's case here beneath some shady eave. "Are you alone this market day?"

"Alexander has just returned home." The news raised then dashed Selah's hopes. "He is zealous to return to the fields and is likely there as we speak."

Selah understood. "'Tis a critical time for farming, especially Orinoco."

"Indeed." An onerous sigh. "Topping tobacco, foremost, and combating pests, mostly those detestable worms." Widow Brodie frowned as she examined an ell of printed cloth. "I fear this year's crop is beginning badly with so much rain."

Spring had been one damp blur. But better than drought, surely. Taking a breath, Selah summoned all her courage. "I should like to call at Rose-n-Vale . . . when the master has time to be interrupted."

The widow's white brows arched. Selah awaited chastisement, a rebuke to her boldness, thus ending her undertaking for Cecily.

"'Tis a private matter," Selah quickly added, and a light dawned in the older woman's faded blue eyes. Did she think . . . ? Selah didn't mean to poke a hole in the woman's matrimonial hopes, at least where she herself was concerned. "Shay has also caught an enormous sturgeon for your table."

"Oh my!" The widow regained her composure. "A fresh fish cannot be kept waiting. I bid you come at your earliest convenience. This afternoon, perhaps? Alexander is oft in his study in the heat of the day."

"Thank you," Selah replied in confirmation, and they both moved on amid the busy marketplace.

Selah continued perusing goods, keeping close watch on her pockets. Though thievery was punished, pickpockets still plied their dubious trade. Bumped by a burly man hefting a large basket, with nary an apology, she was thrust into the path of Helion Laurent.

Removing his plumed hat, the physic gave a courtly little bow, which struck her as more ridiculous than gallant. "Mistress Hopewell, you look all business on market day."

"I am about my father's interests, sir."

"Obviously. But have you no pleasurable pursuits beyond a bargain and the next stall's enticements? Your brother is quite capable, is he not? Yet 'tis you who are most mercenary."

She attempted to move past him, but a throng of shoppers slowed her. "Shay is not yet of age and is still being schooled. He's only lately returned from England, besides."

He returned his hat to his head. "I've always felt it unseemly that a woman of your station conducts business like a man. In Europe such is frowned upon."

She herself frowned and returned her attention to a display of snuff boxes. Would her dismay at his presence never lessen? "You'd best adjust to New World attitudes, sir, when women, including tobacco brides, not only have a place in commerce but own property."

"Indeed. A move of desperation to populate the colony. How else would we lure women to this rusticated outpost without giving them a token of independence?"

"You do not agree with those measures?" Done with his arrogance, she met his eyes. "And yet you sit on the council, the very body that gave them the stamp of approval?"

"I recommend women respect their place and not aspire to dangerous privilege nor masculine pursuits."

They were drawing notice, people pausing to overhear their barbed exchange, including the worst of James Towne's gossips.

Lest she be branded a scold, Selah retreated, relieved when he made no effort to detain her. "If you'll excuse me, sir."

He turned his back on her, falling into conversation with a colony official. Walking toward them were Candace and Cecily, the latter still looking a tad peaked. Trying to collect herself, Selah paused to peruse a display of pipes, turning a particularly fetching one from Port Royal over in her hand. Shay had told her Xander had quite a collection at Rose-n-Vale. Producing enough coin, she paid for the handsomest as well as a pouch of Caribbean tobacco.

"What is it that holds your interest?" Cecily inquired, eyes on her purchases. "Surely you do not smoke!"

Selah held the items aloft. "Perhaps these shall sweeten the deal."

Cecily resembled a cat served a dish of cream. "Well done!"

"Deal?" Candace lost her joviality. "Are you two mischief making?"

"Just being matrimonially minded," Selah reassured her as she continued on, trying to put as much distance between herself and Laurent as she could.

'Twas midafternoon when Selah and Shay took the canoe upriver, his catch netted in the cold water to keep it from the heat.

"Betimes I wish we could keep going," she told him, still pondering her unsavory encounter with Laurent. "The Blue Mountains are bewitchingly beautiful, 'tis said."

"I should like the same, but remember, the wider the river, the thicker the danger. 'Tis foolish to venture past the falls of the James. The Monacans who dwell in the foothills are Powhatan enemies." He suspended his oar, and the canoe continued gliding like a swan. "You suppose Xander has tales to tell of his time away?"

"Perhaps a story or two in exchange for your fine fish," she replied.

Her brother's fascination with the Naturals, not only the powerful Powhatans but the Chickahominy, Mattaponi, and others, had no end. Somehow Xander seemed to stoke that curiosity, bringing Shay arrowheads and other fascinating items, even teaching him Indian words.

As they passed the familiar landmark of Hopewell Hundred, Selah's heart shot from a brisk trot to a breathless gallop. Just around the watery bend loomed Rose-n-Vale, stirring her admiration—and apprehension—anew. Shay beached the boat effortlessly, allowing her to gain ground faster than she had with Cecily. They took the same path, Shay carrying the sturgeon, the pipe and tobacco hidden in Selah's pocket. In the distance dogs barked. Would their coming be welcome? Or more an interruption? Hopefully Widow Brodie had returned from town.

As they came closer a dozen details assailed her. A flower garden she'd never seen lay all abloom, an abandoned wheelbarrow full of thistles and weeds near the gate. A weathervane spun dizzily atop the milk house. Bricklaying on the new wing continued in earnest, and workmen hardly gave them a glance, so intent were they on their task. No sign of Widow Brodie or the master.

Between the summer kitchen and smokehouse was a small courtyard, a well at the center. There they found Xander, shirtless, breeches damp. His sun-darkened neck and forearms made a startling contrast to his paler chest. He poured a bucket of well water over his head and bare shoulders, noisily splashing the stones at his feet. 'Twas clear he was in the fields nearly as much as his indentures.

Rising up, he spied them, his muscled frame glistening in the stark afternoon sun. Selah averted her eyes while Shay called out a greeting. Around the side of the smokehouse came the hounds, rushing them in tail-wagging delight.

"To what do I owe the pleasure?" Xander made no apologies as to his sodden state.

In good humor, then. Relief made Selah nearly lightheaded. He had a fierce temper on occasion, was particularly mercurial after Mattachanna's death. And given the current tobacco crop was beset with woes . . .

"We've come to inspect your scalp after your dangerous foray west," Shay called, holding up the fish.

"A splendid sturgeon!" Xander smiled his appreciation and walked them toward the summer kitchen, where a half-blood cook held sway, her black braid dangling down her thickset back. She took the fish with a nod at his instructions.

"As you can see, my scalp is intact." Xander's gaze swung from Shay to Selah. "Given that, won't you stay for supper?"

Selah's "nay" collided with Shay's "aye."

Xander waited patiently. "So, which will it be?"

At Shay's imploring look, Selah lost ground.

"Please, Sister, what would it hurt to stay and sup?"

On the second floor, a diamond-pane window was rapped, and Widow Brodie's welcoming face appeared through the glass.

"Very well," Selah agreed. Sturgeon *was* her favorite fish. And the matter with Cecily needed settling once and for all.

They moved toward a rear door of the main house and into a stairwell, escaping the blinding sun. Rose-n-Vale had a scantily furnished parlor that seemed rarely used. Instead, Xander led them to his larger study, the leathery-tobacco scent strong. Selah had been here before with her father but rarely. The dogs followed, settling near the cold hearth out of habit, Selah guessed. The rapier above the mantel unsettled her, its shell hilt distinctive. She wondered its history.

"Wellaway!" Widow Brodie appeared, expression vexed, bearing a clean linen shirt. "Nephew, your Powhatan ways make you forget yourself."

Xander grinned and thanked her, donning the garment as his aunt departed.

"A game, aye?" Their host gestured to a table where a chess set rested, Shay's favorite pastime after fishing.

"Aha! I shall best you," her brother boasted, taking a chair. "Is it true what the king says? That chess filleth and troubleth men's heads?"

"What do contrary kings know?" Xander shrugged. "The better question is, what will your fair sister do while we play?"

"Take no thought of it." Shay rolled his eyes. "As you can see, she is besotted with books."

True. Selah was already standing before the tallest book-case, a marvel of mahogany filled to the brim. There were a great many tomes here of manly interest, little that turned a woman's head. Still, agape with the abundance, she read the titles in gilt lettering. One too many agricultural manuals from England, which seemed to have little bearing on Virginia. And a well-used copy of the popular fencing manual by the Italian grand master, Fabris.

Xander and Shay began their game. While they were occupied, Selah drifted unnoticed toward the hall, then out to the summer kitchen for a light. Nearly on tiptoe she returned to the study with Xander's gift. His back was to her as he moved his rook, his arm suspended over the chessboard. While Shay pondered his next move, Selah came to stand behind Xander. The trumpeted pipe bowl glowed good-naturedly, and she drew on it as she'd seen her father do, not so expertly but without a sputter. Aromatic wisps wreathed the air. She inhaled again carefully, then blew the smoke out like a whisper before it crept down her throat.

Without warning, Xander shot to his feet so fast the game table nearly overturned. He turned on her, his gaze half feral. "Zounds, woman! I feared the place was on fire!"

As Jett gave a howl, Selah quickly sobered. Though the fuss was over, Xander still looked stricken. Was he remembering the terrible fire of James Towne in his youth, when a stray spark from musket fire burned all but three buildings to the ground? She prayed not, or her little jest would be in vain.

His expression eased as she apologized. "I've come on a matter of business. 'Tis customary to smoke, aye?"

Reaching out, he extracted the pipe from her fingers. "Unbecoming to a gentlewoman though undeniably amusing."

Shay watched the charade with a grin as Xander examined the new pipe, holding it aloft in admiration, complimenting the design before taking a draw himself. His eyes met hers again, more silver than blue in the late afternoon's shifting shadows. "You have fine taste in pipes, Mistress Hopewell."

"And you"—she gestured to his collection atop the mantel—"hardly need another, Master Renick."

The game momentarily forgotten, he drew again on the pipe and continued to study her in earnest. "What is this business you bring me?"

With an aplomb born of years of store tending, Selah glanced at her brother. "Give us a few minutes of privacy, please."

At once Shay went into the hall and out the front door, the dogs following. A closing thud signaled they were alone.

Selah looked to her shoes, willing her galloping heart to a trot. "I am here on another's behalf."

"Cecily Ward's?"

She nodded, focusing on the smoke rings rather than his bearded face. "I need not tell you why, astute as you are."

Another draw, the pipe stem between perfect teeth. "Mistress Ward fancies me for a husband."

"Bluntly put, aye." She silently chafed at the prospect. Could he tell? "Pray, what is your answer, sir?"

"*Nay* is my answer."

Nay? Profound relief turned to gall at his next utterance. "I have in mind another bride."

This time her eyes went wide. Another? Who?

She dared not pry. Her boldness over Cecily was enough. He was watching her again, clearly enjoying this exchange. Or was he simply flattered by Cecily's audacious offer?

"What shall I tell her?" The question was as tart as Cecily herself.

"The truth."

"But I do not know it," Selah said, unable to kill her curiosity. "Who is she?"

He ran a hand over his jaw. "You have a streak of your father's persistence, asking me such."

"And you would rather I beat about the bush?"

"No one need know the object of my affections."

"I would hope *she* does."

He ceased smoking to admire the pipe again. "I confess I know not her heart."

"But 'tis not Cecily Ward who moves you."

He shook his head, removing all doubt. Excusing himself, he went to the front door and called for Shay to resume their game. Flummoxed, Selah went in search of Widow Brodie, the tobacco bitter on her tongue.

8

Widow Brodie set a lovely table. A linen cloth was anchored by a vase of cowslips, buttery yellow and so fragrant the entire dining room was sweetened. The herbed, prepared fish reclined on a pewter platter amid cobalt-blue porcelain bowls heaped with early garden fare. Despite Selah's warning glance, Shay reached out and snuck a bite from a stack of corncakes fried to crisp perfection. A pot of freshly salted butter and fig preserves completed the feast.

But first they bowed their heads, and a scandalously short grace was said.

"Come, Lord Jesus, be Thou our guest, and let Thy gifts to us be blessed." Xander's voice echoed in the large, mostly empty room. "Amen."

Selah picked up a two-tined fork, its handle of ivory and piqué work unfamiliar. Never had she eaten here. Only Shay and Father had. Xander came mostly to their table, though not for many months after he'd overheard her cross words when he returned alone from England.

Widow Brodie seemed to relish their company. Was her melancholy over the lack of a mistress on its way to being remedied? Though Xander and Shay kept up a merry discourse, supper seemed riven with new tension about the unknown lady of his choice. A miss from Middle Plantation or Point Comfort or Bermuda Hundred? Selah's mind whirled with possibilities as she dined.

"'Tis good the day is long and the moon full for your return home," Widow Brodie told her.

"Summer eves hold a special magic." Selah admired a west-facing window overlooking rolling hills. "The sunsets of late seem like fire in the sky."

"Tell me, is your private matter with my nephew settled?"

Selah took a spoonful of peas. *Not to my satisfaction.* "For the moment, aye."

"You should come oftener to Rose-n-Vale. This house is suited for company, and with the new wing we shall have cause for entertainment."

Selah took another bite, content to listen. Perhaps all this expansion meant Oceanus could come home for good.

"Soon a portico shall be under way. Alexander has drawn up plans with the brick mason." Widow Brodie looked fondly at her nephew. "How far we have come from Virginia's earliest days. I'm sure you've heard your share of your father's stories. I can't recall if he came on the first or second supply."

"The second supply, aboard the *Sea Venture*, sailing straight into a hurricane before landing in the Summer Isles." Selah took a second serving of fish. "I still marvel that Father survived. I'm glad Mother was spared and arrived later on the *Blessing*. Perhaps you were wisest of all, having only recently made Virginia your home."

A grieved nod. "So many have been buried on these sandy shores. Sometimes I long to return to a more civilized Scotland.

But a widow with naught but a nephew is destined to remain right here."

Selah lowered her voice, eyes on Shay and Xander deep in conversation and oblivious to their low chatter. "There is your great-nephew."

"Oceanus, aye. I oft wonder how the lad is faring. If his father was to remarry . . ." Widow Brodie cleared her throat. "But 'tis a mighty big *if*, I fear."

Should she allay Widow Brodie's fears? Tell her Xander's revelation in the study? Pressing a serviette to her mouth, Selah swallowed the urge to share what seemed for her ears only. At table's end, Shay was regaling Xander with his fishing exploits, in which he caught the sturgeon asleep on top of the water and engaged in a watery wrestle till the hook was set.

"I shall take you fire-fishing," Xander told him. "I learned it from the Powhatans firsthand. We'll fit a canoe with a clay hearth raised within two inches of gunwale height. The fire can easily be seen underwater. Then we'll pole the canoe with javelins, ready to spear any fish that surface. Woe to the sturgeons that follow our light."

Xander spun quite a tale. Shay hung on every syllable.

The dining room door opened and Cook entered carrying dessert, a maize-raisin pudding still warm from the bake oven. Steaming cassina was poured, the Naturals' "black drink," which some colonists favored. Conversation dwindled, cicadas chorusing through an open window, the drapes stirred by a sultry breeze.

Though the meal had been delicious, the mood pleasant, Selah felt increasingly sore. Now she must ponder her reply to Cecily. And Cecily, ever prickly, would not take Xander's rejection kindly.

She spooned her dessert to murmurs of "rich" and "flavorful," yet hers seemed tasteless given the leaden lump in her middle. Quietly she waged an unsuccessful war not to look Xander's way without reason. She could hardly fault Cecily for sending her upriver. What woman wouldn't be bestirred by the sight of such a man, bearded and broad of shoulder, as hospitable as he was capable at plantation managing, and dealing peace with the Naturals besides?

As supper finished she was only too ready to say, "We must be away. The hospitality of Rose-n-Vale is much appreciated."

Within moments they were out the rear door fronting the river, Xander accompanying them. The sunset was fading, ribbons of rose gold streaking the darkening sky. Shay ran ahead with the dogs, leaving her and Xander to walk down the wide, grassy hill in tongue-tied silence. When Selah stumbled on uneven ground, Xander's hand shot out to steady her.

"Would you like for me to talk to Mistress Ward personally and spare you the trouble?" he asked. "I've a matter to discuss with your father by sennight's end."

"I admire your willingness. But our guest is not of the temperament to delay and will likely await your answer tonight. Though I shall say nothing of the woman whose hand you hope to have." She took a steadying breath. "Think of all the idle tongues of James Towne wagging about Xander Renick's would-be bride."

"And yours shall make one less, God be thanked."

He helped her into the canoe, wading into the water to send them off, unmindful of his wet boots. Ruby barked as if bidding them farewell, and Shay laughed, the merry sound carrying over the water. Refusing to look back, Selah took up her oar, slicing the water while piecing together the scant facts before her. Xander had said little about his trip to the Naturals. Might he be considering another Powhatan bride? Might it even be one of Mattachanna's sisters?

He'd had critics aplenty when he'd informed the council of his intentions to wed the first time. The letter he'd penned to Virginia's deputy governor had captured her attention and her heart when her father showed it to her privately. Why, years later, did such impassioned wording woo her?

It is she to whom my heart and best thoughts are and have been a long time so entangled, and enthralled in so intricate a labyrinth that I could not unwind myself thereout.

Sadly, Selah recalled the mean-spirited tittle-tattle she'd overheard in James Towne just as readily. *"'Twas an alliance made to further Master Renick's own ambitious ends so the Powhatans would leave him be and yet aid him in cultivating the tobacco that became the pride of the colony."*

She felt a little start when Shay said, "Why are you sighing, Sister?"

"The night is beautiful, is it not?" She paddled with more vigor, determined to return her thoughts to their proper place. "Worth sighing over, truly."

The river bore the moon's full reflection mightily, the smooth sheen of water more gold than black. A multitude of stars blinked nearly as bright.

A true lovers' moon.

9

To Selah's relief, Cecily was asleep upon their return from Rose-n-Vale, still a bit worn down by her recent fever. But the next morning her florid face bespoke much once Selah informed her that her hopes had gone awry. "So Master Renick refuses me."

"He has sound reason, I am sure," Selah told her, heating an iron to press one of her father's shirts. "Goodman Wentz is still calling, is he not? A worthy suitor after Goodman Peacock's failed pursuit."

Cecily stayed sullen. "A far cry from the master of Rose-n-Vale."

Pressing the hot iron to the cloth, Selah curbed her exasperation. Many of these brides were a spirited bunch, unlike their more restrained British sisters, with far more rights and a voice here than in their homeland. Helion Laurent was right about that.

Forging ahead, Selah said, "I've heard you laughing with Goodman Wentz in the parlor. A man of merry temperament bodes well. An industrious planter too. And not overfond of drink as many are."

"His mother must live with us."

"She is a kind soul, mostly deaf and almost blind."

"I sometimes wonder if he courts me mostly as a caretaker to her."

"Widow Wentz is very old and needs looking after, as many do in James Towne."

"Better that than a half-blood son, I suppose. I heard prattle the Renick heir might be coming back."

Selah stared at her, and the hot iron gave off a seared linen smell. She grabbed it free. "Oh?"

"My friend Felicity, now Goody Shaw, told me so. Her husband's brother is a sea captain who vows the boy's passage has been paid."

"The timing is right." Selah resumed her ironing. "Sailing is far preferable in good weather months."

Still, she couldn't hide her surprise. Yet didn't this news dovetail with what Xander had told her about seeking a bride? And might it be Xander's reason for meeting with her father? To announce his decision to remarry? Despite her best intentions, the small blister that had begun in Xander's study began to fester.

Be done with such foolishness, Selah. Think well of the man and this felicitous situation that you, too, will benefit from. Have you not wanted a reunion with the child since he was taken from Mattachanna's lifeless arms? Haven't you lamented Xander's lack of a wife, a mother to his son, a mistress at Rose-n-Vale?

Immediately she righted herself and returned to pressing another shirt as Izella brought more dried laundry.

"Enough of my matrimonial prospects." Cecily leaned in conspiratorially. "What about that man I saw you speaking with in the marketplace?"

Selah frowned. "Helion Laurent? The physic?"

"A Frenchman, *oui*! He is quite the dandy—and seems quite taken with you."

Selah shook her head. "He is taken with none but himself, I fear. Laurent is as full of prickles as a porcupine, and I am quilled every time I draw near."

"On your part, perhaps. Not his. He seems to enjoy bantering with you. Tell me more about him."

Selah's lips parted as a dozen faults flashed to mind. 'Twas sheer work to give a favorable accounting.

A hypocrite with his mouth destroyeth his neighbor.

The timely Scripture tempered her answer if not her dislike. "I know very little. Laurent is French born but trained at the College of Physicians in London. 'Tis said he is the best swordsman in Virginia." And rumored to have killed half a dozen men in duels on his native soil. "He has been in James Towne but a few years and is a great favorite of Governor Harvey."

"I suppose a gentleman and physic wouldn't marry a middling woman like myself." Cecily shook out a wrinkled petticoat. "How I tire of this matrimonial game. The most eligible men are now wed, so I suppose I mustn't dally any longer lest Phineas Wentz look elsewhere."

"I look forward to calling on you as Goodwife Wentz, then."

Done with ironing, Selah looked out the open doorway, past Izella scrubbing laundry, beyond her mother's bent back as she gathered herbs for supper, and over the paling fence to see Xander riding down the road toward James Town. Her tangled feelings, having been schooled into submission, again unraveled at the sight of him.

Would he meet with her father at the store? As it was wash day, she'd stayed home but now found herself wishing she were behind the scarred counter. Her father would be full of news by suppertime, no doubt, if Xander did not swear him to secrecy.

As she thought it, Cecily all but burst out the front door and stormed into the street, nearly sending Xander's mount rearing. Selah felt a warm rush from the roots of her fair hair to her feet. What reason could Cecily possibly have to behave so unbecomingly? Yet Xander seemed to take it all in stride. He removed his hat and smiled down at her, from all appearances unmoved, as if used to women rushing him as he rode.

In a few moments Cecily returned, flushed but smiling. "I asked Master Renick his opinion of Phineas Wentz."

"And?" Selah all but held her breath.

"'A most excellent choice, merry of heart and steadfast of faith.'"

"A sterling recommendation."

"Indeed. Perhaps tonight I shall accept his proposal."

Cecily's and Phineas's laughter floated from the open parlor door. The rest of them lingered at table, Ustis looking especially grave. Surely this didn't bode well after Xander's visit. Usually his company left Ustis jolly. Selah glanced at the ebony and gilt table clock that foretold eight. It had been a long day awaiting any news.

To her great concern, her father's high flush and glassy eyes hinted at the return of the malady that had plagued him all winter. Candace was being overly solicitous, fetching him this or that, including his pipe and tobacco pouch, while Izella brought a light.

"Business was brisk in the forenoon, a great many seeking hilling hoes and scythes and such. Never enough spring tools." Ustis smiled thinly as he lit his pipe. "But I am most concerned with Xander's visit. His news affects us all."

Candace took a seat, hands cupped around her tea. Shay looked up from his cards, his game of All Fours of less interest than what their father had to say. Bracing herself, Selah took up her knitting. Their new kitten had gotten into the basket, making a snarl of her yarn.

"'Tis with a heavy heart that I inform you Xander will soon resign from the governor's council."

Selah paused from untangling her yarn. 'Twas all she could do not to cry out a protest.

"But does not that give Governor Harvey and his faction more room to enact poor laws and act ill-advisedly?" Candace asked. "Ride roughshod over those of us who see reason?"

"Aye, but Xander is done with petty politics. Done with sitting in meetings where in the end honest men have no say and Harvey's arrogance and aggression rule the day." Ustis took a long draw on his pipe, then coughed. "He believes the governor may even create a monopoly on tobacco trade. Harvey is threatening to invalidate the land titles of any who oppose him."

"Is he now?" Candace showed rare ire. "And alienate Virginia's foremost tobacco grower, whose exports are said to keep the entire colony afloat?"

"There is a move afoot to thrust Governor Harvey from office before such happens."

Selah's needles stilled. "I shall pray to that end. But I question the wisdom of Xander pulling out at so needful a time. We can be sure Harvey and his minions shall have a heyday without him."

"Xander will resign from Virginia's council but continue as a member of the House of Burgesses for his own shire. His aim is to effect change from the ground up, not the top down as Harvey does." Ustis held his pipe aloft. "But that is not the end of it."

Every eye was pinned on him, the tension in the room thick. Selah felt she would burst with anticipation. Nay, dread. A wedding announcement?

"As you know, all of Virginia is on tenterhooks, fearing another outbreak of warfare. The few years' peace that was had when Mattachanna became Lady Rebecca is broken, and the tribes are becoming more alarmed by the great number of colonists arriving without end. In an unusual gesture of goodwill, the Powhatans have offered to send some of their children to live among us if we will send some of ours to live among them. Xander has asked our feelings about Shay trading James Towne for Menmend, Chief Opechancanough's domain."

Shay shot up like a jack-in-the-box. "Father, may I?"

Selah had no doubts regarding her brother's feelings about the matter. Their mother was another worry.

"What is at the heart of such a bold endeavor?" Candace questioned.

"To regain trust and further understanding between our people and theirs," Ustis told her. "And you, Daughter, what are your thoughts about all this?"

"'Tis an admirable quest, a fresh bid to renew peace."

Selah sent a bittersweet smile Shay's way. "There's little doubt someone here is already packing his knapsack."

"No doubt, nay." Ustis's voice trembled with emotion. "Though if we agree to such, he'll be sorely missed."

"Father, I am more than willing. And I am unafraid." Shay was as earnest as Selah had ever seen him. "I've oft told Xander I'd like to push further west, see the mountains."

"If Shay goes, when will we see him next?" Candace asked the question uppermost.

"All that shall be decided once Xander meets with the council. But let's not become too concerned with a venture that may well be dismissed as soon as it's uttered."

Selah felt let down. "Nothing else, Father? Only this matter of an exchange between us Virginians and the Powhatans?"

"Aye, one more matter. Some of the Naturals seek to know our God, learn the tenets of our faith. Xander feels, as many in the colony do, that this is a matter of everlasting importance. Even Governor Harvey concurs."

"Ha!" Shay returned to his cards. "Harvey and his cohorts make religion their color when all their aim is nothing but present profit, as has been said."

"John Smith said a great many things." Candace made a wry face. "And you have a remarkable knack for remembering the knave's utterances."

"Let us ponder the matter of our faith." Ustis rubbed his brow. "Save for Mattachanna's unusual conversion, we seem to be alienating the tribes instead of fulfilling the Great Commission to introduce them to the gospel. Needs be we make missionaries of these heathen children by way of the proposed peace exchange."

91

"What do you mean, Husband?"

"By hosting them in our homes, we shall reveal the truth and then return them to their people to share the same."

"The Naturals have resisted our faith till now, understandably." 'Twas Selah's ongoing lament. How could they do otherwise when men failed to practice what they preached? "Perhaps prayers are at last being answered and a way is being made."

But what a sacrifice, with both Indians' and colonists' kinfolk at stake. Yet if things progressed amiably and an end was in mind to return the children in good faith, all would be worth the personal cost. *If.*

More laughter came from the parlor, distracting Selah momentarily. She had no wish to be a naysayer, especially if Xander approved of the plan, but her faith in James Towne's governing body had been shaken and nearly destroyed. There had been so many years of bloodshed and double dealing betwixt the Naturals and whites, and ceaseless quarreling among themselves as colonists jockeyed for position and power. The truth was she didn't trust Virginia's officials if they were to become involved in so weighty a matter.

Unable to concentrate, Selah set aside her handwork. "I've heard Oceanus might return to us."

A smile softened Candace's strain of a moment before. "Isn't that just like the Lord, blessing us amid fresh uncertainty?"

Ustis gave an affirming nod. "The lad is on his way, aye, Xander told me. He's set sail on the *Bonaventure* with his nurse."

Confirmation at last. If the winds were favorable and no accident befell them, the *Bonaventure* would dock and deliver Oceanus and a host of other passengers to their shores. Father and son would be reunited. That alone was reason to rejoice. And somewhere in that mix, Xander Renick would take a bride.

Selah waited for another announcement, something more that her father might have forgotten that would settle the affair once and for all. But no more was heard save the loud ticking of the clock. She checked a wistful sigh lest her mother take note, then looked toward the parlor, where Cecily and Phineas were seated like lovebirds on the sofa.

At least their tobacco bride was well on her way to matrimony.

10

At sennight's end Xander entered the council chamber in James Towne, unsurprised to see nearly every seat taken. In matters with the Naturals, every goodman and official wanted to lend a voice or at least an ear. With their very lives at stake, who could blame them?

All eyes were upon him as he removed his hat, awaiting Governor Harvey's entrance. The chair reserved for the leading official was large and ornate, something a prince or lord might require, and seemed the focal point of the musky, oak-paneled room.

He had come prepared for one last battle before resigning from the council. On behalf of the Powhatans, some would say. His allegiance to the colonial government was continually in question. Some here had even accused him of spy. His foremost adversaries—Helion Laurent and Nicholas Claibourne—were missing, their empty places conspicuous.

The last council meeting had turned forge-hot in mere minutes over the fate of forty settlers marrying Indian women and abandoning the settlement during the last decade. Under old martial law, the penalty for such desertion was death, though most had eluded capture and assimilated.

He'd pleaded like a barrister for his fellow Virginians' right to marry and live as they desired, undeterred by law or king. But the council had instead appointed a sheriff and sent out a posse to round up those living among the "infidels and savages" and incurring the wrath of the Almighty. The archaic penalty remained unchanged.

"Renick, you bring out every man in the colony, even the shirkers and sots." A wry smile worked itself across the face of his friend and fellow planter Emanuel Murray. "'Tis said Governor Harvey rues commanding a lesser audience than you, vainglorious as he is."

"I would rather the meeting be limited to select men, as all this has the feel of theater to me." Xander's gaze traveled to the doorway as more latecomers arrived. Laurent entered, Claibourne just behind. For a few seconds all attention shifted to the two peacocks.

Murray took a seat beside him. "Is it my imagination, or did Helion Laurent just cast you a murderous look? And the proceedings have not yet begun."

"'Tis his usual stance," Xander replied quietly.

Few knew that he and the physic fought a far more personal war whenever they met, be it here or beyond James Towne. Their rancor ran like a scarlet ribbon beneath the more obvious matters at hand, as if they'd crossed swords.

Governor Harvey entered at last, all stood, and a lengthy prayer was said. But not to the God Xander knew and worshiped. Unbidden, a timely Scripture filled his bowed head.

Having a form of godliness, but denying the power thereof: from such turn away.

At their collective "amen," the irascible Harvey brought the meeting to order with an address that tested Xander's patience. True, Harvey had done a great deal to establish the colony, though many of his enterprises and industries had failed miserably and he'd made a great many enemies. While a movement was afoot to depose him, the list of offenses growing, Xander wanted nothing to do with it. His business was straight as an arrow and concerned the Naturals first and foremost.

At last he stood and faced the assembly. "I make a motion that two or more royal commissioners investigate and handle any and all disputes between Indians and English." Sweating from the closed room, a fly bedeviling him, he was as succinct as Harvey had been long-winded. "The authorities must establish accountability and rectify wrongs done."

Barely were the words aired before Claibourne leapt to his feet, a look of utter contempt on his swarthy face. "Wrongs done? May I enumerate for you the base deeds done to us by the savages since Virginia's founding?"

"By all means," Xander replied, "if you are also willing to hear the growing list of offenses committed by the English since sixteen and seven. In my hand I hold Chief Opechancanough's latest grievances. I can assure you and everyone in this chamber that though atrocities have been committed on both sides, we English are the foremost aggressors with our flagrant duplicity and pharisaical self-righteousness."

A rumble went through the room. Not in his favor, Xander knew. He returned to his seat to retrieve a ream of papers while Claibourne continued the verbal assault he'd begun.

"Few here need reminding of the ten years' war that ended only recently and may well begin anew. But for those of us serving on the governor's council who are courageous enough to lead expeditions against the Naturals—"

"Courageous?" Xander turned back around, clutching the papers. "What glory is to be had in burning Indians' fields and destroying enough food to have sustained four thousand men for a twelvemonth?"

"How dare you—"

"Not only burning but keeping much of the plunder from the Indian towns for yourselves." Xander looked from Claibourne to Harvey, who sat in stony silence. "These are the actions that return me to my appeal today—the need of royal commissioners to investigate such acts, which are, by English law, deserving of censure and punishment."

"Are there not laws in place prohibiting trading with the Indians, which you yourself are guilty of?" Laurent stood as a disgruntled Claibourne sat. "I saw with mine own eyes your purchasing a great many goods from the cape merchant's daughter before going west of your own accord. Are there not laws prohibiting such?"

Murray stood in Xander's defense. "Laws that are antiquated and seldom enforced, as free trading abounds, especially on Virginia's borders."

Xander faced his opponents across several crowded benches. "I made no unlawful trade as you claim. As commander of my shire, I went west at the invitation of Chief Opechancanough in pursuit of peace. I brought the requisite gifts as any sensible envoy would."

"Peace?" Laurent all but spat the word. "There's been no peace, nor shall there be till every acre the savages claim is underfoot us Virginians."

Other voices rose, joining in the vociferous cry against the tribes, spewing venom to all corners of the echoing chamber. Xander held his peace as the din grew deafening. He stared down at his papers, upon which he'd penned a lengthy list of Opechancanough's most alarming grievances.

"Gentlemen, I see you all are in a passion, which makes men no longer themselves." Governor Harvey's voice became a hoarse shout. "I pray give a small respite to your anger and recover your reason!"

When the room finally quieted, Xander voiced his second cause—the proposed peace exchange. But how would it end? Chief Opechancanough was ruthless. He was feared. And guilty in the past of pleading peace while plotting mayhem. Most within this chamber would rather draw and quarter him than send Virginia's children into enemy territory or entertain the Naturals in their own.

Xander's gaze swept the florid, frowning faces before turning toward the governor, who seemed more desirous of reconciliation with the Naturals. "I beg you to consider the peace exchange proposed by Opechancanough between the Powhatan nation and the English . . ."

Xander picked a particularly large worm from a tobacco plant, mastering his disgust with the mettle of years in the fields. The pest writhed in his palm before he flung it onto a small fire made for that purpose. Smoke billowed in the early June wind, contained by several indentures intent on ridding the struggling, rain-soaked plants of yet another scourge.

Better the pests of the field than the council chamber.

The thought turned him wry as he looked askance at the clouds. The overcast held no threat of rain and spared his laborers the sun beating down on shirtless backs. Though he'd long grown used to Virginia's climate, he fretted about his indentures, who cycled in and out of Rose-n-Vale's infirmary. He sympathized and prayed. His own seasoning when he'd first set foot on these shores had nearly been the end of him. First the dysentery from foul well water in James Towne, then when he was full grown, a recurring miasma that left him so depleted it was all he could do to pull on his boots.

Mattachanna's coming had changed all that. She'd doused him with her tonics, most of them known healers among the Powhatans, and her practical partnership had renewed his purpose. 'Twas she who'd taught him how to raise maize and beans together, not in unproductive Old World rows but intertwined. Nor would his tobacco be what it was without her expertise. His step lightened in thankfulness before sorrow rushed in.

He picked his way down another row, shadowed by Mattachanna's dire beginnings at James Towne. The dark memory hovered, though he tried to thrust it away as he sent another pest onto the snapping fire.

"Sir." Hosea Sterrett, his farm manager, approached, hat in hands. "I've come to give ye a report."

"A good one, I pray." Xander turned his back on the next tobacco plant and gave the lanky man his full attention.

With a nod, Sterrett glanced at the pluming fire. "Glad to confirm the flax, hemp, and rice are thriving, as well as the black walnut groves."

Xander ran a sleeve across his brow. "Much of our success is because of your oversight."

"Ye give me undue credit when ye yourself work tirelessly, sir." Still, Sterrett seemed pleased. "We're readying a ton of potash to ship to England, in addition to wainscoting and a small quantity of silk from the mulberry grove. For now, I bring ye this." He reached into his pocket and produced a large pink pearl. "From yer oyster beds."

Xander took it, his would-be bride's face flashing to mind. He nearly had enough for a lovely necklace strung on silken thread. "A beauty, mayhap the largest find yet. And such a peculiar color."

"Is it true about the Powhatans, that they amass pearls in their treasure houses, even burying them with their dead?"

"Aye, the chiefs do, yet they tend to ruin pearls by firing them open."

"I daresay ye'd fetch a royal price for this one even in London."

Xander held the gemstone up to the light as the clouds parted. "Not all of Virginia's treasures are to be exported, thankfully."

"Rightly so, sir." Returning his hat to his balding head, Sterrett bade him good day and resumed his rounds.

Watching him go, Xander allowed himself a brief rest. With a word to the workers to slake their thirst, he returned to the house, not trusting himself with so fine a pearl. After retreating to his study, he opened a corner cupboard, hinges creaking, and took out a small, velvet-lined box.

Truly, this new freshwater marvel outshone the last lustrous gray one that was slightly misshapen. A growing collection lay before him. His favorite was a metallic green, the others pale purple and varied hues, gotten from Chesapeake oyster beds. 'Twas said the pearl symbolized purity, loyalty, integrity, and largess of spirit. The essence of his intended.

He secreted the box and climbed the stairs that led to the

nursery across the hall from his bedchamber. The closed door seemed more a wall. He rarely came here, having last entered to read a letter from his Scots kin. He went to the dresser, retrieved the post from a top drawer, and stared down at the page. He'd already committed the contents to memory, returning to the most troublesome lines . . .

I hope that you will consider Oceanus's nurse as more than that. Electa Lineboro has been cast into service due to her family's losses of recent years. She is soon to be five and twenty, of honest conduct and conversation, a handsome, honestly educated maid. Given you have not remarried, I urge you to consider her as a bride prospect. Not only would that ease your son's transition to the New World, it would benefit you at Rose-n-Vale, which is no doubt in need of a mistress, and relieve Miss Lineboro's hard circumstances . . .

The plot thickened. He felt like a character in a Shakespearean play—a comedy, mayhap a tragedy. Just when he was ready to move forward with his own romantic plan, there came an unwelcome twist. He'd married Mattachanna out of affection and a realization that their tie would help bring about peace between the Powhatans and colonists. And here lately he'd begun to allow himself a vision of another bride, one near at hand, one highly esteemed in the settlement, who could have any number of suitors but had chosen to stay chaste.

Enter Electa Lineboro.

The name was pleasing, the prospect convenient, given she was Oceanus's nurse. And on her way to Virginia even as he held the letter between callused fingers. He would be spared the time and expense of wooing her, this woman who was likely not averse to marrying a colonist who peddled tobacco.

Yet his mind—his heart, rather—was fixed on someone else entirely.

He returned the letter to the drawer and began a slow walk around the unused room. No more need for the cradle between the two tall windows. A more fitting bed for a boy of four was against one wall, a new coverlet worked by his aunt atop it. A wooden rocking horse of dapple gray, fashioned in London, awaited beside some colorful blocks and toy soldiers painted scarlet. No expense had been spared for a boy he hardly knew and who hardly knew him.

Lord, help Thou me.

11

"Dearly beloved friends, we are gathered together here in the sight of God, and in the face of His congregation, to join this woman and this man in holy matrimony . . ."

From the women's pews on the seventeenth of June, Selah listened to Reverend Midwinter recite the marriage vows. Try as she might, she could not fasten her thoughts on the nuptials at hand, though she was happy that Cecily was becoming Goodwife Wentz. The groom seemed uncommonly nervous as he stood before the chancellery, murmuring his vows slowly as if tongue-tied. Cecily was more collected, her new blackwork coif covering her upswept hair, her expression serene. Her belongings had been delivered this very morn to the Wentz household east of James Towne.

"I, Cecily, take thee, Phineas . . ."

Selah's gaze lifted to the church's timbered walls and high windows, her thoughts returning to another wedding years before. All of James Towne had crowded into this cloistered chamber the spring Xander wed Mattachanna. Beyond the west wall lay a graveyard, an eternal reminder that Mattachanna was missing. If she had been buried here rather than in England, Selah would have tended her grave, brought flowers in remembrance. Was anyone doing that in the Old World?

Shay shifted on the pew across from her, clearly bored with the proceedings. Ever since Xander had told him the Powhatans' plan, he'd been preoccupied with nothing else, awaiting the council's decision.

As the wedding proceeded, Selah pondered their furious labors since first light. They'd finished the wedding feast, laying tables in the garden for the overflow of guests. Sliced leg of lamb and herring pie crowned the menu, along with assorted sweetmeats and mince tarts. With the help of James Towne's bake shop, a preposterous pile of buns had been created and artfully arranged on a platter and decorated with edible garden flowers, mostly nasturtiums. Punch was mixed with care and chilled beforehand, sure to quench the thirst of all James Towne. Her father fussed if the punch ran low, so Selah and her mother spent the day before concocting and tasting, leaving them a tad woozy by supper.

This morn Izella stood watch in their absence lest hungry gulls or other ravenous creatures arrive first. As soon as the ceremony ended, Selah and her mother hastened home ahead of the wedding party. Governor Harvey led the procession, his betrothed on his arm. His presence seemed to subdue the celebratory mood, though few could deny the soon-to-be Lady Harvey looked resplendent in a gown of silver thread, her serene expression a striking contrast to her escort's familiar frown.

Guests began streaming through both garden gates, intent on making merry. When Xander and his aunt appeared, Selah smiled past her somersaulting stomach, wondering why she'd not seen them at church.

Questions that needed quieting burned her tongue. Should she seek Xander out and inquire about Oceanus and the possible peace exchange?

Bide your time.

At the heart of her curiosity was the matter of his bride. But that was hardly her business either.

"Mistress Hopewell, you are in fine form today, I see."

Selah situated herself near the punch bowl and found Helion Laurent first in line, his black hat with its ostrich plume nearly tickling her face as it was doffed. Again, he gave a courtly bow, looking as if he'd robbed a pirate's ship of plunder. Colorful ribbons decorated the edges of his jacket, his frilled shirt and lace stock a stark white, his mustard-yellow hose beneath ballooning breeches stretching down toward red-heeled, bowed shoes.

She felt plain as a tufted titmouse in his presence. Nor did she feel like sparring with him in the rising heat. With a tight smile, she left the punch to Izella's keeping and sought the next table, making a show of rearranging wedding buns.

He followed, displeasure on his fine features. "Surely you can spare a word for a guest."

"I did not think to find you at the reception, sir."

"When I heard the hospitable Hopewells were hosting, I dared not miss it. I also heard your father continues unwell." His gaze traveled across the garden to where Ustis stood in the shade, several fellow merchants about him.

"Best ask my father himself. I cannot speak for him."

"He is a hard man to corner, popular as he is." Laurent twirled his hat in his hands. "You might mention I wish to talk to him about a survey of land that borders your own upriver."

"Hopewell Hundred?"

"Indeed. Your property that lies fallow." He eyed the wedding buns with apparent distaste. "Such a waste of fertile, cleared acreage. Why not plant tobacco? Wheat and corn?"

"For a physic whose priority should be the sick, you show a remarkable interest in agriculture, sir."

He smiled again, but there was no warmth in it. "Only because my upriver forays to distant patients take me past your idle acreage. One never knows when there will again be a drought or other disaster that requires every kernel of corn, every drop of sustenance."

This she could not naysay. She'd oft wanted to see the land fruitful, but as her dowry was only a part of the whole and she remained unwed, she felt she had little right to speak of it. Besides, her father was too busy merchanting to farm or even seek a new tenant.

"If, by chance, you Hopewells ever tire of landowning, I hope I would be considered first in regard to its sale."

So 'twas land he craved, not her company. "Hopewell Hundred is largely my brother's inheritance."

"Of course. Common knowledge." His gaze sharpened. "But you yourself have a generous land dowry, do you not? Yet you are nearly a spinster."

The word sat like a slur upon his garrulous tongue. How dare he ask. And how weary she was of defending the matter. Why did it concern others if she chose to remain unmarried? Truth be told, she paid little mind to her dowry or dower chest. Such stayed in the shadows, gathering dust along with her dreams.

Another twirl of his plumed hat. "On a more pleasant note, have you heard the council's latest mandate?"

Could her hackles rise any further? Again, she sought refuge in silence.

"You are tasked with accompanying me on calls to the newly wed tobacco brides. Governor Harvey himself recognizes there is none fitter for the task than you, given your successful oversight of the maids coming to Virginia."

"But my merchanting duties—"

"I am sure your brother will stand in your stead."

Everything honest and good within her recoiled. Barely could she eke out a response. "What, pray tell, do these visits require?"

"We shall visit every household with a tobacco bride as its mistress, inquiring as to their health and well-being so that we can give the council a good report."

Dare she pair with him for such a task? But with Governor Harvey behind the plan, who could naysay it?

She batted a fly from the buns, nearly wilting with relief at the sound of her mother's voice.

"Selah, fetch more punch, please."

Excusing herself, she hastened toward the kitchen. Candace's concerned face bespoke much as she returned to her hostessing duties.

Moments later, Selah emerged into bright sunlight, carrying a large pitcher to refill the ceramic bowl. Again, relief washed through her. The physic was nowhere to be seen. A small line had formed at the punch table, Xander at the rear. Excusing Izella, Selah took her place. In the wake of Laurent's unwelcome news, she was all a-fumble, acutely aware of Xander's direct gaze upon her as if he sensed her discomfiture. Mortified, she sloshed punch, spilling some on her lace-edged apron.

When his turn came, he took the cup from her hand with a small, reassuring smile. "My thanks, Mistress Hopewell."

"You're welcome, Master Renick."

He took a long drink, just the two of them beneath the shade of the kitchen eave. Though she was given to making all sorts of counter conversation in their store and elsewhere, all talk flew out of her head.

He took another drink. "Excellent punch."

"A simple *bolleponge*." She smiled past her fluster. "Aqua vitae, sugar, rosewater, and citrus from the Summer Isles."

"Your mother's garden is especially fitting for a wedding."

"Truly." How she hated small talk when other heartfelt matters needed discussing. But small talk they must make. "Rose-n-Vale must be equally lovely now that 'tis summer. All those roses abloom. And a great many robins and warblers and such."

"Don't forget the copper snakes and cougars."

"I'd rather"—she winced as a gull shrieked overhead—"dwell upon all things lovely and of good report."

"I recollect that was the gist of Reverend Midwinter's sermon last time I was churched in James Towne. Before I fell asleep."

She nearly laughed. The reverend, bless him, was notoriously long-winded. "So, you were paying attention?"

"Not word for word, mayhap." He gave her a sidelong glance. "I also recall something about speaking the truth in love."

Startled, she stared absently at her own cup. Might this be the opening she needed? A divine prompting? Summoning all the wits she possessed, she began a bit haltingly. "In that respect, 'tis time I do the same . . ."

He looked at her, his features suddenly earnest. Inquiring.

"I—I beg your forgiveness." The surprise in his eyes left her more tongue-tied. "The asking comes late. I should have done so as soon as I spoke the hasty words once you docked that terrible day. The lapse has haunted me ever since." Even now the old shame of it burned. "There is no reparation I can make for so foolish an outburst."

A weighty pause. "You simply spoke out of your affection for Mattachanna and Oceanus."

She had, but . . . "Does it not grieve you?"

"Not as much as it grieves you." Yet he seemed relieved to have it aired at last. "I am a man not much undone by words or blows or accusations. I am more moved by your softness, your depth of feeling."

For a few fleeting seconds, Alexander Renick lost that stoic, self-possessed manner that marked him. A rare pensiveness turned him vulnerable, his expression easing, features less firmly set. Or was it not pensiveness at all but something else entirely? Reaching out, he took a tendril of hair the wind had pulled free of her coif and coiled it behind her ear.

His touch turned her soft as candle wax. And then just as quickly his hand fell away as if burned. Their locked gazes broke and wandered to the table where the wedding buns were being devoured, bride and groom giving a customary kiss over the great mound of them.

Cecily waved a gloved hand, a lovely satin pair gifted by Phineas, her nosegay of orange blossoms and myrtle clutched in the other. With a trilling laugh, she tossed the flowers Selah's way. They landed at her slipper-clad feet, their ribbon undone. Amused, Selah pressed her fingers to her mouth lest her sip of punch spill out as Xander knelt and retrieved them.

He passed her the tousled blooms after retying their ribbon. "Do you give much credence to the old wives' tale of catching the bouquet?"

"Not in the slightest." Still, she brought the blooms to her nose, inhaling their sweet, earthy scent.

A flicker of something she couldn't name passed over his sun-glazed features. "Is there no man that moves you, Selah Hopewell?"

He wasn't looking at her but at all the color and confusion in the garden around them, yet she flushed to the roots of her upswept hair all the same. What could she possibly say to this? Had he seen her talking to Helion Laurent? Did he suspect . . . ?

Heaven forbid.

"I ask because my aunt asked me," he confided. "And I had no answer."

She stared down at the blooms in her hands. Dare she reveal the state of her heart? "You may tell your aunt that aye, there is such a man, but . . ."

A wicked grin turned him roguish again. "But you will make no more mention of him than I my would-be bride."

She fought a sudden breathlessness. Such a delicate affair. She would not force it. "I cannot help but think of the possible peace exchange and other pressing matters."

"The council's decision should come by sennight's end."

"Is it true that Oceanus is returning also?"

An affirming nod. "He's already at sea, or should be. Pray for a swift, uneventful voyage."

Prayers aside, his leaving England guaranteed nothing. Yet she shooed away any melancholy. "I have no words for how his homecoming heartens me. Four is a delightful age.

110

And Rose-n-Vale must seem a paradise for one so small. My prayers won't cease till he's in your arms again."

"His grandfather wants to see him. His daughter's death and burial in England are not forgotten, nor likely forgiven. He asks if anything of Mattachanna resides in her son."

"I understand, though such is fraught with . . ."

"Complexities," he finished for her.

"Thankfully, your time is your own now that you're leaving the council. You'll not be so often in James Towne."

"Yet I hear dismay in your voice all the same. Would you have me stay and come to blows with the governor and his men?"

"I suspect they rejoice to see you forsake matters here to serve your own shire instead. As for myself, I feel a light has gone out with your leaving."

"You flatter me."

"Nay, Alexander Renick, I speak truth."

"Then let us dispense with surnames and all the rest."

Their eyes met and held. Oh, she was nearly undone. First he'd touched her. And now her name on his lips sounded like a song. She sought some response, but the well of her heart was too full for words.

"Till we meet again, Selah." With a low farewell, he moved away from her just as his aunt sought her out.

"How fare you this joyous wedding day?"

"Very well, Widow Brodie. And you?"

She looked at the bouquet in Selah's hands. "A portent, perhaps?"

"Perhaps." Widow Brodie's expression was so hopeful she daren't say otherwise. "Care for a cup of punch?" At the woman's nod, Selah ladled more of the dwindling drink.

Voices rose near the garden's gate fronting the street as several members of the council gathered there. Selah's alarm swelled. The governing body of James Towne was increasingly divided and bitter, and even amiable occasions such as these were cause for rancor and confrontation.

Thankfully, Xander was at the opposite end of the garden, speaking with her father near her mother's prized weeping willow. Other guests milled about, the four acres offering pleasant distraction, each bed meticulously weeded and watered and cossetted to showcase every color of the rainbow. At the garden's heart, her mother held court, answering questions about certain plants, dispensing advice over which herb was best paired with poultry and which waylaid gout, what thrived in Tidewater soil and what was best left in the Old World.

"So good to speak with you, my dear," Widow Brodie said in parting. "I think I shall walk about before I go. This lovely plot is the talk of all Virginia, and rightly so."

Selah pushed back the wayward slip of hair Xander had righted. Wooziness again smote her. Perhaps she made too much of the gesture. A friend might have done the same. She took a steadying breath and fought for composure. Her stays felt damp in the noonday sun, the sky as sapphire a hue as the newly arrived silk on their shelves.

The reception was waning now, most wedding delicacies devoured. Cecily and Phineas spoke with a few lingering guests as most left to seek the shade of their own homes and workplaces. Selah's gaze returned to Xander now leaving the garden by way of a back street, avoiding the knot of cantankerous men still clustered near the main road. Wise, he was. And bent on a dozen different things that eluded her.

Especially this matter of a bride.

12

At sennight's end, Ustis sat at the head of the table and admired the salted ham Izella placed in front of him. "Our table is bereft of Cecily but about to welcome Watseka."

"Watseka?" Shay was at full attention.

"It means 'pretty girl' in Potawatomi."

"Shall we simply call her *Pretty Girl*?"

"Perhaps we shall ask what she prefers," Ustis replied, taking up a knife and fork to carve the meat. "She shall arrive in a fortnight."

"So, the council has decided," Candace said.

Grieved by the lament in her mother's tone, Sclah awaited her father's answer as she poured small beer. For once, Shay was more interested in Watseka's coming than his supper plate.

"Indeed, the decision has been made, dear wife. With Xander overseeing the exchange, all is in hand. For that we can be thankful."

Shay looked toward their mother as if to allay her fears. "Surely God is in this. 'Tis my dream to go where few have trod, distant though it may be."

"Distant, aye. To Menmend, an encampment few but Xander have seen or lived to tell about. The Powhatans' most recent stronghold." To his credit, Ustis never skirted the hard details. Had his years of misery in early James Towne enabled him to speak the unvarnished truth? "A few other youths will also participate in the peace exchange, lads from Bermuda and Flowerdew Hundred and Middle Plantation."

"How old is Watseka?" Selah took her usual place, Cecily's yawning empty beside her.

"That wasn't spelled out," Ustis replied. "I only know that none of the settlement families are willing to send any but young indentured orphans, though the Powhatans are sending sons and one daughter. Watseka is said to be from the Pamunkey tribe, one of the many grandchildren of Chief Opechancanough."

"I strive to remember such an exchange is sorely needed," Candace said. "Much like Xander and Mattachanna's marriage bringing a prolonged peace, which bore much fruit."

Ustis nodded gravely. "We shall pray to that end."

Joining hands, they bent their heads, Ustis's entreaty a balm to Selah's conflicted spirits. "O most mighty God and merciful Father, which hast compassion on all men and hatest nothing that Thou hast made . . ."

Once the "amen" was uttered, Shay only lent to Selah's barbed edges all over again. "I suppose if I'm old enough to go over to the Indians and learn their language and life ways, I'm old enough to learn what happened to Mattachanna when she was tricked so meanly by our officials."

Candace sighed and buttered her bread, obviously waiting to see who would answer. Selah kept her eyes on her plate while Ustis proceeded cautiously. "There are those among us

114

who forsake the Lord's will and force their own, thus committing all manner of evil. Such was the case with Mattachanna."

Shay began eating, gaze riveted to their father. Though her own knowledge of the affair was as pitted as mouse-eaten cheese, Selah knew it involved Helion Laurent and wanted to shut her ears.

"As you ken, Mattachanna was a Powhatan princess, her people being frequent visitors in the early years of James Towne to treat and to trade."

"Mattachanna turned cartwheels with other settlement children on the common when she came here, Sister said."

"Aye, I remember it like yesterday. Her powerful father doted on her, and rightly so. She always led any visiting delegations, walking ahead of all the rest as a sign of peace."

"But then she grew up, became Lady Rebecca, and died." Shay chewed slowly, digesting the facts as well. "Poisoned by the English, some say, in the Old World."

Selah could no longer withhold a frown. Her brother knew more than they assumed.

A sorrowful nod from Ustis. "Such treachery would not surprise me. But we mortals shall likely never realize the whole story."

"Is it true that something happened on a ship with Mattachanna? And that Captain Kersey and the physic Laurent were involved?"

A pained lull. Ustis studied his son as if weighing how much further to enlighten him. "Aye. Captain Kersey learned that Mattachanna was staying in a near Indian village and, with the approval of a secret council, abducted her. This was done to force her father to hand over English prisoners, tools, and guns stolen in raids."

"And did the chief do as they asked?"

"Not at first. He was incensed that his beloved daughter had been taken, as any father would be." Ustis cast a glance at Selah. Was he wondering how much *she* knew? Or imagining himself in the chief's place?

"Mattachanna was quickly moved upriver and churched by Reverend Criswel beyond sight of James Towne." Selah continued the telling. "After her conversion she became Lady Rebecca Renick."

"Those are the bare bones of it, aye," Ustis concluded. "One day, my son, when you are older, we shall discuss more of the matter. 'Tis unsavory supper talk."

"I'm sorry, Father." Ever agreeable, Shay resumed eating. "Think no more of it."

Selah looked at her untouched plate. Truly, they were all still haunted by the shame of James Towne's sad dealings. Mattachanna's capture was but one of them.

"Will the Indians abuse me, Father, if I go?"

Candace drew in a sharp breath. "We shall pray each day that you are hedged from harm. Surely the Indians mean you no ill. Nor will we harm one hair of any children they send us in return."

Candace's unusual vehemence earned an appreciative nod from her husband. "Your dear mother is right. Keep in mind Xander would not agree to anything he felt would put you in danger. I will admit, however, that I wish another settlement child would be sent in your stead. But to your credit, you have the heart to go, and we are desperate for peace."

Shay smiled as if to bolster them all. "Long years I have waited to join the Indians. Xander has told me much of their ways. And I believe it is as you said, Father, that we are more alike than not alike, despite our many differences. Our souls are the same."

"Aye, just the same. The gospel is for all peoples, every tribe and nation, as Scripture says, for He made us all."

Selah gave Shay a tender, lingering look. What changes would be wrought in him after he lived away from civilization? If James Towne could be called civilized. Would he lose his fleshy frame? Become as tall and lean as a Powhatan warrior? The whole plan seemed ludicrous but for one thing. Xander approved it. Though she didn't endorse all that he did, she'd trust that in this matter he was right.

Still, her sisterly heart was sore. She read the same sort of sorrow in her mother's aging face, which was sure to grow more lined in her only son's absence.

"Xander has told me the Indian fare is quite different than our table." Shay finished his supper. "I shall learn to use bows and arrows and hunt game."

"I daresay you won't miss storekeeping," Candace admitted. "If ever a boy was made for the outdoors, 'tis you."

"I shall do you all proud. I shan't complain. Or be homesick. Or—"

"I do hope you are homesick." Selah blinked away the dampness in her eyes. "We shall certainly be homesick for you."

Shay grinned. "Perchance I shall become so brave a warrior the Powhatans will adopt me!"

Ustis groaned his displeasure. "No warlike talk, aye? You are there to learn their language and their ways, not train to make trouble."

"Very well. What will Watseka do?" he asked.

"She won't mind the store in your place, if that's what

you're thinking. Rather, she'll work alongside your mother and sister, learning our faith, housewifery and gardening, and how to speak English."

"I expect she knows quite a bit about growing things, like Mattachanna did, helping Xander with his crops."

Aye, all too well. Selah forked another bite. She'd begrudged him that too. Making a field hand of his bride, 'twas said. But what if Mattachanna had *wanted* to work alongside him? What if such reminded her of home, her people, and eased her homesickness? Had the wags ever thought of that? Had she?

Selah smiled. "No doubt we shall learn a great deal from Watseka too."

Candace looked a bit relieved that their conversation took a more pleasant path. "If she's anything like Mattachanna, she'll be a delightful addition to our household. And even if she is not—for no one can hold a candle to the pearl we remember—we shall do our best to make Watseka welcome and at ease here."

Shay winked. "Perhaps I, too, shall find a Powhatan princess to marry."

Selah rolled her eyes while Candace gave a chortle of amused exasperation. "At twelve years of age, you are entirely too young to be matrimonially minded, Powhatan princess or otherwise."

"I second your mother, of course." Ustis aimed a pointed look his son's direction. "If I hear of you chasing through the woods after girls and not game, you shall be returned home posthaste."

"Aye, sir," Shay said, still smiling.

Given his amiable bent, he was likely to attract all manner

of friends among the Naturals. Had that been one of the reasons Xander had recommended him before the council?

As Izella served a favored pudding, she gave Shay an extra helping. How would it be with just the three of them at table?

"Selah, are you prepared to go visiting with the physic on Monday next?" Ustis fixed his gaze on her, a note of distress in his tone. "I am unhappy about the arrangement, but Governor Harvey dismissed my concerns and would only assign a servant to accompany you."

"Fret not, Father." Selah forced a smile to allay his worries. If he refused the plan, he'd no doubt incur the governor's wrath. Determined to make the best of it herself, she tried to stay atop her dread. Surely the small gifts she was taking each new bride would sweeten the task. "'Twill be good to learn how the tobacco brides are faring. I suppose we shall even call on Cecily."

"Be prepared to give the council a report." Ustis rose from the table to seek the comfort of the parlor. "The colony's success depends on the happiness of these unions. And take anything else from the store that you think might be of benefit to the new couples. The Almighty has blessed us materially, and we must be generous in return."

13

For once in his tobacco-sated life, Xander was more concerned about the affairs of his household than his fields. How could he not be when his aunt went about the house nearly clucking her pleasure, certain the nurse accompanying Oceanus to Virginia would add more life and color to their spartan existence?

"What a lovely name she has. Electa Lineboro. I wonder if she is as fair? No doubt Oceanus is fond of her."

"Aye, aye," he said, a bit testy from a poor night's sleep.

She pursed her lips in displeasure. "Since learning that Selah Hopewell's heart is taken, I am at loose ends."

She was at loose ends? He raked his mind for a proper reply as she continued.

"One person in particular paid her a great deal of attention at the wedding feast—Helion Laurent. I wonder if he is the gentleman she favors?"

"Laurent is no gentleman." Though he rarely naysayed anyone, the truth would not be denied. "I was unaware he spoke with her."

"Oh, indeed. They spoke at length. I believe you were preoccupied with some of your fellow council members, or rather *former* council members."

"Former, aye," he murmured, a sinking in his chest.

What had the physic to do with Selah? Inquiring about her father's ill health?

They stood on the second-floor landing as the house underwent a thorough cleaning ahead of the arrivals. Duster in hand, his aunt was now staring at his dusty boots resting upon the newly scrubbed floorboards.

"Tell me again when you think their date of departure was."

He rubbed his beard with the back of his hand. "End of April, mayhap, if not before."

"Splendid! Barring storms or piracy, we should see them any day now." Her satisfaction knew no bounds. "How are you feeling about this noteworthy reunion?"

"On tenterhooks," he answered, gripped by another misery.

"That stands to reason. I'd be on tenterhooks too. Not only are you being reunited with your son, you're meeting a woman you might well marry."

He eyed the open nursery door. "You get ahead of yourself, Aunt. 'Tis my kinsman's futile wish for this woman, not mine. Don't make too much of it."

"Well, a doting aunt can dream!" she fussed good-naturedly.

"I have in mind another miss."

She brightened again. "Do go on."

"Would it not be wise to tell the object of my affection first and foremost?" he said.

"I suppose so. And when might this heartfelt revelation happen?"

"Not soon enough for you, I take it."

"Really, Nephew. This hearkens back to your father's courtship. I had nearly given up all hope he'd marry my sister, your long-suffering mother."

"'Tis not as if I've never wed. I am, I remind you, a widower."

"And need I remind you that you gave me my first gray hairs over Mattachanna? Who on earth would have imagined you'd choose a Powhatan princess!"

"I am not the only colonist to take an Indian wife, Aunt."

"None but the chief's daughter!" With a wave of her feather duster she retreated into her new room, only to pop her head around the door frame with a last word. "Whatever your faults, you are not stingy. I adore my new bedchamber and cannot wait for the furnishings you ordered to arrive."

"You kindly gave up your dormer room to Nurse Lineboro. Some recompense was needed."

He began climbing to the third-floor attic, the narrow stairwell little more than the width of his shoulders. The door at the top was open, sunlight spilling into the small space. 'Twas a cheerful, simple room with a princely view. His head brushing the low ceiling, Xander sank to his haunches before a west window, mired in a single thought.

Was Laurent pursuing Selah?

He stared past the glass, mostly unseeing. Here at the roofline of the house the vista was unmatched. Fields formed a patchwork of greens, rolling toward a haze of bluish mountains on the distant horizon that looked more watercolor. Wanderlust danced at the corners of his conscience. Whatever lay on the other side of those rolling, winsome swells beguiled him. Yet he was entrenched here, still besotted with the rivers and tides of coastal Virginia.

And wildly concerned about Selah's circumstances.

He pulled himself to his feet, returned to the second floor, and tried to dismiss his unease over his aunt's revelation. But even Oceanus's room with its abundance of playthings made him no merrier. There, near the cold hearth, was the chair where Mattachanna had sat and rocked him till he grew so big he squirmed to run free. After she died, Xander had nearly burned the furniture, as its presence grieved and haunted him so. But somehow it had returned to being a lovely chair again with a mere melancholy echo.

Was that the work of grief? First the burning anger and numbing disbelief, then the slow slide toward a grudging acceptance of what was forever gone?

Over by a window, the painted, painstakingly carved rocking horse made him wonder. Had Oceanus outgrown such things? Here were enough toys to fill a future king's nursery. Was he trying to make up for two years of absence and regret? Shuttering the thought, he moved to his own bedchamber, which his aunt had just finished dusting. She was downstairs now, humming a familiar hymn.

He stood in the open doorway, aiming for a dispassionate view. The big English oak bed and matching wardrobe were framed by colorful Flemish tapestries of foreign ports and ships. In winter the thick weave kept cold drafts out and the warmth of the hearth fire in. A pair of upholstered chairs nested near the dog irons. Here and there were a few practically placed candle stands. 'Twas the only room in which he didn't allow the dogs. Ruby and Jett knew his preference and obediently waited at the door, watching him.

Would a feminine woman like such a thoroughly masculine room? Would *she* like it?

Again, his thoughts swung in her direction, she who kept to the forefront of his head and heart. Not even a day laboring in his tobacco fields dimmed his growing preoccupation. A fierce longing rent his middle.

How much longer would he put off telling her his feelings were no passing fancy?

Should he decide upon a date to profess his affections? Timing was everything. At night, in that languorous lull between weariness and sleep, he allowed himself to consider approaching her in her garden. Or should he speak with her father first? His desire for her grew by the day, his hopes for a happy home again along with it.

But her regard of him? How austere at times. Hardly a speck of warmth to be had. And yet, sometimes . . . sometimes he felt a turning, a kindling on her part. Laughter lurking in her eyes. Had he imagined it? Nay. More than once there'd been a telling, lingering look. A flicker of unspoken approval. Even . . . dare he profess it?

Desire.

He swallowed past the thickening in his throat. His gaze left the bed and returned to the windows with a view of the orchard. If she'd have him, she would be mistress of Rosen-Vale with all its color and contradictions. He vowed then and there to be an able husband in future. A better father to Oceanus.

God rest Mattachanna's wronged soul.

14

"Sister, what must I pack to go over to the Naturals?"

"Well, let me ponder it." Selah paused in her sewing to study her brother as he readied his knapsack. Another pang. Another bittersweet smile. "I would think, first and foremost, since you are going as their guest, so to speak, you must bring small gifts. The Naturals are partial to brass and beads, as you know."

"Aye, of course. But what about clothes?"

"The Naturals wear precious little of that, at least in the heat of summer."

He grinned and gaped all at once. "So, I shall not only live amongst the Naturals, I must dress like them?"

"I suppose. The council has instructed us to make suitable English clothes for Watseka." She held up a small, nearly finished coif. "I imagine the Naturals would want you to do likewise, out of respect. You don't want to stand out, do you?"

"Nay," he replied vehemently. "I shall see what Xander has to say about the matter."

Selah smiled. Xander this and Xander that. If ever a lad

revered a man . . . Checking the time, she forsook sewing and offered a brief prayer for the hours ahead while engaged in a full-fledged wrestling match with dismay and dread.

"Daughter, I must speak with you." Her father motioned her into the parlor, away from Izella's tidying and Shay's hearing. He went to a painted oak cupboard with their best silver displayed upon the cloth atop it and opened a small drawer. "Needs be you must carry this. For your safety."

She stared at the small pistol he extended. Safety from savages? Or Helion Laurent?

"No need to fear, Selah. Though you've not practiced shooting in some time, you once handled a firearm as well as many men."

But did she remember how to use it? The pistol felt cold to the touch. "I pray I will have no occasion to fire it."

"Hide it on your person. 'Tis meant for reassurance. Though times are more peaceable now, one never knows what could be encountered beyond town." He smiled, but she read something in his eyes that shook her to her buckled shoes.

When the unwelcome knock on their door sounded, Helion Laurent stood outside, a maidservant with him. Selah waited till her father came from the stable with her own saddle mare. In the light of early morn, Ustis looked unusually wan. Withered by the long winter. Where had her hale and hearty father gone? Or did his wan appearance have more to do with this circumstance?

"Godspeed." Ustis's cordial handshake with the physic helped smooth Selah's ruffled feelings about the matter. "I trust your rounds will be done well before the sun sets."

With a slight, noncommittal nod, Laurent reined his horse

north. Selah kept behind him, glad to ride beside the maid-servant. Timid and unsmiling, the girl showed no penchant for conversation, though Selah tried to draw her out.

They were well under way before the bustle of town took hold. Selah all but averted her eyes as they passed no-man's-land with its almost eerie silence, the abode of the dead after that terrible starving time so many years before. Not far from the old James Towne fort, the unmarked gravesites held a great many bones, most of them bereft of coffins.

Midmorning found them farther downriver, where the burgeoning settlement extended. The day was cool for June, the night's rain driving away the worst of the heat and insects. Occasionally they nodded to passersby or drew to the side of the rutted road to allow carts or livestock to pass without flinging mud on their garments.

Eventually Laurent rode abreast of her. "Your father continues unwell."

Selah waved her hand at a passing tobacco bride. "We hope for a full recovery now that better weather is here."

"Why does he shun my services?" Subtle accusation crept into his tone. "As the most respected physic in Virginia, I could serve him well."

"'Tis unnecessary." With a lift of her chin that echoed his own arrogance, she added, "As a skilled herbalist, my mother's ministrations are enough."

"Bah! She is naught but a rustic, woefully lacking in the skills of a London-trained healer."

"Oh? Then why do so many in James Towne and elsewhere seek her out?"

"I doubt she has the council's favor to dispense advice and medicines at will."

"*Sir.*" The term was more epithet. "Why do you continue to bait me at every turn? Is it not in the best interest of a gentleman—though you are hardly that with your badgering—to attend to the business at hand?"

"I rather enjoy our sparring."

"I do not." Selah glanced at the sullen maid. "Nor, I sense, does Ruth."

"The maidservant has no say in the matter. She is simply here at the request of your father, which, regretfully, has deprived Governor Harvey a day's labor in his household."

"You expect me to ride about the country with you alone?" She looked askance at him. "I think not."

His cold smile grated. "Ah, you are all pins and prickles, Mistress Hopewell. Waspish as well as spinsterish. The proper husband might change that."

She fell silent, giving him no grounds to carry the conversation further. By the time the first Hundred came into view with its dozen houses and dependencies, its chimneys puffing smoke, she'd collected herself somewhat. Dogs barked at their approach and turned her mare skittish. Laurent snapped his whip in warning as he led the way.

"Turn aside, Rufus," a man called to the worst offender, a small cur with bristled back.

"We've come to visit your brides," Laurent called out. "Beginning with yours, Monsieur Cassen, if you're willing."

"Obliged." Cassen gave a red-faced nod, gesturing toward his rough-hewn cottage. "She's feeling poorly of late. The dreaded seasoning."

He led them toward a dwelling where a low fire made the close air smoky. As Selah entered in with the maidservant, she heard Laurent behind her, speaking condescendingly to the husband just outside the door. The house smelled of sickness, making her glad she'd brought a few of her mother's tonics.

In an adjoining room lay the former Jane Rickard, a bank of pillows behind her. She rose up briefly, her face flushed with fever. "Mistress Hopewell?"

"Indeed, but I shall make this blessedly brief, given you are unwell."

"Nay, please be seated." Jane was clearly eager for company as she gestured to a stool near at hand. "A visit might do me good." Her inquisitive gaze dismissed Ruth and rested on Selah's burgeoning basket.

"I've brought some things to hearten you, or so I hope." Selah took a seat, settling the basket in her lap. Out of it she drew thread, a thimble, and needles.

Jane looked pleased. "You recall my seamstress ways."

"If you describe your malady, I may have just the remedy . . . though the physic is here too, and just outside, speaking with your husband."

Jane swallowed as if her throat was sore. "Fever. Weakness. Thomas says not to drink the water, but ale just makes me thirstier."

"A common complaint." Selah held her tongue. Sometimes a person was simply made better by a little kindness and a listening ear, tonic or no. "You're adjusting to settlement life, which takes a toll on every newcomer."

"No cure for homesickness, I suppose."

"Aye, time. 'Tis a wondrous cure-all." Selah smiled to bolster her. "What do you miss most about England?"

"Hot cross buns. You could smell them for a league or more on a warm spring morn in Berkshire."

"Oh, I can only imagine it. I've never been to England. But my mother, bless her, makes hot cross buns from Eastertide to Whitsunday."

Jane caressed the sewing notions. "Does my heart good to hear some traditions from the motherland aren't forgot."

"Traditions, aye." Selah gave her the tonic. "Britain is ages old, heavily peopled with so much history, unlike newborn Virginia."

"I don't miss the crowds or the stench. Virginia's air is purer. Sweeter."

"And how do you find married life?" Selah asked with a tremor of trepidation. How was an unmarried miss to hazard such a question?

Jane downed the tonic with a wince of distaste. "Married life suits me. At least when I'm hale and hearty and on my feet."

As she spoke of the travails of colony life, Laurent came in. He greeted and then examined Jane while Selah and the maidservant stood by.

"What is this?" He sniffed the cup that held the tonic and turned a critical eye Selah's way. "Herbs and simples are temporary at best. What you need, Goody Cassen, is a dose of Gascoigne's jelly. With powder of pearl for purification of the blood and melancholia, there's no better remedy."

Watching him dispense his own medicines, Selah tried to dwell on the good. Laurent seemed knowledgeable enough, though the colony boasted few physics and she had little to compare him with. Still, his past misdeeds, his trickery of Mattachanna . . .

Mindful of the other women who needed visiting, they let themselves out. The first call was deemed a success. Hardy as she was in frame, Jane would no doubt survive the seasoning. She had a remedy from both the physic and Selah's basket. At least she knew they were concerned and tried to help.

By midafternoon, Selah and Laurent had made all their rounds of the day but one.

The approach to Wentz Hundred was open, most trees felled, allowing a territorial view that was especially advantageous in times of danger. Framed in a ray of sunlight spearing cindery clouds, Cecily called to her from an open doorway as Selah dismounted. "Is that you, Selah—with company?"

"Aye, 'tis Doctor Laurent and a maidservant and I. Come to see how you are faring in your new role as Mistress Wentz."

"What a pairing!" she said impishly, eyes on Laurent now speaking with Phincas near the stable. "A mercy mission, I suppose. Out and about seeing how we brides are adjusting to these strange husbands of ours?"

They embraced, nearly upending Selah's basket, though it was empty of all but a pot of honey and a small token for Cecily's mother-in-law.

Cecily eyed the amber contents with satisfaction. "Phineas is partial to sweetening. He stands by molasses, but I prefer the work of bees any day."

Selah crossed the well-kept yard, where nary a weed seemed to sprout, a few flowers taking hold around the door stoop. Surrounding outbuildings showed the same careful tending. The house was typical of middling planters, carrying an echo of England with its daub and clay. Over the threshold they went, into a shadowed room where a stoop-shouldered woman sat in a settle near the hearth despite the heat of the day.

"Welcome, Mistress Hopewell," she said with a tremulous voice. "I've known you since you were so small you couldn't see over your store counter, though my failing eyesight has kept me housebound since."

"Good to see you again, Widow Wentz." Reaching into her basket, Selah knelt by the woman's chair. "Mother thought you might like spirits of rosemary."

"For headache, aye." She breathed in the scent as Selah uncorked the vial. "Reminds me so of England—our Rothbury garden."

"The Wentzes have wellborn kin in Sussex." Cecily carried a covered plate to the table. "Phineas has mentioned visiting in future."

"Oh, such a travail a voyage is." Widow Wentz's voice rose in strength. "Blessed am I that I shan't risk another crossing at my great age."

"We shall wait till your heavenly homegoing to take our wedding journey, then," Cecily said matter-of-factly.

Amused, Selah sat as Cecily served oat scones she'd baked. Amid all the barnyard noises outside, they spoke of the latest James Towne happenings as Widow Wentz fell asleep in her chair.

"Seems like an age since I've seen you, Selah," Cecily lamented.

"You look well in your new role."

"Do I? Laboring from sunup to sundown?" With a grimace she held up work-worn hands studded with calluses. "Those colony officials failed to mention the endless work awaiting us. I have little time for pleasure, including my silver lace making."

"It wouldn't matter if you did, sadly. The council has just

passed a law banning the wearing of silver thread and all finery, except for the gentry."

"What?" Her long-lashed eyes snapped. "The council acts as if they've been crowned king! Nor can we spin or weave—"

The old woman snorted in her sleep, halting Cecily's tirade.

"Virginia takes some getting used to, aye, but it has its merits, surely," Selah whispered.

An eye roll was her answer. "Snakes that bedevil and torrid temperatures, a hen that won't lay and two sheep felled by a wild creature, an endless grinding of corn for every meal—"

"A sturdy house to keep the weather away. A husband who adores you. Other wives near for company." Selah took a bite of scone. "Delicious baked goods."

Still appearing downcast, Cecily toyed with the coral necklace upon her bodice. "'Tis our lot, I suppose, to be content with our fate, not torment our husbands with impatient murmurings."

"You are tired and overwhelmed. Would Phineas allow a maidservant to help you?"

"I shall ask him. But who?"

"A pair of recently orphaned sisters from James Towne who are both amiable and industrious and seeking work. Would you like me to arrange a meeting?"

"Please do." Cecily brightened and rose abruptly as the door opened. "Ah, here is the renowned physic himself! Do come in, sir. How pleased I am that you have graced our humble home."

15

Selah and her party returned at dusk, coming back opposite the way they had started. As they neared the outskirts of James Towne, she resisted the urge to kick at her mare's sides and bolt home. They'd visited but eleven brides this day. The rest were far flung in the outer shires. Were more visits on the horizon? She prayed not, at least in the physic's company.

Vexed by the heat, Laurent had grown notably quiet, saying little till the last. "I believe the council will be pleased with our progress. I shall inform them on the morrow of our success. We make a perfect pairing, you must admit."

"I admit nothing," she replied, drying her upper lip with the back of a gloved hand. "Though I am glad to visit at least some of the brides and ascertain they are adjusting as well as might be expected."

"How brusque you are. Allow me to return you home, at least."

"No need, I assure you." Was her glee plain? "I have had my fill of your company. Good day."

His exasperating laugh filled the space between them. "Adieu, lovely Selah."

His free use of her given name nettled her further, as did his honeyed Gallic voice. How could such a man have even a speck of comeliness about him? Casting a sympathetic glance at the maidservant, Selah reined her mare toward Backstreete as all went their separate ways.

Her empty basket dangling from the pommel, her head full of how much Laurent annoyed her, she plodded on, glad the dusty streets were mostly empty this time of day. A few dogs and a piglet ran amok as the night watch assembled to make the rounds.

Down the dusty, rutted street, the light from their store winked gold in the gloom. Was Father at his books again? The front door was locked, the shutters drawn. Selah tied her mare to a post and made her way around the back to the side door, which creaked open with a push of her hand.

"Father?"

No answer. She threaded her way through the storehouse piled with the daily necessities and rare luxuries of colony life. The cavernous room held the tang of leather and reek of vinegar alongside fancy foodstuffs and furnishings. An open case of Venetian glass glittered green as she walked past, small casks of Ceylon cinnamon and Dutch nutmeg heady.

She approached her father's desk carefully. Hard of hearing, he was easily startled. His back was to her, and his head rested on his open account book, quill pen on the floor.

Selah rushed toward him, torn with alarm. "Father . . ." Gently, she placed a hand upon his shoulder. "Are you unwell?"

He roused, shaking off sleep and his spectacles in the process. She caught them in midair and returned them to his keeping.

"I've been a bit more tired of late," he said. "Nothing to fret about. Now, what have we here . . . an empty basket and news of the brides, aye?"

"Fair news for the most part."

"And Laurent? He gave no offense?"

"Offense?" The question struck her as odd. Mayhap he was simply muddled from sleep. She passed him the unused pistol. "The maidservant was a welcome addition wherever we went."

"God be thanked."

He recovered quickly. But she still took note of his high color and the glassiness of his eyes. Setting the basket aside, she knelt till they were eye level. "Let me manage the books tonight. I'm not at all tired, and you seem in need of Mother's care."

"You fret too much, Daughter." But he pushed back from his desk just the same, kissing her brow before making his way to the door. "Alas, I cannot leave you here alone."

"I'm not alone," she replied as a plump gray cat wound its way around her skirts. "Smudge is near."

He sighed, looking as if he'd like to sit down again. "On one condition. I shall lock all the doors and send Shay to fetch you in an hour and escort you to supper."

"Oh aye." Smiling, she feigned a lightheartedness she didn't feel. "I'll get straight to work."

She stood by the window as he left, praying him home. Stoop-shouldered, gait slow, he seemed to carry the weight of both new world and old as he led the mare. Would he not ride instead? Slowly it dawned on her that he had not the strength to mount the horse.

Oh, Father, is there something you are not telling me? Are you beset with some new burden?

136

Perhaps he was missing Shay even before he went over to the Naturals. She expelled a pent-up breath, stung by a smidgen of ire at Xander's tribal dealings. 'Twas all right and good when someone else's son was sent. Would he have done the same?

She sought the desk, moving the taper nearer to finish totaling the ledger of figures Father had left undone. Next, she reviewed the ever-pressing orders, the planters' needs foremost. There always seemed a shortage of packthread for drying tobacco. She wrote down a quick tally of how much to demand from England suppliers.

Each planter had a separate account, some quite voluminous. She stilled when she came to Xander's. A very long list, indeed. In the flickering candlelight, she noted the usual needs. Packthread was at the very top. Next came myriad fishing nets. Sundry tools. A quantity of ribbons, thread, and needles—for his aunt, surely. A games box of the popular trictrac—for Oceanus, likely. At four, he might enjoy learning table games.

But all the rest gave her pause. One oak gateleg dining table. Two candle stands. A walnut armoire.

Eyes widening, she read on.

A four-poster bed with linens of the highest quality. A walnut wardrobe and carved mirror. A pair of ornate tapestry chairs.

Fit for a bride.

The certainty swept through her like a hurricane. Surely a wedding was imminent. Such an order would fill half a warehouse. Yet another reason to disdain him—this bent toward worldly things. But was her family not peddlers of mammon, ensnaring others by their continual commerce?

They themselves lived simply, yet . . . had she no desire for beauty and comfort? No craving for finer things? What did she care if he was outfitting another room at Rose-n-Vale and adding to his personal inventory?

With effort, she corralled her musings if not her soreness of heart, readying the order for shipping along with all the rest. When Shay fetched her, she locked the store and they hastened toward home. If only she could leave behind her many questions as well.

"How is Father?" One look at his empty place at table was Selah's answer even before her mother spoke.

"He's resting after drinking a posset."

Going to a washbasin, Selah prepared for a subdued supper. Shay was already seated, playing idly with his fork and knife. What would it be like to sup with the Naturals? Another pang shot through her. Already missing him, she was. She smiled fleetingly as her mother sat across from her, a venison pie between them. Though she'd eaten little all day, she had no appetite tonight.

"So, tell me everything. How is Cecily especially?"

Selah caught her mother up on all she'd learned, keeping her voice low so as to not disturb her father lying abed in the adjoining room. "All in all, the brides are weathering the change from the Old World well enough. There are the usual worries about so much sickness, menial work, and talk of Indian unrest."

Shay reached for the salt cellar. "The exchange should help with that, aye?"

"Indeed." Candace's head bobbed. "And you are going to

138

be right in the thick of it. One day you'll look back and be proud at the part you've played."

He swallowed a bite, looking thoughtful.

Selah looked at her mother, whose eyes glittered as she studied Shay. "So Watseka will soon arrive on our shores."

"Indeed, and with some ceremony, as befitting so auspicious an occasion. I pray your father is well enough to attend. He would hate to miss Shay's going."

"Father is a graybeard," Shay muttered sagely around a bite of bread. "Needs be he stay in bed and recover."

Selah shot him a chary look. "Perhaps a shop boy should be hired in Shay's absence."

Candace looked grave. "I fear trying to train someone in the ways of commerce is an onerous task and would only add to the strain."

"I shall double up then. Do the work of us both." Selah made a silent vow to rise earlier, forgo the noon meal, and work till dark.

"Nay. You are needed to help with Watseka. I plan to spend the most time with her, but your presence is invaluable to me. Somehow, we will manage merchanting too. And pray your father to a speedy recovery."

Snoring sounded from the other room, for once more reassuring than annoying.

"Sleep is the best medicine." Selah longed to ease her mother's cares. "And when Father awakes, he'll partake of this delicious venison pie. If there's any left." She smiled at Shay, who earned a rap on his hand from Candace as he reached for another helping.

At that they all dissolved into muted, bittersweet laughter.

16

Today was *the* day.

Xander stood before his shaving stand with its looking glass, something he rarely made time for, and took in the man before him. Hardly a gentleman. No powdered wig. No ribbons or bows. No lace. His ruddy Scots coloring, the red threads in his beard, bespoke his roots. He was the image of his rough-hewn father with some of his mother's gentling features. At hand were neatly pressed clothes fit for the governor's chamber, a minor duty before he sought out his beloved.

"On your way, Nephew?" His aunt stood at the bottom of the stairs as he came down them. Her eyes shone. "My, how handsome . . . and fragrant. Such a welcome change from the sweat of your brow."

"Too much sandalwood?" he asked her, smoothing a sleeve.

"On the contrary. Sandalwood is sublime and hints of exotic ports. You wear it well."

She followed him out the riverfront door, where bricklayers paused in their work to watch him pass. He gave a greeting but didn't slow his gait.

"Something tells me the council is not the only place you're headed," she called after him as she veered toward the milk house. "Rarely do you wear such a handsome lawn shirt and doublet."

He let that pass without comment and sought the stables, beset by last-minute doubts.

How would his would-be bride receive him?

Leagues later, his arrival in James Towne left him wishing he'd taken his smallest shallop instead, his dawn bath in the river a distant memory. The pleated falling band encircling his neck was little more than a damp rag, and a fine powdering of early July dust coated all that he wore. But the refined sandalwood scent was intact. Though he was not a vainglorious man, today, the hour that might well decide his future, he wanted to look his best.

He hobbled his horse in New Towne's pasture and skirted Pitch and Tar Swamp to reach the governor's residence, which doubled as a statehouse. The brick dwelling was spared the spiking heat by the cluster of elms providing deep shade. Was he late?

A few of those invited took their seats. Two places remained empty—his own and Ustis Hopewell's. Such did not bode well.

Xander's disquiet didn't settle when Governor Harvey opened the meeting with a lengthy prayer, his clipped English tones a drone in the still room, save the mosquitoes buzzing. "We beseech Thee, O heavenly Father, giver of life and health, to comfort and relieve Your sick servants, and give Your power of healing to those who minister to their needs . . ."

Xander felt a chill. A foreboding. Had Ustis sickened again? He had little time to consider the matter as they delved directly into the all-important exchange, the Naturals expected on Monday next.

Xander had been tasked to handle the proceedings. As translator, having taken part in such affairs since the earliest days of James Towne, he had been delegated all details. With Claibourne and Laurent absent, there were but a few dissenting voices regarding how and where the exchange should occur. These were hammered out to the satisfaction of all in an unprecedented hour, and the meeting adjourned in the forenoon.

Thirsty, belly rumbling, Xander passed outside in the elms' rustling shade and returned his hat to his head.

"Let us take the noon meal at Swan's, aye?" His friend Emanuel Murray began walking that way.

"My stomach will offer no complaint." Xander fell into step beside him. "'Tis good to see you again. My heartiest congratulations on your nuptials at Charles Cittie."

"Mistress Murray and I both thank you for sending round that salted ham with your felicitations." Murray's walking stick tapped a merry beat on the cobblestone path. "She's expressed a desire to meet you."

"Rose-n-Vale's doors are always open to you and your bride."

"Expect it, then. I deeply regret your resigning from council, which means we shall see you seldom. But I suppose your recent acquisition of further acreage requires you to be more at home than here."

"A trifling matter soon forgotten."

"Trifling?" Murray's laugh held mockery. "I would not

142

call a parceling of land that makes you owner of an entire western shire a small matter. Especially since Virginia has but eight of them."

"An entire shire is an exaggeration." Still, Xander felt a beat of pride. "But what is land without indentures to work it?"

"I admire your unwillingness to enslave Africans. 'Tis becoming commonplace." Frowning, Murray kicked at a stone in his path. "My new wife brought several Ashanti to our marriage. House servants. A far cry from indentures."

"I'd rather speak of Ustis Hopewell." Xander tipped his hat to a passing matron. "Do you ken any particulars regarding his health?"

"Only that he's been quite ill the last sennight or so. Much as he was this past winter."

With a sinking inside him, Xander eyed the sign of the swan swaying in the wind above the door they sought. The ordinary's well-kept brick façade with four interior rooms made it the most genteel offering in James Towne. And blessedly close to the Hopewells'.

Several heads turned and hats lifted as the two men entered. Yet Xander felt uneasy anticipating a meal and a pint when a good man lay ill.

He turned his plan for the afternoon over in his mind as they ordered and then ate, the rumble of men's voices around them. Talk was heated regarding the latest furor over the current tobacco inspector, an irascible Welshman who burned more hogsheads in the warehouse kiln than he approved.

"Hard to market the very crop Priddy disdains," Murray said as the object of their ire came into the Swan.

"Ardent smoker he is not," Xander replied, returning his attention to his mutton pie.

"'Twas Priddy who swayed the governor to limit our tobacco cultivation to fifteen hundred plants per grower." Murray lowered his voice. "What are we to make of that?"

"Petition to plant north of the York River on virgin soil that hasn't been depleted."

"North as in Northumberland?"

"Aye. 'Tis our future. The future of tobacco in Virginia."

"And owned in part by Selah Hopewell. A misbegotten dowry, some say, for prime land that sits idle." Murray forked a bite but looked like he'd lost his appetite. "To muddy matters, Laurent is rumored to have been awarded the plantation of your deceased neighbor, which borders both your and the Hopewells' plantations."

Xander stopped eating. "Hearsay, hopefully."

"What's more, he may be making inroads with Mistress Hopewell."

"Laurent? You jest."

Murray flashed him a wary gaze. "Word is she's been accompanying him to see how the tobacco brides are faring. From all reports, they look quite . . . companionable. Fancy gaining the hand of the cape merchant's daughter and prime tobacco land to boot."

Xander managed to finish his pint if not his plate. "God forbid."

Selah bit her bottom lip, the warmth and chatter of the shop fraying her final nerve. Shay ran hither and yon fetching this or that, managing the scales, while she tallied orders and tried to keep up a brisk pace as more customers crowded into the store that held but a dozen comfortably. 'Twas a torment to function normally while Father lay more ill today than he had all the days before. Mother was out of remedies, for nothing seemed to be of much help. By now, most would have called for a physic. But Father had no fondness for Laurent, and other physics were far removed from James Towne.

Selah cast a glance at the back door. At any moment Mother might enter and deliver the dreaded news. Death stalked the colony with little warning. Would they be next?

"Selah."

Her name, though softly spoken, broke through the tumult of her thoughts. Her gaze lifted from the ream of papers she perused. How Xander had navigated his way unnoticed to the counter where she stood trying to add sums was no small feat. She stared up at him without focus, his features undimmed by the shadow of the felt hat he usually wore. Swallowing, she marshaled all her wits and tried to smile.

"Afternoon, sir." *Sir.* What she meant to say, at least discreetly, was *Xander.* Her voice sounded brittle, a testament to all the rest of her.

His hat dangled from one fisted hand. "Might I speak with you in private?"

A bold request. One she hardly had time for. But he was not a man to be denied. His unusually earnest expression had her choose the fragrant, shadowed confines of Father's lair, as Mother oft called it. There they faced one another an arm's length apart.

"You look distraught," he told her bluntly, his eyes never leaving her face, "though 'tis your father I've come to inquire about."

"Father—" Tears that had remained unshed all morn now

145

made her dig blindly in her pocket for a handkerchief, to no avail. "He—"

"He is gravely ill, and your countenance tells me all the rest." He reached into his doublet and removed his own handkerchief. Finely made, it looked out of place in his work-worn hand.

This time she made no move to quash her tears. They fell unhindered, spotting her bodice. Gently, he dried the trail of emotion on her face. The linen held his masculine scent, enveloping her as if he'd embraced her instead. For a time, the shop with all its haggling and clinking of coin faded away. 'Twas just the two of them, caught up in a tender moment, despair and uncertainty suspended.

Finally, she mastered her voice, fisting the handkerchief he gave her. "Mother is urging a move upriver to Hopewell Hundred. She thinks, as Father does, that James Towne's miasmas and swamp fevers are too much for him now that he's nearly sixty."

"I've long thought this a dismal spot to settle." He took her hand and sat her in her father's chair. "There's even an empty warehouse sitting idle near Hopewell Hundred that would serve well for merchanting once he recovers."

If he recovers.

"You have no need of it?" At his nay, she felt a beat of hopefulness. "Perhaps that will suffice."

He looked toward the front, where Shay's voice carried. "I also ken this might not be the best time for your brother to be away."

The peace exchange. Would he send someone else in Shay's stead?

"Please . . . stop and see my father." Selah laid a hand

on his coat sleeve. "Your presence will do him a world of good."

"Consider it done. One more matter . . ." He hesitated a moment, clearly uncomfortable with broaching it. "What have you to do with Laurent?"

"As little as possible." Her stomach turned. What had he been told? "Governor Harvey insisted we call upon the tobacco wives. One visit is behind us, but more are to come."

"My inquiry comes with a warning. Safeguard yourself when he is near."

"I find him disagreeable at best. I—"

"He is not a man to be trusted."

"Then I shall refuse to accompany him further."

"And I shall make sure that is the case."

With that, he let himself out the back into the sunlit lane with all its heated, fetid smells. The safety she always felt in his presence fled with him. Somehow, Laurent seemed to stand between them. Did Xander believe there was more to their pairing than the governor's dictum?

She stared at his handkerchief, noting the lovely embroidery of his initials in indigo thread. His aunt's handwork? Having something so personal heartened her, had her straightening her shoulders and retying her apron. She went back into the fray of the busy store, though her grieved heart followed after Xander on his way to their door.

17

Xander paused at the rear garden gate behind the Hopewells' residence. The short walk from the store had helped clear his head, but in truth, he was more undone by Selah's distress than the news her father lay ill. Removing his hat, he waved it to cool his damp hairline, breathing in the distillation of Selah herself. Climbing upward toward him was a fragrant hodgepodge of carefully tended herbs and flowers.

Though he was earthy and sun-blistered and couldn't rid himself of a tobacco taint, Selah was the essence of all things blooming. On occasion a rose with thorns. Sometimes a bright-eyed daisy. Today a rare, fragile lily. This was as much her garden as her mother's.

He pushed open the gate and let it swing shut behind him, hemming him in with the memory of the recent wedding reception. Every last detail was engraved in his conscience. Every exchanged word.

"Is there no man that moves you, Selah Hopewell? I ask because my aunt asked me. And I had no answer."

"There is such a man, but . . ."

"But you will make no more mention of him than I my would-be bride."

What a game of cat and mouse they played. Yet what if he misread her and she did favor someone else? So far upriver and seldom in town as he was, she could be walking down the aisle and he'd never get wind of it till the vows were said. But at least his fears regarding Laurent were put down. He walked toward the house, wishing she were there and not overwrought and overworked at the store.

"Xander? Do come in!" Candace's voice was hushed—in deference to her husband, no doubt—as he ducked beneath the door's lintel. "You have come at a favorable time. Ustis is sitting up for the first time in a sennight, though the effort has quite worn him out."

She ushered him into their bedchamber, Ustis seated and facing a window. Drawing the door closed, Candace went out. The darkened room was heavy with the smell of sickness. Xander longed to open a window in favor of a cleansing coastal breeze. A sickroom never failed to remind him of Mattachanna's final hours. His uneasiness spiked as Ustis was seized by a coughing fit, sputtering out an unnecessary greeting when he could.

Xander took a chair, knowing Ustis was unable to endure much conversation. "I'm sorry to see you thus, my old friend."

"Old, indeed!" Another spasm of coughing rattled Ustis's ribs. "I've not been so low since I first set foot on Virginia soil."

Tossing aside the usual pleasantries, Xander came right to the point. "'Tis plain to see that Shay is more needed here than with the Powhatans."

Ustis drew himself up in his chair, face glistening from the heat of the day—or his malady? "On the contrary. I'll not be held accountable"—another spate of coughing slowed him—"for the demise of my son's dream. If he cannot go, I fear he will come of age regretting that his graybeard of a father denied him his heart's desire. That, I cannot conscience."

Xander schooled his surprise. "You are sure."

"Never surer. Besides, Selah is quite adept at whatever life hands her. She does the work of two people."

Aye, to my everlasting regret.

Passing a hand over his beard, Xander let go of any romantic notions. Now was clearly not the time to ask for Ustis's blessing on their courtship. Mayhap the most pressing matter was to broach a move upriver. Yet even this brought a new complication if Emanuel Murray's news was true and Laurent was moving upriver too.

"I hear your heart in this matter about Shay, but the offer begs considering before the exchange commences. You can always bow out beforehand." Xander weighed the conflicting emotions crossing Ustis's countenance. "I'm aware of your desire to move away from James Towne. I, for one, can vouch for better living upriver, where I am rarely ill. You have fair land, fresh water, a suitable house, and dependencies that lie vacant from your last tenant."

"Hopewell Hundred, aye."

"I've an empty warehouse with a suitable landing and dock that would serve well for a new enterprise. My indentures can bear the brunt of moving you and your household. What say you?"

Nodding, Ustis made no protest. "I say pray that I can get my boots back on and begin this next venture. I am sick to death of the foul humors of James Towne and its petty politics. Further west means we're closer to Shay, aye?"

"Indeed."

"Trade will be brisk there, as the outlying plantations need our James Towne goods. The store here shall remain open and a clerk appointed." Face red from coughing, he soldiered on. "Though I'm reluctant to rob you of your indentures, mayhap the process will proceed speedily and in good form. I will inform Governor Harvey immediately."

Xander's hopes, which had been sinking fast as a ship's anchor when he arrived, now rebounded. No more unnecessary trips to James Towne. No more waiting for supplies to come upriver. No more wondering what the Hopewells were doing. Could this be the answer to his prayers? Might this move play into his affections after all?

Without asking, he opened a window. "Have you considered alerting one of the country physics? There's a competent man at Mount Malady."

"I may well consult him once we are upriver." Ustis wiped his brow with a handkerchief. "For now, let us be about the business of packing."

Xander opened the bedchamber door, spurred by a sense of urgency. But would Ustis even survive the move?

"Father."

The gentle voice bade him turn.

Selah stood in the doorway, joy sketched across her formerly tear-streaked face. "You are sitting up. Praise be!"

Ustis answered with more coughing as Xander regarded her. Did she ken what a fetching picture she made? Her gaze found his, and she gave him a thankful, fleeting smile. Whatever had passed between them back at the store . . . he craved more of that aloneness. That intimacy. Dare he hope she felt the same?

Ustis found his voice at last. "Good news, Daughter. Xander has graciously offered to help move us upriver as soon as I inform the council."

Behind Selah stood Candace, her face alight with relief and joy. "Our prayers have been answered, then."

"Though I'm loath to separate you from your garden here, dear wife, I trust that the soil upriver is even sweeter and will soon be the pride of the Tidewater."

"I shall begin packing at once," Candace replied, wiping her hands on her apron. "I've enough seed to plant a late garden. A promising beginning, indeed!"

"Then I'll ready my largest shallop to transport what is needed to set up housekeeping and the start of your merchanting there." Xander returned his hat to his head. "Shall we start at sennight's end?"

"No need to delay. Day after tomorrow even, if you can marshal resources and spare the time. I'm determined to move—or die." With visible effort, Ustis stood. All seemed to hold their breath. He tottered a bit, grabbing for the walking stick within reach. Selah came forward and kissed her father's perspiring brow while Candace returned to the kitchen to serve him his midday meal.

"Won't you join us, Xander?" Candace asked him. "'Tis the least we can do to thank you for all your help."

"Once you're settled at Hopewell Hundred, aye. For now, I'd best ready for your departure. Expect a shallop at first light two days hence. Your livestock can come overland. I'll supply a dozen indentures to oversee the move for as long as you need them."

At that, he allowed himself a last look at Selah, who was by her father's side, helping him to the table. She looked up at him just then, almost shyly yet lingeringly, her gaze soft and warm and soul deep. It took all the breath out of him. She held his gaze till prudence returned her to her father again.

At their collective goodbyes, Xander went out whistling. The lightness in his spirit wouldn't be denied. He'd not whistled since Mattachanna died.

The governor was agreeable to the move, given the prosperous James Towne store would remain open. By next morn, the newly appointed clerk shadowed Shay as Ustis sat behind the counter and gave direction when needed. Selah, along with her mother and Izella, turned the house upside down, packing and sorting and parting with all manner of things while running hither and yon to the store when needed. Such gave them no time to have any second thoughts or ponder what they'd miss.

Selah felt borne along by a great wave as their household shrank to dust motes and cobwebs in the emptying. A new venture. A new home. A new garden, even. Though she'd been upriver many times, she'd never thought to live there. Away from James Towne she'd be away from Helion Laurent too, and any further plans to visit tobacco wives.

Candace packed away the last of the crockery and stood, looking bemused. "Daughter, I've never heard you *whistling* before."

Flushing, Selah folded some linens. "'Tis a cheerful way to work."

"Methinks you've picked up some of Xander's habits."

Without answer, Selah returned to her room to sweep the floor as another coverlet was bundled and carried away with all her bedding. Whistling again, she packed the few books she owned in a basket, all the while dreaming of Rose-n-Vale's overflowing shelves. Might Xander allow her a loan of some poetry or Shakespeare?

As promised, the Renick shallop was waiting in the dewy James Towne dawn, and Rose-n-Vale's hands loaded the boat to the gills in the forenoon. Though Selah looked for Xander with a sense of girlish expectation, he eluded her. Perhaps he had business elsewhere or wisely concluded that managing the move was best left to her parents, with the help of so many able-bodied men.

Light of step, she hastened to the waterfront beside the last lumbering wagon bearing their possessions, the vessel's foremast rigged with a small, square sail. Once seated at the middle of the boat on padded barrels, Selah and her mother and Izella faced the direction they were headed, the wind skimming over their flushed features and toying with their coifs. Shay and her father were already at Hopewell Hundred, having left in a loaded canoe earlier that morn.

Soon James Towne seemed little more than an insignificant dot on a map as six sunburnt indentures plied the oars with expert rhythm. Was it almost a relief for them to be spared a day's toil in tobacco fields? Their accents, predominantly Scots, warmed her ears with their rich, Gaelic-laced lilts.

The wind freshened, pushing them along. Despite the boat being laden with so much cargo, they'd see Hopewell Hundred before noon. Silent for the first part of the journey, the women observed great herons along the river's widening banks and bald eagles gliding overhead.

"I fear you shall miss your garden," Selah finally said.

Candace smiled. "A garden is a small matter compared to your father's health. Besides, the new clerk's wife seems delighted to tend it."

Selah looked back over her shoulder. How odd to consider other hands doing their work. "Glad I am we have such a pretty piece of property upriver. Together we shall make it ours in due time."

"Indeed we shall." A rare wistfulness marked Candace's brow. "How I wish we had begun at Hopewell Hundred from the first."

"When you came over from England and Father was waiting for you at the fort?"

"'Twas a true wilderness then. I was expecting his eldest brother, Jon, as you know." She bit her lip as if the thought still saddened her. "Imagine a girl of seventeen, my passage paid, my betrothed dead of a fever on my arrival. A rocky start for one so full of hopes."

"But there stood Father, in mourning, waiting to greet you." The timeworn story never failed to make Selah smile. "And after a sort you set out to woo him."

"Shockingly so, in hindsight." Candace repinned her coif, which the wind had tugged free. "I was drowning in suitors, none of them the least desirable save one. Your father did remind me of poor Jon, but that is not why I chose him."

"You chose well."

"'Twas either marry or return to England. I could not endure another sea voyage, as I'd been quite ill coming to Virginia."

"So you proposed to him on a crisp October day when he showed you Hopewell Hundred."

"Ah, what a time that was." She grew quiet, seemingly lost in the recollection. "Seven and twenty years ago. Your father, bless him, seemed as flustered or perhaps as flattered as I was bold. But our plans to live there quietly were upended when he was appointed a clerk and then cape merchant."

"You've had a good life together."

"Better than most. I cannot imagine a day without him."

How unpredictable life was, as full of twists and turns as this winding river. Selah let go of her expectations, reveling in the wind and the freedom of sailing along on so beautiful a morn, new neighbors and landmarks all around them. There, along the south shore in Warrosquoakeshire, lived the dissenting Puritans causing such a furor among Virginia's Anglicans. Next came Herring Creek near Charles Cittie. On the bluff beyond was the sad spectacle of Henrico, gone to ruin after an earlier Indian war and never rebuilt.

They passed their own dock, a rickety affair of neglected timber her father had promised to right, and moved farther downriver to Rose-n-Vale's larger, far sturdier wharf. Ships oft moored there to offload cargo and take on valuable Renick exports. They drew up to the wharf and the moorings were secured. Selah was helped to land after her mother as indentures began unloading the cargo.

A bridle path skirted the sandy shore, leading to their two-story wattle-and-daub house ringed with shade trees. Doors and windows were open wide in welcome. A stone well stood in a small courtyard, and an arbor led to a fenced if fallow garden. All bespoke a place craving occupants.

Ustis was down by the water in the little cove nearest the house. Still leaning on his walking stick, he started for them, Shay alongside.

"'Tis not a home without a feminine touch," Ustis called out as Candace approached and put her arms around him.

"What say you, Sister?" Stepping in front of her, Shay released a gossamer-winged butterfly from his cupped hands. Its indigo hue was nearly transparent. "Father said these are found in dappled woodlands, of which we have plenty here."

Smiling, Selah watched the butterfly's airy flight back toward the forest, an orange dot on its hind wings. Not one river rat did she see, nor greedy gull.

Shaking off her lethargy from the warm ride upriver, she set to work, intent on making their beds, as they'd likely fall into them at dusk. When she grew tired, she simply drifted to a window or door to find inspiration aplenty to return to her tasks. A bespeckled fawn in a berry thicket. A clump of wildflowers she had no name for. The whisper of water in the cove a stone's throw away. The sooner everything was set to rights, the sooner they could savor their surroundings.

18

Twilight found them atop crates, eating stale bread and smoked fish beneath the front eave of the house. The trestle table was set into place after supper, leaving them all looking forward to breakfast. In the kitchen the huge hearth bore the needful pots and pans, mostly Izella's doing. Their prior tenant, God rest him, had been a carpenter by trade as well as farmer. Little touches everywhere bespoke his artistry—the carved stairwell, the leaf and vine embellishment on the mantels, deep window seats. Each a gift.

Near dusk, the golden wink of fireflies seemed other-worldly amid the deep green woods as the day drew to an extraordinary hush. James Towne was nothing if not noisy. Rarely did it settle, even on the outskirts where their former house had been. But here on a distant shore there was simply the sigh of the wind and crickets' chirrup.

Father was asleep. She could hear his snoring. Mother was reading their Bible by candlelight. Shay was somewhere along the river's edge with a pine-knot torch. Selah found herself alone in the parlor, still trying to make a place for things so that her parents would have one less task upon awakening.

Yawning, she cast a longing look at the stairs. Her bedchamber was up them, across from Shay's, both small yet with a winsome view.

She stooped to dust the dog irons at the hearth, then straightened as a new sound intruded upon the stillness. Hoofbeats? Faint at first and then fading to a barely perceptible walk, as if the rider feared they'd be abed or wanted to surprise them unawares. Her pulse picked up and then settled. Naturals had no horses, though they did try to steal them.

Still feeling a flutter of alarm, unsure where their musket was, she moved to the open front door that faced the small courtyard. The half-moon was generous, outlining the rough edges of woodpile and well and fence.

A horse nickered through the blackness.

She leaned into the door frame, bone weary yet hopeful. "Who goes there?"

"Your nearest neighbor," came the quiet answer. "And his faithful steed, Lancelot."

Xander.

Bereft of words, she stepped outside into the moonlight as he swung himself down from the saddle. "I meant to arrive before dark, but the needs of the day held me fast."

"'Tis good of you to come." Pleasure warmed her voice. "You've met many a need here even in your absence."

"Meaning you Hopewells wore out my indentures." He faced her, smiling. "A fine night for riding. I saw your light from a ways off. A pleasant thing after so much darkness."

She peered into the shadows surrounding him. "No Ruby and Jett?"

"They remain behind to fret my aunt."

This she didn't doubt. "Can I fetch you a drink?"

"Nay." He came nearer, head turned toward the river's edge where the fireflies were the thickest. "Is Shay fire-fishing?"

"Aye. He seems to need no sleep."

"He's safer here than at James Towne. No unruly sailors or sots." He reached into his pocket and withdrew something that was all a-rattle as he passed it to her. "Needful seed."

"*Nicotiana tabacum*?" she teased. "Sweeter than the breath of fairest maid, said one poet."

"None of the noxious weed, nay."

"Thank you. Mother will be especially grateful. We're anxious to start planting in the morning, test your upriver soil and see what grows here."

"Tobacco foremost."

"I shall leave that to you. And Oceanus, in time."

"Mayhap sooner than later. He's due to arrive any day. You should see the nursery—" He halted, as if uneasy delving into such personal matters. "His bedchamber resembles a small battlefield, complete with wooden soldiers and a rocking horse and all manner of amusement."

'Tis not play-pretties he needs, but you.

She held her tongue. She'd not repeat her foolish foible upon his return about leaving Oceanus behind. Nor follow with another wrenching apology.

"A welcoming home awaits him." Her heartfelt words seemed to ease him. "I'm sure you've left no stone unturned as to his coming."

"And you?" He looked toward the house, light framing the windows.

"I sense I shall feel at home here too. Moving seems to have given Father a new vision, new hope. And as I said, Mother is ready to plant a garden."

She gestured to a makeshift bench made up of barrels and a wood plank. They both sat, a respectful space large enough to fit Shay between them.

"Why do I ken there's more than what you're saying?" He leaned forward, hands fisted. "Are you homesick?"

"Homesick for James Towne? Nay. I simply long for a more settled life," she confided. "One in which I don't fear some tattooed warrior or skulking malady might rob me of those I love."

"Life in this New World has always been full of obstacles and dangers."

She looked up. The stars seemed bright and sharp as glass away from the smoky haze of town. "Do you ever feel the tug to return to Scotland?"

A thoughtful pause. "Scotland has its own pitfalls, starting with a ship's passage. If we're to win this new land, we must stand firm right where we are. Raise sons and daughters to come after us and carry on what we have started."

"You must think me a spoilsport with all my murmurings."

"You're no spoilsport, Selah Hopewell. Simply a lass in need of a fresh apron and a good night's sleep. One who has better things to do than sit with a Scotsman when they both must rise before first light."

She looked to her apron, knowing it was a soiled, wrinkled mess even in the humid dark. She pulled at the strings, then balled the apron between her hands. Neither of them made a motion to go. That solaced her too. The space between them had shrunk by half now. Had he moved? His face was cast in craggy profile, the scant, silvery light giving her a glimpse of the aging, bearded man he might one day become.

Another bittersweet pang shot through her. Time was so fleeting. Yet all of life's uncertainties seemed sweetened by company. Starlight. The dwindling close of a busy day. She dug in her pocket and produced his handkerchief, clean and folded into a tidy if wrinkled square.

Holding it out reluctantly, she offered its return. His hand did not rise to meet it.

"Mightn't you keep it?" Pitched low, his voice held a rare poignancy. "Though I hope you have no need of it."

Oh, I shall indeed have need of it. When you take your leave tonight. When Oceanus arrives. When Shay goes.

In answer, she returned it to her pocket, sensing a tiny thrill. A heartfelt bridge had been built. He could not know how she had treasured that small bit of cloth, even putting it under her pillow when she slept. Nor had she wanted to wash it and remove all trace of him. And all the while she had wondered . . .

How would his hand feel upon her hair again? Her skin?

A tickle was her answer—the barest brush of his knuckles upon her heated cheek. They swept downward till they rested beneath her chin, tilting her head upward ever so slightly. Slowly he leaned in and closed the distance between them as her heart beat fast as a captive bird's wing. Would he . . . kiss her?

But his hand fell away as a rush of footsteps had them both looking again at the river.

"Xander? That you?"

"Who else?"

"Look at this!" Shay held up his catch with one hand, the

spear with which he'd caught it in the other. At Xander's praise, his smile widened. "Father shall have a fine striped bass for his breakfast."

"No doubt you'll teach the Naturals some fishing tricks."

"Ha! I should like to teach and not only be taught." He passed inside the kitchen doorway, leaving them alone again.

But the sweet moment betwixt them was lost. Or simply postponed?

Selah stood reluctantly, bringing an end to their unexpected meeting. "You must be weary from a day's labor and then graciously calling on your new neighbors."

He didn't deny it. "Fare thee well, dear Selah. It sits sweetly with me that you're not far."

With that, he called for his horse and swung himself into the saddle with a seamless grace she never failed to note. Though her head tugged her inside, she let her heart sway her into watching him till the darkness swallowed him whole, the faint sound of his whistling unable to alleviate the sudden lonesomeness in his wake.

19

Soon their new home was nearly unpacked, and the warehouse along the waterfront opened its doors. A mere half mile separated the two and was easily had by a brisk walk or by horse. Most of their upriver trade came by boat, some by horse and wagon.

Though their start was smaller and the warehouse not yet full, business was brisk once word spread that outlying plantations didn't have to venture clear to James Towne for supplies. Since Ustis knew nearly everyone in the colony, hearty shouts of welcome and parting farewells rang out from morn till late afternoon. Somewhat revived, he did not rely on his walking stick as much.

Selah marked time by Shay's going. Only a few more days and they'd return to James Towne for ceremonies initiating the exchange. For now, as she stood in their new garden, making rows and hills and watering the precious seed Xander had given them and that which they'd brought, all else faded beneath the glaring Tidewater sun.

"Mother, should we plant the rose cuttings here or over

there?" Selah asked, blinking in the glare, her thoughts mired in moonlight and Xander.

"Train them up against the kitchen wall." Candace's voice reined in her daughter's woolgathering. "Thankfully, the honeysuckle planted by the last tenant is full of health and vigor."

Selah gave an appreciative glance at the luxuriant vine shading the arbor between house and kitchen.

Hours later, their backs pinched from bending over, the garden was done. Purslane, French beans, lettuces, parsnips, artichokes, maize, and Ustis's prized potatoes. A lush if late harvest to put away for winter and to share with those in need.

Ustis returned from the warehouse, his hymn singing heard far down the shore, ahead of supper.

Selah didn't miss her mother's relieved expression. "I was about to ring the bell."

"Forgive my tardiness. Business continued brisk till the last and has quite worn me out." He all but fell into his chair, smiling despite it all. "I see the lines of worry about your face, dear wife. But I assure you I am better than when I left James Towne."

"I think we are all better than when we left James Towne. And have better neighbors."

Selah did not miss the glance cast her way by not one but both of her parents. Warming like the sassafras tonic she held, she couldn't help a fleeting smile.

"I dreamt I heard hoofbeats a few nights ago. Mayhap a midnight visitation of the manly sort?" Ustis inquired, and Candace could not withhold a chuckle. "Does our fair daughter have something to report?"

Selah set the cup in front of her father. "Only that Master Renick came by, inquiring about your health."

"Kind of him." Candace took a seat nearest her husband. "Did he mention Oceanus's return?"

"He did, indeed. Any day now."

"How welcome it will be to have him close. We're so near Rose-n-Vale I expect we shall hear the lad's voice carry."

"A pleasant thought."

"I hope he'll find a playmate in Watseka." Candace grew grave. "An only child can be quite lonely."

"Which reminds me that today the widow from Martin's Hundred came to buy," Ustis said. "The one with a great many children. She inquired after you and Selah—and Xander. She said she'd heard he'd helped us move."

"Widow Hastings? She is said to favor him." Candace took a second cup from Selah's hands. "He certainly has the means to support so large a brood, and Oceanus would have a great many brothers and sisters."

Ustis sipped, then winced with distaste. Sassafras was not his favorite. "I've lost count of how many children have the Hastingses, yet I fear their great number contributed to their father's demise."

"Ustis!" His droll remarks did not deter Candace's chastening. "Need I remind you that children are a heritage from the Lord, all eleven of them."

"Merciful heavens," he replied. "Though I do recall a brood of seventeen at Flowerdew Hundred . . ."

Selah listened, the mere power of suggestion sending her into a swirl of discontent. Little wonder the widow favored Xander. More than the widow, in truth. Withholding a sigh, she went to the door to look for Shay.

"I doubt he'll be home till our resident owl begins hooting," Ustis said of the creature who roosted in a near oak. "Shay is exercised by the notion that gold is to be found hereabouts and is best spotted in the dark."

"The fanciful imaginings of a lad," Candace replied, breaking into soft song. "'Thy crimson stockings all of silk, with gold all wrought above the knee; Thy pumps as white as was the milk; and yet thou wouldst not love me.'"

"'Greensleeves,'" Ustis murmured, closing his eyes.

Selah walked outside to look for Shay. Foolishly, she'd hoped he'd keep to home, spend his remaining time before the exchange with them. But there was simply no curtailing her brother's rambles or predicting his wayward timing once he did return home.

She pressed her fingers to her lips, pondering that interrupted, would-be kiss, till a sudden rustle in the brush emptied her head of such. Whirling, she stared into the tangle of overgrowth that led deeper into the woods. A deer, perhaps. A wily raccoon. Or one of the dreaded poison snakes so common in Virginia.

Beset with gooseflesh, she sent up a breathless call to her brother. "Shay, please come home!"

He appeared soon after, clutching a small lump of ore shot through with glittery specks. "See, I am fine, Sister. No need to worry way out here. I was simply looking for gold and found this. What say you?"

"Rock crystal? A fetching addition to your collection."

With a last look at the secretive woods, Selah followed him inside, shutting the door and barring it soundly behind them.

Come the Sabbath, the reality of their upriver existence took further hold as they gathered for worship at the edges of Renick land. There, in a comely little glade, stood a church set upon a cobblestone foundation and crowned with a wooden roof and belfry. One of the "chapels of ease," as the mother country called it, erected in shires far from James Towne. Behind the church was fenced ground where sunlight spread yellow light over too many crosses.

Xander stood with several men near the open chapel door as congregants from across the shire gathered. Though church attendance was required but once a month, this building looked filled to the brim. Oft settlers came merely to socialize, but who could blame them?

In moments, Xander greeted the Hopewells, looking pleased they'd come. "Welcome to our parish. You'll find we stand on no ceremony. Here we have no altar but pulpit, no priest but itinerant preacher. Keith is his name."

"If the gospel is preached, all is well, aye?" Ustis took his walking stick from Candace while Shay hobbled his horse. "Such progress since sixteen and seven, when James Towne's first church was held outside beneath an old sail for an awning!"

"Surely there's no prettier place to worship in all of Virginia, or to be laid to rest," Candace remarked. "I recall you had this chapel's foundation laid soon after you settled at Rose-n-Vale, or Renick Hundred as it was once called."

"It took several years for all the bricks to be had, but 'tis finally finished." He excused himself as a man sought his attention about some matter inside, leaving Selah slightly openmouthed as she watched him go.

Shay elbowed her. "Sister, are you struck dumb?"

Was she? Another window had been flung open, allowing her to see Xander in a new light. "I'm rather surprised to find so comely a chapel in the woods, is all."

Congregants moved slowly through the chapel's open doors, trading sunlight for welcome shade. She did not miss the Sabbath parade of James Towne officials in their finery commanding the foremost pews. Here there were mostly indentures and small planters dressed in their humble best. A few married men with families. A knot of older good-wives. As Selah moved toward the entrance, another star-tling realization took hold. Might they—the Hopewells—be considered gentry among these people? They were drawing noticeable stares and whispers.

When she tarried on the step outside, Shay turned toward her. "Sister, will you not enter in?"

Aye, and repent of thinking Xander a heathen.

Duly chastened, she bent her head as the bell ceased tolling above them and followed her family to their seats.

Forgive me, Lord.

The service opened with a morning prayer and Scripture reading. Most of Virginia's pulpits were empty, awaiting cler-ics to be appointed by the Bishop of London. But few men of the cloth wanted so rustic a church.

"Lay not up for yourselves treasures upon earth, where moth and rust doth corrupt, and where thieves break through and steal: But lay up for yourselves treasures in heaven, where neither moth nor rust doth corrupt, and where thieves do not break through nor steal. For where your treasure is, there will your heart be also . . ."

Selah's head was bowed, but her gaze strayed to the men's side. Though she'd heard the scriptural admonishment all her days, the words seemed to leap to new life. Xander seemed turned to stone on the front pew, though a muscle twitched in his bewhiskered cheek.

Was he . . . convicted?

Was ambition not her foremost concern about him? Vainglorious pursuits? He was amassing earthly treasure like no one she knew in all Virginia. And forever emboldened to do more with Virginia's unceasing efforts to prove its worth to the king.

She looked to her hands folded primly in her lap, her lace cuffs painstakingly made and imported. Was such finery necessary? Did she not take pride in the stares of the plainer goodwives here? Could they who were considered "the better sort" not get by with less? Less tobacco? Less indentures? Less Indian land? Yet still they toiled and spun, all of them . . .

If she felt even a pinprick of self-righteousness, such was swept away by Keith's next swordlike thrust.

"Judge not, that ye be not judged . . . And why beholdest thou the mote that is in thy brother's eye, but considerest not the beam that is in thine own eye?"

'Twas as if heaven itself came down and smote her. She blinked, the board in her own eye a painful distraction. Who was she to know Xander's heart, his aim? Who was she to task him with being a better father? Could she fault him for working tirelessly? Would she rather he be a sluggard?

The service came to an end, its brevity blasphemous. Worshipers began filing out into fresh air while Xander lingered, exchanging a few words with those nearest him. Clutching her *Book of Common Prayer* in a gloved hand, Selah made her way out of doors in no hurry. With work forbidden on the Sabbath, their cooking done the day before, they were free to tarry.

Ustis took a seat beneath a shady elm while Shay joined other lads his age near a creek. Candace greeted the good-wives, their coiffed heads identical, Widow Brodie among them. Matrons all, few of them Selah's age or station. She put a hand to her own coif. Her freshly washed hair had taken a sheen of beeswax to settle into braids. Even now a flyaway wisp dangled in her eye. The very one Xander had righted on Cecily's wedding day. With a whoosh of breath, she sent it out of her line of vision.

"How is your teething babe today, Goody Phelps?"

"I vow I spied a savage in our very woods whilst gathering herbals."

"My husband lies abed with the sweating sickness."

"She is no good wife, selling a firkin of butter with stones in it!"

As the feminine voices rose and fell, Selah skirted their circle, intent on the fenced graveyard. She'd always regretted that graves be so near places of worship, but the powers that be enforced such, just as they'd declared an annual day of the dead to mark the occasion of the last Indian massacre.

A robin alighted on a fence's rough railing, its repeated chirp rising above the hubbub in the churchyard. Somewhat assuaged by its sweet song, Selah counted seventeen grave-stones of all sizes. Their world, though not as fragile as when first founded, was still a delicate endeavor.

Xander missed his hat. He didn't wear it on the Sabbath but now found his hands idle and empty, his heart overfull, his thoughts distracted. Ustis was telling him about the latest tariffs, usually a riveting topic, but try as he might, Selah kept stealing his attention. He swallowed, trying to track what Ustis was saying, for he really was interested, just not as interested as he was in the man's daughter.

Framed by the emerald green of early summer, even with the crosses beyond, Selah lent a grace and peace to the otherwise melancholy scene. Hard to fathom he'd once found her paleness uninteresting, her fine features lacking depth and character. She was as comely a lass as the Almighty ever made.

She turned around just then, her gaze meeting his across the expanse of ground that separated them. Ustis's next question failed to take root. Xander's gaze fell to his leather boots. Everything within him urged some decisive action, some heartfelt declaration. Yet now was not the time to ask to woo the daughter of a man soon to part with his son.

Besides, he might have misread her, been blinded by his own intentions. Selah, independent minded as she was, might tell him to go to blazes. Might even suspect him of trying to marry her to gain her land dowry.

". . . I am prepared to part with my son on the morrow. Is all as it should be regarding the exchange commencing at James Towne?"

"The exchange . . . aye." Xander returned to full attention. "At first light, we'll take the shallop that brought you upriver and return to James Towne. The formalities shouldn't be complicated, and we'll be home by dusk, Lord willing."

"We'll be ready," Ustis replied with a wheeze, getting to his feet.

Selah crossed the grass, eyes for her father alone, worry

tightening her features. Not one word to Xander had she spoken. Might Selah begrudge him separating an ailing father from his son, despite Ustis's insistence?

Xander walked behind the stooped figure, ready to step in if he stumbled, as Selah placed her hand on her father's arm in silent support. Candace and Shay joined them, all assuming a slower pace.

"Won't you join us for the Sabbath meal, Xander?" Candace's gracious invitation was tempting, but he wouldn't intrude on their remaining time together before Shay departed even if he had no excuse.

"We're hosting the preacher today. Another Sabbath, mayhap."

His aunt joined them, finally extricating herself from the garrulous goodwives. "Perhaps you Hopewells can join us at Rose-n-Vale next time."

With a few last words that he'd see them in the morning, he turned to go.

"Soon we shall have a few more seated around our own table," his aunt said as he helped her into a pony cart.

More than the Hopewells, aye. A stranger of a nurse. A stranger of a son. The prospect lent to his loose ends the nearer he drew to the unknown date of their arrival. Uncomfortable as he was making small talk, shepherding children, and entertaining guests, how would he manage? Though his aunt was elated at having more than Ruby and Jett for company, he held fast to the habit of answering to no one, of working through meals and into the night it warranted. The world as he knew it would soon change. Again.

Lord, help Thou me.

20

Truly, heartfelt conversations required no words.

Pondering it, Selah left the churchyard to walk home as Xander and his aunt went another direction. Only Father rode, the two-mile stretch too much in his recovering state. He plodded along on his old gelding, an amiable creature that preferred a slow walk. They all kept a companionable silence, and Selah looked back but once.

As did Xander.

The smile she couldn't hide she felt to her toes. Proof she wasn't conjuring castles in the air. Were they not going to extraordinary lengths to hide their unprofessed feelings while forgetting their eyes had a language all their own?

Dismay and delight did a bittersweet dance inside her. Dismay that she could be so easily swayed by the bearded tobacco lord whose work habits and earthly strivings she disdained. Delight that love, even unconfessed, might have come to them at last, triumphing over the struggles and heartaches of years.

Shay trailed behind with her, a telling light in his eyes.

"Sister, why are you whistling? 'Tis unbecoming of a lady, some say."

⊱≎⊰

The next morn, brazen sunlight beat down upon James Towne as two hundred or more English and Naturals assembled on the grassy common. Xander's smallest shallop was but one of many, the Powhatans' vessels foremost and far more colorful. Selah saw Cecily and others she knew at a distance, but with the crowds so thick, a fleeting glance was all that could be had.

"So, my beloved son, are you prepared for this momentous day?" Ustis's voice held a beat of regret, at least to Selah, as they took their places near the English officials.

"Aye, Father. I shall do you proud." Shay's gaze ricocheted to Candace. "Mother, are you ready for Watseka?"

"Indeed. We must have someone to replace you, even if she wears a skirt."

Shay laughed, no skittishness written upon his boyish features. "I shall miss you all. But when I return, I shall fill your empty ears with adventures!"

A hush came over the assembly as a procession of Powhatans came up from the shore. Every eye seemed riveted to Chief Opechancanough, who rarely left his own territory. Formidable and half a foot taller than the tallest colonist, he was marvelously made, covered by a cloak of feathers that fell to his knees. His sharp features were paint blackened and slashed red with puccoon, a valuable plant gotten farther south. His aging face held a thousand stories.

All that Mattachanna had once confided returned to Selah now. Hard to fathom that this man, the emperor of the Powhatan nation, was Mattachanna's kin. Perhaps he wouldn't look so fearsome if not flanked by so many werowances and weroansquas, those favored attendants with special standing. If fear could be felt, it was here, weighting so many solemn white faces in the chief's presence.

A silent prayer rose from Selah's chary heart. For Shay's and the other children's protection. For peace. For the success of this exchange that seemed so fraught with risk.

At the crux of the ceremonies was Xander, first to greet the dark delegation as head interpreter. Once the Naturals assembled, his English words, when translated, were still cloaked in native imagery.

"We desire to open a path between nations, to remove the brush and briars, to enact a peace that will last as long as the sun provides warmth, the trees give shade, and the rivers run with water."

Beside Governor Harvey's stiff self-importance, Xander's apparent ease and eloquence were jarring. Selah felt naught but shame as the officials oozed an unseemly arrogance, which had surely sent her father upriver as much as James Towne's marshes and miasmas. Unlike them, Xander showed no impatience for the long speeches or the elaborate gift giving, nor the sun's heat as it climbed overhead. Beside him was Meihtawk, an especially welcome sight, who came regularly to their shore.

Though a great many warriors were present, there were few Indian women. Those Selah did see were at the back of the throng. Wives, perhaps, as the chief had several from nearly every Indian nation. That custom scandalized all Virginia, though it consolidated Powhatan power.

Somewhere in the throng were the Powhatans' peace children. Earlier, Laurent had examined all the youth inside the church, both English and Indian, deeming them fit. Reverend Midwinter had led in prayer. None wanted illness or death on either side. Now, standing beside the governor and his officials, the physic's searching gaze settled on Selah.

Though the day was hot as Hades, his scrutiny sent a chill clean through her. To escape, she stepped behind a burly Virginian.

The chief was speaking now as Xander interpreted, all attention on the English peace children. "I lift you up from this place and set you down again at my dwelling place . . ."

At last the Powhatan children appeared. A low murmur passed through the gawking colonists. Selah softened as her gaze fastened on the sole girl. This must be Watseka. She was by far the youngest, perhaps six or seven years of age, and clad in the whitest doeskin. The fringed garment draped over one small shoulder and fell to her knees. On her feet were equally white moccasins embellished with shells and glass beads. A stout braid dangled down her back, dark as tarred rope. Her oval face was missing a smile. She seemed rather awed by her newfound circumstances, or perhaps confused by all the fuss.

Governor Harvey was speaking now, and Selah strained to hear his clipped English words. Something about opening a school for Indian youth. Many pounds of sterling were being raised by English churches to teach Indian children useful trades and train them as missionaries to their own people.

When the ceremonies ended, a group of goodwives rushed the Hopewells, nearly bowling Candace over in their eagerness.

"What a burdensome task you've taken on, you Hopewells.

I say train the little urchin in spiritual matters foremost, with the Bible writ large, as well as the psalter."

"Do not forsake the catechism. The child must recite it perfectly."

"Needlework and a sampler seem in order first. Every young girl needs to learn a good vocabulary of stitches and general housewifery."

Wishing they could go straight to the shallop, Selah watched her mother free herself from the busybodies to follow Ustis to where Xander waited with Shay. On her brother's back was a knapsack stuffed so full the straps bulged. She'd secreted sweetmeats within as well as a letter she'd penned for times of doubt or discouragement, though she prayed there'd be none.

"Farewell, Sister." Shay brushed her cheek with a hasty kiss as Xander looked on. "I am feeling particularly brave."

She tried to smile, emotion choking her. All she could manage through an impossibly tight throat was one word. "Godspeed."

Candace embraced him, her tearful goodbye tearing at Selah's heart. But 'twas Ustis who left her most undone. He bowed his head as if to master himself before murmuring a few hard-won words in Shay's ear, looking frail and withered beside his strapping son.

"Meihtawk will continue as emissary during the exchange," Xander explained once they'd collected themselves. "If something should happen Shay needs knowing about—a summons to return home—he will convey that posthaste."

Ustis and Candace embraced their son a final time, pride and sorrow mingled on their faces. "God be with you."

In moments, Meihtawk brought Watseka by the hand to

where they stood. This close, Selah marveled anew at the child's appearance. Slight of build, the girl had fine, dainty features. A delicate shell necklace encircled her throat.

"She is a granddaughter of Chief Opechancanough. Her mother, a Mattaponi, died of the running-sores sickness after she was born," Meihtawk told them in accented English. "She has been raised by her aunts until now."

Selah knelt in the grass till she was eye level with Watseka, feeling dry as an abandoned well. Sadly, Mattachanna had taught her few Powhatan words, hungry as she had been to learn English. "Wingapo."

Pleasure flashed in Watseka's wary yet lively eyes.

Selah held out her hand and felt a glimmer of relief when the child took it. Once Ustis and Candace made their own warm introductions, they began a slow walk to the water past their former house and garden to reach the Renick shallop. Xander spoke with Watseka in her tongue, pointing out this or that, as they pushed away from James Towne's shores.

With a yawn, Watseka laid her head upon Selah's lap in a manner all the more remarkable given their short acquaintance. Candace's face softened visibly as she took in their charge. Ustis seemed lost in thought. Xander was near the bow, the oarsmen maintaining a rhythmic silence in the face of a contrary wind.

A summer storm threatened over the Chesapeake, heavy clouds as gray and purling as smoke. Likely it was already raining at James Towne and would travel upriver in time. As she thought it, the oarsmen seemed to renew their efforts. Rain was needed, but thunder and lightning were another matter, especially on the water.

By the next bend in the river, large drops had begun to pelt them. Xander quickly made an awning of a worn sail, beneath which they sought shelter. He scooped the still sleeping Watseka up in his arms and continued to hold her as they neared Hopewell Hundred.

Seated near Selah, he reassured them about Shay's journey as well. "They'll likely press on despite the weather and make camp along the Pamunkey River tonight."

By the time their recently restored dock came into view, lightning was lashing them, sending them all scrambling for shore. Xander still held Watseka, who was fully awake now and looking wide-eyed over his shoulder. The oarsmen hastened away, the weather preventing their return to fieldwork.

Once home, they all began removing sodden garments. Selah's beaver hat with its wide brim was soaked through, rain dripping from the peak of her nose. She hung her hat from a peg to dry, removed her apron, and tied another on, then started for the door again to fetch what she'd been secreting for Watseka. As she went out, she heard her mother's voice behind her, ever ready with an invitation.

"Xander, you must stay on for a meal, or at least till the weather clears. Izella is preparing a bountiful supper. Shay's bed is yours for the taking too."

"I second the notion," Ustis said. "Let us not bid you farewell only to find you lightning struck."

Without hearing Xander's reply, Selah made her way beneath the eave to a small shed, a scratching at the door muffled by the rain. Not wanting the pup to traipse through the widening mud puddles, she scooped him up and hurried back to the dry house and Xander's answer.

Watseka's expression grew more animated as Selah shut

the door on the noisy weather and released the wiggling ball of fur onto the plank floor. "From a litter at Flowerdew Hundred."

Watseka looked to Xander. "*Attemous.*"

"Dog, aye," he replied. "*Attemous.*"

Getting on her hands and knees, Watseka began growling as the inquisitive pup sniffed her doeskin dress and began nipping at the fringed hem with tiny teeth, which set them all to laughing. Next, she caught the pup up in her arms, its tongue a flash of pink against her merry face.

Excusing herself, Selah left for the kitchen to help with supper preparations. Candace soon joined her, finishing what Izella had started before she left to do the milking.

"Though I am happy for Watseka, I fear the wee hound will have its way with our fowl," Candace lamented as she fried beef collops. "A kitten might have done as well."

"We shall make sure the pup respects all poultry." Selah poked at a kettle of greens, wondering if Xander favored ramps and onions. "Our last cat was carried away by an eagle, if you recall. At least a pup stands a fighting chance."

Nodding, Candace brought forth a cake that had been soaking in a cupboard for a sennight. As she removed the linen wrap, the scent of spirits quashed the potent greens. "I do hope *The English Hus-wife* does not disappoint."

Selah eyed the concoction as well as the receipt book open on the kitchen table. "Your cake, you mean?" Big and round and the color of an autumn nut, the cake boasted the best dried fruit and spices to be had, nutmeg foremost.

"Watseka's welcome cake." Candace eased it onto a platter. "Let us hope she likes it."

"'Tis a wonder you kept it from Shay before his going.

I daresay Father and Xander will waste no time with it, if Xander stays."

"He is to stay, aye." She stole a look at Selah as if gauging her reaction.

Heartened—and flustered—by the thought, Selah took down their best pewter and glass. There seemed a special intimacy about sharing a meal. She'd sensed it especially at Rose-n-Vale. Remembering the lovely posies set upon that linen-clad table, Selah dashed outside again, only to find little could be had but a few sodden wildflowers.

When supper came, Ustis and Xander took the table's ends while Watseka sat by Selah across from Candace, hardly leaving them room to miss Shay.

"Xander, would you honor our table by blessing what we are about to partake?" Ustis asked.

Selah sensed Xander's surprise, her spirits sinking. *Oh, Father, can you not pray instead?*

They joined hands and bent their heads, even Watseka, who was a fine mimic.

"Guide us, Lord, in all the changes and varieties of the world, that we may have evenness and tranquility of spirit, that we may not grumble in adversity nor grow proud in prosperity but in serene faith surrender our souls to Thy most divine will, through Jesus Christ our Lord."

Their joined hands released. Dumbstruck by the beauty of his prayer, Selah sat unmoving for several seconds. Beside her, Watseka squirmed off the bench to approach the hearth's fire, where she offered the dying flames a small portion of the meat upon her plate. A satisfying sizzle sent her back to the table.

Xander had a ready explanation. "'Tis Powhatan custom

to throw a bit of food into the fire as a thanks offering before eating."

Ustis harrumphed while Candace simply managed a small smile as supper commenced. Out of the corner of her eye, Selah watched Watseka try her first English meal. Bypassing her utensils, she partook with her fingers very neatly and carefully, savoring every bite of her collops. Corn pone and greens, familiar to her though perhaps prepared differently, also disappeared.

At the serving of the cake, Watseka gaped. Though the night was overwarm, Selah poured the girl some herbals in a tiny cup.

Cake promptly devoured, cup empty, she began yawning again, clearly worn out from her long day. Who knew how far she had traveled before coming to James Towne? And Shay? Was he even now seeking shelter? She turned her uneasiness into a silent prayer. The damp did her brother no favors, oft leading to chest infections and the pursuit of some remedy.

Removing Xander's dishes, acknowledging his murmured thanks, she kept her eyes down, glad for the steadying routine. When the men moved to the parlor, she wiped the table clean, wishing her topsy-turvy feelings were as easily discarded as the supper crumbs.

21

Ustis, exhausted by the day's events, his chest rattling with that stubborn cough, took to his bed, Candace following. Once their bedchamber door shut, 'twas only Selah, Watseka, and Xander in the parlor now. Rain mellowed from a downpour to a patter, and the house finally cooled. Full and dry, they sat and watched Watseka play with her pup. To her delight, Xander untied the leather string binding his hair in a careless queue and gave it to her as enticement.

Leaning back in Ustis's chair, clearly the most comfortable, he stretched out his legs and crossed his boots at the ankles. With Selah beside him, near enough he could catch the herbal scent of her, he pondered spending the night. His aunt didn't expect his return till tomorrow, and his tarrying might ensure Watseka's adjustment was more comfortable for all concerned.

But none of that explained his dallying.

'Twas this sudden closeness, so beguiling, that kept him rooted and opened the door to pondering their future. A future far beyond this sodden eve that might well thwart the coming harvest to a languid winter's night before his own glowing hearth, Selah by his side, and nothing more pressing to ponder than choosing a favorite pipe.

Thus ensnared, he threw caution to the wind. "I suppose this might well count as courting."

A stunned silence. And then Selah laughed. A laugh so high and musical it had the ring of a bell. She looked sideways at him beneath long-lashed eyes. "Are you making sport of romantic matters, Xander Renick?"

"Nay. I just do not know how to proceed."

"Are you seeking my permission?"

"I have been seeking your permission for some months."

"But not in words."

He shook his unkempt head. "A lingering look. A tarrying."

She smiled then, somewhat shyly, her eyes never leaving his. "Have you spoken to my father?"

"Not yet. The timing continues unfavorable. Besides, you know I am not one for bowing to custom. Mayhap it bears considering to court as the Powhatans do."

"And how is that?"

His gaze veered to Watseka, leather string in her mouth as she played tug of war with the pup. "A warrior presents his would-be bride with a gift, often some delicacy to be eaten, that conveys his ability to provide for her."

Selah's gaze swept his buckskin breeches and linen doublet. "I see no food on your person."

"Alas . . . given that, you are free to decline my verbal offer."

"And if I accept? What then?"

"I approach your parents. Pay a bridewealth to them."

"A bit like the tobacco brides, perhaps."

"Something like that, aye. Next comes the wedding feast."

"Are we then considered married?"

"Not until I prepare a place for you. Rose-n-Vale should do. Then we'd marry at your parents' home." Caught up in the moment, he'd unwittingly made it more personal, but from the look on her face she didn't mind. "An elder officiates, breaking a string of beads over our—the couple's—heads. The wedding feast follows."

Another smile. Her eyes seemed to dance. And then the warmth fled her gaze. "Like you and Mattachanna."

He gave a nod. The memory, so distant now, seemed almost to belong to someone else. "We married first before her people, then the English in church, if you recall."

"I do. Yet somehow, courting you seems to tread on that memory."

"How so?"

"You were—mayhap still are"—she looked to her aproned lap—"in love with her."

"Is that your only reservation, Selah?"

"Nay."

"There's more, then."

"A great many things. Shay leaving. Father continuing unwell. I'm needed now more than ever here."

He fell silent. Such plain speaking led them down a path thwarted with weeds and thistles. Shouldn't love be more glad-hearted? Willing to take risks, come what may?

Watseka's soft giggling defused the tension of the moment. The pup had the leather string, flinging it back and forth between his teeth.

"Are you always driven by duty, Selah? What of your heart?"

"My heart . . ." Wistfulness filled her face. "'The heart is deceitful above all things, and desperately wicked: who can know it?'"

"True, aye, as is this—'a continual dropping in a very rainy day and a contentious woman are alike.'"

"Shall we exchange Scripture for Scripture?" she asked, seemingly chided *and* amused. "As for me . . ."

He waited none too comfortably for her answer.

"I am not at peace with your working night and day and your preoccupation with plantation matters."

"Is that all?"

"Is that not enough?"

"I sense your resistance goes deeper, is what I'm saying." His tone was firm, yet the searching words were soft. "Let us have the matter settled between us once and for all, here and now."

Tears glittered in her eyes. He'd not meant to issue a challenge. Ruing it, he wanted nothing more than to take her in his arms, no matter what her answer would be. Finally, it came.

"I would have you remarry for heartfelt reasons, not base practicality like the tobacco brides. With a genuine depth of feeling, a sincere heartfelt commitment, nothing less." Her shimmering gaze turned him on end. "Is it wrong for me, nearly a spinster, to want to be the object of your best thoughts and intentions?"

That look she gave him. Entreating. Expectant. It rent his open heart. If not for Watseka he would take her in his arms and silence her endless queries.

He leaned forward, hands outspread. "Selah, how can I prove to you—"

A storm of coughing sounded from the bedchamber. Selah

187

stood as the door opened and Candace appeared in her night-cap and gown.

"Daughter, can you bring dried horehound leaves mixed with honey? Perhaps that will soothe your father's chest and help him sleep."

"Of course."

Xander pulled himself to his feet. "Is there anything I can do?"

"Your being beneath our roof is comfort enough." Selah started for the kitchen. "If Father takes a turn for the worse . . ."

"I'll retire, then, but am ready if the need arises." He started for the steps with a candle, having been told Shay's room was to the right of the landing.

He kept his tread light, not wanting to aggravate an already sleepless situation. On his way he gave a passing glance at Selah's half-open door. A small bed, a washstand, a desk and chair within. One small rug lent softness and color. Still, it looked so spare he felt a qualm over his own sumptuous bedchamber.

Shay's room was even more spartan, deprived of both his presence and possessions now on their way to the far frontier. Xander shut the door and opened the sole window. Sitting, he tugged off his boots and sank atop the feather mattress, which was far too warm for a summer's day and much too short. Shay was more round than tall.

But sleep was not on his mind tonight, his thoughts over-full of their storm of words with every attending emotion below. In time he heard Selah climb the stairs, her feet a whisper on wood. Her door shut, yet another barrier betwixt them. Within the confines of her room he heard a faint rustling as she and Watseka readied for bed.

He had made a stab at courting Selah, and the outcome was less than he had hoped. But he, of all men in Virginia Colony, was known for his persistence. In tobacco cultivation.

And now in courtship.

⟨✿⟩

Yawning, Selah arose before first light, leaving Watseka asleep upstairs. All were still abed but Izella, who laid the fire for breakfast. Assuming Shay's chores, Selah first fed the chickens, then let the pup scamper about untethered as dawn lit the eastern sky. Heart full of last night's honest exchange, she paused beneath the garden's tattered arbor, the tangle of coral-hued honeysuckle most fragrant at first light. Her gaze rose to the roofline and Shay's open window. No doubt Xander was an early riser—

"Morning, Selah."

The low voice bade her turn. Skirts swaying, she faced him as he approached from the well, water buckets filled to the brim. How had she missed him?

"Good morning, Xander." Oh, his name tasted sweet. For a few fleeting seconds this seemed their house, their dewy morn. "You must be anxious to return to Rose-n-Vale."

"Not particularly." His eyes were smiling. Reassuring.

She'd not slowed his pursuit then. All her naysaying of last night fled with him so near.

"The work will always be there." His gaze left her and took in the sunburnt yard already inching toward midsummer. "But moments like these, nay."

He strode past her and set the fresh water within the kitchen's open doorway while she began pulling weeds in the garden, mightily distracted. Taking hold of the wheelbarrow, he rounded the stable to the woodpile and set the axe to ringing, sparing her father the exertion. A gentling stole through her that this man, the best of Virginia, would perform so menial a task.

Soon finished with the early morning chores, they stood together and watched the sunrise, a glory of red gold that kept them captivated till the sudden appearance of Watseka. Naked as a jaybird, she flew out of the house to greet her pup. The sudden commotion started the rooster's crowing and Xander laughing. Selah rushed toward Watseka, scooped her up, and returned her to the house and the clothes they'd made her. Within minutes, looking considerably more uncomfortable, Watseka returned outside dressed in a miniature version of what Selah herself wore, down to the coif covering her black hair. But her tiny feet stayed bare.

"'Tis her custom to bathe at first light." He swung Watseka up onto sturdy shoulders. "A practice the odiferous English should follow."

Selah warmed all over at his bold words, thankful she'd bathed just yesterday. "Then I shan't prevent her in future."

Watseka sank her hands into Xander's tousled hair and asked him a question in her tongue. Replying, he set her on the mounting block, only to see her scamper toward her pup as fast as her English clothes allowed.

As Selah watched, he left the courtyard to turn the cow to pasture, then retrieved his horse, signaling he would soon depart. But first breakfast.

"Can you help me cook?" Selah called to Watseka once they were in the kitchen, passing her a long-handled wooden spoon. Though Watseka understood little English, she stood raptly by the porridge pot.

"*Supawn.*" She pointed her spoon at the bubbling contents.

"*Supawn,*" Selah repeated. "Mush?"

As the mush simmered, frying bacon commenced. Curling her nose, Watseka eyed the pork with suspicion. Was sweetening shunned as well? Selah took out the Caribbean sugar and put a bit on Watseka's tongue, a wide smile her reward. One front tooth was missing, giving Watseka a slightly lopsided look.

Candace came in, making much of their little charge. "Well, I see all is in order. Watseka proves a great help in the kitchen." She moved to where an apron hung on a wall peg. "I fear your father did not sleep a wink last night due to his coughing, which surely kept those of you upstairs awake as well."

"Nay," Xander assured her as he stepped into the kitchen.

"I'm sorry to hear Father is no better." Selah began ladling steaming mush into bowls while Watseka set out spoons. "I shall tend the store today. Thankfully, only churning the butter and making small beer remain for Izella. The other chores are mostly done, thanks be to Xander."

"A far cry from your usual duties." Candace looked at him fondly as he seated himself and took a first bite. "We don't mean to keep you any longer, though we do appreciate your help."

"I can carry Selah to the store on my way to Rose-n-Vale," he replied, reaching for the bacon.

"No need." Selah took her place, at war within herself once again. "The store isn't far yet is a bit out of your way."

"As you wish," he replied quietly, winking at Watseka as she added more sweetening atop her mush.

Seeing the exchange, Selah let her heart have its say. "On second thought . . ."

Xander looked at her in question.

Heat filled her from head to toe at her sudden reversal. "A ride would be a fine thing, thank you."

A beat of amusement crossed his face as he began speaking in Watseka's tongue, leaving her giggling more than eating. He took a small piece of bacon and fed it to the pup, who wagged without ceasing at their feet.

Still giggling, Watseka responded with a veritable volley of musical words.

"Her pup is to be called *Kentke*," Xander told them. "'He dances.'"

"Oh?" Delighted, Selah tried out the strange word much as she'd done *supawn*. "Kentke."

"The pup certainly does dance, for he never stops his wiggling." Candace rose at the sound of Ustis's hoarse voice from the bedchamber. "If you'll excuse me . . ."

Finished with breakfast, Xander murmured something to Watseka, which led to her helping clear the table. When he wandered outside, Selah felt the void before she realized he'd gone. But he was not far, just beyond the door, and would soon carry her to the store.

Blowing out a little sigh, which caused Watseka to look her way, Selah hung the kettle over the flames and prepared her father's tonic. Lord willing, she'd serve Xander no more nays and excuses. For once her heart would trump her head and curb her reason.

22

From atop Xander's horse, the view of the river and surrounding countryside was sublime. Xander pointed out various things only a true native would know, making the distance to the warehouse and wharf lamentably short. Crates and hogsheads lay about, some empty, some still full of wares. Faced with all that still needed doing, Selah all but mumbled an apology. There simply weren't enough hands, Shay's foremost. Already the wharf was lined with watercraft, the bridle path along the shore muddied with those approaching to buy, barter, or trade.

"Your work is cut out for you this day." Sliding to the ground, Xander helped her down and hobbled Lancelot. "I'll do what I can, though I am no cape merchant."

"You'll do plenty." His steadying presence bolstered her as she unlocked the back door with the keys her father had given her. "I rather like these joint endeavors."

Once she found the scales, Xander opened the front entrance to the men living on outlying Hundreds, most vaguely familiar to her but better known to him. He greeted them all by name and a handshake, inquiring after their welfare and their families, making introductions when needed.

And she thought James Towne was busy.

The forenoon found her buried in tobacco receipts but scant coin. And then came a blessed lull. Securing the coin in a metal box, Selah looked up to see Xander at counter's end.

"Needs be I return home," he told her.

She nodded, so grateful for his help a mere thank-you seemed inadequate. Crossing to where he stood, she reached for his hand and gave it a heartfelt squeeze. "You're a fine man, Xander Renick."

He laced her fingers in his, drawing her closer until she was in the sanctuary of his arms. Held so, her cheek against his chest, his heartbeat rhythmic and enduring beneath her ear, she felt . . . sheltered. Safeguarded amid their tenuous circumstances.

"Here and now, Selah, I declare my intentions to you." His whispered words were warm against her temple. "I would have you as my bride, the mistress of Rose-n-Vale, if you decide that is what and where you want to be."

Her heart welled and then her eyes. Her arms stole around his waist, anchoring him to her, giving him a half answer. When he cupped her chin in his hand and tilted her head back to look up at him, she felt little more than a puddle at his boots.

"'Twould be wise, if you're to help manage in your father's absence, to let Watseka accompany you some days. Consider a shop boy. In the meantime, if you or your kin need anything at all, send for me." Reaching up, he lifted that same stray tendril and tucked it into her coif.

The longing in his gaze—did it mirror her own? She still

had hold of his waist, though a niggle of impropriety bade her release him. Ignoring it, in a show of surrender she stood shamelessly on tiptoe, all but asking him to kiss her.

Begging.

With a chuckle deep in his throat, he brushed her forehead with his lips in a maddeningly gallant gesture. For a widower having tasted the fruits of marriage, he was a marvel of restraint. "I will not give you what you are yet unsure of, thus forming a bond between us that might well break."

Closing her eyes again, she let the moment be what it was. Cherished the tense, excruciatingly sweet tie that begged strengthening.

"Fare thee well, Selah."

He rode off, his horse's hoofbeats once again no match for her thudding heart.

He'd stated his intentions toward Selah. Spent the night beneath the Hopewells' roof. Nearly kissed her during those last heady moments alone in the warehouse. Yet he'd withheld the promise she'd not be a tobacco widow. How could he do otherwise when years of toil and ever-extending territory drove him still?

Now, three days hence, he contemplated telling her the truth about his and Mattachanna's tangled relationship. Settle her insecurities that the memory she feared they trod upon was not what it seemed, but far more intricate and buried grave deep. Share the secret that no amount of labor and sweat or success could temper.

Such was uppermost in his mind as he inspected his tobacco fields, judging the quality and vigor of this year's crop, which was nearing harvest. A crop that should have left him elated. No Orinoco yet had yielded so well, the color a coveted greenish-gold. England was now importing over a million pounds of leaf, Rose-n-Vale's the leading export. Still, there was little rest, a host of unseen challenges to come, a never-ending list of goods gotten and debts settled both here and in the Old World . . .

Hardly time for a new bride, a returned child, and an unknown nurse.

He rode on till he came to his maize, the tasseling stalks blocking his view. Here at the cornfield's heart with the gourdseed variety topping eighteen feet, not a leaf stirred, turning his shirt sodden before he'd escaped its suffocating grip. Planted in nearly as many acres as his tobacco, it promised food and forage for a lean winter, of which they'd had many.

He rode on, drawn to a haunting spot on the edges of Renick land. Time had turned it nearly unrecognizable save the stones and wooden crosses that marked two graves. What he'd give to have Henry Renick here to ken firsthand that his stake in the New World hadn't been in vain. His father had lived barely the three years required to receive the lion's share of land grants awarded those first settlers. And Xander had been with the Powhatans for most of it.

His beloved mother, pale like Selah, had been an uncommon woman, a tower of health and strength whose pride was her only son, his success the joy of her heart. But now? At five and thirty, past the prime of life, he'd best be concerned about more than tobacco, as Selah said. Build memories with those he loved rather than simply add another wing to Rose-n-Vale.

"Good day to ye, sir."

A voice pulled him back to the present. Another of his farm managers stood by a long chain of scaffolding used to air the cut tobacco.

"We've finished the drying racks ahead of the harvest, as ye ken. But with so many men fevered, progress has slowed on the packing and prizing house."

"How many are down?"

"Thirteen, mostly new arrivals."

"Needs be we sun-cure more than fire-cure the leaf, then." His indentures, most of them the heartiest of Scots, didn't shirk work. His concern was their working when ill, sickening further and sometimes dying. "Another five and twenty men are coming. Though they're inexperienced, if we train them properly they might suffice and let the ailing men recover."

Yet Xander well knew the promise of a ship was but a dream till it docked. More than a few had been lost at sea or intercepted by Spaniards.

"We're ready to house them, sir."

"You've done well overseeing their new quarters. Is the roof finished?"

"Just this morn, aye." The man took a long drink from his flask. "Another matter, sir. The slave traders have been by again. Wanted to part with a dozen or so Africans. Said they ken our need."

Xander shifted in the saddle, struck by the plea to reconsider in the manager's beleaguered face. "I'll not sell my soul to own another's. Not even if it means saving the harvest."

"I won't mention it again, sir. The Africans were sold to

197

the Frenchman instead. He's begun work on the land east of ye."

Laurent. The physic turned planter. The would-be wooer of Selah Hopewell. And now his neighbor. Looking toward the land in question, Xander schooled his reaction to the news, tantamount to a kick in the gut.

"Prepare to harvest by mid-August. Mayhap the ailing men will be recovered by then. I'll make the rounds and see if more medicines are needed from the apothecary. There's an able physic at Mount Malady I'll send for."

"Bethankit, sir."

The man rode off, and Xander turned in the direction of the indentures' quarters, a scattering of mud-and-daub dwellings with a rutted lane betwixt them. Only a few had wives and children and required a separate house. Virginia's woeful lack of women was an ongoing lament, as was the law that forbade these bound men to marry without his permission. Another brides' ship was needed. But even a dozen of them wouldn't be enough.

The sun bore down blisteringly, surely adding to the ailing men's fevered misery. He'd lost count of the indentures overcome by disease. Though he made sure their provisions were ample, their quarters orderly and clean, they still succumbed. Wives would help remedy that. Children would give them something to live for. Many of them were homesick, longing for the familiar. They'd not had the benefit—or the scourge—of being born here.

One of the women met him as he dismounted at the end of the lane. Her worn features beneath a soiled coif bespoke little sleep and trying to do for too many men. Was she also ill?

"Are ye well, kind sir?"

"Well enough, Goodwife McTulloch. And you? Your husband?"

"I'm middlin', but my man's poorly. A great many men are ailin'. 'Tis a wonder ye stay standin' in this heat."

"When you're born to it, it doesn't wear on you so badly." He removed his hat, the barest skim of breeze riffling his damp hair. "Expect a physic and more medicines from Mount Malady. And a quantity of fresh fruit from the Summer Isles on the morrow, if you and Goody Allen could distribute it."

Her flushed face bespoke relief. "Ye look well t' the health of yer men, ye do." She gave him a last, searching look. "Prayers for yer own health, sir. A wee bit shilpit t' my eye, if ye dinna mind me sayin' so."

Shilpit?

Though his Scots was rusty, he knew the word well enough and supposed he did look a bit haggard given the season. Bidding her good day, he started for the first building on the road—the barracks, he called it—hosting the bulk of the unmarried men. Even from a distance the stench of illness and overused chamber pots called a warning. Bracing himself, he let himself in after a loud knock.

A murmur of respectful greetings sounded from all corners. He stood in the room's center so he could be heard by all. "It grieves me to see you suffer, some of you not even on Virginia soil a fortnight. I've relief coming in the form of fresh foods and medicines. A physic should arrive shortly. An itinerant preacher is also making the rounds. Bring any other needs to the attention of Hosea Sterrett, who'll relay the matter to me. I'll return again soon to see how you're faring."

He went from house to house, taking stock of anything

else that needed addressing in addition to the ailing men. A decrepit roof. A dry well. More fence posts for gardens and livestock.

Xander was admired—and mocked—for his treatment of his indentures and his refusal to own Africans. Let a man work the land in exchange for his ship's passage and soil of his own in a few years' time. That he understood. But let no man be owned by another with no hope of ever being free.

Late afternoon, he'd finished his rounds and returned home another way, skirting the very boundary stones between Renick land, the Hopewells', and now Laurent's. How the physic had come by such prime acreage he didn't know, but his hackles rose at the mere thought.

Not a soul was in sight—not even the Africans Laurent was said to now own—just rolling hills awaiting twilight, a few trees along a watercourse breaking up the summery landscape. Xander loosened his hold on the reins and looked toward the river. There seemed a special poignancy to the dwindling day as it took a final breath. A subtle yearning that called for Selah by his side.

He was surrounded by people who felt themselves beneath him—his indentures—and those who felt themselves above him—Virginia's gentry. The latter despised his success, and the former held him in high regard as the standard they hoped to reach. He remained in the lonesome middle, a vacuous place where few men lived, a position that afforded few friends. He counted Selah a friend.

Once past her guardedness, he had warmed to the woman beneath. She was not shallow of soul. Not frivolous in nature.

The heart of her husband doth safely trust in her . . . She will do him good and not evil all the days of her life.

But did he love her? Aye, he did. 'Twas a different sort of love than the wild, reckless passion he'd felt for Mattachanna in his youth. The better question was . . .

Would Selah let him love her?

Till then, he had Rose-n-Vale. Mattachanna's son. A beloved aunt. Two doting dogs. An ample table. A comfortable bed. A favorite pipe.

An almost sweetheart.

23

"Glad news, Daughter! The ship bearing Oceanus has docked."

Selah stared at her father as she entered the warehouse with his midday meal, the welcome words no less upending because the homecoming was expected. "This very day?"

"Indeed." Ustis adjusted his spectacles, looking more delighted than she'd seen him since Shay's leaving. "Xander got wind of it early this morn and has gone to meet them in James Towne by shallop. Of course, his new indentures will be kept overnight there for the usual requirements on arrival, but Xander should return with Oceanus sometime this afternoon."

Soul lifting, Selah set down her basket, hardly believing the happy news. Soon Oceanus would step ashore, into their waiting arms and hearts. Hardly the baby Mattachanna bore but a nimble boy, whether resembling more his father or his mother they would soon discover. Or perhaps a pleasing mix of them both.

"I'll remain here with you till they come." Selah began unpacking the basket while Watseka roamed the store, poking a small finger at this or that, finally holding up a mustard pot in undisguised fascination. "Surely Mother and Izella won't mind an afternoon alone."

"I daresay they will not," Ustis agreed, partaking of a roast chicken leg. "Miss Mischief never tires. What I would give to greet the day running like she does."

Selah bit her lip. How keenly the old nickname brought Mattachanna's memory back.

"She's adjusting well to our ways, though 'tis a struggle to keep her clothed." Yet who could blame her? The Naturals' dress was far more practical, allowing one to leap and dance and run without hindrance. "Needs be we reserve her English clothes for Sundays."

"A worthy suggestion." Ustis stifled a cough by taking a drink of ale. "How goes her schooling?"

"Her mind is lively, so much it astounds me. She shows remarkable ability with her sewing." Truly, the small sampler Watseka had begun was nothing short of an astonishment. "I suppose her aunts have taught her a great many things."

"The women of her tribe are particularly skilled with handwork and have long been partial to our sewing notions." He looked from Watseka to Selah. "But what is this I hear about a sparrow? Your mother says one alights on her head nearly every morn when she goes outside."

"It even sings a song for her. I've never seen anything so charming." Smiling from the delight of it, Selah handed him a mince tart. "Have you not witnessed it?"

"I haven't had the pleasure yet. But mayhap she needs a playmate more than a bird or a puppy. Oceanus is near her age and will be exercising a growing independence from his nurse."

"Perhaps today he and Watseka shall meet." Selah looked out the open doorway to the wide river empty of all but a passing canoe. "The wind has freshened and is in their favor."

"A memorable day for Rose-n-Vale." Ustis stood at the sound of distant voices. Never idle for long, he readied for more business.

Selah observed his half-finished meal. "Shall I stay on and help you, Father?"

"Not today, Daughter. I feel more myself, God be thanked. Go enjoy this glorious afternoon."

Selah called for Watseka and led her outside as half a dozen indentures passed inside. Doffing their caps, they eyed Watseka curiously, likely unaware of the exchange that had taken place. Virginia was swelling so in size that any news was often belated. The outlying plantations heard last.

The day was indeed glorious, the heat tempered by a cooling wind. Watseka soon had an apron full of ribbed mussels so common alongshore. She held out her dripping apron. "*Tshecomah*."

Selah nodded, thinking Watseka's native word more winsome. "Shells."

With a smile so wide her missing tooth was apparent, Watseka made it clear Selah was to load her own apron.

"We need a basket." Selah backtracked to the warehouse for that very item, wishing for a tiny, clean apron too, if only to appear tidy when Xander and Oceanus docked. But did it even matter when every eye would be on the long-awaited lad?

By the time she'd returned, Watseka's English clothes were in a little mound on the beach, the apron holding the shells protectively, her lithe self underwater in the river.

Selah sank onto the warm sand by the discarded clothes.

She'd grown used to Watseka's ways just as the girl adjusted to theirs. Each day she performed her daily rituals, offering a smidgen of food to the fire, bathing in the river, searching for tuckahoe roots in the marshes. What she wanted with the mussels was a mystery that surely would be solved in time.

As playful and graceful as a river otter, Watseka splashed and rolled and amused as Selah waited for the shallop. "How I wish I could join you," she said to no one in particular.

Her thoughts drifted toward Shay, gone nearly a fortnight. What had her brother gained and discarded during his time with the Powhatans? She missed him terribly, his empty room across from hers now occupied by Watseka, his vacant chair at table an ongoing reminder of how far he had roamed.

Shrugging aside any melancholy, Selah removed her shoes, stockings, and garters and left them on the sand. As she waded into the cool river, Watseka came up with a mighty splash, dousing her.

"You little imp!" Selah splashed her back, their mingled laughter floating across the water.

By four o'clock, she was weary of dismissing vessels floating by. Then at last a speck of wood and sail took shape before her searching eyes.

"Come and make ready," Selah called over her shoulder as her feet left the water, the urgency in her voice getting Watseka's attention.

Fully clothed if slightly disheveled, they stored the mussel basket to carry home later. Hurrying back toward the wharf and warehouse, they joined several colonists coming or going, either laden with goods or waiting to load them. Selah's wish to meet Xander and party with no onlookers was quickly discarded.

"See who comes?" Selah gestured to the shallop as it approached. "A young friend for you, or so I hope."

Watseka, likely understanding little beyond a sense of expectation, trained her dark eyes on the river. Ustis came to stand beside them, lifting Watseka onto his shoulders in a surprising show of strength.

Selah's heart seemed to beat out of her chest as the vessel finally docked at wharf's end. Her gaze skimmed over the six oarsmen to Xander in the stern, a stranger with him. Seated near the mainsail was a woman. Oceanus's nurse? Near the bow was Oceanus himself. Tall. Spare. Looking little like the toddler she remembered. Not one speck of Xander did she see at first glance. All was Mattachanna.

"Oceanus," Selah said to Watseka, wondering if the Powhatans called him by a different name. "Master Renick's son."

This was the moment she'd dreamt of, yet in the glaring light of reality the dream faded. First to step from the shallop was the nurse, hardly the gray-haired matron she'd envisioned. Every bystander's head turned as the woman, holding Oceanus's hand, disembarked and walked gracefully toward them.

Chestnut hair beneath a lace-edged coif. Pale skin unmarked by the pox or the sun. Clad in a gray gown neither highborn nor low, the cloth none the worse after a long sea voyage. Her expression was unreadable, and she was seemingly oblivious to so many stares. Selah's gaze fell to the boy beside her, his eyes fastened on his buckled shoes.

Would he not look up? Allow her to see the cast of his features?

At that very instant he did. His dark eyes ricocheted from her to Watseka, who stared back at him unflinchingly. Truly,

Mattachanna was engraved in every line and furrow of his small face. 'Twas her black hair that hung about his shoulders, her nose and jaw etched into his beloved features.

Occanus weaved a bit as if his sea legs had yet to catch up with solid ground. With a word to him, his nurse stepped off the pier near several hogsheads to await the rest of their party. Xander made introductions as they all gathered in a circle.

"Oceanus fared well on the crossing, as you can see." Xander's hand rested on the boy's shoulder as he stood beside him. "Nurse Lineboro accompanies him and may make her home in Virginia. My factor from London, Bazel McCaskey, is an unexpected but no less welcome guest."

"We are Rose-n-Vale's nearest neighbors." Ustis shook hands with the man and made introductions of his own. "This is my daughter, Selah, and our charge from the Powhatan nation, Watseka."

"An Indian child? How extraordinary!" McCaskey's gaze passed from Watseka to Selah. "Mistress Hopewell, is it?"

She smiled in affirmation, warming to this swarthy Scot, whose open countenance bespoke a warmth and congeniality oft missing in fractious Virginia.

"We've long prayed for your safe arrival," Ustis said. "Now we shall pray the New World treats you kindly. Your transport is waiting. We shan't delay you any longer, though we hope to see you on the Sabbath."

"Not only the Sabbath," Xander announced, hat in hand. "Once our guests gain their land legs, Rose-n-Vale will host a gathering."

"Sounds delightful," Selah said, catching his eye.

Pulling free of Selah's hand, Watseka crossed to Oceanus. He took her gift of a mussel shell with a slightly bewildered smile, turning it over in his hands before Watseka all but skipped back to Selah's side.

"Thank you," Oceanus said when prompted by Nurse Lineboro.

Xander gestured toward the waiting wagon where baggage was being loaded. "Not so fine as your Old World conveyances, but the journey isn't far."

"'Tis good to feel land beneath my feet. I'd rather walk beside the wagon." The factor stared into the distance as if already envisioning Orinoco fields. Reaching into his pocket, he turned back toward Ustis. "In honor of Virginia's hospitality, here is a gift from the mother country."

"Honored, thank you." Ustis accepted the brass tobacco tamper with a nod of his grizzled head. "A welcome addition to my collection."

Looking slightly crestfallen, Watseka spoke a single word as they departed. "*Pa-naw*."

'Twas enough to turn Xander around with a smile. "Farewell, Watseka, till we meet again. *Pa-naw*."

Watching them depart, Selah felt cast adrift from the tall, hatted man with his back to her, a jumble of new people and events between them. Yet had she not just stood with him in the warehouse shadows several days before, weak-kneed over his wanting her to be his bride, the mistress of Rose-n-Vale? Such a forceful, passionate declaration now seemed no more substantial than river mist. Nor, understandably, had he paid her much attention today beyond the usual polite exchanges.

His last words returned to her like a cold tide, prickling her skin and leaving her shaken.

"I will not give you what you are yet unsure of, thus forming a bond between us that might well break."

24

Overnight, Rose-n-Vale assumed the feel of a tavern, its chambers no longer suffused with a dusty, sunlit stillness. Now the house seemed small and a bit moody as Xander bumped into guests at every turn, the factor's unexpected arrival adding another unsettling element to a burgeoning household.

"My, Nephew, our abode overfloweth." His aunt's brows rose in wonder when he appeared earlier than usual the next morn to gain a few minutes of undisturbed quiet.

As if sensing his mood, she served his cassina in silence before retreating to the summer kitchen to give instructions to Cook for the meals of the day. Alone in the dining room, he sat in his usual place, eyeing empty chairs that were no longer simply chairs but would soon hold complex strangers. Nurse Lineboro foremost.

Dismissing his uncle's glowing letter about her, he pondered Oceanus instead. Though bearing his mother's mark, the boy showed little of Mattachanna's fire and free-spiritedness thus far. Had being reared in the shadow of an overbearing relative and an especially attentive nurse made him a bit guarded and withdrawn? Seasick at the start of the voyage, he'd then fallen ill with a chest ailment. His rattling cough concerned Xander. Mayhap once Oceanus regained his health he'd come into his own.

"Good morning, sir."

Xander pulled his gaze from the diamond-paned windows to greet the nurse. She approached the table hesitantly, eyeing a porcelain pot on a tray, the fragrance of cassina potent.

"Your aunt tells me there are no servants' quarters in this house." Selecting a cup, she poured the brew, then cooled it in her saucer once she'd sat down. "Might I ask what it is I'm drinking?"

"A native beverage."

She took a sip, steam obscuring her pale features if not her distaste. "I'm finding little about Virginia that resembles Britain, including sitting at the master's table."

"You are welcome to Cook's table in the summer kitchen, if that is your preference."

"I offer no complaint, sir. 'Tis just that your choice of guardian was an exacting man." She sighed, confirming what he'd suspected about his aging uncle. "Children and servants remained out of sight below stairs unless sent for."

He took another drink. "Brave New World, indeed."

"'Twill take some getting used to, these little freedoms." Opening a fan, she began wafting it about. "I'm afraid Oceanus had a fitful night, given the insects and the heat."

"He'll adjust soon enough." Xander looked again toward the windows. The sun rode the horizon, shimmering over the river in its sultry climb. Newcomers fared badly in the summer, especially the sweltering days of August. "He's fast asleep, or was when I looked in on him before breakfast."

"His chest still ails him. I suppose you heard him coughing in the night."

The troubling sound added a new layer of angst. Suppose Oceanus was sickly from a lack of fresh air and exercise? "I've sent for a physic to examine him. Expect his arrival later today." Done with his cassina, Xander eyed the clock, ready to begin his morning ride. "Now seems a good time to tell you I want the boy breeched."

"Breeched?" Her cup rattled when she set it down. "Oceanus is but four."

"Four seems a great age, when boys here are oft put out of coats sooner. His hair needs cutting too."

Without his blackish mane, Oceanus would be far cooler, yet Nurse Lineboro was regarding Xander as if he'd called for a scalping instead. Heat seared his neck at her reaction, leaving him more at sea about parenting the lad.

He forged ahead. "Tomorrow morn we'll have a meeting about Oceanus's time in Scotland, his schooling and life there. My kinsman sent a number of reports the last two years, but you no doubt have your own thoughts as his nurse."

"Indeed I do, sir."

When his aunt came back into the room, the stilted silence had her casting him a questioning look. A heavy tread on the stairs led to McCaskey's appearance, his jovial nature a balm for what had gone before.

"Cassina, ye say? I must try it." Sitting, he took an appreciative sip once Widow Brodie filled his cup. "Bracing. Like a stiff Scots headwind. And . . . maize? Corn pone? Nae bannocks?"

"Nae oats, nae bannocks," Xander replied. "Corn abounds here but only a wee bit o' wheat."

"I'll nae complain." McCaskey smiled at Nurse Lineboro. "A pleasant night, I hope?"

"Not in this heat, I'm afraid. Nor did Oceanus fare any better."

"A pity." McCaskey's joviality dimmed. "I've heard some Virginians have their Africans cool them with feather fans at bed and table to combat both the insects and the weather."

The nurse turned inquiring eyes on Xander. "Might that be arranged?"

Arranged? He set his jaw to quell his aggravation. He usually shunned unsavory talk at table, though these new-comers were understandably curious. "You'll find no slave labor here. I can easily recount for you all the woes Virginia has inflicted on itself since the first ship carrying Africans docked."

"God forgive us." His aunt shut her eyes for the briefest second. "Let us forgo the details."

With a wince, McCaskey took another sip of cassina. "Still, more slavers are bound for Virginia than any other port. And most planters prefer slave labor over indentures."

"Yet Rose-n-Vale's tobacco exports outstrip every planter in the Tidewater without them." 'Twas Xander's best defense.

"To my great pleasure as yer factor." McCaskey's smile showed uneven white teeth. "Such a frightful clamor for Virginia's Orinoco. British buyers continue to prefer yer leaf o'er all else, and now 'tis on the continent, especially sought after by the Dutch, making the Spanish seethe with indignation."

"Is it true the Spaniards inflict the death penalty for any selling their tobacco seed?" Nurse Lineboro asked as she sampled a corncake at the urging of Xander's aunt.

"They threaten, aye."

"Our ship's captain reports Spanish vessels are oft sighted in Chesapeake Bay." Her anxious eyes sought Xander. "Virginia remains on alert for the Spanish threat, do they not?"

"Spanish spies, mostly. But the truth is the Spaniards have set their sights on the Caribbean and Florida and are no longer the hazard they once were."

"Britain has a solid foothold here." McCaskey heaped his plate with bacon and bread. "I might well decide to forsake Scotland for America in future, but I'll not settle amongst those prim Puritans with their ban on tobacco."

"The Puritans reside mostly in Massachusetts Bay, though a small remnant live just across the river," Xander told them.

"What is yer number now outside Virginia?" McCaskey asked.

"Eight other colonies exist, the most recent being Maryland."

"But none so old or so prosperous as Virginia."

"Oh aye, the colony is a braw age, truly, nearly as auld as I am," Xander replied, to McCaskey's amusement. "What would you like to see next?"

"Yer water-powered sawmill." McCaskey lifted his eyes from his dwindling plate. "With Virginia's timberlands, ye colonists have no lack while all of Britain cries for wood."

"And all Virginia cries for laborers." Nurse Lineboro frowned. "Yet your port officials detained Rose-n-Vale's indentures who put to shore with us just yesterday. The French physician raised a concern about their health."

A concern? More uproar. Laurent had threatened to send them all back to Scotland, citing suspicion of a contagion among them. The consulting Mount Malady physic dismissed the concern as groundless, yet Xander's bondsmen were still in quarantine, little better than gaol.

"Another reason to consider Africans." McCaskey brandished his fork like a weapon. "Think what more could be done here with them."

Xander leaned back in his chair, his patience thin. "Must we come to blows over the matter?"

"My apologies." McCaskey reddened. "I am your humble factor. If ye continue exporting the quality Orinoco you do, I'll say nae more about the matter."

Xander looked toward the clock. "We'll return for the dinner hour, after which I plan on showing Oceanus his pony."

Nurse Lineboro frowned. "He's not ridden before, sir."

"Time to begin then." To his aunt, he said, "I'll leave his riding clothes to you. I believe you've made something suitable for him."

She nodded. "Oceanus is so tall I might need to adjust them. But 'twill be done in time for your first ride."

Breakfast finally over, Xander went out, McCaskey trailing, leaving the women to whatever women did in their absence. His aunt would oversee Nurse Lineboro and Oceanus in the meantime.

⁂

"She's an industrious child," Candace remarked as she and Selah paused from their gardening to watch Watseka at work beneath the arbor. "Her aunts have trained her well. Sad, though, she is missing a mother."

While Candace returned to her weeding and watering, Selah took a stool and sat beside Watseka in the shade. Truly, she was a wonder of productivity. Beside her was the basket of ribbed mussels—*tshecomah*—they had gathered on the beach the day Xander came upriver with Oceanus. Ever since, Watseka had been toiling tirelessly at breaking the mussels into small pieces.

Though it had taken some help from Ustis and a great deal of misunderstanding due to their inability to speak Powhatan, Watseka finally obtained what she was after—a handmade drill.

"I believe she is wanting to make the mussel shell beads the women of her tribe are known for," Ustis finally said. "I recall some of her people bringing *rawrenock* to James Fort early on."

The word brought a telling sparkle to Watseka's eyes. "*Rawrenock,*" she repeated with joy over and over.

"She means to make a necklace," Selah mused, helping her whenever she could.

Though some might naysay the child's efforts, Selah sensed it was important to her, a tangible tie to her roots in a very white world.

"I am glad to see her happily occupied. She's an able helper in the garden and kitchen, but I sense those don't satisfy like her bead making."

Selah sought a great length of leather string in anticipation as Watseka rasped each shell on a sharp rock to a uniform size.

"'Twill take weeks," Ustis murmured in a sort of awe at the child's efforts. "In the meantime, I wonder what Shay is doing. I doubt he is as hard at work bead making."

Despite a bittersweet twinge, Selah had laughed. "Fishing and hunting in buckskins, likely."

They gathered beneath the arbor in the shade after supper,

even Izella, Ustis preparing his pipe with the tobacco tamper Bazel McCaskey had given him. The gift turned their conversation to Rose-n-Vale, though Selah's thoughts never strayed far from its master.

"An invitation should be forthcoming, something about a gathering or frolic, if I remember correctly," Candace said, arranging her handwork in her lap.

Silently, Selah counted the days since she'd last seen Xander. An appallingly long fortnight. "With the harvest near at hand, such seems a stretch."

"A little merrymaking sweetens the work, aye?" Ustis settled in for a smoke, leaning back against an arbor post. "No doubt the indentures deserve a frolic of their own to hearten them before the harvest. Much sickness at Rose-n-Vale of late, or so I've heard."

"I've some tonics to help with that." Candace plied her stitches without looking up. "I wonder how Oceanus and his nurse are faring? I've prayed the dreaded summer seasoning would pass them by."

"The nurse has a frailty about her that doesn't bode well in Virginia. She reminds me of those English roses brought over on the second supply. They failed to thrive here with the drought." Ustis studied Selah. "I do wonder if you and Nurse Lineboro will be friends."

Hope welled up at the words. Away from the bustle of James Towne and their ties there, did her father sense she was sometimes lonely?

"Perhaps we shall," Selah said, watching Watseka abandon her shells to play with Kentke near the stable. "I have high hopes Oceanus will befriend Watseka too."

"Why not go to Rose-n-Vale tomorrow if the day is fair?

Take the needed tonics." Candace perused her stitches in the fading light. "Widow Brodie always welcomes company."

Dare she? Their long summer days were a blur of endless tasks—harvesting, preserving, distilling—which left them tumbling into bed each night with no thought of the morrow save what needed doing next. "Can you spare me the time, Mother?"

"You've been toiling from dawn to dusk with nary a rest. Izella and I can do without you for one day." With an encouraging smile, Candace removed any doubt. "As your father said, a little merriment sweetens the work."

Needing little prodding, Selah fetched a towel and clean smock from the house, then made her way to a secluded spot along the river where the rushes and cinnamon ferns hid her from view. She disrobed, removed her cap, and unpinned her hair to wash it. The cool water embraced her, sand firming beneath her feet as she walked in up to her chin.

At her back came a familiar giggle. With a splash, Watseka joined her, her despised English clothes forsaken. Lately she had lost her cap, a shoe, and an apron. While Candace tried to impress on her to be more mindful of her appearance, Watseka seemed not to understand or care. Though she was young, her Powhatan roots went deep. Since the Hopewells saw the practicality of her people's garments, they could not scold or blame. Selah had half a mind to make herself a buckskin dress, though if James Towne's ruling body found out, they might well sentence her to a public dunking on the ducking stool at the next full tide.

"A-visiting we shall go," Selah sang as she scrubbed her hair and Watseka's, trying to make her aware of tomorrow's visit.

Watseka parroted back a few precise words. "Visit . . . boy
. . . Oceanus." She ducked beneath the water, stripping the
remaining soap from her hair.

At bedtime, when they knelt to pray, Watseka surprised
Selah by mentioning Oceanus again. Her quicksilver mind always seemed to leap ahead of them despite the many changes
and challenges. Was Shay adapting so readily? Was Oceanus?

Selah tucked Watseka into Shay's bed, crossed the landing,
and crawled into her own bed. An owl hooted. The night
wind bespoke a blessed coolness. Already she was craving
not autumn with its colorful leafing but the icy silences and
new-fallen snows of winter. Such spelled a rest from their
toil. And more time.

Her last thought was of Xander. Always Xander. Hearts
were such restless things, her own forever craving more. More
of his company, his heartfelt words.

His kiss.

25

In the forenoon, Selah and Watseka took the bridle path alongshore to Rose-n-Vale. Rarely had she seen Renick land in summer, tied as they'd been to James Towne. Bright blue mist flowers in the open meadows gave the lush grasses a bluish hue, the same serene shade as the river on a cloudless day. Even now she imagined the burned taint of Indian summer in the air and the subtle shift of the landscape.

When Ruby and Jett came bounding over the rise to meet them, Watseka shrieked and hid behind Selah. Truly, the dogs were a frightening pair to one so young.

"They mean no harm," Selah reassured her as the dogs began sniffing and wagging their long tails. "Gentle giants, truly. One day Kentke may be as big."

Shading her eyes from the sun, Selah started up the rolling rise to the house with the gamboling dogs so glad of their company. Midway there, she turned back to take in the river that Xander continued to call the Powhatan. Whatever it was, it flowed serenely past on this windless day, toward Shay.

At the back of the house were carpenters, not the bricklayers of before, erecting what looked to be a portico. A little thrill of discovery went through her. Brick by brick, column by column, Rose-n-Vale was coming into its own. Again, that feeling of sneaking up on the main house from behind and not approaching the proper if little used front door nagged her. Last time they'd found Xander at the well. Where was he now?

They passed the formal flower garden with its arbor, every inch abloom with aromatic roses. Watseka peeked in a window of the summer kitchen, the din of crockery within rivaling the hammer-wielding workmen. Selah's heartbeat seemed nearly as clamorous, her tongue tied the closer they came. All aflutter she was, and they'd not seen one whit of the master.

"Welcome, Selah!" Widow Brodie appeared at a side door. No matter that she had a houseful, Xander's aunt made them feel at home. "And this must be Watseka!" She winced as a hammer struck. "Come inside at once. We shall reward your long walk with refreshments from the Summer Isles."

Into the shadows of the main house they went, the river-front door soundly shut on the dogs.

"I've brought some of Mother's tonics for the indentures who are unwell," Selah told her, darting a gaze into Xander's empty study.

"Glad I am of that. You could have carried nothing better." She took the basket. "Mount Malady's physic came and went but dispensed little. These will certainly help relieve the misery."

"Let us know if more are needed. Mother is filling the new stillroom with every conceivable remedy, both from the woods and our James Towne garden. Thankfully, Father seems on the mend."

"God be praised." Widow Brodie led the way into the

small parlor and shut the door on the din. "I pray all this racket is done by the festivities."

Selah hardly minded the noise. The sound of progress, Father always said. "I'm quite smitten with your portico. I hope you smother the posts in roses."

"You must tell Alexander the very same. Men can be so . . . practical. That we have any flowers at all is Mattachanna's doing. Otherwise all would be planted in tobacco."

Selah smiled. "Orinoco-n-Vale sounds quite unpoetic."

A rare cackle. "Quite!"

As their hostess took Watseka by the hand and excused herself to bring refreshments, there came the light tap of footsteps on the stairs.

"Mistress Hopewell?" Into the parlor stepped Nurse Lineboro. "You caught me napping—or trying to." She rolled her eyes as the hammering resumed. "I heard talk of tonics. A sleep remedy is sorely needed."

"Oh? I shall do what I can. You're welcome to our still-room should you want to visit in future."

Nurse Lineboro took a leather chair that looked newly arrived from England. "Such a masculine domain. I confess to not feeling entirely comfortable here."

Selah made no reply. For a servant, albeit a nurse, the woman seemed a bit high-minded and free with her opinions. Yet the refinement in her voice and carriage bespoke a genteel upbringing. "Handsome is as handsome does," Mother would say. Mulling it, Selah took a seat. She'd make no hasty judgments as she had with Xander. Whatever her foibles and faults, Electa Lineboro was lovely to look at, her gown a deep blue, its slashed sleeves embellished with white satin ribbon, her hair covered by a lace-edged cap.

"'Tis too hot here to enjoy the outdoors. And this house, though large, has few amusements. I confess that I—" A horse's high whinny cut short Nurse Lineboro's words and sent her to the nearest window. "The men are back—with Oceanus intact, I hope. He's frightfully afraid of horses."

The tramp of booted feet and another door opening deep within the house led to Ruby and Jett's frenzied barking and Watseka's sudden appearance. Selah didn't miss Nurse Lineboro rolling her eyes again as she faced the open parlor door. Amused by the melee, Selah stayed near the window as dogs and children and men poured forth into the small space, followed by Widow Brodie with too few refreshments. Out the door she went again to remedy such before anyone said a word.

"Mistress Hopewell." Xander pulled off his hat. "Brave of you to join us."

"Indeed, Master Renick. Rose-n-Vale hums like a hive."

Oceanus stood beside Watseka, clearly pleased at having a pint-sized companion. From a pocket he withdrew the shell she'd given him as if to show her he'd not forgotten. "May I go out and play now, Father?"

Xander gave a nod. "Aye, you've earned it."

"Don't you want something to slake your thirst first?" Nurse Lineboro asked him.

"From the well?" He looked at Xander again.

"Or the kitchen. Cook has more than well water."

"I shall show Watseka my new pony on the way. Mayhap she can help me name him."

Xander winked at him. "Even a Powhatan name is most welcome."

Nurse Lineboro took him aside but not out of earshot. "Be ever mindful that ponies kick and bite."

Dismayed by her chastening, Selah took in Oceanus's riding clothes, the miniature doublet and dark breeches. On his feet were the buckled shoes he'd arrived in, not boots. Bound for the cobbler next, no doubt. His long hair, so bountifully black, was shorn. Overnight he'd achieved full-fledged boyhood. As he left, he gave a courtly little bow, further tugging at her heart.

"He's quite the wee gentleman, obedient and obliging," McCaskey said in earnest approval. "But a bit of an old soul for one so young."

"Lord willing, the latter will change." Xander stepped aside as his aunt reappeared bearing a tray.

She served sugared lemon water in pewter posset cups, fresh mint atop each. Selah sipped hers gratefully, wishing they were on the half-finished portico instead as they took the seats scattered about the parlor.

"How does Oceanus take to the saddle?" Selah ventured.

"He's asked to bring his pony inside the house." At her smile, Xander added, "He wants nothing to do with the wooden rocking horse in his bedchamber."

"Save it for a brother or sister then." McCaskey grinned, looking to his right. "D'ye not ride, Nurse Lineboro?"

"I've had little opportunity to do so, though I might need to master it if I stay on in Virginia."

"I thought I overheard you discussing your departure plans with Widow Brodie."

"I've not yet decided." She flushed, gaze traveling to Xander. "Master Renick hasn't said he no longer needs my services."

Xander held his tongue, and the room stilled uncomfortably.

"I confess Virginia has cast its spell on me." McCaskey drained his drink with relish. "In the words of one former colonist, I am overcome by the 'fair meadows and goodly tall trees, with such fresh waters running through the woods as I was almost ravished at the first sight thereof.'"

"Stay on, then," Xander said. "Cast your lot with the rest of us, a motley assortment of men and not nearly enough women. Here you'll no longer be concerned with importing tobacco as factor but growing and exporting your own."

McCaskey stroked his clean-shaven jaw. "I suppose I must grow a beard as you ruffians do."

"Nay, all that is required are callused hands, a willingness to work, and a sound knowledge of Orinoco."

As the men talked, Selah took out her fan and stirred the heated air. To her relief, Xander went to a window and opened it, hinges creaking. McCaskey began questioning him about indenture contracts, leaving Selah to manage conversation with the now sullen nurse.

"I can only imagine how hard coming to a strange land must be," Selah said quietly.

"I had little choice in the matter. My circumstances forced me into the role of nurse since my parents perished in the last plague that swept through Britain." Nurse Lineboro looked to her lap, smoothing a fold of her skirt. "I thought by coming to Virginia I might better my chances of marrying bereft of a dowry."

"Husbands are as prevalent as tobacco, truly."

An arched brow. "Yet you remain unwed. Have you no suitor?"

Did she? Though Selah's entire being coaxed her to look at Xander, she would give nothing away.

"Of late, I'm needed more at home. My brother is away, you see, and my father continues unwell."

"Your father . . . a kind, capable man, Widow Brodie says. A friend to the Indians. How is it having an Indian child beneath your very roof?"

"Watseka is delightful, and mastering English much faster than we are her tongue."

"Isn't it unusual for so small a girl to participate in such official dealings?"

"On the contrary, her presence signals the Powhatans' peaceful designs," Selah explained. "Women and children always do."

As the hall clock struck eleven, Oceanus returned with Watseka, smelling of the stable, straw sticking to their hair and garments. Nurse Lineboro looked aghast.

McCaskey, ever a foil to her straitlaced ways, burst into laughter. "Jumping in the haymow, no doubt."

Oceanus gave a sheepish smile. "Watseka is fond of my pony. She calls it *Aranck*. What means she?"

"*Aranck* means star, likely for the star on your pony's forehead," Xander said as the children came to stand before him. "Well named."

"We have rumbling stomachs, Father."

"And I thought it the sound of thunder." Chuckling, he plucked some chaff from his son's tousled hair. "Have Aunt Henrietta fetch you some cheese and butter bread from the milk house."

"Aye, sir."

"Remember your table manners," Nurse Lineboro put in. "Sing not, hum not, wriggle not."

Her terse words chilled Selah's heart as much as Xander

warmed it. Oceanus said nothing, though his face darkened and grew shuttered. Beside him, Watseka picked at her own frayed braid, darting a glance at Selah as if seeking her approval before they went out again. Sensing Xander's aunt might need a hand, Selah pocketed her fan and excused herself. Xander followed her as the factor and nurse resumed their parlor conversation. By the time she reached the riverfront door, he'd overtaken her.

"We're to have an evening's entertainment Saturday next." Resting against the door frame as if in no hurry, he looked down at her. "Will you come ?"

She nearly sighed. Could he sense her utter delight at being asked so personally? "A host of warring Powhatans couldn't keep me away."

"They're not among the invited guests." His wry smile was her complete undoing. "You are the very first."

She turned breathless, her pent-up feelings magnified by his nearness. "Rose-n-Vale has never had a frolic, to my remembrance."

"'Tis time, mayhap." His gaze sharpened in intensity. "Time for a great many things."

Her heart beat out a question she could not ask. *Many things?*

"Why did you come today, Selah? Was it simply to bring Watseka?"

"Nay. I also brought stillroom remedies for your ailing indentures."

"But none for me."

"You?" Her voice became a troubled whisper. "What is your malady?"

"Insomnia. An acute pain here . . ." He took her hand

and pressed it to his chest, where she felt the bold beat of his heart. "Something akin to mental torment."

She laid her other hand along his bewhiskered jaw, more touched than amused by his teasing. "I suffer the very same. But even if I had a cure, I hope you would not take it. I would not."

"Nay." His fingers tightened around hers.

"Verily, there's no relief for so fatal a malady but this . . ." Standing on tiptoe, she brushed his lips with her own, so fleeting it was less kiss and more maddening tickle.

She sensed his surprise—and profound pleasure. Out of the corner of her eye she saw a sudden movement in the parlor. Stepping back, she turned on her heel and fled through the back door toward the dependencies, as abuzz and addle-pated as the bees hovering near straw skeps in the kitchen garden. All around her pulsed the rhythm of plantation life, so different from Hopewell Hundred. Rose-n-Vale resembled a small village.

Was that Xander's intent? To become so self-sufficient that he had little need of imported British goods?

Widow Brodie ushered the children out of the milk house, their mouths and hands stuffed with bread and cheese. "Dear Selah, I hope you will bring Watseka to Rose-n-Vale as often as you like. Things can be dreadfully dull for a lad with a busy father, an overbearing nurse, and an ancient great-aunt."

"And I was just thinking how impossible it would be for Oceanus to be bored here. I doubt he'll have hours enough."

"Speaking of hours enough, did Alexander mention the coming frolic?"

"He did. Are you overburdened with preparations?" Though

strained at the seams at home, Selah could not deny her help. "Can I relieve you in some way?"

"I simply covet your advice. I'm sorry to report this heat has flattened our supply of ale for the coming guests."

"Mother would tell you to boil it with honey, which seems to revive it."

"Oh?" They began a slow walk toward the summer kitchen. "Perhaps you can assist with the menu. Fish, of course, with some sort of sauce? And mutton? Or perhaps a fricassee? I have few banqueting dishes in mind."

"Perhaps baked marrow pudding? Or string beans with almonds?" Selah paused. What dishes did Xander favor? "Virginia's tastes run to New World succotash and Indian pudding. Cherry tart is also a favorite, though I noticed some early apples in your orchard. Perhaps apple tansy. Father may even have marzipan at the warehouse."

"Splendid, all. Two heads are better than one." Widow Brodie seemed relieved. "As I said, feel free to bring Watseka to play any time you please."

26

The stillroom released a vinegary scent in the rising August wind. All morning they'd been at work blending spices and preparing crocks for preserving. Selah felt quite pickled herself, her apron splotched, her hands reeking of brine. She gave Izella a weary smile as she brought in the last basket of beans.

"What shall you put on for Rose-n-Vale's frolic?" Candace wore the same frown as when she'd perused Selah's simple wardrobe that morning.

"I've no idea, but I did see some pretty printed fabric on the last supply ship. Though I'll be surprised if Father hasn't sold it, with all the business of late."

"Why don't you take Watseka and see if there's enough cloth to be made into gowns for the both of you?" Eyeing the crocks of finished vegetables, Candace returned to the garden. "We can put off more preserving to sew."

"Go too?" Watseka looked at them from the open doorway, always ready for the warehouse and Ustis's store of sweetmeats.

"Of course!" Selah removed her soiled apron. "But let us hurry. We've pretty frocks to make!"

Spurred by anticipation, they set off, making a footrace of it. Watseka won by a good stretch, the pup at their heels. Winded and thirsty, they schooled themselves to a walk as the wharf and warehouse came into view. Scooping Kentke up in her arms, Watseka followed Selah through the back door. Ustis was at the front, out of sight, talking to customers.

Standing in the middle of all the merchandise, hands on hips, Selah got her bearings. A darkened corner boasted cloth of all kinds, ell after ell of osnaburg common among indentures alongside a host of blues favored by servants. Her hands sorted, uncovered, restacked. Was the coveted fabric gone? When first uncrated midsummer, it had stolen her breath. Weeks at sea had not diminished its luster.

Lost in her feverish pursuit, she almost started when a voice called from the adjoining doorway, "Searching for something, Daughter?"

"Indeed I am, Father. That lilac chintz from the East India Company. But you may have sold it."

"Not after I saw you looking at it longingly, nay." With a knowing smile, he went to a small trunk and unlocked it. "Nothing on earth could induce me to part with it, so it has remained hidden. 'Tis yours, Selah."

The fabric was even more beautiful than she remembered. And soft, so soft. Eyes damp, she embraced both the chintz and him. "I hope to make a pretty frock for Watseka and myself to go to Rose-n-Vale."

"Ah, the frolic. Of course. But I doubt there's cloth enough for two gowns. Perhaps this printed cotton would be suitable for Watseka's new dress?" He pulled a lovely lemon-hued fabric from another hiding place. "What do you think, child? Shall you dress up like the sun? Twirl about like a yellow butterfly?"

"*Keshowse*. Sun." Setting down Kentke, Watseka fingered the soft fabric and smiled her approval.

Selah bit her lip. Squeezed for time, could she fashion two frocks? She was an able seamstress but no mantua-maker or milliner. None existed, not even in James Towne. Heaven forbid she arrive looking like a seed sack. "We must run all the way home and start sewing."

"Not until you have a pocket of sugared almonds, surely." Ustis went to a stone jar where he kept such, Watseka by his side.

Pockets full, Selah and Watseka were off again, half running in the unclouded joy of expectation. Selah had not had a new gown in many months and none so fine as this fabric.

Once home, she set to work, assembling scissors and sewing notions, nearly scowling at the tick of the clock.

"I shall sew Watseka's," Candace told her, examining the cloth with a practiced eye. "Such a lovely lilac ground, and all those tiny trailing vines and leaves in ivory. Dreamlike, truly, while Watseka's is brilliant like the sunbeam she is."

"Father said the same."

"Where is she?"

A sudden rasping from outside gave the answer. Busy with her shells beneath the arbor.

Candace went to the open doorway to better see her. "What on earth might she intend for them?"

Selah smiled and began rummaging for a brass thimble and linen thread. "Perhaps she means to wear a bit of jewelry with her new dress."

The portico was finished. All but sawdust and a few mis-placed nails remained in the trampled grass at its edges. His aunt swept her broom across the expanse of new boards with relish, heels making a little tap at every turn. Xander walked the length and breadth of the long porch, examining the finished work with a critical eye.

"I've a mind to add the same to the front of the house in time." He'd already talked to the master carpenter. "A great many lessons were learned with this one. But we shall save any future construction for cooler weather."

"The craftsmen did admirably. I'm glad you rewarded them handsomely too." She came to stand nearer him. "How are the ailing men in quarters?"

"Mistress Hopewell's tonics seem to be of help."

"That and prayer." She rested her hands atop the broom. "Thankfully the governor saw fit to release your newest ar-rivals from quarantine since none showed signs of contagion after all."

"Aye." Xander wouldn't say what Laurent's misdiagnos-ing and dallying had cost him. "Hopefully all the workers will be on their feet for the coming frolic. Have you enough hands in the kitchen ahead of Saturday?"

"I believe so. Cook has nearly trained the new kitchen girl, and some of the indentures' wives will help. I also asked Selah her ideas for banqueting dishes." Her casual air did nothing to hide her intent. "She is quite a hand with such things."

"Oh aye, no doubt."

"Not to mention the copy of *The Country Housewife's Garden* you gave me last Christmastide."

He'd completely forgotten.

"And I do hope you'll trim that beard of yours," she scolded lightly. "We can't have you mistaken for one of your indentures."

He ran a hand across his scratchy jaw. "Careful, you might turn me foppish."

"You? Never! I do take pride in having the handsomest nephew in all Virginia. You can't begrudge me for wanting you to look your best. Now I must bid you good night. We've much left to do. Saturday is but day after tomorrow."

With that, she disappeared into the house with her broom, leaving him alone on the portico save Ruby and Jett, who were sniffing at the addition as if debating its merits. Was he half mad to consider a frolic? Though he considered himself equal to most tasks, becoming reacquainted with Oceanus, navigating his nurse, and familiarizing McCaskey with the workings of Rose-n-Vale exceeded the day's hours.

He returned to the hall, carried out a chair, and sat down. All he lacked was a pipe, but in truth, he was too spent to cross to the summer kitchen for a spark with which to light it. Besides, thoughts of his beloved didn't need clouding with smoke. In his mind's eye Selah was still sitting in his parlor, looking all the world like she owned it, trying her best to make conversation with a fractious nurse and a flirtatious factor amid two rambunctious children. Then hazarding a surprising half kiss before she flew away like a bird eluding his net.

If he'd only gathered his wits and kissed her back.

Twilight was filling in all that was left of daylight, the sun a spectacular splotch of gold as it rode the horizon to the mountainous west. From this portico he could both greet the day and oversee its ending. How much sweeter if such glories could be shared.

Selah, what must I do to finally win your heart?

His gaze was drawn upward at the rapid wingbeat of a dove. Waiting for its mate, likely, its mournful cooing adding to his own hollowness in Selah's absence. Before the week was out, a gathering of twigs would be beneath the eave. While the male provided the materials, 'twas the female who built.

In the same vein, he offered Selah himself and Rose-n-Vale, but 'twas she who would make a house into a home. A husband out of a widower. A motherless boy more whole.

Lord willing.

27

Selah held up the half-finished gown to the dimming light. Her sewing skills had been stretched to the seams in crafting such. Still, she pressed on, inspired by never having owned such a garment before. Now, two nights before the frolic, she lacked finishing the skirt seams and the ribbon pleating. Could she manage it? 'Twas a simple design turned fancy by a sumptuous fabric. Fit for a ball. A wedding.

Oh, Xander, will you dance with me?

Every stitch seemed woven with all that remained unspoken. Possibilities. Promises. Tongue between her teeth in concentration, she plied her needle with a dizzying array of stitches. Herringbone. French knot. Eyelet. Cross. Stem.

"What a glorious gown!" Candace eyed the ivory ribbon, which set off the sleeves and bodice. "Might you catch a certain gentleman's notice?"

"I aspire to no such thing," Selah murmured, then bit her tongue at the half-truth.

Candace took a seat, her fingers caressing the finished sleeve. "Needs be we discuss the matter further."

"What means you, dear Mother?" Selah did not look up from her zealous stitching.

"I can only hope this frenzied labor is fueled by your heart-felt affections."

"You believe I am smitten with Xander Renick."

"I would be delighted if so, as would your father."

Selah finished another whipstitch. "Xander has not spoken to Father about such."

"Oh, but he has. First Xander spoke to me since your father was unwell—even before he approached you. And your father has since told him he has our wholehearted blessing."

Selah's needle slipped. She met her mother's eyes. "I don't know what to say."

"How about 'aye.'" Her gray gaze lit with exasperation. "Yet I sense you are unsure."

With effort, Selah stilled her hands. "I am not unsure of my feelings but his."

"His?" Candace questioned gently. "When he has made plain his intentions?"

"Intentions are not affections."

"Your father and I began our marriage with mere intention and little affection. We are quite well suited and content. There is no reason to think you and Xander would be otherwise."

"I simply want to be chosen for the right reasons, not simply to warm a man's bed nor mother a child nor manage a growing plantation."

"Many women marry for far less."

Such truth. Selah's conscience pricked her, sharp as a pin. "You think I have overly romantic notions."

"That is between you and Xander."

Sitting back, easing the ache in her neck and shoulders, Selah focused on Watseka's finished dress hanging from a wall peg. "I still wonder about Mattachanna at times."

"How so?"

"Their marriage."

"You saw her very little after her captivity and even less after they wed, other than the times she came to the store."

"And when I did, I sensed a sadness about her. Even after Oceanus was born, she seemed a bit melancholy. I'm ashamed to say I laid the blame at Xander's door. His overwork. His ambition."

Candace shook her head. "Mattachanna parted with a great many beloved things before she became mistress of Rose-n-Vale, which was likely the root of any mournfulness. Under the reverend's care, she became so homesick for her people that her sisters were sent for, even before she married Xander."

"I shall never forgive Helion Laurent and Captain Kersey and those officials who did her harm." Ire made her eyes burn. She stared down at the chintz that was no more than a purple puddle. "Such men deserve naught but Hades as punishment."

"God shall be their judge." Candace reached for Selah's needle and thread. "Let me finish this for you. Step outside and walk about. Breathe the fresh air. I believe you are not just overtaxing your eyes and fingers but your mind."

Glad to relinquish the task, Selah did as she bid and sought a seat in the arbor's shade facing west. Though she couldn't see Rose-n-Vale through the forest and fields separating them, she craved a glimpse.

Forgive me, Xander. Perhaps I don't deserve you, thinking such things.

Forgive me, Lord. Not even You threw a stone, though You had every right.

Closing her eyes, she rested them and dwelt on a verse she'd taken to heart but seldom put into practice.

Finally, brethren, whatsoever things are true . . .

Xander cared for her. And she loved him.

Whatsoever things are honest . . .

Xander had declared his intent as an honorable man would.

Whatsoever things are just . . .

Xander honored his indentures and the terms of their contracts. He opposed slaveholding. His fair dealings with the tribes were second to none.

Whatsoever things are pure . . .

Xander had asked her to join him in holy matrimony as his bride.

Whatsoever things are lovely . . .

Rose-n-Vale was surely one of the loveliest spots on earth.

Whatsoever things are of good report . . .

Xander was known far and wide as an honest, God-fearing, albeit driven man.

If there be any virtue, and if there be any praise, think on these things.

The evening was young, unspooling before Xander with endless possibilities. Their fevered preparations had dwindled to the tuning of a fiddle and the rearranging of benches on the portico. All bespoke guests to come. He doubted he'd sit down once the festivities were under way. Servants ran from house to summer kitchen, laying out a table the likes of which Rose-n-Vale had never seen. Pitch-pine torches dipped in pennyroyal blazed here and there, casting light and scattering insects. His aunt had prayed for no rain but clouds, a curious order that got her exactly that, as if Providence was the first guest to arrive and orchestrated the weather as requested.

"Alexander, can you imagine what would ensue if the heavens opened and there came a thunderstorm? The house would be stuffed to the gills!" She sighed as she tied on a new apron. "I cannot help but recall Governor Harvey's last entertainment when such a calamity occurred. Someone even made off with the silver and no one was the wiser!"

Stepping off the portico, Xander glanced at the attic dormer. No sign of Nurse Lineboro, nor McCaskey in his quarters. The expanding lane to the dependencies beyond the summer kitchen was yet another reminder more housing needed to be built. Two housemaids and another kitchen maid were coming on the next supply ship at his aunt's request.

"Sir?"

He turned around to see his farm manager approaching. "Welcome, Sterrett."

"Indeed, sir. Most of the workers will be joining us. There are but three still ailing and abed. The rest consider it a special privilege to be invited up to the house."

"There are no airs or social distinctions here," Xander replied. "Unlike Britain or even James Towne."

"A freedom we're slowly taking to heart." Sterrett turned toward the river, unmistakable awe in his gaze.

Tonight the Powhatan was misted, a deep pearl gray. The mourning doves were cooing on high, undisturbed by the melee around them. Xander spied Oceanus coming out of the summer kitchen, nearly spilling the punch bowl he was carrying. How keen he'd been to help, yet from the look of things, that might not be happening. Biting his tongue, Xander swung his attention in another direction.

Walking uphill from the bridle path alongshore was a sight that set his heart to beating hard as a smitten boy's. At the front, skipping merrily along, was Watseka, bright as a candle flame in her yellow dress. Behind her at a more sedate pace were Selah's mother and father. Ustis was leaning on a cane, always seeming a step shy of recovery.

And his beloved?

Selah had her head bent as if navigating the uneven ground in new slippers. Her skirts swirled becomingly as if she were dancing with the wind. And her gown . . . purple as a Scottish thistle. Did she know it was his favorite color?

Pleasure gave way to guarded hope. If they could somehow secret themselves away for even a few minutes tonight . . .

McCaskey moved in front of him, blocking his view. "Renick, a fine gathering you're hosting." Already at the ale, he held up his tankard in a sort of toast. "Your first, so your aunt said."

And mayhap my last.

Other guests were appearing, his nearest neighbors on foot or horseback, others by water, the distant wharf now teeming. Virginians enjoyed these gatherings. Hospitality wasn't something he paid much attention to, though his aunt often set an extra place at table for any who might come by, even if it never happened.

"Are we among the first to arrive? Rose-n-Vale has never looked so festive." This from Ustis, speaking in winded bursts. "Selah told us about your new portico. A worthy addition."

"I've been wishing I'd seen to it earlier. There are chairs if you want to take in the view." Xander gestured toward them as Candace smiled her appreciation.

Selah appeared from behind her father. Smiling coyly at him. Watseka was standing nearer him, and he gave a little bow, complimenting her new dress. She chattered to him in her tongue, asking about Oceanus.

"Last I saw, he was wrestling the punch bowl."

With a little laugh, she dashed toward the house, and he noticed her pockets were bulging. What was she up to?

"Where are your faithful hounds?" Selah asked as he fell into step beside her.

"Tied behind the smokehouse and nursing a bone, well away from the guests. My aunt rightly insisted."

"Of course. We shut Watseka's pup inside the stable lest he follow us all the way here." She smiled at him again. In fact, she hadn't stopped smiling. "You're looking in fine form since I last saw you. I feared with all the illness of late and your own special malady—"

"Which worsens by the hour." He came to a stop by the rose arbor. "When was it I last saw you? I've lost track of the time."

She looked up at him, pushing back that maddening tendril of hair he'd once righted. "Five days, eleven hours, and fifty-six minutes."

His own smile could be no wider. "You flatter a man."

"Only you. And 'tis not flattery, truly." The light of a pine torch illuminated the flush of her features. "The time seems long without you."

"Agreed." He studied her, wanting to imprint every detail to last him once she'd gone. "Your gown . . . Purple looks well on you."

"Thank you." She raised a hand to the lace falling band covering her shoulders, appearing suddenly shy. "Don't look too closely or you might see a great many hasty stitches."

"You could say the same about my weskit. My aunt's eyesight isn't what it once was."

"Yet handsome nonetheless—"

"Master Renick, what a fine occasion you're hosting!" The warm voice turned them both around. "I have yet to welcome Mistress Hopewell upriver."

The wealthy widow from Martin's Hundred? Selah greeted her warmly. "Good to see you again, Mistress Hastings. I hope all your family is well."

"Aside from the usual summer maladies, quite well, thank you." Her smile didn't reach her eyes. "I'm surprised to find you two quite clannish by the garden."

"Clannish, nay," Xander returned easily. "Rather reacquainting ourselves after a long absence."

"Ah, I see," she replied, stepping nearer him and leaning in to smell a blooming rose. "Such a lovely garden."

Selah turned back to him, brushing his coat sleeve with the tip of her fan. "Perhaps we shall meet up again before the night is over."

"Count on it," he replied, schooling both his longing and his disappointment as she made her way toward the portico.

28

So, they were being clannish? Guilty as charged. The obviously smitten widow had simply called out the obvious. Selah felt a startling realization that Xander now possessed the ability to shrink her world to one. No one else existed or much mattered, even at a public frolic. Engrossed in his company, she all but forgot her manners. Little wonder others took notice or made mention of the breach.

Her restless gaze roamed through colorfully clad ladies and gentlemen as fireflies came out in flickering force. She spoke with Nurse Lineboro and others she knew, aware of Xander being the gracious host as the party swelled in size. With so many guests she'd likely not get another word with him, and some of the gaiety went out of her.

"Ah, the unforgettable Mistress Hopewell." McCaskey sidled up to her, offering a cup of punch. She thanked him, his slurred speech raising her alarm, though he seemed steady enough on his feet. "I saw you coming up the hill on foot. Surely a lady of your station deserves better."

"I'm no grand dame, I assure you. Nor have I ever seen a wheeled carriage in these parts." She sipped her punch.

"Most ride horseback or rely on river travel. Virginia's roads are frightful, I'm afraid."

"A shame you can't travel in style. I suppose you ride?"

"I do, though I'd rather walk."

"Why don't we take a turn through the garden, then? The lawn is getting overrun."

Her refusal was needless as the call to supper came. Mc-Caskey took his place in the supper line. Slowly guests made their way through Rose-n-Vale's open doors to the new wing. Selah could hear children's buoyant laughter, though she'd lost track of Watseka and Oceanus in the melee. She tarried till the portico emptied, her parents just ahead of her. Ustis whispered something in Candace's ear. Her low laugh assured Selah all was well.

Oh, Shay, how do you fare?

Thoughts of her brother overtook her at curious times. Might those promptings signal her brother's need? She breathed a silent, open-eyed prayer for protection. Wisdom. Peace.

"If you lack a supper partner . . ."

Xander was behind her, bringing up the rear. No wealthy widow was near. Again, that delicious sense of being singled out took hold. Any anxious thoughts of Shay scattered.

"I've never had a supper partner," she confessed. "Shall we sit at table?"

"There's no formal board but a great many chairs." He smiled at her, his words for her ears only. "And a private bench at the back of the garden."

She warmed to the invitation. The dining room and parlor were thick with guests, supper provisions ample, even the banqueting dishes she'd suggested to Widow Brodie. Selah placed some of the fare on her plate, Xander just behind.

In the hall she spied Governor Harvey and a few officials conversing at the foot of the stairs, punch in hand, Laurent among them. How had she overlooked his arrival? Her appetite fled. Eyes down, she passed by them. Invited or not, these men made their presence known at various functions, if only to flaunt their authority. Aware of Laurent's eyes on her, she took a side door. Nearby sat Watseka and Oceanus on the steps, sharing a plate.

In her quest to avoid the physic she'd likely lost Xander too. No longer was he shadowing her. Passing beneath the rose arbor, she took a shell-strewn path to the bench, pulse picking up when she heard a footfall behind her. Laurent?

Lord, nay.

Teasing laced his tone. "Don't think you can elude me."

"'Tis not you I wish to elude." Relieved, she sat, finding Xander's hands empty. "What, no supper?"

"Somehow a gathering like this steals my appetite."

Did he mean Harvey and his minions?

He took a seat beside her. "I'll have my fill when all go home."

"But there might be nothing left." She took a piece of salted ham between her fingers and held it out. He leaned in obligingly, his arm about her back as she fed it to him.

A fiddle ground out a tune in the background, the hubbub of voices nearer the house rising steadily. The guests were enjoying themselves, as was their absent host. She took a bite herself, then gave him the next, content to stay hidden at the back of the garden for as long as time allowed them.

"I never thought to feed the master of Rose-n-Vale," she began as he leaned in again.

A burst of giggling from the hedgerow turned her rosy.

With a rustle of bushes, Oceanus stepped out, Watseka following. Beneath Xander's inquiring gaze, they stood chagrined, and then Watseka approached, something in her outstretched hands.

The shell beads? In the dark they glistened and gave a faint tinkling sound. All the time and care Watseka had spent crafting the beads—was it for them?

Xander took the gift as Oceanus looked on, perhaps as mystified as Selah herself. Lifting one strand of beads, Xander put them over Selah's head, where they cascaded down her bodice.

"A gift," he told her. The other strand he wore. Against his dark blue doublet, they made a striking contrast.

Without a word, the children slipped back into the hedgerow, leaving them alone again. "You're smiling." She set down her plate and fingered the new necklace. "You welcome the gift of her hands and heart."

He took her fingers in his. "I welcome the meaning behind it especially."

"Oh? All I see are beautiful beads that took a little girl a very long time to fashion into something wearable. That itself is remarkable. Is there more?"

He gave a nod. "Watseka is wiser than her years." He took the shells from around his neck and slowly wrapped them around their joined hands. "In a Powhatan wedding ceremony, beads encircle the bride and groom. Such symbolizes unity. Hearts as one."

"Hearts as one . . ." Joy sang through her at his poetic phrasing. "Beautiful . . . romantic."

With a mesmerizing slowness, he unwound the beads binding them and placed them again about his neck, then he stood and brought her to her feet. They were so close she could feel the beads bedecking them through their garments. Was that his heart she also felt? Or her own, pulsing like a hare released from a snare?

He bent his head, kissing her as she'd never dreamt of being kissed. 'Twas a declaration. A whirlwind of sensations and emotions. Gone was the uncertainty, the hesitation.

"Selah . . . I am taking this as your *aye*."

"Aye," she echoed. "Aye to everything."

She kissed him back, so many kisses she soon lost count of them. Lost in the moment. In the sweet exclusivity of his embrace.

When they drew slightly apart, she felt bereft. Foreheads touching, they welcomed the new world that had just opened to them, no longer two separate souls but nearly one.

"Lest my aunt send out a search party for me"—the amused lament in his tone brought her to her senses—"I'd best return to my guests."

His lips met hers a final time before he left her. She followed him with her gaze, waiting to make a discreet entrance herself. Dancers swirled past the tall windows of the new wing as she made her way toward the portico and her parents, nearly colliding with Nurse Lineboro.

"Oceanus needs to be abed. The hour is growing late." Her pointed gaze took in Watseka flitting about with the other children. "I'm afraid his companion grows wilder by the hour."

Downcast, Oceanus looked at Selah, his high spirits gone. Knowing she had little say in the matter, Selah simply called for Watseka and took her hand.

"What are those curious beads around your neck?" Nurse Lineboro asked.

"The work of Watseka, fashioned from shells." Smiling down at her, Selah relived the tender moment all over again.

"A far cry from the Virginia pearls one hears about." Nurse Lineboro turned away, leaving Selah hoping Watseka had no grasp of the sour words.

Seeking a diversion, Selah pointed toward the house. "Shall we try some comfits I spy coming from the kitchen?"

Intercepting the large tray, they sampled the sweets, Watseka wide-eyed despite the late hour. Above their heads the moon foretold eleven o'clock. A few guests were departing, but the merriment carried on for most. Near the summer kitchen came the bellowing voice of McCaskey, telling a shipboard tale that made Selah want to cover Watseka's ears. With the sheriff on hand, the factor might well be arrested for public drunkenness.

Selah led her further from the noise. "Let us stay outdoors. Soon we shall take our leave."

As pine torches were replaced, the light of one illuminated Helion Laurent stepping off the portico. Would the darkness hide her? Nay. He approached, his swagger loosened by spirits. Rum, from the potent smell of it.

"Ah, Mistress Hopewell. So soon away?"

She drew Watseka nearer. "The hour grows late."

"A pity soon consoled. Now that I'm residing upriver, I shall see you again soon enough."

Dismay lodged like a stone inside her. Few welcomed the news that Laurent was spending more time upriver away from the hornet's nest that was James Towne. "Will you turn farmer as well as physic?"

"I have an eye toward my future." Reaching out, he lifted the beads from her bodice in a startling display of familiarity. "I daresay your jewelry is most peculiar. Surely there is a story behind it."

Freeing the strand from his bold fingers, she took a step back. "A gift."

A reassuring hand grazed the small of her back. Xander came forward, torchlight illuminating his wary gaze like a lightning flash. Laurent seemed to recoil. In the ensuing silence roiled hostility, loathing, a palpable ill will. She felt nearly blackened by it.

"Your father has had enough merriment." Without a word to the physic, Xander took her elbow and steered her toward the stables.

In his wake was her mother. "Xander has lent us a pony cart to ride home in."

"Aye, let us depart." Ustis brought up the rear, his beloved face strained.

Near the stables a groom was readying their ride. Selah and Watseka would walk behind with a pine knot. Passing Selah the light, Xander accompanied them to the bridle path near shore and saw them safely off.

"Soon, Selah." Xander's last, heartfelt words to her carried her home.

29

By daylight the shell necklace was even prettier than when she'd been given it, a tangible reminder of her and Xander's newfound tie. The frolic's afterglow still lingered, adding a deep-seated joy to the next few days' tasks. Less busy in the kitchen, Selah had more time to help her father. The bridle path between Hopewell Hundred and the warehouse was well traveled now as autumn encroached. Watseka oft accompanied her, Kentke nipping at their heels.

This morn, with her father downriver at James Towne, Selah traipsed after her mother into the near woods, empty baskets on both arms, intent on wildcrafting.

Candace eyed the shell necklace her daughter wore night and day, a knowing spark in her eye. "Our little Watseka is a clever matchmaker, so it seems, and not only a bead maker."

"Older and wiser than her years, aye."

"Well, I am a firm believer in beginning your lives as one without further ado. You're clearly Xander's choice. Why wait?" Candace began tearing boneset leaves from a bush in such haste it underscored her words. "If I've learned one lesson in Virginia, 'tis brevity. Many do not have the luxury of the morrow."

"Given the season, I cannot simply load a cart with my belongings and hie to Rose-n-Vale." Selah wandered farther into the woods toward a persimmon tree heavy with fruit. "Not till after the harvest."

"All in good time, I suppose." Candace turned grave. "It does not help that Helion Laurent has designs to pay more visits to the tobacco wives in the outlying shires. He approached your father at the warehouse just yesterday. It seems the governor is insistent—"

"Nay." Selah straightened, ready to defy Harvey himself. "I shan't accompany Laurent again at any time."

"Your father told him the same. Vexed, the physic was." Candace paused in her gathering. "If you were to marry, you would be safeguarded from Laurent's plans and purposes."

"His schemes, you mean." Selah bit into a ripe persimmon, the juice dripping onto her bodice. "I trust him not."

"Because of his trickery regarding Mattachanna? Or is there more?"

Much more, I sense, though I know none of it.

Selah tossed the pit away. "Xander has warned me to give him wide berth."

Candace cast her an aggrieved look as they moved through the brush in search of more boneset. "Then you'd best heed your betrothed's—for I shall call him nothing less—warning."

"I shall, never fear." But she did fear, goose bumps rising on her arms at Laurent's latest ploy.

They fell silent, lost in their search, and their baskets soon overflowed with papaws and medicinal plants to stand them in good stead for the coming winter. Their wandering had taken them far, almost to the edges of Laurent land.

Though there'd been no cause for alarm today, no presentiment of trouble, Selah cast her skittish gaze wide, unable to shake the feeling of being watched. A rising wind added to her angst, leaves flying and twigs snapping and causing movement in every corner.

At last Candace called over her shoulder, "Come, let us hasten back and see how Izella and Watseka are faring with their applesauce making."

Xander helped Oceanus onto the mounting block, a telling skittishness in the lad's movements. His pony waited patiently, a handsome gray just twelve hands high, rescued from a wrecked Spanish galleon a year past. From a distance Nurse Lineboro watched, a speck of linen on the portico.

"Nurse says I might snap my neck." Oceanus looked from the portico to Xander, his eyes wide beneath his sweep of dark hair. "What means she?"

It means Nurse Lineboro will soon be sent away.

"Only that you take care to learn all you can about horses so accidents don't happen," Xander replied. Selah aside, he desired nothing more at that moment than to wipe away the distress marring Oceanus's face.

"Nurse Lineboro is a fretter."

Xander smiled. "Some women fret, aye. Some don't."

"Great-Aunt Henrietta is a fretter too."

"Aye, that she is."

The pony nickered and tossed its starred head, returning them to the matter at hand.

"Remember, you always begin with your left foot." He touched the boy's new left boot. "Meanwhile, your left hand is on the horn of the saddle while your right hand belongs on the cantle."

Oceanus did as he bade, not sliding off to one side and tumbling to the ground like he had yesterday.

"'Tis all about balance," Xander told him, using a loose lead rein to coax the pony into a walk and then a gentle trot.

Shoulders squared in a show of confidence, Oceanus bounced along atop the pony as Xander quickened the pace. "Why hasn't Watseka come again to play?"

"She is busy at the Hopewells', I suppose. Would you like to visit them?"

"Aye. But Nurse says I need another playmate."

"How about we see if we can find Watseka tomorrow? After my morning ride about the estate?"

The sheer delight on his son's boyish face hardened Xander's resolve. He'd delayed the tobacco harvest by a sennight due to the crop needing more time, a prime opportunity to give Oceanus time too. He didn't need reminding how important it was for the boy to be with other children. Besides, Xander needed to see Selah. The want of her was never ending.

"What about the pony course, Father?" Oceanus looked toward the pasture behind the stable. "Going around the circles and blocks and poles and such?"

"Soon. Once you feel you're ready," Xander replied, wanting him to have some say in the matter. "Soon you shall learn fencing and swordplay. Be a brother of the blade."

"Truly, Father? Shall I have my own rapier?"

"Aye. And your own fencing master."

"I would rather you teach me. Great-Aunt says you are the best."

"Alas, I have traded fencing for farming tobacco." Sensing Oceanus was growing tired, he halted lessons. "Why don't you find Cook and wheedle some gingerbread out of her? I believe that was what I smelled when I passed by the kitchen."

With a hasty adieu, Oceanus rushed headlong toward the building in question. Returning to the house, Xander faced Nurse Lineboro. She sat on a bench beneath the eave, awaiting Oceanus's afternoon lessons. Though the hospitality of his house continued, he found her company . . . taxing. As did his dogs, from all appearances, as they reclined on the opposite end of the portico.

"Beginning tomorrow you will continue Oceanus's morning lessons but leave his afternoons free," he told her.

She seemed taken aback by his quiet words. "But his studies shall suffer, sir. He must learn mathematics, history, celestial navigation—"

"You'll also cease teaching him French."

Her naysaying knew no bounds. "But French, sir, is what his guardian required, along with Latin and—"

"In addition to fewer studies, Oceanus needs more time for sport and friends."

A furious flush stained her paleness. "I suppose next you'll have him laboring in the fields."

Into the tense lull came a low growl from Jett. With a quick rebuke, Xander finished what needed saying. "If Oceanus is to inherit Rose-n-Vale, he needs to learn how to be crop master at my side. Tobacco is a fickle if profitable endeavor that requires careful training."

She stood, no longer meeting his eyes. "I sometimes suspect you are a slave to it as much as your indentures are."

"You're not far from the mark, but 'tis the way of the New World."

Her expression tightened. "I am weary of the New World."

He stepped onto the portico. "Have you given any thought to remaining in Virginia? Or should I arrange passage on a future ship to England?" At her silence, he said kindly but forthrightly, "Oceanus has outgrown the need for a nurse. He's to have a male tutor in time."

Color high, she fiddled with the watch pinned to her falling band. "I shall need another month or more to decide my future. I beg you to allow me that."

"As you wish," Xander replied.

If she did return to England, it wouldn't be for lack of offers. Not in deprived Virginia. Nor did he feel the slightest qualm about severing her tie with Oceanus. Despite the two years she'd minded the boy, he failed to sense any sort of sincere affection on either side.

"Good morning." McCaskey cleared his throat, shielding bloodshot eyes from the sun's glare as he joined them. "My disheveled head is pounding, my wits lagging. I must say, your Caribbean rum and port are second to none."

Xander eyed him without sympathy. "You'd best hie to James Towne if your thirst continues to exceed my supply."

A rueful chuckle. "Meaning my intemperate habits tax you greatly." McCaskey took the bench the nurse had abandoned. "You are not the sot I am, to your credit, Renick."

"The harvest commences soon, so a clear head is a boon. You'll need to earn your gill of rum with all the rest."

"I suppose I should sharpen my tobacco knife." McCaskey

sighed, then raised his voice, breaking into song. "'Hail thou inspiring plant! Thou balm of life, well might thy worth engage two nations' strife; exhaustless fountain of Britannia's wealth; thou friend of wisdom and thou source of health.'"

"How tiresome." Nurse Lineboro motioned to Oceanus as he neared, gingerbread in hand. "Come and let us resume our lessons. After today, your afternoons will be spent otherwise."

"Thank you, Father." Oceanus looked relieved. "I dislike so much study."

"As I once did." Ruffling the lad's shortened hair, Xander led the way as they went inside. He sought his study and opened the windows, the dogs circling before lying down. From the parlor, Oceanus began his lessons.

Until the nurse and factor departed Rose-n-Vale, Xander wouldn't marry. He wanted Selah to come to him without any guests beneath their roof. Though their impassioned time in the garden settled a great many questions between them, he sensed Selah still needed more time. More proof of a courtship rather than a business transaction. She also needed telling that her family, Shay included, were welcome to live at Rose-n-Vale permanently, if needs be.

"Nephew?" His aunt rapped at the closed study door, voice muffled. At his bid to enter, she did so, shaking her head all the way. "I bring ill news. Three salted hams have been robbed from the smokehouse. Cook believes it happened last night."

"While the dogs were inside and we were sleeping," he surmised. He didn't set a night watch. All his indentures were needed in the fields. "Mayhap we should turn the dogs loose and add a padlock, though we've had no need for such till now."

"I do think that would be wise. Though I daresay it frightens me to think the damage the dogs might do a starving thief."

"Better that than the hangman's noose." Virginia law didn't fit the crime, he'd always thought. Not to those first settlers who remembered the pinch of prolonged hunger. "'Men do not despise a thief if he steals to satisfy his soul when he is hungry.'"

"Ah, Scripture has an answer for everything. Do not forget the last part, Alexander—'but if he be found, he shall restore sevenfold; he shall give all the substance of his house.'"

He gestured to a chair. "I suspect 'tis Africans from a neighboring plantation."

"Helion Laurent's, no doubt." She sat, looking as aggrieved as he felt. "I've heard what happens under his oversight. The harm done those slaves."

"If so, the brunt of the blame should be laid on those who made them hungry and fail to relieve them."

"God deliver them." She sighed. "Such prized hams. I do hope the starving souls savor them. We won't butcher again till November, after the first frost, so will be woefully short on pork. And you know my distaste for wild game."

"There's beef to be had." He studied her, sensing more than thievery on her mind. She never resembled his mother so much as when she was vexed.

She met his gaze, ire giving way to fear. "Speaking of Laurent, you no doubt saw him consorting with colonial officials at our gathering. I hesitate to bring it up now, but I fear his presence bodes ill. It certainly unearths all I've tried to bury since Mattachanna's passing."

Going to the mantel, he reached for the pipe Selah had given him. 'Twas too early in the day to smoke, but he needed a distraction. "It soured the evening, aye."

She looked out a window, chin atremble. "You are a man of great endurance and restraint. 'Tis a wonder you've held on to your temper and not run him through."

His gaze lifted to the sword mounted on the far wall. "Bitterness is a disease, sickening he who harbors it. Our chance to avenge Mattachanna died with her."

"Will you tell Selah?" Her chatelaine clinked as she took a handkerchief from her pocket. "As your bride, should she not know what transpired with Laurent? The debacle that led to your marrying Mattachanna?"

"I'm undecided. It seems to have little bearing on the present."

"I beg to differ." She dried her eyes. "'Twas all I could do to not confront the scoundrel the other night and assure him his sins will find him out."

"Laurent is hardened to any evildoing. I see no evidence otherwise." His mind was a-scramble trying to recall what his aunt knew and didn't know from that heinous time. She didn't ken the truth about one matter. But she knew all the rest.

"If he is hardened to his evildoing, we shall see more of it, surely." She stood, so shaken she seemed a bit unsteady on her feet. "And now that embossed carbuncle of a physic is closer than ever before."

He stood, finding no humor in her Shakespearean slur. Nor was she aiming for levity. Taking her elbow, he walked her toward the door. "I sense all this company and entertaining has gone hard on you."

"I'm not as young as I once was. And my gout pains me more than not, despite Candace Hopewell's remedies. Speaking of the Hopewells, have you not seen Selah since the frolic?"

"Tomorrow."

She smiled. "If ever a man was marked for marriage, 'tis you. Those Indian beads of yours raise my hopes. I suppose you've hidden them away somewhere."

"Rest assured, Rose-n-Vale will have a bride."

"But after the tobacco harvest?"

"Selah will decide."

"I pray she is as impatient as I am."

She stepped into the hall, turning to give him a last, worrisome look and prompting him to say, "Leave any matters about Laurent to me."

30

Selah awoke, not because of her father's loud, sawlike snoring, but because of its absence.

Treading carefully, she felt her way in the dark from bedchamber to stair and then parlor. Outside all was shimmering starlight, the harvest moon in full flower, the night too fetching to sleep.

One sweep of the now familiar homeplace told her where he was. Beneath the arbor, the most fragrant bower to be had by day or by night. She approached in his line of sight, not wanting to startle him. Mother must have been tired indeed to not have missed his presence.

"Dear daughter, what are you doing awake?"

She sank down beside him on the bench. "I missed your snoring."

A chuckle softened his craggy features. "Yet your mother sleeps on, God rest her. She has been tired of late."

"Why are you out here, may I ask?"

"Is it any wonder?" He gestured to the sky. "'Lift up your eyes on high, and behold who hath created these,' so said the prophet Isaiah."

"Methinks there is something more besides."

The warmth of his hand on hers assuaged her worry. "You are a most perceptive daughter."

"What is it, Father?"

"I am simply missing Shay, as surely you must be."

"Has it been but a month since we stood in the dust and heat of James Towne common and bid him goodbye? It seems far, far longer."

"Love doesn't wait well. Love is always missing the other."

Truer words were never spoken. 'Twas the same with Xander. An aching restlessness. An endless absence.

Father continued in quiet tones, "We shall soon have news of Shay. Xander told me he will go to the Powhatans once the harvest is under way."

"Glad news." Selah squeezed his hand. "Still, it makes me miss Shay no less."

They sat in silence for a time, the chirrup of crickets an enduring night song. A wolf howled in the far reaches, so distant it lost its threat. 'Twas a velvety darkness—the warmth, the moon-washed blackness.

When he took a deep breath, she detected that dismal rattle in his chest. "Wherever Shay is, we are beneath the same sky, the same heavenlies. Somehow that seems to lessen the distance."

"A comforting thought."

She tilted her head back, gazing on a particularly bright North Star. There'd been such a star guiding them home after Rose-n-Vale's frolic. The beloved memory made a woozy melt of her middle. The bench. The beads. She'd lost count of Xander's kisses. He'd not only kissed her back. He'd kissed her soundly. And left her in a sort of lovestruck trance ever since.

In the presence of her father, shame crouched at the door of her heart. She and Xander were not yet betrothed. Was there such a thing as a chaste kiss or embrace? Had they done wrong in the garden, wooed by the beads and the seductive secrecy of finding themselves alone?

"Good night, Father." With a last squeeze of his hand, she left him, praying he'd be abed again soon and sleep the night through.

As for herself, thoughts of her beloved kept her wide awake. Marriage beckoned, sanctifying untoward desires. Any day now he would come for her. Their time would be at hand. She would be Xander's bride. Selah Hopewell Renick.

How sweet the sound.

Before dawn, her mother gently shook her awake. "Needs be you tend to the merchanting today, Daughter. Your father is having one of his spells."

The unwelcome news brought Selah upright. Father's difficulty breathing seemed to worsen in the dog days of August. She dressed and breakfasted hastily. A sloop was expected with supplies, having docked at James Towne the day before, where the larger store took the lion's share.

Candace's brow was pinched with worry. "Perhaps Watseka should accompany you. I don't like the thought of you alone."

"I'm hardly alone, Mother, especially on supply-ship days. In the afternoon, send Watseka with something to tide me over till supper if you like."

"Very well. But should you need anything . . ." Candace laid a hand upon Selah's cheek. "Would that one of Xander's greyhounds went with you."

"Father's flintlock is hidden in the storeroom if needs be."

The reminder only earned her a pained look. Selah pressed a kiss to her father's perspiring brow and started off, trying not to let any concerns rob her of morning's glories.

Before her the broad river, bestirred by a humid east wind, wore a ruffle of white lace. By the time she reached the wharf, the sun at her back had dampened her stays and whetted her thirst. This early, none were at the store. She unlocked the doors and entered in, then prepared the scales and ledgers, rearranged ells of cloth to better display them, and restocked depleted wares.

Before long the day's business commenced. She preferred these upriver folks. They had an earthy honesty far removed from the airs and eccentricities of James Towne. Usually few goodwives happened by, but today two came with their husbands, making much of the merchandise and asking a plenitude of questions Selah was happy to answer.

Mother had worried needlessly. The wharf and ware-house kept a brisk pace, and then the anticipated supply ship docked, landing her waist deep in hogsheads and crates and tubs. A few willing men helped her open them, unleashing a flurry of examining and dickering and buying. Most upriver purchases were made with tobacco receipts.

By midafternoon her head was filled with names and amounts, the little coin that had been transacted deposited in a locked box. Stomach rumbling, she caught her breath during a lull and looked east, wondering when Watseka would come. The storeroom had emptied, people carrying home their goods. A few men lingered on the wharf, one fishing off its end.

"Good day, Mistress Hopewell."

The familiar voice turned her around. In the doorway stood Helion Laurent.

"How fortuitous to find you here when we hardly exchanged a word at Renick's gathering." He began to move about the store, poking this or that with his ivory-headed walking stick as if loath to touch recently handled goods. "I am seeking a few items for my plantation. I expected your father to assist me."

"Father is home today." She wouldn't say unwell. News traveled fast, ill news especially.

"No matter. Your help is all I require."

The way he said it—and the look he gave her—left her nauseous. A glance out the open door showed an empty wharf. Were they now alone? Her mind made fearsome leaps. Had he told the loitering men to leave?

"Father may well appear at any moment to assist you." The half-truth nipped at her, but fear turned her defensive.

"So how do you find being upriver?"

Grim with you so near.

"I do not miss James Towne," she said.

He moved on, his back to her now, but ever nearer. "Even though you are no longer there, I hear reports of you. One distressed me particularly." A close perusal of scarlet hose and a canvas doublet trimmed in white lace revealed his penchant for vanity. "I came here today not only to transact business but to warn your father. Since he is absent, I will tell you."

"If for my father's ears, best wait till he is here."

"But the matter concerns you."

What could she say to this? He would tell her no matter what. She escaped to the far end of the counter, making a pretense of adjusting the scales.

"You should know I have it on good authority that Renick woos you not for your person but for your land dowry. Such would make him the largest plantation owner in Virginia, greater than any of our more worthy officials. 'Tis no secret *that* is his chief ambition." He gave a tight, hollow smile. "Be forewarned."

The accusation dropped into the sultry afternoon like shards of ice.

Watseka, where are you?

Laurent was perusing the chains now, those fetters and foot cuffs used for Africans. Father usually put them out of sight at the back of the warehouse. Why were they out front?

Whenever Laurent moved, she moved too, as far as possible from his reach if not his gaze. Her hands straightened, dusted, rearranged goods as her mind whirled.

He could harm me, and none would be the wiser.

If only the supply ship had not gone farther upriver to unload more goods. If only Watseka would come. If only Father were not unwell. If only Xander . . .

Laurent's harsh allegations slithered through her conscience. If she did wed Xander, her dowry would become his. Legally she would relinquish it all. But did it even matter? He was already the foremost tobacco lord in Virginia. Was it true he wished to trump the foremost officials with his landowning? Could that truly be the reason for his pursuit of her? Some ignoble motive? Though her whole being cried out against the lie, the slim shadow of doubt remained.

Hoofbeats broke through the tumult of her thoughts, followed by childish voices. Weak with relief, she traded the shadowed warehouse for stifling heat and found Xander dismounting in back, Oceanus and Watseka greeting each other amid the mess of unpacked goods.

Xander looked askance at Helion Laurent's horse, hobbled and ripping noisily at the marshy weeds nearer shore. His gaze swung to Selah, a dozen questions in its depths. She could not even stammer out a greeting, she felt so besmirched at having him find her with the very man he'd warned her about. She was hardly aware that Watseka approached with a small basket.

Thanking her, Selah shook her head. "I'm not the least hungry. Why don't you and Oceanus have a picnic by the water? Find a shaded spot."

They ran off happily, leaving her alone with Xander but for Laurent. He called to her from the store, and she squared her shoulders, overcoming her revulsion, or trying to.

"Trouble with the physic?" Xander asked her quietly. He stood before her, features sharp with concern.

She stared back at him, entreaty in her eyes. There were no words for the wariness that uncoiled in her at Laurent's presence, the same sick dread that overcame her when she encountered a poisonous serpent.

Saying no more, Xander went ahead of her into the warehouse. She hung back, making sure the children were situated on the bank, if only to delay her entrance.

Laurent raised his voice, obviously displeased with Xander's arrival. "Renick? I thought you'd be deep into tobacco by now. I've not known you to wait so long to harvest."

Xander gave the customary merchant's reply. "What is it you buy?"

The rattle of chains was the answer. Selah winced, returning to the ledgers while Laurent made a frightful noise coiling the chains atop the counter.

"I've need of a branding iron."

Selah firmed her voice. "We have none."

"A blacksmith is required, then, to make the brand." He turned toward Xander, who stood, arms crossed, watching Laurent transact his business from a few feet away. "How about your smith's services, Renick?"

"My smith's not for hire. He's never worked a brand, nor will he."

"Still, a brand I must have. I shall seek the James Towne smith to make my mark. For now, these fetters will do."

Selah wrote what was owed in the ledger, but her quill halted in midair at Laurent's next remark.

"So, your half-heathen boy is back. He looks a great deal like your late wife. I see very little of you in him."

Xander drew nearer. "What concern is that of yours?"

"'Tis a wonder you returned the child to Virginia." After paying in silver coin, Laurent draped the chains over his shoulder. "One would think you wanted to be rid of him permanently."

Selah's soul went still. She stared at the figures she'd written down, the ink a black blur.

"Scripture says there is one who speaks rashly like the piercings of a sword." Xander took the remaining chain off the counter. Slowly he wound it about the physic's neck, twisting till it tightened and pinched. "Much enslavement is self-made. No shackles are required."

Laurent's stare held cold annihilation. "What is that to me, Renick?"

"'Tis your everlasting soul I fear for, Laurent."

With a jerk backward, he tried to free himself from the chain's hold. It fell to the floor with a dull, clanking thud as

Xander released his grip. Movements stiff with fury, Laurent picked up the chain along with the others and strode out of sight.

Selah stood turned to stone by the quarrel.

Xander spoke into the lull once Laurent had ridden away. "I owe you an explanation."

"All this has to do with Mattachanna, does it not?"

"Aye." He leaned against the counter, eyes on the river beyond the open doorway. "How much do you ken of Mattachanna's ordeal among the English?"

"After Captain Kersey and others brought her to James Towne against her will, you mean?" At his nod, she dug unwillingly for what she knew. "Only that the council wanted to use her to bargain with her father, the chief. For a great quantity of corn and the return of stolen goods and English captives."

She came out from behind the counter to stand beside him. The children were wading in the river. Soon Watseka would peel off her English clothes. But for now, Selah only cared about the troubled man beside her.

"Mattachanna was taken to James Towne by night and kept in the household of an official secretly. Word was sent to Opechancanough that she would be released with his cooperation."

She nodded. "But her father was slow to meet the English terms, so Mattachanna was kept."

"Opechancanough met most of the council's demands but not all of them, not to their satisfaction, nor in the time they dictated." He paused, gaze still on the river. "Time passed and Mattachanna grew more dispirited. She missed her people. Since she'd always treated the English with great favor and generosity, she felt they had dealt her an immense blow, a betrayal."

"'Twas exactly that." Even now Selah recalled the shock her own family had felt at the treachery done to a young woman who meant no harm. "She was soon removed from James Towne to another unknown location upriver." Here Selah's knowledge unraveled. Amid such secrecy, she had been denied a visit to her old friend, leaving her to speculate where Mattachanna was. How she was. "There Reverend Criswel supposedly watched over her and instructed her in the catechism and our faith."

Xander ran a hand over his bearded jaw. In the harsh afternoon light it glinted red. "She was placed in Criswel's care, out of sight of James Towne, because she was with child."

With child.

The straightforward words failed to take root. Selah simply stared at him as all her preconceived notions came crashing down.

"During her early captivity in James Towne, Helion Laurent, acting as physic, forced himself on her."

The sharp intake of breath was Selah's own.

"To hide both his wrongdoing and her pregnancy, the council decided upriver was best. But Mattachanna grew ill in both body and spirit. Her sister was sent for as Criswel feared she might die." His grieved gaze met hers. "I was sent for."

"You? Why?"

"I was one of the few who could speak freely with her in her native tongue. She trusted me. I knew her father, her many kin, from living amongst them as a youth. She told me what Laurent had done to her."

Selah looked to her knotted hands. "Carnal knowledge
. . . such is a punishable offense in Virginia."

"An accusation easily made and hard proved."

"But—"

"If you are as well connected as Laurent, especially so.
After he had offended the chief's daughter in such a way,
all was silenced lest another war ensue. Even the Powhatans
punish such a crime by death."

Never had he looked so troubled, the slight grooves worn
by time and weather in his handsome features taut. She
schooled her ire and listened, though she wanted to cover
her ears instead.

"I met with the governor and his foremost officials and
told them what Laurent had done." The dismal outcome
was mirrored in his hard expression. "Their response was
that carnal knowledge resulting in a child necessitates consent."

What? Was there no justice? No recompense? Selah tried
to tamp down her welling dismay. "And so Laurent escaped
the hangman's noose. But what of Mattachanna?"

"Reverend Criswel—a good, God-fearing man—knew it
would be best if she came under someone's protection by
marriage. I was the logical choice." At last a sliver of light
came into his face. "By that time, I was thoroughly enam-
ored with her. We were wed. Rose-n-Vale became her haven.
Oceanus was born, the son I had long hoped for but who
was not my own."

Nay, not his own but his sworn enemy's.

From outside came the sound of bubbling laughter. Not
Watseka's but Oceanus's. The joyful intrusion spread a balm
over the ill feeling left in Laurent's wake. Yet in the ensuing

silence, a new sorrow began to unspool inside Selah. How she had misjudged Xander.

Her mouth felt dry, her tongue tied. "I have a confession."

He looked at her, his eyes glittering with emotion. If ever a man could undo a woman in a glance . . .

"I have thought wrongly of you for years." Tears nearly closed her throat. "I've been a fool to believe you sent your son far away from you in a callous gesture when he is not even your son, when his very presence must remind you of what that vile—"

"Nay, Selah." He swallowed, the cords of his own throat tightening. "He is all I have of Mattachanna. And I choose to believe her beauty and her character trump any evildoing Laurent did her."

She slipped her arms about his waist and laid her head upon his chest. Long moments passed as the truth took root. She let go of the lie that Xander wanted to wed her for ignoble reasons. She would not even give that voice.

Outside the laughter ebbed. Oceanus appeared at the door, holding out Watseka's English garments. "She says she is a beaver."

With a sudden, bottomless laugh, Xander banished all remaining tension from the room. "Soon I will take you to pay a visit to your grandfather the chief, and you will see that most of your kinsmen do not wear a great many clothes in summer. Watseka is only following her custom."

"She isn't the only beaver hereabouts." Selah took the clothes and impulsively kissed Oceanus on the top of his thoroughly wet head. "*Meegwetch.*"

"That means 'thank you.'" He smiled up at her. "*Meegwetch.*"

"Good words." She smoothed his hair back, wondering when Xander had had it cut. Perhaps at breeching, as was common. She searched for any telltale sign of Laurent in his sweet face.

Lord, may it only be Mattachanna I see.

With another smile, he ran off with the boundless energy of a boy not yet five.

"Where is your father?" Xander's question turned her around.

"Unwell, thus I am here in his stead."

"What happened here today before I came? With Laurent, I mean."

"Nothing of consequence, as you arrived soon after. But if you had not come when you did . . ." She all but shuddered. "Save for the Almighty, rogues such as he are hard to redeem."

"I suspect 'tis not only Mattachanna who has suffered at his hands." Xander's gaze held a warning. "Or who else will."

Selah returned to the counter and closed the ledgers. "If you would see me home . . . I have no heart for merchanting today."

Together they toted most of the remaining goods inside the storeroom before locking up, then called the children to follow once Watseka was dressed again. In the bright sunlight, with the river gliding on as before, the shore soothed by a freshening wind, Selah could almost believe nothing had changed. Yet in the span of a tense hour, her small world had turned on end. Everything before her held a different cast, including the man whose saddle she shared. The boy running ahead of them after Watseka. The precious memory of Mattachanna.

She herself.

31

Once home, Xander helped Selah dismount, his hands lingering at her waist. "Have you given any more thought to the beads?"

Smile returning, she looked up at him. "I can think of naught else."

"Nor can I." His countenance eased. Had he somehow been unburdened by all he had told her? "Once the harvest is well under way, Oceanus and I will head west to the Powhatans. Have you anything for your brother?"

"I'll gather some small things to give him. How long will you be gone?"

"Long enough to ascertain how the exchange is faring. When I come back, we'll talk more about the future."

She blinked into the glaring sunlight that snuck beneath her hat brim, wishing she could go with him. How she missed Shay. The world he'd gone to was strange, indeed. She craved but a glimpse.

Behind them came Ustis's raspy voice beneath the arbor. "Home early, Daughter?"

"For today, Father."

"I'll explain if you want to go inside," Xander told her.

Her first thought was to leave the matter to him. But what would he share? That Laurent had bought chains and made insulting remarks, and a fight had nearly ensued? That she sensed the presence of evil every time he drew near?

"Please." She touched Xander's sleeve. "Say nothing to Father. His health cannot take it. I shan't return to the warehouse alone. Surely that is caution enough."

"I'll ask him for your hand, then."

Would he? Could so much happiness and heartache coexist in one day?

Stunned, she walked toward the house. Her mother was near the well, listening to Watseka and Oceanus tell of their picnic. Selah sought the empty parlor, still able to hear the murmur of her father's and Xander's voices outside.

With effort, she bent her thoughts toward the small knapsack to prepare for Shay. Some sweetmeats, perhaps. A trinket or two for him to share with new friends. Nothing that would slow Xander. Already she missed him. Though she tried to push today's confrontation aside, it seemed to set the stage for another acrimonious encounter. Some retaliation by Laurent. 'Twas not only for herself she feared.

Removing her hat, she stole a look at herself in a looking glass. Pale as frost. Surely that bespoke her turmoil. And yet, Xander was even now asking for her hand—

"Selah."

Xander had come into the parlor. Was he leaving? The day had flown. Four o'clock shadows were creeping across the courtyard behind him. Yet another goodbye. The harvest and the journey would soon be upon them. Time in all its sweet fleetingness seemed to gather round, causing her to impress his beloved features on her heart like flower petals between pages.

His voice held a jubilant beat. "Your father has given his blessing."

"I didn't doubt it. You're like a son to him already."

"When I return, we'll name a day. Your parents are welcome to make Rose-n-Vale their home as well."

Gathering her in his embrace, he kissed her more than once. These weren't stolen garden kisses in the scattered light of pitch-pine torches. These were kisses of farewell and separation and longing. Hope and glad-heartedness and promise.

"Something to remember me by," he murmured into the closeness between them, again smoothing that wayward flaxen strand beneath her coif. "Though I would rather take the pins from your hair . . ."

Never had he seen her hair unbound. Such was a husband's privilege. Would he be surprised it fell nearly to her knees?

"I'll stop on my way west to collect anything you have for your brother." Taking her face between his callused hands, he kissed her lingeringly a final time. "Take steadfast care, Selah."

Already she felt a widening chasm both inside her and around her, as if some protective buffer were being removed. "I wish I could go with you."

"You do go with me, in both head and heart." Looking like he wanted to kiss her again, he turned and left the house instead, calling for his horse and Oceanus. Both came posthaste, though Oceanus immediately asked when Watseka could play again.

Xander helped him into the saddle. "Mayhap on the Sabbath after our journey. We'll likely meet at divine service." Swinging himself up, he met Selah's eyes.

"Godspeed." She reached out and squeezed his hand. "I'll watch for you. And pray."

Selah missed him. Missed him so much she pocketed her father's pistol and rode with Watseka to Rose-n-Vale. There she earned the curious looks of farm managers and indentures as she stood apart from the fields and watched the last of the tobacco harvest unfold. Most of the crop had already been transported to Xander's barns before he'd gone west. There it would cure for several weeks, allowing him to take Oceanus to the Powhatans. Lord willing, he'd return before the striking began, the next step after harvest.

Factor McCaskey approached. He and the farm managers had been left in charge during Xander's absence. "Mistress Hopewell, what brings ye out on such a Hades-like day?"

Selah peered at him beneath the wide brim of her beaver hat as he swiped the sweat from his brow with a grimy sleeve. "Living in James Towne, I've rarely seen Orinoco cut, at least not on this scale."

"'Tis a sight to behold, truly. And such an excellent harvest to boot."

She nudged the horse nearer the biggest barn and stood in its powerfully scented shade. Since childhood she'd become accustomed to tobacco drying, familiar with its peculiar aroma, the very essence of Virginia.

"Marry you the tobacco man?" Watseka's oval face shone with delight as she craned her neck round to look at Selah.

Selah reached into her pocket and withdrew the shell beads in answer. Wonder engulfed her. Here she was amid fields as far as the eye could see, poised to be Rose-n-Vale's mistress. And Xander had graciously made provision for her parents. Would they all not benefit, coming under Xander's protection by marriage?

"When I return, we'll name a day."

She would wear her purple gown. Sew a new coif that bespoke her married standing.

For now, she looked west, to the land Watseka knew so well and would soon return to.

My beloved, hurry home.

Was being four so . . . absorbing?

Since the start of their journey, Oceanus had not lagged behind. He'd forged ahead. Now that he was away from his nurse and the routines of Rose-n-Vale, something seemed to have unlocked inside him. No longer was he the old soul who'd landed. Out in the open without clock or tie to tether him, Oceanus missed nothing around him—the call of a bird, the shift in the wind, a tortoise beneath the river's surface. Xander was riddled with questions, some he gladly answered, some he couldn't, glad the lad had a quick wit and a ready memory.

As for himself, the journey west seemed less arduous than before. Mayhap because of fair weather. Or Oceanus's company. Or because he had finally confessed all and revealed the truth of the lad's origins to Selah? Whatever the cause, Xander felt lighter in both step and spirit. Oddly, he'd begun to view Oceanus through a different lens since. Not as Laurent's son. Not as the result of a vile act. But as a youth who'd inherited his mother's intrepid spirit, her love of the land.

"Father, how shall I greet my Indian grandfather? When do I give him the gift we brought?" Oceanus touched the pouch in which the ivory compass was encased. With its fly and needle, it would be well received, even awe inducing. "Shall I speak of my mother?"

Xander pondered his reply as they traded walking for riding, Oceanus sharing a saddle. "Your grandfather the chief will be surrounded by a great many warriors and werowances. You'll be held in high honor as his grandson. 'Tis wise to speak little and observe much, at least at first. There will be a feast and gift giving to welcome us. You'll soon find you have as many kin as grains of sand."

"But not Watseka."

"Nay, she remains with the Hopewells for now. But you will meet Shay, the Hopewells' son, who is living there."

"He is not Powhatan like me?"

"Shay is British to the bone but desires to learn all he can of the Naturals' ways, just as Watseka learns about the English, the Tassantassas."

"I am not much afraid."

Xander almost chuckled. The lad was *greatly* afraid. The nearer they drew to the Powhatan encampment, the more hunched his small frame became. For a few fleeting moments Xander was beset by doubts. Was Oceanus equipped for such a visit? Would he even remember it in time? Mayhap the changes dealt him—an ocean voyage, a new world, an Indian grandfather—were too much for one so young.

"You have nothing to fear from your grandfather's people," Xander reassured him. "Tomorrow we will come to the Chickahominy River and pasture Lancelot till our return. You have the unmistakable look of your mother. That is sure to please Chief Opechancanough."

The yellow pine canoe on the river's banks seemed an almost eerie acknowledgment that their arrival in Powhatan territory had not gone unnoticed but was highly anticipated. White oak paddles lay in the dugout's rough-hewn bottom. Shoving off from the shore sunwise, east to west, Xander navigated as Oceanus sat on the loose board seat in front of him.

Here the landscape altered and became a vast, swampy expanse between southern bluffs and gentler northern hills. Cypress trees, their fringe a smudge of green against overcast skies, intermingled with tallow shrubs heavy with berries, their spicy-sweet scent reminding Xander of the candles Mattachanna once made.

"Father, what is that?" Oceanus pointed a finger at endless miniature mounds of mud along the river's banks.

"Crayfish burrows," Xander replied, paddling around a fallen birch with a fierce tangle of branches. "You cannot see these creatures by day. They come alive at night."

"Can we eat them?"

"Some do, but they make better bait, as you shall find once you learn to fish."

A woodpecker began a raucous tapping, the echo like a hundred hammers in their ears. Mallards and herons paid their swift, silent passage no mind, though a lone doe eyed them warily from a thicket. Soon, small Chickahominy towns appeared on both south and north banks, the Naturals gathering in small knots to bathe as was their morning custom.

Xander raised a hand in greeting, deciding it never amiss to teach a New World lesson. "The Chickahominy made friends with the English when we first set foot on their soil. Once they were our allies. They taught us to grow and preserve our own food. They even promised to supply us with bowmen if the Spanish came to fight us."

'Twas a fragile, tentative alliance, further strained by the land-stealing English. Once, Xander had plied these waters in trade with the very Indians now estranged. Did they regard him with animosity and suspicion? Might Oceanus be in danger? Clearly the two of them were at the mercy of Providence above and Xander's own earthly reputation here below. Not once had he cheated these people. Not once had he abused their trust. Would his previous fair dealings allow them safe passage?

At the next bend in the river, taking them away from the stone-faced onlookers, Xander felt a palpable relief. The very presence of a child, always a token of peace, boded well. And with his ebony hair, dark eyes, and tanned skin, Oceanus looked far more Natural than English. God be thanked.

Lord, is it low of me to ask Thee to hide any likeness of Laurent in the lad? Any and all baseness of spirit?

The desperate prayer swelled his heart. How could he parent the lad if he grew to resemble such a wicked man? When every glance at him was a reminder of the evil act that had spawned him?

Yet the child was not evil.

For I am fearfully and wonderfully made: marvelous are thy works; and that my soul knoweth right well.

Hope took hold, lighting his soul. With Selah by his side, he would see the boy raised right. Oceanus need never know about his true origins. What mattered was God had made him, made him fearfully and wonderfully and marvelously. As such, there was no impediment to his becoming an upstanding, God-honoring man in time.

All that his earthly father was not and might never be.

32

Selah awoke, the moon outside her bedchamber pouring pale light through the open window. Had she only dreamt the unusual sound, intermingled with the pup's barking and other barnyard noises? Perhaps Father was awake, roaming about restlessly as he sometimes did.

Leaving the soft warmth of her bed, she trod barefoot to the door, hesitating at the top of the stairs. Through the nightly din of cicadas and frogs came another sound that roused her further. A rustle of brush. A footfall. Just beyond the bolted doors and shuttered windows.

She felt her way down the steps and into the parlor, then paused at the front door. The distressed whinny of their mare forbade her to venture further. She stood still as her heartbeat quickened, causing a roaring in her ears. Some prowling creature, perhaps. Father had mentioned seeing catamount tracks near the henhouse. Izella slept in a room off the summer kitchen. Surely she'd awaken if needs be.

Selah hugged the wall till she came to her parents' bedchamber. Pushing open the door, she moved nearer till she could ascertain their rhythmic breathing and undisturbed forms in the shadows. Though she was unable to see the clock, instinct told her it was nearly break of day.

Returning to the parlor, she listened. Night seemed to have settled again. Not one untoward sound did she hear. Kentke's barking had ceased. Slowly she went up the stairs, ever mindful of Shay as she passed his bedchamber. Lest she wake Watseka, she stepped gingerly across the worn floor toward her bed, stifling a yawn. The moon, snuffed by clouds, reappeared, slanting pale light across tousled bed linens . . . and an empty mattress. The chamber pot in the far corner had no one perched over it. Despite their admonitions, Watseka sometimes preferred to go outside.

Selah's hasty return downstairs had her stumbling on a step and careening into a wall. To her dismay, her parents were on their feet, Father waiting as she descended the steps.

"I cannot find Watseka." As a precaution, she took out the loaded musket from its resting place. "There was a commotion outside, so I came downstairs and checked all the locks. On my way back to bed, I found hers empty."

"I shall go out and have a look myself while you return upstairs and stand watch by your bedchamber window." Father cleared his throat. "Your mother will bolt the door after me. Make no move till you hear my voice. Perhaps the child simply went out to check on her pup."

Selah balked. "But the doors are locked—"

"But not the upstairs windows, your mother says."

Selah had forgotten. In the heat, she'd left the windows open. How could she have been so careless? Could Watseka have climbed out . . . or might someone have climbed in?

Xander had entrusted Watseka to their care. The appalling certainty that the girl's disappearance was Selah's own fault nearly buckled her knees. She would not see her ailing father suffer for her lapse.

"Give me the gun, Selah." Father's firm tone belied his weakened state.

She took a step back, her clutch tighter on the musket. Turning, she reached the door and rushed headlong into the last of the night.

At last they came to Menmend. Ever since they'd sighted the sprawling encampment with its haze of woodsmoke, Occanus's skittishness had spiked visibly. Xander knew that Chief Opechancanough, ever shrewd, would sense it, to the lad's discredit.

"Father, I am not feeling brave."

The whispered words brought Xander to one knee. Hard as it was for him to show any outward affection, he set aside his unease and embraced the boy. At first stiff, Oceanus finally leaned into him and laid his head upon Xander's shoulder.

"'Tis natural to feel fear betimes. But remember the biblical queen Esther, who did bravely before the king despite her fears. And the shepherd David, who defeated the giant. Courage bears its own rewards." He stroked Oceanus's silken hair, so like Mattachanna's. "Be stout of heart. Your coming will please your grandfather. Remember, you are a valiant soul crossing an ocean and now venturing further west. I am proud of you."

With a nod, Oceanus lifted his chin and looked toward the outline of the village situated along the picturesque Pamunkey River. Domed dwellings spread in all directions, a multitude of reed-covered shelters offering shade and repose. Smoke from countless cook fires thickened the sultry air.

The lively if distant shouts of children at play surely tickled Oceanus's ears.

Before they'd gone much farther, a tattooed escort appeared from a stand of oak and fell into step beside them, their official welcome to Menmend.

"Welcome, True Word."

Gaze never settling, Xander looked for signs of Shay. Their meeting would hearten Oceanus too. For the moment, he was regarding their guide with silent wonder, gaze riveted to the headband he wore with its colorful feathers.

They passed palisaded walls much like those of the English before coming into the heart of the village and reaching the council house. Here there were at least a hundred werowances gathered beneath a bower of saplings that shaded their chief. Xander knew some of them and considered them sound men. Others, full of superstition and animosity, he avoided if he could.

As usual, the chief was expecting them, alerted by spies whose watchful gaze Xander had felt since the Chickahominy River. There was no deducing Opechancanough's feelings about the moment. Faced with his favored daughter's son, his grandson, the nearest living link to Mattachanna he had, the chief remained wooden. Oceanus regarded the mantle of raccoon skins the headman wore with such awe it seemed to make him forget his fears.

Without warning, the assembly gave a collective shout. Expecting Oceanus to start, Xander reached out a reassuring hand, but the lad did not so much as flinch.

A bowl of water was brought by the chief's most favored wife. Xander paused to wash as was customary, as did Oceanus. After drying their hands with feathers, they drew nearer

Opechancanough, who regarded them both with an unnerving intensity before breaking the silence.

"Is this my daughter's son?"

"It is he, aye, and desirous of seeing you."

Though the chief knew English, he spoke to Xander for several moments in Powhatan.

The lad needed an Indian name.

He had the look of his mother.

Was he hungry after so long a journey?

All the while, Oceanus stood in watchful, respectful silence.

Finally, Opechancanough placed a hand on the boy's recently shorn head. "It is good you have come to see your grandfather. My heart has long been on the ground since your mother sailed to the land of the English king and failed to return. We must feast to celebrate your coming. But after, I have an important matter to discuss with your white father that concerns you."

As they gathered to eat, Xander spied Shay. Disbelieving, he blinked to clear his vision. Gone was the oft clumsy, ham-fisted Hopewell. A stone or more had been shaved off his thickset frame. His longish hair was shorn on the left to accommodate his bow hand as was Powhatan custom, the right side braided, a lone feather dangling. But his infectious grin was the same, his successful adjustment to this new way of life evident. He approached Xander and Oceanus as they were seated at the feast, joining them cross-legged upon rush mats.

"Oceanus has grown up." Shay extended a hand in friendship, retaining the English custom. "I am the brother of Selah Hopewell."

"Selah, who lives with Watseka?" Oceanus glanced at Xander. "The one you will marry?"

At this, Shay's hopeful gaze swung to Xander. "Am I to call you brother?"

"Lord willing, aye." Xander pulled Watseka's shell beads from beneath his shirt and let them dangle down his shirt-front. "Not long after I return to Rose-n-Vale."

With something resembling a subdued war whoop, Shay signaled his appreciation.

They commenced eating, partaking of endless bowls of smoked fish, succotash, roast squash, maize, and far more. Upwards of two hundred Powhatans consumed the feast, the bounty never ending. Such a grand welcome was for Oceanus whether the lad realized it or not.

Sated, Xander contented himself as the dancing and entertainment unfolded. Observing the color and whirl about him gave him room to mentally roam. The chief wanted something from him, something that would delay his leaving. But the matter wouldn't be broached tonight, he wagered. Unlike with the English, time was neither consulted nor considered. They knew no such thing as hurry. Events unfolded as they would.

For now, Shay took care to explain to Oceanus what was happening, who was dancing and why, which noisemakers were being used, the significance of each. The lad's trail-weary legs were at rest, the blisters made by so much walking relieved. Tonight they would sleep near the heavily guarded chief's lodge, mayhap close to Shay.

Hours later when Oceanus's head was sagging and the dancers grew exhausted, all dispersed to their beds. Shay led them to their lodging, taking up his own mat near them. But sleep was long in coming for Xander.

Insects buzzed about them, but as he smelled of smoke from the tribe's fires, few alighted. He lay awake on his back, gaze fixed on the most brilliant star. Sirius shone upon them, brightest during the dog days of summer.

Turning on his mat, he wished for a pillow, his own bed, the peace to be had on his porch in the gloaming. He yawned, turned again. 'Twas Selah who kept him awake long past his prayers. He smiled into the darkness. Might she be pondering Sirius this long, sweltering night, same as he? The distance between them chafed. Already he was anxious to return. Name a wedding day.

Start life anew with the woman he loved.

Panic propelled one to rash acts. As dawn smudged the sky, Selah traded the security of the house for the courtyard and realized the truth too late. Within seconds of being in the open, she heard a horse move in the woods behind the stable.

"Watseka, where are you?"

Whoever had been prowling rode hard away. At once her father was behind her. In one hand he held a pistol.

"Daughter, come inside." The breathless words had no sooner left him than he clutched at his throat and then his chest. With a groan, he sank to the dew-damp ground.

"Father—" Stricken, Selah moved toward him when his pistol discharged.

The early morn was rent open by the jarring sound, wrenching her ears even as she grappled with searing pain. Her musket gave way and fell to her feet.

Hit.

Woozy, she sank to her knees, curling her legs to her chest. Scarlet soaked her nightgown, certain to render it nothing but a rag. 'Twas her last fleeting thought.

33

As the next day unfurled, Opechancanough met with Xander privately, though the werowances who usually hovered were not far. "Tell me how my granddaughter Watseka fares with you."

Xander could not stay a smile at the question, the memory of her playful ways never far. Nor could he staunch his surprise. So much of what was discussed regarding Indian-English relations was grim. He was only too pleased to talk of more cheerful matters.

"She is learning the English tongue and English ways," Xander told him. "Just as the son of Ustis Hopewell is thriving, so, too, is Watseka."

They spoke at length between long pauses of pondering and reflection. Tobacco curled from their shared pipe, the aromatic yet somewhat harsher blend of the Naturals that most English disdained. Xander gave a favorable report of the children living among the English and listened as the chief spoke of the children in the Powhatans' care.

"When will you depart?" The chief's penetrating gaze made Xander reconsider his leave-taking on the morrow.

"Once I meet with the English in your care and give them tokens and such from their families."

The chief eyed him unflinchingly with a look Xander knew too well. Something was afoot. His suspicion was confirmed by Opechancanough's next words.

"My grandson has been separated from his mother's people for many seasons. It is time to reacquaint him with our ways. I ask that you leave him here till the moon of white frost."

Late fall. November.

Xander passed Opechancanough the pipe. Dismay cut a wide swath through him. What could he say to this? Denying the chief so heartfelt a request would be taken as a grave offense. Oceanus was his grandson. True, he had many. But no others from his favored daughter. Nor did the lad have other surviving grandparents.

No doubt Oceanus would thrive much like Shay if left in the Naturals' care for a few months more. What could it hurt? The small qualm he felt was a selfish one, given the boy was all he had of Mattachanna. That, he would miss.

His delayed response seemed to surprise the chief. Trying to quell the last shred of resistance inside him, Xander stared unseeing through the smoke at an array of fine beaver pelts dangling from a support pole.

Opechancanough's eyes narrowed. "Would a few furs make the separation more agreeable?"

"I would simply ask that Oceanus be told and consent to the plan. He is young and has withstood many changes of late. He still mourns his mother."

The chief gave a nod of assent, and Oceanus was sent for. He entered the council house with his usual reserve, though

Xander had heard him happily shouting and playing with other children moments before. Now, facing his grandfather, he darted a glance at Xander as if to ascertain what was about to happen.

Xander put a hand on his shoulder. "Your grandfather would like for you to have a visit with him while I return to Rose-n-Vale."

Oceanus fell silent for several strained seconds. "May I have a bow and arrow like Shay?"

The question seemed to please Opechancanough, who agreed.

Bolstered by his approval, Oceanus addressed him personally. "Can I learn to hunt and swim, Grandfather?"

Opechancanough again agreed. "You will have a Powhatan name as well, in time."

At that, Oceanus went out to resume his play. All the levity vanished with him.

Opechancanough's eyes glinted hard as flint. "Tell me about the white chief Harvey. Is it true that he has erected a palisade between the great rivers across leagues of land not his own?"

Was her very life's blood flowing out of her? Would it spell her demise? Selah shook so hard her teeth hurt, her head dangerously aswim. Even as her mother's voice broke through the darkness, she couldn't grasp hold of her meaning. Vaguely she was aware of being carried inside and someone shouting for rags.

Where was Father?

When she next opened her eyes, it was light of day. Murmuring ebbed and flowed around her like the tides around James Towne. Not Xander. Not Father. Other masculine utterances she had trouble deciphering.

Rose-n-Vale's factor, McCaskey?

Nay, the sheriff.

"Tell me what happened with as much detail as you recall."

Her mother's voice, broken and disbelieving, hurt her ears. Selah breathed in the shocking scent of hartshorn as it passed beneath her nose. The dark shadow taking slow shape before her was equally abhorrent.

Laurent. Posing as the physic she was desperately in need of.

"You've suffered a great loss of blood." His voice was low as his fingers probed her torn flesh. When he neared her stinging wound, she all but hissed at him.

"Becalm yourself or I shall administer valerian, which you well know is vile to the taste if soothing to the mind."

Jaw set, she let him do as he purposed, cleansing then wrapping her arm. As soon as the linen was in place, she could feel the blood's flow again. But 'twas the feel of his hands on her—and the knowledge of his hands on Mattachanna—that had her gathering all her strength and shrinking back from him amid the bed linens. The soft pillow held the scent of her father. Had he not fallen in the courtyard before dawn?

Her voice was a whisper. "How is my father?"

A prolonged pause. "Your father, God rest him, will be buried posthaste due to the extreme heat."

At that, she slipped back into the blackness. She came to her senses again as her mother's soft, tear-laden voice droned on in the shadows. "The window was left ajar . . . my daughter went to look for Watseka . . ."

The beloved name nearly brought her upright.

"There's every reason to believe the Indian girl beneath your roof has simply run off to rejoin her people." The sheriff's words were clipped, certain.

Nay, nay. Watseka would not run. The girl did not have a fleeing bone within her small body. She'd been content in their care. The peace of the entire colony might well hinge on her well-being. And Xander's own life was at stake. The tension between the English and Naturals was always asimmer. Watseka's vanishing might well lead to more warfare. Another massacre like 1622.

Laurent was still hovering. "I have prepared a posset for you."

Something touched her lips. She sputtered, finding it bitter. But it was not valerian.

Mayhap poisonous.

Wrenching her head to the right, she refused, spilling the posset across the bed linens.

"Confound it! You minx—" The epithet was said through clenched teeth, and then he nearly shouted at Izella to clean up the mess.

At last the dark shadow that was Laurent moved away. "It is I, Nurse Lineboro, come to help care for you."

Selah stilled, eyes closing to stop the room's dizzying spin. "How is my mother?"

"She is unharmed but, as a new widow, understandably stricken."

Father.

How she loved him. The fact he'd been ailing—failing—lessened the ache not one whit. How they hoped he'd be well in time. Had prayed to that end. Already the house felt odd

without him. Shay was the heir, the head of the family now.
And he but a boy far from home.

"Can you sit up, Selah? Take some nourishment?" Nurse
Lineboro prodded. "Water, at least."

Selah raised herself up against the pillows Izella bunched
behind her. The effort seemed herculean. But drink she must,
if only to stay clearheaded enough to keep an eye on Laurent.
A knot of men remained in the parlor, the physic among
them. Though she had no proof, she felt him behind Watseka's baffling disappearance.

"Pray becalm yourself, as the physic said. Think of your
poor mother."

"How did you come to be here?"

"We heard a weapon firing clear to Rose-n-Vale."

"Has Watseka been found? I fear the physic has somehow
done her harm."

"On what grounds?" Alarm flared in the nurse's eyes. "I
know little of the law in James Towne, but I caution you
against offending Helion Laurent. You are useless to your
cause if you give him reason to bring a charge against you."

True, but this did little to relieve the fury asimmer inside
her, a fury that would only subside with the return of Watseka if not her beloved father. A fury so consuming that only
Xander could douse it.

Downing more water, she lay back, restless for her mother.
In time, Candace was at her side, her eyes puffy from weeping.

"Your father has gone from us." She clasped Selah's hand.
"Though we mourn, we are not without hope. Our concern
at present is the here and now. Seeing you well."

"What felled him?"

"I believe 'twas his heart, but only the Almighty knows."

Her stalwart father rarely complained, but when he did it was about his chest. Being roused from sleep and pitched headlong into a fright had done him no favors either. A prick of guilt arose, but she countered it. Finding Watseka was now their chief aim.

"Will a search party be sent?"

Candace's plump shoulders rose and fell as the men's voices mounted. Pain had ever sharpened her temper, causing her to fling a rebuke over her shoulder. "Have a care, gentlemen! Will you not take your squabbling out of doors?"

The offended silence might have found her pilloried for insolence save for her grief. Without another word, the men betook themselves outside through the open door into sweltering sunlight.

Selah shifted beneath the linen sheet and watched her mother move slowly about the house as if lost, touching this or that. Her father's beaver hat. His keys hanging on a nail near the door. His pipe and tobacco pouch. The toy flute he'd given Watseka.

Her heart burst anew as she watched her father being laid out upon a settle in the parlor. Bitter sobs she tried to choke down burned her throat before filling the still room and her ears.

The terrible sight was blocked by the return of Nurse Lineboro, who sighed and touched her brow as if she had a headache. "I am to sit by your side, the physic says."

The men were still outside, the sheriff's voice foremost. She thought she'd heard McCaskey's voice, but all was ajumble in her mind. The grief that pressed down on her ebbed, if only for a moment. Laurent's presence most concerned her.

"Please tell the factor I must speak with him." Why was

her breath coming so hard? Her voice so winded and strange? Had Laurent given her something and she was unaware of it? "Watseka must be found."

"Such seems the least of your worries." A crease marred Nurse Lineboro's brow. "I do think she's run off, as the sheriff says. Such a wild little thing. One would think you'd be glad."

Glad? Had she no knowledge of what Watseka's absence spelled? The grim consequences? "Please summon the factor now."

Nurse Lineboro, used to obeying orders, did as she was bade. Outside came the sound of departing horses.

Soon McCaskey drew up a chair where Selah lay. "Tell me again what happened this morn."

With effort, Selah recounted her rising before first light and finding Watseka missing, the commotion outside, the fateful moment she'd rushed into the yard with her father following. A nightmare from which she wanted to shake herself awake.

Selah set her jaw against her throbbing arm. "What is the sheriff saying about Watseka?"

"Very little."

"Will there be a search party?"

"Nay. The men cannot be spared from the harvest and other responsibilities."

"Will word be sent to the Powhatans about Watseka being taken?"

McCaskey shook his head. "The consensus is she has not been taken but has run away."

"She has not run. I would swear to it. 'Twas a horse I heard in the woods behind the stable and kitchen. Surely that speaks of foul play."

"The officials advise waiting till Renick returns and they hear his voice in the matter."

"'Twill be too late. She may be hurt, suffering—"

"And you would have me, a lowly Scot, take on all Virginia as to how things should proceed." The thinly veiled mockery in McCaskey's eyes told her he knew them for what they were—pretentious, petty men who would waste no more time searching for an Indian girl than they would a stray animal.

"Do they think Chief Opechancanough will respond kindly when he learns we did not even hazard a search for his kin?" Selah hissed. "Perchance the Powhatans shall come down on us in retaliation and without warning, as they once did, when scores died by fire and hatchet. Will these officials not count the cost of their indifference? Their arrogance?"

The unusual ire in her voice returned Candace to the bedchamber. "Daughter, take heart. The sheriff did say he will appoint an armed musketeer to watch over us till we women determine what we shall do next. For now, the passing bell will toll in James Towne to announce your father's death. I shall begin sewing his woolen winding-cloth." She took a deep breath, tears close. "Needs be we return downriver as soon as possible."

34

Laurent returned on the morrow.

'Twas all Selah could do not to lambaste him as he entered the fragile sanctity of their home. A musketeer was outside, his presence providing small security. As it was, Selah regarded the physic coldly and silently as he approached with his portmanteau.

"And how is Mistress Hopewell today?" he asked, coming to stand over her as she reclined upon her parents' bed.

"I have no need of your services, sir."

"Your injury may well portend otherwise." He began unwinding the bandages while Izella went to fetch water at his request. "You are lucky 'tis a flesh wound and the lead ball went awry. The bone is still intact."

Selah averted her eyes. Luck? Nay. Providence had spared her. She might well have been killed instead. Still, how could a flesh wound cause such pain? She could not sleep. She had no appetite. Yet 'twas nothing like the hole in her heart. Everywhere she looked told of her father's passing. Another cape merchant had been appointed, a necessary but grievous occurrence. Goodmen came bearing her father's coffin, an onerous leaded box of elm lined with velvet, soon to be interred at James Towne's church.

She'd lost count of the people hastening upriver to pay their respects. Even now feminine voices floated from the parlor, Xander's aunt among them. Had she news of his return? Looking toward the open door, Selah chafed. What was taking Izella so long? She didn't like being left alone with Laurent.

He was examining her arm, his features a mask but so close she saw the black velvet patch on his left temple, the placement signifying dignity. Of which he had none.

She spoke so low that none but he could hear. "Where is she?"

He stilled. "I know nothing of whom you speak."

"Oh, but you do. And we shall get to the heart of the matter soon enough."

"We?"

"When Alexander Renick learns how you came here under cover of night, taking a helpless child and thereby killing my father—"

"You Jezebel." His long fingers encircled the wrist of her wounded arm, tightening till her voice finally faltered. "Take care with such accusations. I can assure you I did not do whatever it is you accuse me of. I would as soon brand you a liar before all of Virginia."

"If not you, then one of your minions instead." She tried to pull free of him despite the crushing ache. "As I said, any treachery and deceit shall be found out."

Izella returned with the requested water. The very air seemed to spark with animosity. If she noticed, she gave no sign, dark eyes down, face as much a mask as Laurent's.

Selah shut her eyes as he applied a potent-smelling salve to the wound, then bound it up again.

"You shan't be able to go to your father's burial." His tone was low and insistent. "Your wound may well fester. Strict bed rest is called for."

She marveled at his falsity. Here he stood, playing the part of a capable physician, while he was likely the man whose actions had led to her injury?

"I shall return after the burial at James Towne and look again at your wound." With that, he excused himself, leaving her alone with Izella.

Selah met the servant's eyes awash with unshed emotion. Though Izella could not speak, she could feel. Father had taken her in when she'd been irreparably injured by a slave trader, who'd exchanged her for food once they reached Virginia's shores. Was this uppermost in Izella's mind and heart? Reaching out, Selah clasped her workworn hand and squeezed, relieving some of her own festering ache.

Her mother entered in, carrying the finished shroud and a vial of brass pins. Behind her, Widow Brodie held the chin strap used in preparing the body for burial.

Selah touched the woolen cloth, brought it to her face, and dried her tears. *Father . . . Father.* There were not words enough for the ashes inside her. All that solaced was the simplest of God's holy promises.

Precious in the sight of the Lord is the death of His saints.

Widow Brodie settled on the edge of the bed. "My dear, I sense there is much turmoil inside you, which neither my presence nor consolations can mend. I hope Alexander can set things right concerning Watseka. I pray continually for his speedy return, as I do your return to health."

Selah made no reply. She lay back as they went out to prepare her father to lie beneath the heavy ledger stone inscribed to bear witness to his life's work.

Here Lyeth the Body of Ustis Hopewell
One of the Ancient Planters
Cape Merchant, Virginia Colony
Aged 64 Years
Deceased the 19th of August 1634

The next sweltering day wore on feverishly. Xander was not yet at peace leaving Oceanus again, though he was heartened by how readily the lad took to native life. Mattachanna's heart would leap for joy to see her son stripped to buckskins and bow and arrow, running free with Shay and the other youth. He took to the water like a river herring and was soon swimming and diving for shellfish. Already his head and shoulders bore the red paint of the Puccoon root.

By the time he returned home ahead of Christmastide, Oceanus would boast a Powhatan name and speak their tongue. While Xander wanted the son of his heart, his heir, to escape the noose-narrowed English perspective with its damning prejudices and pride, he also wanted him safe from the abominable superstition and mysticism of Powhatan werowances. Free of hatred for the Tassantassas, the English. A tall order for a child of mixed blood.

That night before he would leave the Powhatans, Oceanus's voice came to him in the wee small hours, slurred by sleep. "Father . . ."

"I am right beside you."

"I am happy here. But I shall miss you, Father."

"And I you."

"Sometimes I cannot remember what Mother looked like. I cannot see her in my head. Only in my dreams."

"But you feel her in your heart, aye?"

"In my heart . . ." He yawned and turned over again. "Always."

Blinded by tears as much as the heavy darkness around them, Xander drew the boy nearer into the curve of his large frame.

His desire to hurry and return to Rose-n-Vale ebbed.

The day of Father's burial was fraught with wind and heat lightning. The river roiled and tossed, lapping at both shores with foamy spray, the water not tranquil blue but churlish brown. At dawn Selah rose with the rest of the household, intent on taking the shallop to James Towne. But when she stood too suddenly and nearly fainted, her mother was quick to remind her she was unfit to travel and the physic had forbidden it. Widow Brodie would accompany Candace overland in a wagon driven by Rose-n-Vale's indentures.

Mindful of the solemnity of the day, Selah sat in the parlor, dozing and reading by turns. The mantel clock seemed to stand still. Widow Brodie had brought her a basket of books—fairy tales and Shakespeare's sonnets. These she could manage with one hand. Her sewing remained untouched, the garden with its colorful squash and late corn all but abandoned. Gradually the wind waned by suppertime, a meal mostly untouched. When her mother returned at dusk, she said little.

Selah greeted her with an embrace, alarmed by her washed-out pallor.

"I am going to retire, Daughter. I'll share details about your father's interment later. Please tell Izella I shan't be having supper."

The days following left Selah feeling a prisoner to four walls. Bereft of both Father and Shay, their days assumed a hollow emptiness naught could mend. Visitors had ceased, and Laurent was summoned to another shire to treat an outbreak of some malady there. Izella was at work in the kitchen, and the musketeer was down by the river's edge. Thus the cage of Selah's grief cracked open and sent her tiptoeing out of doors while her mother sat napping near a window, her mending in her lap.

Unable to saddle the mare, she rode without, though it took all her strength to mount the block and gain the horse's broad back. Winded and in pain, she slowly made her way into the sunlit brilliance of the afternoon toward Rose-n-Vale.

Even from a distance, the main house brought her to tears. Xander's absence was keenly felt, especially here. Just this morn Mother had prayed again for his return, a new lament in her tone that bespoke a fear something might have befallen him. What would he say when he learned all that had befallen them? Would he suspect Laurent as she did?

Dashing a hand across her damp cheeks, she rode along the borders of Renick land. Striking was in progress, a great many hands removing the dried leaf onto waiting wagon beds for the sweating and sorting to follow. Riding alone, her arm in a sling, was sure to draw notice or comment. Still, she pressed forward toward Laurent's newly awarded acreage.

Never had she come here. She had no wish to visit it now, yet something drove her past her trepidation.

Oh, Father, you are not coming back. But Lord willing, I can do something about Watseka.

The sight of so many Africans clearing the land of trees and stumps to prepare for future planting was a sore sight. Fieldwork never ceased but for the harshest winter snows. In the distance were a few outbuildings and an unfinished barn. 'Twas said Laurent's previous tobacco in a small plot near James Towne had succumbed to mold, a complete ruination. Was this why he continued to ply his trade as physic?

Tobacco cultivation, even by a crop master's exacting standards, was chancy, always one step away from disaster. Many had failed while Xander succeeded, his Trinidad seed well established, his brand with its bow and arrow above a sheaf of tobacco leaves well known. Yet tobacco was not her preoccupation this day.

Thunder sent a shudder through her. The scent of rain pervaded everything. Lost in thought, she'd failed to heed the weather. She veered into a stand of ash trees, her gaze never settling. Where had Watseka been taken? What if she had been not just taken but killed, her body hidden in the woods and hastily buried? Hatred ran high in Virginia. Selah had tried to shut out the violence of the past, but it was part of their New World tapestry, each bloodred thread vivid and unforgotten. What could she, a lone woman, do?

Never had a separation seemed more an eternity. She didn't just miss Xander. She ached for him. Only he could set things right. He had the clout and cunning that she, a wounded woman with little voice, did not. The longer he delayed, the greater the threat to Watseka. To them all.

As the first warm drops began to fall, so did more tears, intermingling with the rain dripping off her hat brim. Weary of horseback, she slid off the mare and dropped to her knees in the weeds. Too late did she realize she had no mounting block to help her back into the saddle. 'Twould be a long, wet walk home. Cradling her slow-to-heal arm, she prayed yet another broken prayer amid the wood's noises around her.

35

Xander's return to the white world was far faster without Oceanus. Whereas he'd been cautious with the five-year-old by his side—aye, five, as his birthday had just passed—he now pushed himself to his own seasoned limits. Their parting had gone easier than expected, their goodbyes brief if heartfelt. Xander had swept Oceanus up in a bearish embrace, their first, with none of the awkwardness that had marred their affection before.

"You must tell my father I am missing him and will be glad to don English garments and return to merchanting." Shay's infectious grin warmed Xander like the sun on his back. "And kindly tell my mother I miss her beef steak pie. And Selah her teasing."

"I shall." Xander hoisted his knapsack onto one shoulder, considerably lighter than when he'd come.

"Have no fear about Oceanus. I will keep special watch over him. Already he's taken to their ways faster than I when I first came."

Kneeling, Xander prayed over his son just the same. For

protection. Favor. Their future reunion. Oceanus and Shay then waved at him till he stepped beyond their sight.

Though he'd been twice Oceanus's age when he'd gone to live with the Powhatans, he recalled his own internal shift as his English mind grappled with that of the Naturals, his slow shedding of his regard of them as savage and the English superior. Each had much to learn from the other, if they would. Mayhap then the New World would be less fraught with warfare.

The day wore on, endless ruminations keeping him company as the landscape changed and challenged him. He slid down a rocky cliffside that nearly poked holes in his moccasins, then paused to drink from a mossy spring. Thirst slaked, he filled his sweat-stained hat to the brim before returning it to his head. The deluge of cold water did him good. To the east, pewter thunderheads amassed like cannonballs, snuffing the sun and promising rain.

What was Selah doing on so contrary a day?

Thoughts of her quickened his pace. How should he come to her? Just as he was, an unshaven, gut-foundered, overeager rogue? Or by way of Rose-n-Vale and a bath? Impatience and longing discarded the latter. By now, under the watch of McCaskey and his farm managers, Rose-n-Vale's leaf should have been bound into hands and left to sweat beneath barn eaves, the last step before inspection. Surely all was in hand enough for him to go straight to Selah. He'd prove to her she came first, business second.

The next morn he sprinted to the grassy glen where he'd pastured Lancelot. So winded his ribs ached, he leaned into an oak, the soughing wind cooling his brow. Well rested and fortified, his horse nickered at the sight of him. And then, ears snapping forward, head lifting, he gave a distraught snort.

Lightning flared on the horizon, thunder after it. Before Xander could reach him, Lancelot bolted. Biting back an epithet, he watched his hopes gallop away till the animal was but a dot of black on the stormy horizon. Xander trod half a mile more, then the skies tore open and soaked him, the ground beneath his feet no longer dust and brittle leaves but sinking muck.

It would be a long, hard slog to Rose-n-Vale.

Candace stood staring at Selah as if she were a ghost. A very sodden one. "Daughter, I was nigh frantic when I awoke and found you gone!"

"Forgive me, Mother. I didn't mean to stay away so long." Selah entered the house and set her dripping hat on the table, not hanging it beside her father's just inside the door like usual lest she burst into fresh tears. "I've been out looking for Watseka. I shan't rest till I find her."

"But your wound." Her mother's face seemed to have aged doubly overnight. "The physic fears it might fester."

"I would rather it fester than seek his services. 'Twas my wish from the beginning that another be sent for."

"Mine as well, yet the Mount Malady physic has not come."

"No doubt Laurent has contrived to stop him somehow."

"Laurent is too fond of you, I fear." Candace moved toward a window, near tears herself. "I hear someone coming, and it may be him of whom we speak."

Selah removed her muddied shoes and left them behind

as she climbed the stairs to her room. Her steps seemed lined with lead, her spirits little better. Was this grief? This bone-deep weariness, this teeth-on-edge existence? Or was it mostly fear for Watseka and the future?

Her bedchamber was smothering, the curtain motionless. Through the shut window she heard voices alongshore. Laurent's voice carried the clearest. Soon they would dock. He'd obviously returned from seeing patients downriver. Dread pushed against her like a cold wind, buckling her knees till she sank onto the bed's corner. She'd not go looking for Watseka again with him so near.

She began shedding her damp dress with difficulty. Her mother was needed, as she couldn't manage with one arm. Selah called to her from the landing, and the task was soon completed. When Laurent's knock sounded, she prepared to face him. How different Xander's homecoming would be. 'Twas him her heart beat for and her every hope hinged upon.

Nearly lightning struck, Xander sought cover beneath a rocky overhang once he passed from Powhatan territory to the westernmost land now claimed by the English. Here he waited till the storm had spent its strength. Night was encroaching, drawing a murky curtain over the sodden landscape. Once the thunder rumbled away, he pressed on despite the wet and his weariness, every step engulfed by darkness.

Something inexplicable thrust him forward beyond his gnawing need to see Selah again. Every delay now scraped at him like the briars he'd pushed through. If only his horse would return. If only he could continue in the moonless dark.

At last he bedded down, still alert for signs of Lancelot, ready to launch to his feet if he heard the familiar tromping or a neigh. For now, the night insects began a chorus broken only by a whip-poor-will's soulful song. Soon, this too would be silent as the first frost fell across the land. By then, would Selah be at Rose-n-Vale by his side, awaiting Oceanus's return?

All the time they'd lost through misunderstanding and pride . . . Did she now wait for him with the same yearning, the same half-wild eagerness, anticipating a life together that had till now been denied them?

He'd long carried one recollection of her like an old cameo in his pocket. She'd been but a bashful girl. Upon his return from living among the Naturals years before, he'd come into their store, buckskinned and befeathered. She'd mistaken him for an Indian, so long he'd been with them. How dumbfounded she'd been to hear his Scots lilt, her pale brows peaked over rounded eyes, cheeks red as a Pippin apple. Betimes she wore that same flush now.

Selah, I am coming.

On the borders of the westernmost English settlement, Xander breathed in air that was no longer pure but singed his lungs. At first it was only a searing trace. But half a mile more left him fighting for a clean breath. There, in the foothills that afforded a windswept view of east-lying lands—Renick land—his ongoing fear materialized.

Fire.

Though he'd not stopped since first light, all exhaustion deserted him. Abandoning everything weighting him save his essentials, he began a long sprint toward the flaming horizon.

O merciful God.

His barns. The year's harvest.

Smoke, thick and pluming, was almost fragrant, redolent of prime curing tobacco. Enough leaf to fill thousands of exported hogsheads to England. To settle the debts owed his creditors. To ensure the plantation's workings for another year. To fund the passage of more indentures.

Gone.

The leather fire buckets in the main house and all the dependencies were little more than a few drops amid such a firestorm. By now every hand he had would be working to stop the blaze from spreading, if it could be stopped.

Xander ran on toward the worst of the danger, unsure of what awaited him, praying his aunt and everyone within his care was unscathed.

How odd that even in the midst of death, the natural rhythms of life never lessened. One must eat, sleep, pray. Yet so oft of late Selah and her mother had little appetite, sleep allowed them no escape, and their prayers seemed to reach no higher than the ceiling.

Increasingly Selah sought the sanctuary of her room. But here were shadows too. An artificial flower she'd made with Watseka lay atop her dresser, the red paper folds resembling a Rose-n-Vale rose. The window was open, an everlasting reproach. Though she'd shut the door to Shay's bedchamber across the landing, she could not do the same to hers with Watseka still missing.

Lord, be with her. Comfort her. Lead us to her.

A flutter of the curtain caught her eye. In that instant came a sparrow's insistent chirp. Selah all but held her breath. The sparrow chirped again, perhaps looking to land on Watseka's small shoulder. The bittersweet sound brought Selah's hand to her mouth to hold back a sob.

Something more than the bird drew her to the window. The sky, blue as a robin's egg only a quarter of an hour before, was now besmirched. How had she not noticed the acrid air? Her gaze sharpened and turned to disbelief, all her heartache engulfed by a pluming wall of gray coming from the direction of Rose-n-Vale.

"Fire!" Her feet made a great commotion on the stairs as she hurried down them and all but burst into the parlor. "I fear for Rose-n-Vale."

Candace emerged from her bedchamber, blinking sleep from her eyes.

"Mother, can you not smell it?"

Without waiting for her answer, Selah ran toward the stable to fetch the old mare. Behind her, Izella was already at the well, filling buckets in case the fire came near. The musketeer joined her, searching the sky with slack-jawed wonder. He said not a word as Selah rode west.

36

Xander had not expected to encounter Selah amid so much smoke and danger. Renick land was indeed aflame, but just how badly was hard to decipher. Every indenture he had was on his feet, even those he'd left ill, trying to fight the fire with whatever means were at their disposal. When they saw him, he read visible relief on their faces. But there was little he could do against such a hellish wall, where the heat and smoke and wind overcame anything in its path within seconds.

Mounting a pastured horse, he rode by fiery tobacco barns that billowed and threw heat so far it seemed to sear him as he passed. He continued toward the main house to ascertain that his aunt and servants there were unharmed. A bucket brigade had formed at the well, indentures watering the lawn lest cinders threaten the main house. Some men had climbed ladders to the roof, giving it a thorough soaking despite the danger to themselves.

He dismounted behind the garden. Almost immediately, Ruby and Jett bounded to his side. There, through the smoke and melee, he saw Selah and her stricken mother. His aunt stood beside them near the summer kitchen as the flames advanced uphill toward the house. All was summer scorched, so dry that sparks exploded and crackled. Selah grabbed up a blanket and raced downhill toward a burning wheelbarrow as if intent on smothering it.

He followed on foot, overtaking her easily, and wrested the blanket from her arms. His eyes fell on her bandages, a dozen questions clamoring. "You're hurt. From the fire?"

She stared at him through bloodshot eyes, her face so drawn he knew at once something else haunted her. "There's no time for explanations—do what you must to save this place!"

He took her hand when what he wanted was to take her in his arms. "Stay far from the fire, Selah. I'll not see our future go up in smoke like the rest of Rose-n-Vale. There's precious little to be done but attempt to save the house. Keep near my aunt. We shall talk soon enough."

She nodded, turning away, her wounded arm drawn to her chest.

As he worked with the indentures to hedge the encroaching fire, he prayed for the wind to abate. Till it calmed there was no accounting the damage.

"Renick!" McCaskey came alongside him, emptying a bucket on the charred grass at their feet. "Thank heaven yer back. But ye've returned to a maelstrom, this fire being but one of several grievous matters."

Xander emptied his own bucket, and they returned to the bubbling spring that cooled the milk house. "What means you?"

His factor swiped sweat and soot from his brow with a dash of his sleeve. "Ustis Hopewell lies buried, and the Indian girl who lived with them has gone missing. And now this."

The dire details poured forth, making the scorching all around them fade. Ustis dead? The news left him feeling gut shot. And Watseka . . . missing? He stared unseeing as the fire licked closer. What was property—even tobacco—compared to loss of life and a peace child unaccounted for?

Choking on the smoke, Xander drew more water, his mind careening, hardly aware of what he did.

"There's naught to be done but wait," McCaskey told him. "We cannot even ride to inspect the damage without doing further damage to our horses and ourselves."

"Best surround the house then. Wet down the grass. The stables are secured, are they not? The horses removed to safer ground?" Xander listened for answers even though his gaze never settled, probing the smoke and the forms of those who rushed back and forth atop the rise.

"Aye, the horses are secure. Now best be thinking who is to blame."

"Not lightning from the latest storm."

"Nay. 'Twas deliberate. I am sure of it. Someone knew ye were away and wasted no time devising all manner of mischief, starting with the Indian girl."

McCaskey's plain speaking had never been more appreciated. A wave of smoke billowed between them, acrid and menacing.

"Pray for rain," Xander shouted to any near enough to hear. He left McCaskey to oversee the containment of the fire, which was thwarted in its uphill trek from the west by nearly a hundred men. Reeking of smoke and sweat and now blackened with soot, he approached Selah as she stood on the portico with the women.

"Alexander, you look a fright, but never have I been so

glad to see you." His aunt embraced him, her white coif and apron singed with sparks. As if sensing his intent to speak with Selah alone, the other women went inside, coughing all the way.

Placing a hand at Selah's back, he urged her inside as well, into the somewhat cleaner air of his study and an almost hallowed quiet. This was not the homecoming he'd anticipated, and he knew she felt the same. She sat by a closed window without saying a word, eyes on him, hands fisted in her aproned lap.

He groped for composure as he sat beside her. "I have no words regarding your father."

The sheen returned to her eyes. "'Twas no secret he was unwell. But one is never ready when death comes."

He swallowed hard, throat so parched it thinned his voice to a rasp. "Tell me what you believe happened to Watseka. But first, what of your arm?"

The story poured forth, leaving him stunned and disbelieving.

"So, the sheriff and his men refused to form a search party." The ire he'd felt upon first hearing it was barely banked as Selah nodded in confirmation. "For the life of me, with peace hanging in the balance, I cannot fathom why they would not at least attempt one. They blamed it on the harvest? Other matters? Such doesn't ring true to me."

"Nor me."

Xander tried to track the details in his benumbed brain as they talked. "How is your mother?"

"Strong in spirit. To her credit, she carries on, knowing she'll join Father in time."

"He lies at James Towne church?"

At her aye, Xander settled another matter. Without Ustis or another male presence, the women couldn't be at Hopewell Hundred. A musketeer meant little. "You and your household will stay here for the time being. I'll get no sleep tonight, but the thought of you near would hearten me."

"Where is Oceanus?"

"With the Powhatans." Restless, he stood and looked out the window ahead of returning outside. "His grandfather the chief has asked he stay on till late autumn."

"Better he be away at such a tumultuous time. And with Watseka gone . . ." She stood and faced him. "Glad I am Shay is away too. He'll take Father's death hard once he hears, but I'm relieved he was spared the spectacle of him passing that frantic morn."

He put his hands on her shoulders, wanting to hold her close but for his bedraggled state. "Go upstairs to my bedchamber and rest." He half expected her to argue, to exert the will of old. "A maid will bring hot water for a bath."

Visibly relieved, Selah gave him a half smile. "I'm no good to anyone, tired as I am. And now I'm to have a look at your lair."

Despite it all, he chuckled. "Sleep will help you regain the use of your wounded arm. In the meantime, I'm in need of one of Watseka's garments. I trust you have something of hers at the house. Something that would let Jett track her."

"In my upstairs bedchamber, aye."

"I'll send someone, then."

⚜

Up Rose-n-Vale's staircase they went, Widow Brodie leading her to Xander's bedchamber before leaving to retrieve a suitable nightgown. Selah stood on the threshold, breathing in her beloved's very essence, a rich comingling of leather and linen, Castile soap and ambergris. The spacious room was a feast for the eyes. Sumptuous by Virginia standards. A heady moment for one raised in an austere household. The intimacy of staying here was one step away from matrimony. Was that where all this was leading? Why did she feel like naught but a trespasser?

A maid brought buckets of water, filling a copper hip bath hidden behind a paneled leather screen. Selah's wound needed cleaning, so the bath was especially timely, though it required her to grit her teeth to manage it. That done, she rested her arm along the tub's rim and leaned back. As she'd been unable to snatch more than a few hours of sleep since her father's passing, she nearly dozed off in the tepid water. But the frequency of men's shouts, the beat of horses' hooves, and the sudden, shocking drone of rain roused her.

Rain. An answered prayer. She stepped out of the tub, toweled dry, and donned the borrowed nightgown, light-headedness landing her in the nearest chair. When had she last eaten? Before she could recall, there came a knock and Widow Brodie appeared with supper.

"God be praised! Just as I was leaving the summer kitchen, the heavens opened!" She set a sodden tray on a small table. "I shan't complain, and I suppose you shan't either, if the bread be damp."

Selah managed a smile. "All I care about is Xander's safe return home and that Watseka be found."

"Lord willing, we shall soon have her among us." With capable hands Widow Brodie went about pouring steaming dittany tea into a cup, while Selah eyed the bowl of sugared nuts beside a pewter plate heaped with sliced apples, cheese, and buttered bread.

Famished, she bent her head and murmured grace before her hostess even left the room. As she ate, wind-whipped rain buffeted the leaded panes and freshened the air, promising the fire had met its end. At least the house was spared. Though she itched to look out the window before the last of daylight faded, she feared what she would find.

She darted a glance at the canopied bed, turned down and waiting. The masculine chamber seemed more guest room, not even a dust mote in evidence. Without rising from the chair, she began acquainting herself with the contents of this unfamiliar lion's den. Twin tapestried chairs. A bathing cabinet. Silver candlesnuffers atop a low table. A massive wardrobe commanding an entire wall. On the mantel was a pair of porcelain dogs reminiscent of Ruby and Jett, alongside an overflowing vase of August blooms.

From the very garden where he'd kissed her.

Wooziness and weariness collided. Unable to keep herself upright any longer, Selah climbed the bed steps to lie atop not one but five feather ticks. Obviously, Rose-n-Vale's master liked his bedding soft, same as she. Lying back atop a bank of pillows, she was beginning another prayer for Watseka when sleep overtook her.

37

The damage done to his tobacco, fields, and barns was beyond calculating. But the main house was spared, and all within it. None of his indentures had been hurt aside from minor burns. For now, Xander's every thought belonged to Watseka. He set about gathering a search party of determined if worn men just before midnight. He'd not wait till morn.

McCaskey, not wanting to remain behind, insisted he accompany them, leaving the charred plantation to farm managers. Xander assented, looking over the soot-stained, red-eyed lot of them. Only Ruby and Jett seemed up to the task, ever spirited, only settling when Watseka's garments appeared. They sniffed thoughtfully, able to follow a scent on the air and the ground.

"Can they search after a soaking rain?" McCaskey questioned.

"Most assuredly," Xander replied. He had little doubt his hounds, equipped with harness and tracking lines, were up to the arduous task. His only doubt was if Watseka would be found alive. The sobering thought lined his soul with lead.

They began at the Hopewells', the last place Watseka had been that fateful night. As they stood before the empty house, the musketeer gone, there was a hushed, weighty silence as Xander bent his head and prayed for wisdom and direction.

In the light of pitch-pine torches, the hunt began. Xander was tossed between hope and dread with every step they took, by turns yanked and at a standstill as the hounds sniffed and searched, noses to the ground and then the air. Their extraordinary powers were fueled by more silent prayers. The men fanned out around them, some on horseback and others afoot, all eyes on the landscape as they followed the dogs' leading.

Why was he not surprised when the scent led toward Laurent's land?

The closer they came, the darker his thoughts grew. With the physic's dim regard of the Naturals and how snug he was with Governor Harvey, the matter would likely never be investigated even if harm had been done the girl. Just as Xander knew to his core that the Naturals would respond to such a heinous crime against a peace child by retaliating in kind.

Why did he feel even now he was walking toward his own demise? Could evil be felt? Aye, it could, as every fiber of his being urged him to turn back. To retreat. Was he putting the search party in harm's way?

Evildoers shall be cut off: but those that wait upon the Lord, they shall inherit the earth.

Unbidden, the timely Scripture assuaged the ragged parts of him. He halted the party at the boundary stone of Laurent land. "I need but one man with me. The rest of you wait here. Put out your lights or seek cover where you can't be seen."

"I shall shadow you," McCaskey said.

There was no argument. All sensed the risk. Coupled with the utter darkness, even a sliver of moon denied them, the night turned more menacing, even haunting. The dogs, till now stealthy and quiet, reached fever's pitch, straining at their tethers, clearly growing closer to whatever was riveting them.

As McCaskey watched, Xander turned Jett loose.

"Is that wise?" the factor murmured.

"If he finds Watseka, he'll return and lead us to her."

"Aye. But not Ruby?"

"Jett is the keenest tracker and rarely goes wrong." Xander pitched his voice low, eyes on Jett as he disappeared into the darkness. "If we encounter anything threatening in the meantime, Ruby will protect us."

Understanding dawned on the factor's sun-weathered face. He cast a look back at the men fading into the woods to wait, no longer visible save a few flickering lights. Ruby led them on, nose to the ground. Soon they would come to Laurent's dwelling, a rough-hewn blend of wattle and daub with a thatch roof, a far cry from his framed-timber rowhouse in James Towne. But first they passed by the rude hovels of his Africans.

Again, Xander's hackles rose. The stench of their quarters was like a fetid wall. Denied even the simple right of bathing as well as eating? Even a privy pit?

A sudden movement to the left halted them, Ruby poised like a statue. The night watch? A lantern flared some twenty yards distant. Holding it aloft was a gaunt African, eyes huge in his bony face. Fearful. Questioning. One of Laurent's slaves.

"We mean you no harm," Xander reassured him. "'Tis a lost Indian girl we seek."

A burst of gibberish followed, likely Angolan. Slavers oft went to the slave-trade port of Luanda. Laurent's Africans knew little if any English, being so new to Virginia.

"He looks so weak he can barely stand." McCaskey spat into the grass. "God help the Indian girl if she is indeed here."

At their approach the man sank to his knees, his lantern casting pale light on the wet grass. McCaskey pulled him to his feet. Sunken eyes on Xander, the man gestured to his mouth and then his belly.

McCaskey released his hold on him. "I believe he may be your smokehouse thief and believes you've come to whip or hang him."

"Aye. He's too afraid to be merely hungry." Pity overrode Xander's exhaustion. "I simply wish he understood our mission."

The cords in the man's neck constricted as he swallowed. He began backing up as a rustle to their right drew their attention. Jett emerged, attention on Xander. Without a word, Xander stepped in the hound's direction and they started west, still in pitch darkness save the torch, leaving the night watch behind and moving nearer Laurent's own dwelling.

Xander braced himself for the confrontation to come. The pistol at his waist was a dire reminder of the course the night might well take. When Jett gave a short, shrill bark nearer the house and a moving light shone from inside, Xander faced the main doorway, McCaskey just behind him.

Laurent all but spilled out the entrance, whether muddled

by sleep or spirits Xander did not know. The answer was in his aggravated, slightly slurred voice.

"Who goes there? Renick, is that you, you rakefire? Trespassing in the dead of night?"

Xander held fast to Ruby's lead. "Aye, and I'll not leave till I have answers, even if I have to search every inch of your acreage."

Laurent cursed and came nearer. "Is that your foul factor with you? Zounds! A pox on the both of you! I'll have you hauled before all James Towne—"

"Step aside while I search your dwelling." Xander wasted no more time. "As commander of this shire, 'tis my right."

"You'll take no such liberties—" Laurent lunged toward Xander, but McCaskey intervened with a swift shove, cutting him off in midsentence besides.

"Ye muckspout!" McCaskey held the light nearer Laurent. "'Twas ye I saw riding near the Hopewells' the morn the Indian girl disappeared. What say ye to that?"

Laurent lunged again, but McCaskey dodged him with a low laugh. Leaving Ruby behind, Xander grabbed the factor's light and gained the house behind Jett, passing through the door Laurent had left open. Here disorder reigned. Everywhere he looked were piles of goods, the four rooms with their connecting doors more a narrow maze that a heavyset man could not manage.

"Watseka, are you here?" he shouted in Powhatan.

He listened hard as Jett moved around the clutter, leading him upstairs to two chambers. The distaste Xander felt upon entering Laurent's private quarters soured his stomach. The tousled bed. A stash of brandy and a silver brandy bowl. Medicines and bottles. But Watseka was not here, despite

Jett's earlier agitation, though she might well be buried beneath the mess.

Jett gave a low whine near an empty cupboard before leading him downstairs again. Had Watseka been brought here at some point?

Outside, McCaskey and Laurent were exchanging heated words if not blows. Ruby was between them, ready to take down Laurent if the need arose. Laurent, if memory served, disdained dogs.

"I shall report you to the authorities come morning, Renick!" The threat lent no backbone to his slurred words. "No man—not even the shire's commander—has the right to storm another man's home and property without a warrant or assent from the sheriff."

"Do what you will. Till we find Watseka, we shan't stop our search, with or without consent."

"Watseka, is it? Your heathenish bent has no bounds. I've no doubt you are a Powhatan spy."

"Stop yer blabbering." McCaskey spat as Xander began to walk away. "Yer in need of a scold's helm to tame yer blasted tongue, though I'm hoping it's the gallows for ye after what ye've done."

With a roar like a wounded bull, Laurent charged, ramming McCaskey square in his middle. Down the two went in an explosion of punching and grunting, setting the dogs to barking and the rest of the search party running.

At Xander's bidding, two of his heaviest indentures intervened and separated the brawlers. Undaunted, the dogs continued nosing the ground between them till Jett began to sniff Laurent's muddied breeches.

He took a step back, letting loose another curse while

flinging a final warning their way. "If I encounter you further on my land, I shall shoot on sight."

Xander swung round and faced him. "Thus adding a charge of murder to your suspected offense of kidnapping, which caused not only the death of the colony's cape merchant but inflicted a grievous injury to his daughter, my betrothed. And now," he said with growing surety, "fire setting and the malicious destruction of property."

"You can prove nothing!"

"I shall prove everything."

With that, Xander walked away into the night. McCaskey and the search party followed, the chase far from done.

38

Who could sleep on such a night?

Selah pushed aside the bed linens at dawn, looking out Xander's windows with their sweeping views. Smoke writhed from the damp ground in places, no longer a threat but a reminder of all that was lost. In the distance the farthest fields were shadowed in a gray haze along with the remains of ruined barns and outbuildings. Nearer the house it seemed a boundary line had been drawn, blackened grasses on one side, withered, seared grasses on the other.

Rose-n-Vale had been dealt a harsh blow. But the mansion was still standing, and she'd overheard Xander say burned fields reaped hidden benefits. Still, it all paled when compared to recovering Watseka. What had the night's pursuit borne?

Dressing hastily, she went downstairs in yesterday's soiled clothes to find her mother and Nurse Lineboro in the dining room with Widow Brodie. They ceased speaking when she entered, their expressions guarded.

"Has there been any word of Xander?" Selah asked, joining them at table.

"I doubt he'll return without Watseka. Though he is needed here to superintend the damage done the plantation, the child is his chief concern." Widow Brodie reached for a teapot and coffee urn. "To celebrate that these walls are still standing, I've made both Turkish coffee and Chinese tea, which your mother kindly gifted me, compliments of the Dutch East India Company."

"Coffee, please." Selah smiled, feeling more herself than she had since their ordeal began. Xander's homecoming had struck one worry from her list, at least.

"We were just praying for the search party." Candace set down her cup. "Perhaps it's best we stay on here at Rose-n-Vale for now."

In case there's further trouble. Selah heard all her mother did not say. How safe she felt here in company. Cocooned from Laurent especially. Even her grief seemed blunted. She had no wish to return to Hopewell Hundred. Not now. Perhaps not ever.

"Have breakfast, my dear." Widow Brodie had hold of a savory dish. "Cook has made a delicious pumpkin pudding."

Selah took up a spoon, her mind not on the fare before her. "Surely we can be of some help, not just sit waiting. I shan't be a loiter-sack."

"Well said by the future mistress of Rose-n-Vale."

A delicious warmth stole through her. Had Xander made known his intentions? She smiled back at Widow Brodie, noting the nurse's surprise and her mother's undisguised delight.

"I doubt Alexander will want you laboring like an indenture," Widow Brodie said. "Perhaps we can sew men's shirts and breeches, knit stockings. The indentures' quarters are half burned, their belongings with them."

A plan was made to retrieve their sewing notions and other personal belongings from Hopewell Hundred as soon as possible.

"I can't thank you enough for making us all feel so welcome," Candace told her. "Izella seems quite content in the kitchen helping Cook."

"She's an excellent hand in the garden too. We've been needing more servants with Rose-n-Vale expanding. Betimes my nephew forgets the household and just supplies the fields."

"I can certainly join you making garments," Nurse Lineboro said. "Earn my bed and board till I settle elsewhere. Master Renick no longer needs my services, especially with Oceanus gone over to the Naturals."

"Have you made plans to return to Britain?" Widow Brodie was good at ferreting out most anything. "Or is Virginia more to your liking than when you arrived?"

"I'm still undecided." She gave a small, mysterious smile. "I shall ponder it more thoroughly while I ply my needle."

Selah breakfasted, listening as they spoke at length of the fire's devastation. The sun was up, streaming through the windows like a benevolent guest. It cast the room in a palette of yellows, making it seem their hard circumstances were naught but a bad dream. If only Father were here—and Shay and Watseka. If only the fire had never happened. Their thoughts could be happily occupied with other things, like a wedding—

A sudden barking sent Widow Brodie to a window, where she blinked at the glorious light. "The search party has returned at last."

Abandoning her breakfast, Selah passed into the hall, already feeling at home in the house. A dozen questions clamored, though no doubt she'd have her answers when she first saw Xander's face.

He came in the back door, leaving Jett and Ruby outside. He was red-eyed and unshaven, sweat- and soot stained from his collar to his boots, his eyes telling a long story, though he said nary a word. Never had she seen him so spent. She daren't ask him anything.

She laid her head upon his wrinkled shirt as her good arm stole about his waist. "Promise me you won't go out again till you've eaten and slept."

A prolonged pause. His bristled jaw rested atop her coif. "Marry me, Selah."

'Twas the last thing she expected to hear. Her answer was no less startling. "I will, Xander. Today, if you like."

He looked down at her. A smile blurred his exhausted edges. Just a ghost of a smile, but it left him looking more like the handsome man she loved.

"You see, the hospitality of the house is bursting. I've nowhere to put you. I've run out of room." He studied her, all levity aside. "So we'd best get the deed done. Today, aye."

"I heard the itinerant pastor's voice but a few moments ago." She looked toward the half-open door. "Surely he'd pause to perform a wedding of only a few minutes' making."

He drew her close again. "Promise me you'll wear your purple gown. The one I'm partial to."

"'Tis at Hopewell Hundred and needs sent for." She wouldn't say *home*. Home was here. Nothing mattered so much as now. With circumstances as they were, they had no promise of tomorrow.

"I don't want you to go alone, nor your mother, not without an escort. I'll send a wagon with you to bring all that is needed back here as well."

"We can go right away. The day's young." She looked into his eyes with certainty. "And what a glorious day it is for a wedding."

He lifted her hand and kissed the back of it. "But first a word, aye?"

He led her back toward the feminine voices in the dining room. All quieted when they stood before the three women still at table.

"I've no good news but our nuptials." He gave Selah a sidelong smile, their fingers intertwined. "We'd like to be married today with little ado save a simple wedding supper."

Widow Brodie clasped her hands together. "Just the tidings we need to weather such a turbulent time."

"But mustn't the banns be read? Three Sundays in a row?" Nurse Lineboro's face darkened as she looked to Selah. "And are you not in mourning?"

"Mourning is seldom observed in Virginia," Xander told her. "Here in the outer parishes, a clerk issues a license, and if one is underage, parental consent ends the matter."

"Of which I freely give, though you have no need of it." Candace rose from the table, looking considerably cheered. "Quite fortuitous that both preacher and clerk comprise the search party."

Xander nodded. "Needs be we wed in the shire's chapel rather than here. A New World custom I heartily approve of."

"With pleasure." Selah looked at him, feeling a dizzying pull to get it done. In the last few days, waiting had seemed frivolous when life and death played out around them. "Best hasten to lay hold of my gown."

"A walk in the sunshine shall do us good." Candace moved toward the door. "I'll fetch my hat."

"And I shall consult Cook about the wedding supper." Widow Brodie was the first to leave, smiling all the while.

By six o'clock in the evening, the chapel stood tranquil, doors open to catch the slightest breeze. Only a scant few gathered, Xander's houseguests foremost. Though marriages in the forenoon were most common, an evening wedding was not amiss. Selah truly felt like a bride in the purple gown, her hair decorated with Rose-n-Vale's white roses, more than happy to don a married coif. The pearl necklace Xander had given her as a wedding gift now rested upon her bodice, Watseka's beads beneath. His tender gaze told her she was beautiful. To her great relief, he'd finally slept and bathed, his trimmed beard and best suit of clothes wooing her as much as his steady gaze.

Even if the circumstances they now found themselves in left them on tenterhooks, they joyfully entered into the sacred moment and pledged themselves to each other before God.

". . . keep her, to love and entreat her in all things according to the duty of a faithful husband, forsaking all others during her life; to live in holy conversation with her, keeping faith and troth in all points . . ."

The vow saying paused as Xander pulled something from his pocket. A posy ring? Pleasure overrode her surprise as he placed it on the third finger of her left hand. Decorated with quartz crystal, the gold band glittered in the shadows. Was something inscribed within the band's circle?

Xander leaned in and whispered in her ear, "Time shall tell I love thee well."

Any remaining doubts she'd had about his devotion faded to the furthest reaches.

Hands clasped, they faced the small gathering as husband and wife. Clapping and fiddling accompanied them on their return to Rose-n-Vale as a tenant played the traditional wedding tune "Black and Grey." Supper was already laid on the dining room table, a bounteous offering of late summer's best, every dish and platter laden with seafood and garden fare, even a bride's cake and groom's cake. Izella and the maid wove in and out of the full dining room, replenishing cups and empty dishes.

Selah fought back tears as a toast was made by her mother in her father's stead. But sorrowful as they were that Ustis and Shay and Watseka were not among them, they made the most of the occasion. For just a few sweet hours, the darkness of the present was swept into a shadowed corner. In the new wing still bare of furniture save a few hastily assembled benches and chairs, Selah and Xander led a dance, then bade the festivities continue without them.

Slowly they climbed the stairs while the fiddling continued below. On the threshold of their bedchamber, he swept her off her feet into his hard arms and carried her in with a defiant spring in his step, the trill of her laugh following.

39

Well before first light they awoke. Though the sun had not yet tiptoed into the room, a new day lay ahead, a blank canvas waiting to be filled by them both. Xander propped himself up on one elbow and slowly wound a tendril of his bride's fair hair around one callused finger.

"Selah . . . Hopewell . . . Renick." A smile of genuine joy broke over his face. "Mistress of Rose-n-Vale."

"Good morning, Husband." She yawned behind her hand. "Such feels right. Content." She kissed him, long and lingeringly, growing used to the brush of his beard. "If I can make you forget your troubles for just one night, I am a happy woman."

"'Tis not as I would have it, our beginning."

"But we are together, and that is all that matters." Selah kissed him again, longing to remove the regret in his gaze, the pressing cares of the coming day. "Our pleasures are doubled, our griefs halved."

"Aye." Xander lay back, one sinewy arm behind his head. "How shall you spend your first day as mistress?"

"Drinking cassina. Eating leftover bride's cake." Pondering

all the possibilities, she laid her head upon his bare shoulder. "Have devotions with Mother in the parlor. Consult Cook as to the bill of fare."

"Dinner?"

"Of course. What are your favorite dishes?"

"Anything that is set before me. With gratitude. I am ever mindful of the starving time not so long ago."

"A fine ham, perhaps."

He turned his head and kissed her temple. "The smokehouse was robbed, remember."

"Oh . . . I do recall your aunt lamenting that. Sturgeon, then. I shall pick fresh flowers for the table. Examine your garments and see what needs mending or making. Meet with the new maids and learn their names." She studied his thoughtful profile. "How do you spend your days?"

"I usually begin with a routine ride to all four corners of the plantation." Releasing her, he swung his legs over the side of the bed and reached for his shirt. "Dinner. Desk work. Fieldwork. Supper. Sit upon the portico." He sent a roguish grin her way. "Adore my wife."

She flushed and pushed back the covers, retrieving her purple gown. "I shall wear my bridal attire all day to remind you."

"I assure you that shan't be necessary." He began dressing in the fading dark. "Needs be I remind *you* to stay close to the house."

Her joy slipped a notch. He was so careful with her. She sensed all that weighted him, all he did not say.

"I don't mean to alarm you, Selah. Just make you somewhat wary."

"I understand."

"I've sent word to Mount Malady for the physic to see to your wound."

Her arm, healing slowly, was still very tender but not festering, God be praised.

A smile returned to his voice. "But nothing needs doing before our first cup of cassina together, aye?"

Twin maids. How was she to tell them apart?

Giggling, they stood before Selah after giving her a clumsy, unnecessary curtsy. Tabitha and Clarity. A third maid, Primrose, had been at Rose-n-Vale for a few months, the twins but a fortnight. All indentured orphans. Widow Brodie said the trio needed training, a taming of their high-spiritedness. Selah simply saw unschooled girls eager to please, who'd eaten too much wedding cake and drunk too much punch the night before.

"We shall meet together every morn in the new parlor to discuss what needs doing." Selah reached out and straightened Clarity's coif with a smile. "You can request certain duties if you like. Widow Brodie says Primrose is fond of the milk house."

"Jings, mistress!" Primrose's Scots speech unfurled. "I'd blister otherwise in this infernal heat! It's so verra cool within those stone walls, I fancy myself a kelpie."

Kelpie? Selah paused. She'd ask Xander what that might be.

"You can tend to the morning's milking and churning, though any cheese making won't be had till the weather cools." Her gaze narrowed to the twins. "I heard you sisters are skilled at housework. For now, there is plenty of that to be done after last night's revelry. I'll be in the garden should you need me."

They betook themselves to their respective places in a flurry of petticoats. Selah passed onto the portico, where her mother was sewing with Nurse Lineboro, a basket of brown cloth between them. Xander's aunt was in the kitchen with Cook and Izella amid a banging of pots and pans. The last thing she wanted was to usurp the older woman's authority, so she stayed clear of the kitchen and made a beeline for the kitchen garden.

But what she really wanted to do was hunt for Watseka.

Anything else seemed foolish. Frivolous. Why could she not rest in the knowledge that Xander had taken Jett and gone out with another search party right after breakfast, leaving Ruby behind as watchdog? Even now the russet giant looked at her moodily from her tethering beneath an oak's spreading shade.

Bending her mind to her task, Selah took stock of what needed harvesting in the heat-scorched garden. A great many English gourds, melons, and cabbages sprawled at her feet. Herbs ran riot, mingling with flowers and lettuces gone to seed. A soot-blackened kitchen wall supported sprawling currants and gooseberries. No rhyme or reason to this garden patch. Might she and her mother make better use of it in time?

Her gaze rose. Over the paling fence stretched a field of maize, beans, and pumpkins as far as the eye could see. A few indentures' wives were already at work there. She dipped a bucket into a rain barrel and began watering, thoughts of her first night as mistress beneath Rose-n-Vale's roof warming her as much as the sun upon her back. She nevertheless kept to her humble task, knowing she'd not be content to sit still on the portico like the other women.

While she watered the thirsty soil, she prayed. That Watseka would be found. That Xander and the search party would be safe. That Shay and Oceanus would return to them sooner rather than later.

Slowly a dark thought wrapped cold tentacles around her and nearly stopped her in her tracks. If Watseka was not found, or was found harmed, then they had more than the Powhatans' coming down on them to contend with. What if the Indians refused to return Shay and Oceanus? Or did them harm?

Xander released the search party and stood alone at the Hopewells'. How quickly everything went to seed when a place was vacated. After going through the empty house again, including the bedchamber that had been Watseka's, he passed out of doors to sit in the arbor's shade. Jett lay beside him, panting after covering a vast amount of territory in a few hours.

To no avail.

Now late afternoon, the sun sank behind a drift of clouds on the horizon that hinted of rain. All was quiet save a lone sparrow perched atop a wending honeysuckle vine, its piercing trills sending a dart of sorrow through him.

Watseka, where can you be?

He could not ignore the slight possibility the child had run off, rejoined her people. If so, they were expending a great deal of time and worry needlessly. But neither could he return to the Powhatans yet, not while his lands lay in ruins and the fire setter was free. Not till he'd left no stone unturned regarding Watseka's whereabouts here.

He took a breath, expelling the turmoil within, only to take it back up again. If the chief's granddaughter was not found or had been harmed, woe be to the English. The Powhatans' wrath had been triggered by far lesser matters. Hindsight buffeted Xander with regret. Had he but refused Opechancanough's request to keep Oceanus till the autumn . . . Had he but known about Ustis's death and insisted Shay return to the Hopewells . . . As it was, more than Watseka's life was now in jeopardy.

The sparrow piped another shattering song into the stillness. Xander pulled himself to his feet and froze. The nicker of a horse drew his attention to the near woods as Jett gave a low growl.

A trespasser?

With a whispered caution to Jett and a tug on his halter, Xander quickly led him out of sight behind the main house. In seconds, Laurent rode into the courtyard atop a sleek sorrel horse Xander had never seen. He turned toward the stable and rode inside. Xander heard the thud of his boots hitting the ground as he dismounted.

Long minutes passed. Xander remained hidden, awaiting Laurent's next move. Thus far he was keeping to the stable.

What was afoot?

Selah smoothed her new coif with its lace edge and stepped onto the portico in anticipation of Xander's homecoming. Her first day at Rose-n-Vale left her glad but guarded. But for Watseka, she would have reveled in her tasks, her new surroundings. Widow Brodie was a thorough teacher, acquainting her with the dependencies and their workings as well as every corner and crevice of the main house itself. She confessed herself only too glad to give the burden of management to Selah, as she hadn't the strength of years past. She much preferred to sit with Candace, sewing and conversing, for they had much in common at their age and station in life.

"Come, Daughter, and join us." Candace set aside the linen shirt she was making and gestured to a chair. "You've been on your feet all day."

Selah obliged, taking in the river and landscape of late afternoon. Each hour gave Rose-n-Vale a different glow, a different mood. Now in the throes of midday, all was dry and sweltering, a bit testy.

"I've not seen Nurse Lineboro for several hours." Widow Brodie looked up from her knitting. "'Tis not like her to be away so long."

"Nurse has no charge to tend," Selah answered, taking a cup of leftover wedding punch from the tray Izella brought. "Factor McCaskey mentioned he's teaching her to ride."

"Oh? I didn't think she cared much for horses." Candace took her own cup. "But I suppose we're all at loose ends, what with the fire and Oceanus being away."

"Rather bored, she is. But the factor can hardly spare the time for riding lessons, can he?" Widow Brodie's face fell. "Not with so much rebuilding going on with the barns and the like. And then the ongoing search for Watseka."

"I suppose everyone needs a reprieve from their labors." Candace brightened. "Might another romantic attachment be at hand beneath our very noses?"

"Nonsense!" Widow Brodie shook her head. "Not between the nurse and factor, surely, though I did spy her dancing with Helion Laurent at the frolic more than once."

Selah listened without comment. She'd seen the same, but the physic had danced with several women that night, just not herself. As for the factor and Electa Lineboro, Selah had sensed a softening of late in the nurse's regard of him. But with all that was happening, she'd not given it much thought.

"Her tenure here is at an end." Though Widow Brodie kept her tone light, Selah knew she'd had several run-ins with the nurse. "Alexander has sent for a Scots tutor. His arrival should coincide with Oceanus's return from the Powhatans."

"You showed me the schoolroom this morning, down the north lane nearest the spinning house." Selah's mental map was quickly taking shape. Rose-n-Vale was expanding before their very eyes.

"The tutor's quarters are upstairs. Quite cozy and smelling of sawdust, 'tis so new. Alexander regrets his own lack of learning as a boy, being largely self-taught."

"Such a self-made man has little need of books, surely, and even less time to read them," Candace replied.

"I believe the library is changing for Oceanus's benefit."

"I can attest to that." Selah recalled her surprise as she'd unpacked two crates of books but an hour ago. "The shelves now bear primers, fairy tales, and fables."

"How glad I'll be to have the boy back again." Widow Brodie's gaze settled on Selah. "And I trust he shall soon have a brother or sister. Twins run in the Renick family, did Alexander tell you?"

Selah's eyes rounded. Twins? "He did not. Perhaps he wants

to surprise me. Thankfully, I have many hands to help with any newborns, including yours and Mother's."

"How delighted your father would have been." Candace continued to smile despite the sheen in her eyes. "Perhaps, if it's a boy, you shall name him Ustis."

"Don't forget the cradle in the attic." Widow Brodie was equally delighted. "With the new wing we have plenty of room. Surely Shay shall stay on as well rather than return to Hopewell Hundred. He is but a boy yet, after all."

"His father's death shall make a man of him." Candace lost her easy air. "Xander spoke of sending word for him to return to us. But he won't be told the sad news till he gets here. We shall tell him."

Wise, that. No need to burden Shay on the long journey back to them. Let him learn the hard facts surrounded by their love and care. *Lord, let it be soon.* Selah's gaze strayed beyond the portico again, wishing Xander back, restless when he was away. The taint of smoke still hung in the air, the heavy odor of burned land surrounding them. Faint hoofbeats grew louder. Her heart rose like a lark in anticipation.

"How is your arm, my dear?" Widow Brodie inquired. "I overheard Alexander say to expect the physic from Mount Malady. Might that be him now?"

Her answer came as the factor rounded the house on a borrowed mount. He reined in before the portico. "Good day, ladies."

Widow Brodie asked the obvious. "Where on earth is Nurse Lineboro?"

"Comfortable enough in the saddle that she's enjoying a jaunt on her own while I return to work here. Namely to rebuild the main tobacco barn."

"We shan't detain you, then."

Without another word he cantered down the lane past the dependencies to the fields beyond.

"Fancy that, she's out on her own. I expect my nephew to ride in next. 'Tis the hour he usually appears."

They fell quiet for a time, each lost in thought, Selah adjusting to the notion of twins. Oceanus would make a fine big brother no matter what the Almighty sent them. In the meantime, she'd seek out the cradle in the attic, see if it was big enough for two babes. Begin sewing tiny garments and pray for a babe to fill them.

They'd not spoken of Watseka or which room might be hers. The omission bespoke a lack of confidence in her recovery, of hopelessness gaining the upper hand. Selah stared down at her unfinished punch, puzzling out where to house Shay. But for the moment the soreness in her heart was so acute she couldn't grab hold of the joy before her.

40

This had been Selah's dream of many months. Watching the sunset from Rose-n-Vale's portico with Xander by her side. Breathing in the sights and sounds of the estate as it settled. The faint whiff of smoke from the summer kitchen. The lowing of a milk cow in the pasture. The doves in their nest beneath the portico eave. Tonight the sunset was a spectacular firestorm of russets and gold, heralding the coming autumn.

But where exactly was her husband?

She journeyed down the lane to look for him, past the dependencies where maids and stable hands milled about in the twilight, Ruby and Jett at her side. The dogs seemed to be leading, she merely following. Did they know where their master was? Xander had left after supper to meet with a party of indentures who'd returned from searching for Watseka. But that was two hours ago.

Down the hill she went toward the smallest tobacco barn. It sat beside a scorched field, the only barn unscathed by the blaze. There she found him, an alarming sight with his rapier, fencing with an imaginary opponent. She entered quietly behind him and pressed her back against the barn's rough wood. The dogs, ever obedient except when it came to Widow Brodie, sat on their haunches and watched him too.

On guard. Advance. Lunge. Parry.

For being tall, he was remarkably quick on his feet. She all but shivered at the whistle of the sword as it sliced the air. Her father had spoken of Xander's skill. He'd been trained by a fencing master from the first supply in his youth. She'd come across books by fencing masters in his study. But she'd not thought to see him at practice. It seemed to bode ill.

He turned and walked toward her. The rapier glinted in the fading light.

"You are very skilled," she said, a bit awed.

"And you are very biased." He sheathed his weapon and cupped her elbow, leading her out into fresh air.

"Why have you returned to fencing?"

"I am rusty as an old sword." His smile was thin. "And I promised to teach Oceanus upon his return home."

Was that all? She prayed so. She discarded the worry as they walked uphill to the house. "'Tis been my dream to watch the sunset with you . . . and the dogs."

"You are a long-suffering woman." He glanced at the dogs fondly as they jockeyed for position beside him. "Little wonder they adore you."

They stepped onto the portico, two chairs awaiting them. The rest of the household was abed. Lost in the luxury of aloneness, Selah took a seat, savoring the remaining sunset as it melted onto the horizon.

He reached for her hand. "Now seems the time to ask you if a move to the new wing would be favorable. Our present bedchamber would become your mother's. The dormer room the nurse occupies would be Shay's."

"A wonderful plan." The very thought cheered her. "I overheard Factor McCaskey say he'll be sailing with your first tobacco shipment. I thought he and the nurse might make a match. He seems fond of her and has openly teased her about returning to Scotland with him."

He looked toward the river all ashimmer with the last of daylight. "Which brings me to another matter that will likely make you blush."

She returned her gaze to him, overwarm already.

"'Twould seem Hopewell Hundred has become a trysting place. I was there earlier today after another search when Laurent appeared and then Nurse Lineboro."

Her sharp intake of breath caused Ruby to raise her head, looking sleepy-eyed. "They are . . . a couple?"

"I didn't stay to find out. But aye, they did meet. Thankfully I remained out of sight, though Jett did growl when Laurent first appeared."

"Oh, Xander . . ." Selah kept her voice to a whisper, though she hardly knew what to say. "What a riddle this is."

"Keep the matter between us. We shall bide our time and see how it plays out. That they are hand in glove is now apparent, but we cannot ken what that signifies. Not yet."

"Regarding Watscka, you mean. And the firing of your property."

"Aye. Thus far their trespassing at Hopewell Hundred is all we have."

"Earlier today McCaskey returned alone, saying he'd given the nurse a riding lesson and she chose to continue without him. She must have met up with Laurent next." She looked at him, knowing he was far more schooled to worldly ways than she. "Might it be a love triangle?"

"I suspect. Though I believe the nurse is the only one aware of it. I'd wager both McCaskey and Laurent are in the dark."

"She's in a hard place. A woman alone." Should they not give her the benefit of the doubt? "She seems . . . shrewd. Discontent. Perhaps she's simply undecided which suitor to choose."

"What a rosy picture you paint." Their eyes met, his skeptical. "Though I don't want to belittle her without cause, I feel to my marrow there's more afoot."

Selah squeezed his hand. "I'll keep my eyes and ears open and my mouth shut."

They sat in silence for a time. Fireflies winged around them, tiny lights in the gloaming. Thankful as she was for this shallow moment of tranquility, all she wanted was an end to this uncertainty, the endless searches and speculations.

Turning her hand over, he kissed her palm. "For now, why not do a little trysting of our own?"

She smiled, only too glad to return to the matter of their honeymoon. "Is it true there are twins in your family?"

With a wink, he stood, bringing her to her feet. "Let's find out."

For the present, all else was forgotten.

Early the next morn a wagon was sent to Hopewell Hundred to bring beloved belongings and furnishings to Rose-n-Vale. Indentures roamed the main house, carrying furniture up and down stairs, turning all topsy-turvy, and the maids scurried about with feather dusters. Pulled a dozen different directions, Selah was happy to supervise her and Xander's nest in the new wing. As there were a great many more windows, she rejoiced. Drapes were hung, sofas and chairs and tables rearranged in the blue-and-white parlor adjoining their first-floor bedchamber.

All the while her mind remained on the possible love triangle. Standing on a stool, hanging a framed piece of art, she paid little attention when a maid said, "Mistress Renick, would you like this small clock on the mantel or here on this side table?"

Stepping off the stool, still trying to grow accustomed to her new name, Selah said, "On the table, please. I believe Master Renick wants the Venetian mirror hung over the mantel."

Beyond the window glass came a flurry of movement in the peach orchard. Selah paused as the maids went out again to bring more items from upstairs. Was that . . . the nurse? She moved toward the window, keeping to one side so she wouldn't be seen.

There, in the heart of the orchard, stood Electa Lineboro with McCaskey. Her arms were raised as if to strike him, but his hands encircled her wrists, preventing it. She tried to pull free, but he held fast, easily overpowering her. Anger stiffened his every move, and though she fought back, even kicking him in the shin, he pulled her behind a fully leafed tree, hiding them both from view.

Was she hurt? In danger? Selah hurried out a side door and all but ran toward the peach trees, then drew up just as abruptly. Down one particularly leafy row the nurse and factor were locked in a heated embrace, as if their fighting of minutes before was naught but playacting.

Stunned, feeling hoodwinked, Selah backtracked to the main house on fast feet, nearly colliding with Widow Brodie as she entered the hall.

Exasperation showed on her aged face. "Last night a thief got into the henhouse. We've no eggs this day. And Cook says two prized Nankin chickens are missing."

"The same thief that robbed the smokehouse, perhaps."

"'Twould seem so."

"But the dogs—"

"Out with a search party, the both of them. Alexander takes nary a precaution, not even a simple padlock on the smokehouse door. Why, I cannot fathom. Betimes I think an armed guard is needed for all this trouble of late."

"Glad I am we've brought our poultry from Hopewell Hundred." Selah gestured toward the new wing to distract her. "Come see all we've done this day."

Despite Selah's satisfaction at all they'd accomplished, she could not wash her mind of what she'd stumbled upon in the orchard. Yet what did it signify? Nothing more nefarious than a heated, stolen kiss? Had Nurse Lineboro shifted her affections from physic to factor?

When another search party turned up empty-handed in late afternoon, Selah received the news with spirits that could sink no further. Her memories of Watseka were still keen, but she feared in time they would wane like the passing of seasons, once bright but eventually turning to rust. Her ready, toothless smile. Her joyful laugh. How she'd lit up their home with her irrepressible, pint-sized self.

Lord, wilt Thou not help?

Every hour lost seemed another sad, delayed answer. Still, Selah met Xander at the riverfront door before supper with a brave face, vowing to welcome him home with a smile despite what the day dealt them.

Xander freshened up at the washstand, changed into a new linen shirt, and looked approvingly at the way Selah had arranged their bed and furnishings. Though he was little concerned with such matters, he admired her feminine touch. The tang of sawdust lingered, though all had been swept up and a colorful Persian carpet covered the pine floor. When he stepped into the adjoining parlor where she waited, ready to escort her to the dining room, she surprised him yet again.

"We'll dine alone here tonight."

His shoulders eased. Did she ken he craved time with her apart from the others? Surely she shared that same desire. 'Twas their honeymoon, after all.

Twin tapers shone gentle light upon a small supper table dressed with dishes he'd not seen before. From Hopewell Hundred, likely.

"I could get used to this." He sat, looking across at her as she poured him applejack. Her wedding ring shone gold on her slender hand. She wore a pale blue gown he liked nearly as much as her purple one. "So, tell me, why *are* we alone?"

She smiled, allaying his concern. "Nurse Lineboro pled a headache and is in her room. Mother and your aunt claim the heat has stolen their appetite."

He nodded. "And McCaskey is laboring till dark with the indentures on another barn."

The parlor door opened, and Izella came in on quiet feet, to serve them chicken fricassee left from midday dinner, stewed pumpkin, and corncakes. Selah kindly waited till he'd finished eating to say, "I'm sorry to report a thief has struck the henhouse."

He swallowed the news along with his supper. "Mayhap a fox."

"Your aunt believes 'tis no animal. She wanted me to ask you about tethering Ruby and Jett to both the smokehouse and henhouse."

"Nay."

She looked at him, inquiring.

"I've reason enough to refuse." His eyes held her own, seeking understanding. "Just trust me."

"Then I shall say no more about it." Taking up a spoon, she sampled dessert. "Izella has been putting up brandied peaches for days. 'Twas Father's favorite. Cook told me you're partial to fresh ones, so I picked some for supper."

"You were in the orchard?"

"Twice." She took another bite. "First to gather fruit this morn and then again this afternoon to find Nurse Lineboro and McCaskey there."

"And they weren't picking peaches." Beneath his wry gaze her skin pinked. "Did they see you?"

"Nay, they were blinded by a blaze of ardor."

Despite the circumstance, he chuckled. Abandoning his half-eaten supper, he lit the pipe she'd brought him and looked out the nearest window to the orchard. A west wind riffled the heavily leafed branches, sending ripe fruit to the ground. Those trees would be bare once autumn's tumultuous winds blew.

She set down her spoon. "Tell me about today's search."

"'Twas the most promising by far." He inhaled, enveloped in a fragrant cloud. "And the most frustrating. We combed all of Hopewell Hundred again, to no avail. Given Laurent was in James Towne, or 'twas said, we took the liberty of exploring the far west corner of his plantation that is heavily wooded."

He paused and she looked at him, expectant, eyes full of heartache and hope.

"Jett led us to a heavily traveled thicket. A few chicken bones and eggshells were scattered about."

"What?" Her eyes rounded. He read her thoughts. The thief?

"It might be naught but a passing vagabond. The ground bore an imprint—some sort of crate or container."

"Was it gone? Had it been moved, perhaps?"

"Dragged through the dirt and brush, as best we could ascertain. It might signify nothing, but . . ."

She looked as perplexed as he felt. Tears shone in her eyes but remained unshed. "I think of little else but Watseka, even more than Father. Questions torment me continually. Is she hurt? Sick? If we don't find her, what then?"

"You don't believe she's run away and rejoined her people."

She gave a vehement shake of her head. "I believe she was happy here. We did all we could to make her comfortable. Given the commotion that I heard outside the exact hour she went missing, I suspect foul play."

"I agree." Pensive, he drew on his pipe a long moment. "As I pray and search, I sense she is still alive. That she is not far."

"You've looked for days now. Will you keep up the hunt?"

"Until I find her, aye."

"I worry about you encountering Laurent again. He was in such an uproar when you searched his house. I do wish we knew why he met with Nurse Lineboro at Hopewell Hundred."

"After which she returned to Rose-n-Vale for an orchard

tryst with McCaskey. The plot does thicken." He set down his pipe, of no more mind to smoke than to eat. "We will be vigilant and watchful. Even eavesdrop if we must. McCaskey will soon take his leave. I'll press the nurse on her plans if only to hasten her departure. I won't abide any double-handedness beneath my roof."

41

A sennight passed as Selah adjusted to her new role. This morn, she was in the milk house, straining the pails Primrose had brought her from the dawn milking. Soon the shelves bore a great many shallow, glazed earthenware dishes as the milk cooled and the cream rose. 'Twas one of Selah's old tasks she was loath to let go of, if for no other reason than the milk house reminded her of church. Here in the shaded, almost hallowed shadows she poured out her heart along with the milk.

Gone was the stilted formality of past prayers. Out of a sense of urgency and growing heartache, she began calling more familiarly on the God who had made her. No doubt she'd be branded a heretic in James Towne, talking to the Almighty as if He were not only her heavenly Father but her friend.

Lord, each day of waiting seems to take Watseka further away from us. She is so small. The nights will soon grow cold. Please hedge her from all harm. Bolster her spirits. Help us leave no stone unturned. Deliver us from the snare of the fowler and from the noisome pestilence. Help us be not afraid of the terror by night nor the arrow that flieth by day. And let no harm befall Oceanus and Shay. Return them to us in Thy perfect timing—

"Mistress Renick."

She spun around, nearly upsetting a dish. Shay stood in the doorway. Taller. Leaner. All the boyish lines that once defined him were missing, his once irregular features more in harmony. Stepping inside and closing the door lest flies or dust disturb the whitewashed confines, he caught her up in a bearish embrace.

"There, Sister. Nothing to cry about."

How like Father he felt and sounded. How thankful she was to have him back. She dashed a hand across her damp eyes. "But how did you come to be here? Xander said nothing to us."

"He relayed word to Meihtawk to escort me home. The chief seemed sorry to see me leave but understood that Xander's summons was not to be taken lightly." Releasing her, he ran a hand over his hairless left scalp. "I shed my skins lest you fear I was a Powhatan. But there's no help for my hair, shaved with a sharp shell to not encumber my bowing."

"'Twill grow back like a proper Englishman, I suppose."

"In time."

She drank in his sheepish grin at her scrutiny, his beloved presence a tonic for her heart and soul. And then solemnity rushed in.

"Mother just told me about Father. But I'm most concerned about you." He looked askance at her bandaged arm, which she waved to reassure him. "So much has happened. And now Watseka is gone."

"But not to her people."

"I heard no word of it, nay, nor saw any sign of her."

354

She hugged him again, breathing in the smoky, sweat-stained scent of his former English clothes, the breeches too short. Where he'd once come up to her chin, he was now eye level. "We must put away any sadness for now and rejoice in your homecoming."

"Homecoming, aye." The wry look he gave her was so like Father she wanted to both laugh and cry. "Fancy returning to find your sister wed, your father dead, and your new abode Rose-n-Vale."

"Hopewell Hundred is yours to do with as you wish."

"I've given it little thought till now."

"How fares Oceanus?"

"Reveling in being a son of the forest. His mother is strong in him, and he took to their ways like a duck to water."

"Glad I am to hear it. And you? Are you . . . sorry to return?" She'd oft wondered if he would be and now held her breath for his answer.

His smile swept away all doubt. "Nay. I was oft homesick. Their ways are not our ways. I'm needed here to help with the rebuilding, comfort Mother, and pester you as usual."

At a raised voice outside, they traded the cool shadows for the September sun. Widow Brodie stood on the portico, waving them inside.

Shay's gaze trailed the tray Izella carried across the sun-scorched lawn from the kitchen house. "I'm much changed, Sister. But ravenous as always."

At nightfall, they all gathered in the new blue parlor. Though the mood was subdued given their circumstances, Selah felt especially grateful that Xander had quietly reunited them with her brother. Shay's return seemed to cheer him. He embraced her brother heartily more than once, even exchanging a few words in Powhatan. Near at hand sat Meihtawk, having been alone with Xander in his study the long afternoon.

As the conversation ebbed and flowed, Selah kept a discreet eye on McCaskey and Nurse Lineboro playing a game of loo at a corner table. Was she still meeting secretly with Helion Laurent?

The factor, brash and less than genteel, was quite a contrast to the physic's carefully honed artifice. And the nurse? Selah reckoned someone so dour had no romantic designs, but appearances were deceptive. Something told her at least one of the trio knew Watseka's whereabouts and were wiser than the rest of them about so paramount a matter. The certainty prickled the hair on her bare neck.

As the clock struck nine, Izella served nuts and fruit and replenished their cups. At Selah's bidding, a maid went upstairs to ready their rooms. Shay would sleep in Oceanus's bedchamber till the boy came home.

If he came home.

Was Xander on tenterhooks at the thought? Had he told Meihtawk about Watseka? Her new husband was not a man used to being thwarted. Though his endurance was one of the qualities she most admired about him, these repeated searches took a toll. He uttered no complaint, but Selah sensed his own hopes slowly eroding as he grappled with the repercussions of a peace child gone. Soon he must tell the Powhatans.

She returned her attention to Shay, trying to put off any dour thoughts and simply relish having her beloved brother within arm's reach. At the moment, he was clearly enjoying being the center of their attention.

"I have no great desire to move to Hopewell Hundred just yet. Not till I come of age." Shay's gaze traveled from his mother to Xander. "I can be of more use to you here, surely, with all that is to be done to prepare for next year's harvest."

"We'll start by having you hunt through the rubble for nails to reuse," Xander told him. "My blacksmith has fallen behind, making so many new ones."

Shay nodded. "I'll put my hand to anything to help Rose-n-Vale rise again."

Such talk was heartening, bringing the eventful day to an end. As the clock struck ten, Nurse Lineboro was the first to bid them good night. McCaskey's gaze followed her as she left the parlor, a smug expression on his face.

Who could decipher the gist of his thoughts?

Dawn found Selah wide awake, her feet touching the floor even before Xander, a notoriously early riser. She laced herself into stays and donned the oldest of her gowns, a faded red India cotton, and an apron. No longer did she need help. She tiptoed to her dower chest, opened it, and retrieved a coif embroidered with wildflowers and strawberries in gilt thread. Carefully closing the lid lest she wake Xander, she startled as strong arms enfolded her from behind, nearly lifting her off her feet.

"Good morning, my bride." He embraced her, nuzzling her neck and making her laugh at the tickle of his whiskers. "You've no dressing table yet. No looking glass. How can you pin up your hair?"

She sank onto a stool as he took up her hairbrush. Unbound,

her hair cascaded onto the floor. Such a mass kept her warm on bitter winter nights but in summer wound round her and felt suffocating.

"Pure gold." Xander ran the brush through the length of it, teasing out every tangle. "I've ne'er brushed a woman's hair. Yours carries the scent of the garden."

"Mother's concoction. Rosemary water and mint." Smiling, she closed her eyes, patient beneath his hands. He plaited her hair, forming a sort of crown by entwining the braids.

She felt atop her head. "My coif will be towering!"

"Like the queen you are. Where are the pins to hold it in place?"

She pointed to his washstand. He gathered up the pins and returned to finish what he'd started. All thumbs he was, but persevering. She smiled at the do-or-die look on his face. And bit her lip when the pins poked her scalp. Finally done, he stood back and admired her. Flushing, she looked about for her shoes, but he found them first, even kneeling and placing them on her feet.

Touched by his attentiveness, she looked to her wedding band. "Time shall tell I love thee well."

He stood, seeming unusually pensive. "Is there any doubt?"

"Nay, no longer. I am the most blessed of brides—"

"Nephew?" An abrupt banging on the door ended the intimate moment.

Xander crossed the room to admit his aunt, her face a stew of displeasure. "My apologies for barging in so. But Nurse Lineboro has gone. Up and fled during the night with no explanation!"

Xander took in the outburst in stony silence while Selah felt little but relief.

"Has she not simply gone out?" he asked.

"Nay. Her belongings—and some of ours—have gone with her. She's robbed a pair of silver candlesticks and a snuffer and who knows what else!"

Selah moved toward the hall to find her mother coming down the stairs. Leaving Xander to handle matters regarding the nurse, they went in to breakfast. Shay was still abed, the dining room empty. But Izella was already at work, given the jugs of cream and molasses and a heaping platter of corn-cakes at table's center.

"I suppose there shall be one less guest at breakfast." Candace sat, looking far less perturbed than Xander's aunt. "I don't quite know what to make of it."

"Nor do I." Selah took her usual place. "I long for a time of . . . boredom."

At Xander's entrance, Selah looked up expectantly. His bearded face betrayed none of the turmoil of the moment as he greeted her mother and sat at the head of the table. McCaskey soon followed, and cassina was poured. Once they said grace, a brief lull ensued.

The factor was piling his plate high when Xander looked his way. "Good to see you this morn, McCaskey. I feared you took flight with Nurse Lincboro."

Nearly dropping his plate, the factor stared at Xander, who sipped his cassina without expression.

"Electa—" McCaskey set down his plate with a clatter. "*Nurse* is gone?"

"Sometime in the night, aye, with all her belongings."

"And some of ours," Widow Brodie added with a frown. "But at least we shan't have to go looking for her. She obviously left of her own free will."

Clearly McCaskey was ignorant of the scheme. Selah felt a beat of sympathy as he grappled with the ill news, which seemed a bold rejection of his suit.

"She left no letter? No explanation?" He looked about the table as if searching for answers, lingering on Xander longest. "I—she—unfortunately I do not ken where she's gone. She made no mention of leaving. At least to me."

Xander resumed eating, and the conversation turned to the plans for the day. To Selah's relief Shay appeared, calling out a bright good morning, unaware of the night's events. Rounding the table, he kissed his mother's cheek before taking a seat beside her.

"I am ready to go nail hunting," he announced as he reached for the molasses. "Or whatever else needs doing."

Xander nodded. "Eat your fill first, and then you can accompany McCaskey to the fields. I'll be searching with Meihtawk and the dogs today."

Selah's heart sank, as she knew Xander was needed at Rose-n-Vale instead. But what else could be done till Watseka was found? As for McCaskey, he sat in stricken silence, staring at his untouched plate, his face florid. Distressed.

Selah struck a lighter note. "If you need me, I'll be in the kitchen making small beer since Cook is unwell."

Xander met her eyes, appreciation in their depths. "Have the maids clean the garret. Shay might enjoy his own bedchamber since Oceanus will return in time. The view is unmatched."

"I shall be content no matter where you put me," Shay replied between bites. "'Tis good to be back, though I do miss my Powhatan friends."

"You can accompany me on future visits if your mother

approves." Xander pushed his empty plate away. "Once Watseka is found—"

With a choked cry, McCaskey stood so abruptly the table shook. Every eye was upon him, breakfast forgotten.

"I confess—I hardly know how to say such—" Eyes half wild, McCaskey looked to Xander. "The Indian girl is Nurse Lineboro's doing. She goaded me into taking her. Said she wasn't fit company for your son. She promised to marry me if I did the deed, and so I—"

"Spare the women your ranting." Xander stood nearly as abruptly. Never had Selah seen him so riled. "Withdraw to my study."

McCaskey moved toward the door like a chastised schoolboy. As Xander followed him out, fury stiffening his stride, Selah put a hand to her throat, trying to calm the swirl of her stomach. 'Twas the last thing she expected to hear.

"And to think we've hosted two such scheming plague sores beneath our very roof!" Widow Brodie's chin shook with emotion. "I knew no good would come of the factor's drinking— the plan was no doubt hatched under its influence—and now that no-good nurse has fled!"

For a few moments they sat in benumbed silence.

Candace finally murmured, "Be sure your sin will find you out, as Scripture says."

Fork in midair, Shay frowned, and Widow Brodie resumed her ranting. "Well, McCaskey will lodge here no longer, nor act as factor, I'm sure, after Alexander has his say. Imagine taking a helpless child and blaming it on that fopdoodle Laurent, foul as he is!"

Nauseous, Selah excused herself, feeling shock and deep sorrow not only for Watseka but for the evil that drove men to do such grievous things. Though McCaskey had confessed to a great deal, what would be gained? Would he lead them to Watseka?

Lord, let it be.

The kitchen was blessedly quiet save the buzz of a horsefly in the rafters. All was orderly, pots and pans scrubbed and set to rights, the scent of drying herbs and the last meal lingering. Izella's brandied peaches stood in jars of amber perfection on a near table. A low fire smoked and snapped in the cavernous hearth. Poking it, Selah stoked it to greater life.

She'd grown used to doing things in a one-handed way as her wound healed sufficiently. Of late, except for an occasional twinge, she was nearly whole. Taking up a kettle, she went outside to a rain barrel and drew enough water to begin making small beer, her mind not at all on the task before her.

As the water came to a boil, she tried to familiarize herself with Cook's domain. The molasses was easily found, but yeast was another matter. She'd all but given up on powdered ginger when Izella returned from gathering eggs, unearthing both yeast and ginger before leaving again.

As the hearth's fire grew hotter, Selah opened a window, inviting in a cooling coastal wind. Though she was bodily in the kitchen, her mind was in her husband's study. She spilled the ginger, dropped a cask of raisins, and singed her apron.

What else was McCaskey confessing?

At last the kitchen was redolent of the sugary-spicy drink ready to ferment. Or so she hoped, as she felt so addled concocting it.

"Selah." At her name so tenderly spoken, she swung round, nearly singeing the hem of her skirts.

Lost in thought, she hadn't heard Xander enter the kitchen. She'd simply stood stirring the concoction in the kettle, her back to him. Now, facing him, she braced for ill news, his expression unreadable.

"The last time McCaskey saw Watseka, she was alive."

Alive? Overcome with relief, she closed her eyes, a dozen more questions dancing on her tongue.

"If McCaskey is to be believed, there's still hope, though his conduct is inexcusable. He and the nurse caged her and placed her at the farthest reaches of Laurent land."

"Caged?" Her heart was so heavy she wasn't sure she could bear it. "Like an animal?"

"They fed her occasional scraps till the day she disappeared. They couldn't decide what to do with her once they'd caged her. They debated whether or not to kill her."

She shuddered, such depravity flipping her stomach. "They don't know where she is?"

"He claims she was moved. By whom he doesn't ken. A sennight ago, I came upon the spot at the far west corner of Laurent's land where she was being held, which may confirm his story."

"But what of all the rest? The fire and Nurse Lineboro's liaison with Helion Laurent?"

"She told McCaskey 'twas Laurent who started the fire. When she learned what he'd done, and the dire ramifications under Virginia law, she decided McCaskey was her choice. Their intent was to implicate Laurent for both the fire and Watseka."

Selah stared at him, grappling with all the facts and implications. 'Twas a love triangle gone dangerously awry as both men sought the favor of one woman.

"The nurse may have returned to Laurent after all." Xander's ire was evident, his tone tight. "For now, we'll renew our search for Watseka."

"Of course." The bubbling kettle drew her notice, and he swung it off the fire to rest on the hearthstones for her. "What are you going to do with the factor?"

"If Watseka isn't found, I'll turn him over to the Powhatans. I told him so after he confessed to Meihtawk as well. McCaskey has a great deal at stake."

"What if he runs too?"

"Meihtawk will shadow him. For now, McCaskey will continue to search with us."

She leaned against the kitchen table and raised the edge of her apron to dry her damp eyes. "I fear for Watseka if she's in Laurent's hands. After his treatment of Mattachanna—"

"Say no more, Selah."

Their eyes locked, the depths of their distress communicated in a single, wordless look. He didn't want the past to impose upon the present, which was disturbing enough. This she understood, though she felt like wringing her hands.

"I'll continue to pray," she told him.

What more could she do?

42

Suppertime came, but no Xander.

As her mother, Shay, and Widow Brodie ate, Selah pushed her food around her plate and listened hard to every sound outside. Table talk was nearly nonexistent, each of them silently entertaining their own questions and concerns. The dwindling day brought a soft rain, muting the hoofbeats she longed to hear. Search parties usually ended by late afternoon. What could be keeping them?

Tomorrow was the Sabbath. A blessed reprieve from work if not worry. Dwell on the good, Father would say. And so she would. Thankfully, Cook had seemed better once Candace gave her a medicinal posset. Shay lent a hand wherever he could and had found a great many nails to be reused in the rebuilding. The maids cleaned the main house from top to bottom, not only the empty garret.

But no hoofbeats. No husband.

Her imagination made fearsome leaps. Had they had another confrontation with Laurent or found Nurse Lineboro with him? What if McCaskey had run after all? What if all three of them turned on Xander?

She ate a bite of fish without tasting it. Poked at a potato.

Declined dessert. In the distance she finally heard what her heart craved.

Candace looked to the windows. "God be praised, if 'tis them."

Abandoning the table, Selah went into the hall to the riverfront door. *Lord, please . . . let it be good news.*

But no sign of Watseka did she see. Only harried, weary men damp with rain and in need of supper, scattering in different directions. Xander came through the door with a simple shake of his sodden head. She swallowed her questions as he shrugged off his coat and crossed into their new rooms.

"Have a supper tray brought, aye?"

"I'll ready it myself," she answered.

Returning to the dining room, she met three pairs of inquiring eyes. "He's said little yet, but there appears to be nothing new. He'll take supper in private."

They nodded in understanding, their relief at his return as palpable as their dismay at his coming home empty-handed. Selah filled a plate with the foods he usually enjoyed but doubted he had any appetite for them. At least he was home. Safe and sound.

While he ate if for no other reason than to have strength for the days ahead, she took up a book and tried to read, but the words on the page escaped her.

At last he put down his fork. "There's to be no more searching."

Her heart seemed to stop. "Is Watseka—" She could not say the hated word. Everything in her rebelled.

His voice was quiet and measured. "If I'd heeded the Scripture of this morn during our devotions, I'd have saved us another futile afternoon."

Her thoughts reached back to the early dawn hour that had marked their Bible reading.

"You ken how timely Psalms is. How it oft speaks to our circumstances."

She sighed, her mind still muddled. "I was but half awake, having passed a near sleepless night. I recall it not."

Pushing his half-finished supper aside, he reached for his Bible, which lay open to this morning's reading. "'Rest in the LORD, and wait patiently for him: fret not thyself because of him who prospereth in his way, because of the man who bringeth wicked devices to pass.'"

She took in the words, trying to reconcile them with their predicament. *Rest. Wait patiently. Fret not.* She was failing at all.

His shadow-rimmed eyes bore a hole into her. "You ken we are to do no more."

"Nothing?"

His gaze returned to the Psalms. He seemed strangely at peace. "We simply wait. Pray."

"But . . ." The whispered protest died on her lips.

"The outcome of all that concerns us is more to be trusted in His hands than ours."

This she couldn't deny. But to simply do . . . nothing? While Watseka was suffering?

Could she trust God in this?

Could she trust her husband?

⁂

The Sabbath broke golden and cool, the walk to church pleasant. Still, Selah could not grasp Xander's sudden peace about matters. Rather than settle her, it chafed. Fatigue turned her testy. She felt as nettled as in days of old when she'd been caught in the cobwebs of misunderstanding him. Of misjudging him.

Walking alongside her, Candace regarded her anxiously as if sensing her internal struggle. They made a subdued party as they passed through the open doors of the chapel.

This morn, all eyes seemed to be on them as a couple. News of their marrying was spreading slowly over the Tidewater. Xander reached for her gloved hand, his comforting touch somehow intensifying her misery. Memories of Father and the last Sabbaths they'd spent with him inside these walls only lent to her sagging spirits. Not even Shay with his steady if concerned smile made a dent in her melancholy.

Where was her faith? Her trust? Such seemed crowded out by confusion and hurt.

A hush descended. The order of service began with the Psalm reading. She nearly missed the itinerant pastor's sonorous words with her ruminating, and then the faintest glimmer of light illuminated her clouded mind.

"'Rest in the LORD, and wait patiently for him: fret not thyself because of him who prospereth in his way, because of the man who bringeth wicked devices to pass . . .'"

He read on, but the next words were lost to her. Were he and Xander in league? Nay, her husband looked as surprised as she at the choice of Scripture. Was this not blessed confirmation that they were indeed to do nothing? Releasing a deep, steadying breath, she let go of her tight tangle of worries to the only One who could help unravel them.

Early the next morn Xander left for James Towne by shallop. What business betook him there he did not say, nor did she ask. She was practicing rest and patient waiting. Her morning was spent in the orchard with her brother, picking endless wheelbarrow loads of apples, which Shay rolled back and forth for cider making. Xander had told him to keep near the house in his absence while McCaskey and the ever-present Meihtawk took to the fields.

Midday she joined her mother and Xander's aunt on the portico as they were wont to do, sharing details of their days. Newly made garments for the indentures—brown linen shirts and breeches—overflowed a large basket. Though gout had slowed the older woman's fingers, her efforts were unflagging.

Selah sat on the steps and arranged in various vases the flowers she'd picked, her eyes on the river, which was growing more restive. She smelled a heaviness in the air, the bite of the coming autumn.

"I fear we are in for unwelcome weather." Widow Brodie scanned the darkening skies. "Cook predicts a northeaster by nightfall. Though I can abide a bit of wind, 'tis lightning that frightens me."

"Will the shallop hazard such?" Candace asked the question Selah didn't.

"Alexander is an able sailor but won't take risks. He's not forgotten the hundred-year storm all Virginia lived through years ago." She returned to her sewing. "He may wait in James Towne till the morrow if the wind worsens, though he won't like the delay."

Nor would Selah.

Where would Watseka spend the storm?

Lord, yet another petition to bring before Thee. Of late I fear I'm in danger of storming heaven's very gates.

She stood to search for the maids, leaving her flowers. "Best batten things down."

By three o'clock, lightning had licked the horizon and the indentures were pulled from the fields. Selah could see them hurrying toward their rebuilt quarters from her perch in the garret beside Shay. Though Nurse Lineboro had gone, her heavily perfumed scent remained. Selah waved a fan to banish it, the heat of the garret unrelieved by the closed windows. Before her watchful gaze the storm played out like theater. Wind wailed about the rafters. Rose petals scattered and fences bent from the storm's force. Yet no rain slashed the glass.

"I spy our resident wrongdoer," Shay remarked with no mirth. "Better here than gaol, I suppose."

True enough, McCaskey disappeared into his quarters, only to be locked inside. Meihtawk remained outside, prowling about the main house and dependencies, occasionally disappearing into the summer kitchen, where he passed time with Cook.

Come twilight, no shallop moored in the wave-tossed water off Rose-n-Vale's wharf. The wind strengthened, blowing with such force it flung sand against the windowpanes.

All retired but Shay, who lingered in the hall with the dogs. Glad for his nearness, Selah kept watch in her bedchamber, alone with a flickering taper and her thoughts. Sleep held no escape lest she have bad dreams. Of lostness and Watseka and Father. Of that terrible morn when their world turned upside down.

Xander, my beloved, stay on in James Towne lest you

*put yourself in danger. I am not good at waiting, but we
shall make out all right tonight. Though I feel great anxiety
for Watseka, that particular Scripture oft returns to me and
keeps me from falling to pieces.*

She nodded off in the uncomfortable chair. Only when
Shay shook her awake did she rouse. He held a candle, the
flame adance in a draft. His face was drawn, his eyes too
huge in his tanned face.

"Sister, we are in grave straits."

She started from her chair. "What means you?"

"An African has come to us in this storm, only we can't
understand a word he says."

"Where is he?"

"Meihtawk is with him in the hall."

Shaking off sleep, she followed him through the midnight-
black parlor, their candle snuffed in a draft. They kept on,
hand in hand, till they reached the lantern-lit hall. There
stood a tall man, little more than bones. Meihtawk stood regarding him as though he were a ghost, his musket dangling
from one sinewy hand. But nary a growl from the dogs as
they sniffed and circled the man. Surely this was a favorable
sign?

He was one of the enslaved, but she did not know whose.
Tenderness smote her at his terrible scars, upraised and scarlet even in the dim light. She'd not seen him before, to her
recollection, except perhaps at a distance in the fields. His
sunken eyes fastened on her, and he waved his arm rapidly,
ever agitated, as if asking them to come.

"He puts himself at great risk being here." Shay's face
showed a rare perplexity. "Though in such a storm this may
be the only time he can come in secret."

"Lord help him if he's branded a runaway, if his master knows he's missing." Reaching out, Selah clasped the man's trembling hand, if only to quiet it. She squeezed the bony fingers in some sort of wordless affirmation. He still beckoned with the other, gaze pleading.

Thunder resounded like cannon fire. Even now branches and untethered things clattered across the house's exterior. How could they follow him, if that was indeed his intent? But how could they not?

What would Xander do?

She let go of him. "My husband—he is not here. But we will help you if we can."

Her speech came to naught. No kindling lit his restless eyes. No sign that he understood the slightest word. A chill passed through her that had naught to do with the wind's battering. Was this Laurent's slave? Had Laurent made those heinous scars? Was he even now searching for his property?

Time was against them. She sensed it to her marrow. The four of them hovered in agonizing suspension, precious seconds ticking by. When the hall clock struck ten, Selah seized a fire bucket full of sand along one wall and dumped it onto the floor. Her brother and the African gaped.

Selah looked at Shay. "Fetch me an iron poker from the hearth."

At her summons he moved quickly. Praying for clarity, Selah took the poker and drew a dog in the sand with the tip. Her poor attempt gave her pause, but immediately the man's face cleared. As he gestured to Ruby and Jett, Selah nearly wilted with relief. A blessed start. She held out the poker to him. He took it without hesitation.

Shay raised the lantern higher as the man began drawing

in the sand. Lines emerged. An outline. Bars? A rude drawing of a . . . cage. Xander seemed to whisper in her ear. *"He and the nurse caged her . . ."*

She startled as both dogs set up a tremendous barking and charged past them, their nails clicking on the hall floor.

"Someone comes." Shay looked toward the locked front door, which was seldom used.

Xander? Selah's fleeting hope faded. Ruby and Jett never barked at their master.

Shay's eyes narrowed. "I fear 'tis Laurent."

"Stay here and hold your ground, then. Say nothing of what has happened tonight." Selah looked to Meihtawk and the African. "Jett shall go with us three."

Resistance replaced Meihtawk's usual mask. "You stay," he told Selah, no doubt thinking of Xander.

"Nay, I cannot in good conscience," she told him, then followed him and the African to the riverfront door.

43

Something ominous settled in Xander's spirit at the onset of the storm that had nothing to do with the weather. Although all of James Towne and the coastline had gone tapsalteerie, he'd seen worse. As Rose-n-Vale's shallop tugged at its moorings, confirming his return upriver was futile, he sought a different route.

His business with the tobacco inspector done, he sought refuge at Swan's to sit out the tumult. The ordinary's four rooms were mostly empty, a few lone travelers happening by.

A serving of oysters and two pints of ale later, Xander stared out the window as barrels careened down streets and brush and leaves whipped past along with a hat or two.

"You look on tenterhooks, Renick." The proprietor stood at table's end as a serving girl cleared away his empty dishes. "Shall I ready a room?"

"Rather a bold horse."

Swan scratched his head. "You've never been one for flinching at shadows, but falling trees are another matter. Gaining Rose-n-Vale without injury to you or your mount is chancy."

"At least there's no rain," Xander told him. "And the dark is a way off yet."

With a nod, Swan turned aside. "I'll send word to the stables, then."

Xander paid his bill and stood at the back door to wait for a mount, the wind tugging at his hat and yanking at his coattails with fierce talons. Northeasters wreaked special havoc on the coast, as ships and piers were oft dashed to pieces. Inland would be less fractious, or so he hoped. Selah was in good company, thus he had no fear on that score.

As he swung himself into the saddle, a Scripture leapt to mind, chilling in its force if comforting in its promise.

Yea, though I walk through the valley of the shadow of death, I will fear no evil.

Meihtawk could lead blindfolded, even in the dark. Never had Selah seen so capable a woodsman. Wisely he kept to open ground, well away from the trees shuddering and cracking at the forest's fringes. In the dark their reverberating upon the ground sent a tremor through her. She'd tied her neckerchief about her bent head as sand and twigs stung her exposed skin. Betimes she clutched a fence to stay upright, the raw wood driving splinters into her ungloved hands. All the while she clung to one verse like a rope, an anchor.

And a man shall be as an hiding place from the wind, and a covert from the tempest . . .

She would not lose heart. The African had not hazarded so dangerous a mission to let fear have sway. Too much was at stake. A great deal to be gained.

Unless he was a pawn of the enemy, luring them into a trap.

Surely this scarred, gaunt man had no guile, even at Laurent's behest. His face was too beseeching, his eyes too haunted. His crude drawing of a cage struck her to the heart. It could lead to none other than Watseka.

But would they find her alive?

For the first time she felt thankful Laurent's land adjoined their own, if only to speed their chase. As for Shay and what lay behind that front door, she could only guess. And Xander? Where was he in the midst of all this?

On they pressed through the last wind-beaten remnants of summer. How long they'd been walking she did not know. Chest heaving, she felt chilled and heated by turns. She tripped repeatedly, her skirts a nuisance. Weariness sank bone deep.

Without warning, Meihtawk slowed his pace and let the African lead. A loosened branch raked her cheek as the wind shifted with a moan. With it came a parting of the clouds.

Moonlight streamed down in silver ribbons, hastening their steps, taking them into a copse of woods that looked dangerously black. Jett plunged in first, nose to the ground. When Meihtawk held up a hand, halting her, she watched the African swallowed whole by the darkness. Breathless and light-headed, she dug her heels into the dirt to stay standing, Meihtawk's sturdy shoulder against her own. The African finally reappeared, bidding them come as a flash of lightning lit the sky.

Lord, spare us any evil.

Briars tore at her skirts and skin as they entered what seemed a dense blackberry thicket. The men went ahead of her, standing tall one minute, then crouching the next. Tearing away underbrush. Digging. Had they been led to a grave? Everything within her recoiled.

Nay, nay. I cannot bear it.

The African was speaking in his strange tongue. Excitedly. Hurriedly. Thunder snatched his words away. Selah crept forward to where the men hovered, her pulse rapid as a bird's wings. Reaching out, she touched something cold. Rough.

Iron.

Despite her shaking, she thrust a hand through the bars of the cage and felt . . . flesh. "Watseka?"

Over and over she called the girl's name, fingers roaming desperately to find answers. Was she merely hurt? A cold rain began falling, driven sideways by the wind. It stole any reassurance that Watseka was alive. Her skin . . . so cold to the touch. And damp. Selah's searching hands told her what her eyes could not. Watseka was encased in an iron cage used for criminals. The padlock confining her hung ponderous, denying them her freedom.

Meihtawk's voice rose above the din. "Stand back."

She obeyed, landing on her backside as he began hacking at the lock with his hatchet. Only this might open the cage too ponderous to move. Picking the lock was denied them in the dark. As he leveled blow after blow, Selah bent her head and prayed for deliverance.

Xander dismounted at Rose-n-Vale's stable, sent the lathered horse into a stall, and woke a groom to tend him. Hurrying to the main house, he was heartened by a sudden bark and the flicker of light within. The riverfront door opened and Shay stood before him, Ruby wagging fiercely at his side.

Relief eased Shay's tight features. "I feared 'twas Laurent again."

Again. Xander's hackles rose as he came through the door into the sanctuary of the still hall.

"To her credit, Ruby tried to have him for supper." Shay moved to set down the lantern as a gust of wind slammed the door shut behind them. "So much has happened. I hardly know where to begin."

Xander shrugged off his coat, none the worse for the tempestuous miles dealt him. "Start at the beginning."

With a nod, Shay took a breath. "Not long after nightfall, when a gale shook the very rafters, an African appeared. We understood not a word, but he seemed to want you. We told him you weren't here and tried to make out his purpose, to no avail. Finally, Selah cast down a sand bucket. With a poker, the African drew a picture that looked to be a cage. He bade them follow, so she left with Meihtawk and Jett and told me to stand watch here."

Xander's eyes sought the hall clock. Nearly midnight. "How long ago?"

"Full dark. Ten o'clock or so. I've no idea where they've gone to. Laurent came as they went out. Said at least one of his slaves was missing. He suspected the African came here." Shay shook his head in disgust. "'Twas clear he'd been drinking. He left, murmuring threats against you."

Xander called Ruby, his every thought of Selah. "Lock everything till I return. If Laurent reappears, do not open the door or exchange a word."

He passed into his study and opened a cupboard where his

weapons were kept. Selecting a flintlock, he shoved it into his pistol pocket before returning to the stables for fresh horses, Ruby on his heels.

ᏉᎶᏉᎶ

Meihtawk was growing tired fighting iron. His efforts began to lag, Selah's hopes along with them. She crouched in the rain, a sodden lump, one arm thrust through the back of the cage with a hand on Watseka's bent head.

Lord, please lend Thy strength to the blows.

Before she finished the prayer, Selah heard a final clang and the lock was cleaved in two. She scrambled to her feet as Meihtawk yanked open the heavy door of the cage. And then raw force faded to tenderness as he extracted Watseka. In his sinewy arms, her body hung limp. Raising her hands, Selah took the girl from him. Light-headed again, she sank down upon the muddy ground. She lowered her face to Watseka's nose and mouth and tried to detect the faintest breath. The barest flicker of movement. But the weather showed no mercy and denied her knowing.

A miracle, Lord. One is sorely needed.

Meihtawk uncorked a flask and dribbled water into Watseka's open mouth. Gently Selah shook her and called her name, to no avail.

She'd nearly forgotten Jett till the big dog lowered his head and began licking Watseka's face. The long, rough tongue did a thorough if gentle work.

Could it be? Watseka moved her head ever so slightly.

Selah swallowed down a sob of gratitude, tears streaking her cheeks like rain. Just as hope soared, fear swooped in like a devouring raven. A great rustle of brush sent the African fleeing as a horse charged into the thicket. For a moment even the rain abated. The rider jumped to the ground, the fickle moon sliding behind a bank of clouds. Selah's heart seized.

Laurent? They were on his land—

"Selah?"

Xander. She went weak with relief, her answer lost to another gust.

He sank to his knees, hands roving Watseka, assessing, much as hers had done. "I've brought two horses. Meihtawk will carry Watseka, and I you."

"Where is the man who brought us here?" She half believed him to be no African but an angel in disguise.

Xander shook his head. "There's none but us four. At least now."

Selah released her burden to Meihtawk, only too glad to return to her husband's arms. Atop the horse they took a different route to Rose-n-Vale, the wind giving way to deafening thunder.

44

The shutters were closed in Oceanus's room, the dim morning light soothing. Watseka lay on her back atop the bed, eyes closed, her face a frightful spectacle of scratches and insect bites. Freshly bathed and dressed in a loose smock, she had a linen sheet pulled to her middle. Selah perched on a near chair as Candace and Widow Brodie came and went with food, drink, and tonic. These sat mostly untouched under Selah's sleepless gaze. Though her eyes stung and she needed a good soaking of her own, she wouldn't leave the girl's side. Not yet.

Xander stood by her at intervals, having summoned the Mount Malady physic. They listened for his arrival as the sunny morning lengthened, making their travail of the night before naught but a bad memory.

"She is so still," Selah whispered. "Alarmingly so."

"After such an ordeal, rest will restore her better than anything else."

"Mother has made sure she is well watered. She ate but a few bites of porridge, then fell back asleep. But she's spoken nary a word."

"I know one unerring remedy."

She looked up at him in question.

He smiled. "Oceanus."

"Shall you summon him?"

"Meihtawk is already on his way."

The news rose inside her like the sun. Reaching out, she stroked Watseka's bug-bitten arm, the welts covered by a poultice. "Oceanus will help restore her, aye."

He kissed her before returning downstairs to his study. Stifling a yawn, Selah started to rest her head on the bed's coverlet when a noise at the front of the house sent her to a window instead.

Below on a large gray horse sat Nicholas Claibourne, a fierce if former opponent of Xander and all his endeavors on the governor's council. A friend of Laurent's, he had an equally rakish reputation. Selah watched him dismount and walk to the front door, where a housemaid admitted him after a loud knock.

"Kentke." The soft voice was more warble.

Surprised, Selah turned and moved toward the bed. Watseka's eyes were open. She repeated the word, this time more clearly.

"Your pup? Last I knew he was with Shay in the orchard." Selah smiled and squeezed her hand. "Would you like me to fetch him?"

A nod. Selah was hard put to contain her joy. She hurried downstairs just as Claibourne entered Xander's study, the door shutting soundly behind them. Ignoring the dart of worry his presence wrought, she hurried outside to find Shay. He was at work cleaning up the battered orchard, the ground littered with ripe fruit and windblown limbs and leaves. Several trees had toppled. Nearby, curled up in a patch of sun, was Kentke, asleep.

"Watseka is asking for her pup." Selah scooped the furry creature up, his gangly legs a testament to his growing. He licked her face with a dart of his tongue, reminding her of Jett reviving Watseka.

Shay smiled. "So, Miss Mischief has come to her senses at last."

"'Twould seem so. Being missing for more than a fortnight takes a toll."

Shay looked past her to the house. "Why has Claibourne come?"

"I know not. He and Xander are confined in the study."

"'Tis not a good sign." He grimaced and tossed aside a worm-ridden apple. "He's in league with Laurent, no doubt."

Kentke squirmed in Selah's embrace, hastening her to the house. "Pray," she said over her shoulder. "And be on your guard."

✺

"I am here as Helion Laurent's second, to challenge you to a duel."

"A duel." Xander faced Claibourne across a desk littered with work left undone. "While my fields lie in ashes and I've just reclaimed a peace child."

"Indeed, a duel is required." Claibourne's eyes narrowed to slits in his pockmarked face. "For impinging on Laurent's honor."

"*Honor?*" Xander did not hide his disgust. "He has none to defend."

Flushing, Claibourne rapped his coiled riding whip against

the side of the desk. "How dare you, Renick. Your words bear the craven mark of a coward."

Xander crossed his arms. "Let us return to the matter at hand. Why a duel?"

"For trespassing on Laurent land. For spreading malicious accusations that a gentleman of his merit would stoop so low and set fire to your acreage—"

"I spread no accusations. The truth has an uncanny way of surfacing. As for trespassing, did Laurent not do the same when he showed himself last night at my very door?"

"He simply wanted to reclaim his wayward African and challenge you himself. Denied that, he sent me instead to secure a date and time. Not pistols but swords."

"Your arrogance knows no bounds." Xander moved to the study door and opened it wide, when what he wanted to do was grab Claibourne by the throat and let him fly. "Get off my land lest I fight you after I finish him."

With an epithet beneath his breath, Claibourne went out and slammed the front door after him.

Watseka's face brightened when Selah appeared with her pup.

"Kentke has missed you. See how he wriggles at the sight of you?"

The pup gave a little bark, which led to Watseka's first smile since her return. She stretched out her arms. "Kentke. He grows big."

Risking Widow Brodie's ire, Selah turned the pup loose atop the clean coverlet. "I'll return in a few moments and see what merriment you two have been making."

She sailed back down the staircase and into Xander's study. He stood at the window, arms crossed, as the hoof-beats of their visitor grew fainter. Though she'd heard not a word of their exchange, ill will suffused the room and made her choose her words with care.

"Claibourne is an unwelcome caller."

Xander turned toward her. "He comes to issue a challenge as Laurent's second. A duel."

She put a hand to her throat. "You have more reason to call him out than he you."

"Aye. Pride blinds them both. I expected the challenge, but I will not bow to it."

A sigh of relief escaped her. "His sword is formidable, some say, but no match for yours. If you did fight and best him, he'd surely go to his eternal punishment. At least alive he stands some chance at redemption."

"Well spoken by a wise wife whom I have no wish to worry." He came and rested his hands upon her shoulders, his gaze tender. "How is our charge?"

"Playing with her pup." She smiled past her weariness. "I'm going to fetch something more from the kitchen and coax her to eat."

"The physic should be here shortly, though we might have no need of him, God be thanked."

"She's more herself by the hour, truly. I pray she has no more bad dreams." Last night had been fraught with them, Watseka's restless tossing and cries only soothed by Selah's whispered words and soft embraces.

"You need to sleep." He touched her cheek. "My aunt will watch over her tonight."

She nodded, needing little convincing. "Enough about me. What of you?"

"For now, I need to ride about the estate and assess the wind's damage."

"Take your weapon." Though she hated to say it, she could not avoid the truth. "Watch your back."

"Look for me at supper." He kissed her, his ire of minutes before gone. "We shall have a peaceful eve, Lord willing. And we'll continue praying for Oceanus's safe return."

Once Kentke was returned outside, the physic arrived and spent a thorough hour examining Watseka and talking with Selah.

"She's a hardy little soul." He shut his portmanteau at visit's end. "I see no cause for bloodletting or any treatment save bathing in chamomile-infused water for her irritated skin. An extract of lemon balm should help her sleep more soundly. Be especially vigilant about her eating and drinking."

Once Watseka ate a bowl of broth, Selah herself grew drowsy. The maids went about on tiptoe, shutting the door of Oceanus's bedchamber as the afternoon wore on. Selah nodded off. They slept till supper, finally rousing when Xander came in.

"Ah, our Powhatan princess is good as new." Taking her from Selah, he tossed her into the air and gained a fit of giggles before carrying her down to the dining room.

Seated on his knee at supper, Watseka ate from his plate, then moved to sit with Selah when Izella served apple tansy for dessert. This she ate two bowls of, though Selah feared she would be sick. Understandably, Watseka was ravenous in her recovery.

"We shall ask her no questions of her ordeal and torment her further," Xander had said when they'd found her. Yet so many questions remained. Selah nearly grew dizzy from guesswork. After Nurse Lineboro and the factor had stolen her away, it seemed Laurent had foiled them by moving her to where she'd been found. Somehow the African knew where Watseka was. He might have seen Laurent move her or aided him somehow. But for the heinous scars upon his back and bony shoulders, Selah would still rather believe him a guardian angel.

"How much storm damage, Alexander?" Widow Brodie dabbed her lips with a napkin at meal's end. "Precious little, I hope."

"Mostly fencing down in the pasturelands. Felled trees that will make fine firewood. Nothing of lasting damage." Xander took a drink of small beer. "Hopewell Hundred needs visiting next. Shay and I will see what begs repair."

"I've a hankering to return," Shay told him, "and collect a few of my belongings."

Xander nodded. "We'll go on the morrow and take a wagon. I have need of some empty barrels from the warehouse."

"Take care." Candace looked at them fondly. "Till this matter between McCaskey and Laurent is settled, I'd be very wary. And now Claibourne has come calling . . ."

The room stilled. Selah stroked Watseka's silky braid, her mind on Claibourne's challenge. As second, should he not address McCaskey instead since the factor had laid the blame at Laurent's door to begin with? Yet McCaskey was not considered a gentleman, just a middling merchant, and only gentlemen dueled. She'd seen little of him since he'd been banished to the quarters and was now shadowed by a farm manager in Meihtawk's absence.

"No sign of Nurse Lineboro, I suppose?" Widow Brodie still nursed her displeasure. "Surely she is at the heart of this misguided tryst with both men and should be punished. I would like to retrieve those candlesticks, besides."

To his credit, Xander eyed her with amusement. "A loss of silver is far preferable to her duplicitous presence here, aye, Aunt?"

She gave a wry chuckle. "Well, framed such as that, I must agree."

Watseka yawned and ended the matter. Easing the child onto her feet, Selah stood, hardly able to stifle her own yawning.

"'Tis my turn to spell you tonight, Selah." Widow Brodie intervened, taking Watseka's hand. "Go to bed, the both of you. My nephew looks worn as yesterday's breeches."

"I'll not deny it." Xander stood, eyes on Selah as she came toward him. "A peaceful good night to all, then."

In the hall lay Ruby and Jett, their comforting presence an added safeguard to doors and windows shuttered and locked. Still, a whisper of alarm crept past Selah's exhaustion.

With matters still so unresolved, what would the morrow hold?

45

Wagons ambled along the rutted road from Rose-n-Vale toward Hopewell Hundred as dawn cracked open the sleepy eastern sky. McCaskey and half a dozen indentures followed Xander in the lead. Shay sat beside his brother-in-law, looking pleased as a fox in a henhouse to be holding the reins. But for one matter.

"I've rarely seen you with a sidearm other than your pistols."

"Pistols are wildly inaccurate." Xander shifted on the seat, the rapier riding his hip safely in its scabbard. "Swords rarely miss."

"You are taking no chances with Claibourne or Laurent, I'd wager."

"I hope to have no need of any weapon. 'Tis precautionary," Xander told him as they rolled to a stop beside the warehouse.

Since Ustis's passing, Xander felt a bit melancholy coming here. Ustis had been a trusted friend, a wise counselor. He would have made a treasured father-in-law. His business acumen was second to none. Though a new supplier was needed for the upriver plantations, nothing had been done, the want left unfulfilled. Mayhap at the next general assembly he'd make a motion. In time, Shay could assume the position, if he was willing.

A few boats bobbed at their moorings along the waterfront, mostly upriver visitors, a few vessels familiar. A small, unknown shallop at wharf's end drew Xander's notice, but he gave it no more than a passing glance as he took out a key and opened the warehouse. His indentures filed in, intent on the empty barrels. They weighed a thousand pounds each when prized with tobacco but were easily hefted when empty.

"Now is the time to fetch your belongings," Xander told Shay. "And see how the house fares idle."

Shay's expression turned pensive as they took the path leading to the Hopewells'. He'd not been home since his return from the Powhatans. He'd only heard secondhand how his father had fallen. Did he blame McCaskey? The factor, Xander had noticed, gave Shay wide berth as if guilt dug a chasm not easily bridged.

No sooner had they disappeared into the shoreline's leafy shade than a commotion made them look back over their shoulders. Into the clearing near the warehouse came a procession nearly silent but for the rattle of chains and the clang of bells. Xander summed it up in a glance. Laurent and Nurse Lineboro on horseback. Six men in the coarse garb of indentures on foot. And one fettered slave.

"'Tis the African." Shay sucked in a breath. "The one who came to Rose-n-Vale and told us of Watseka."

The starving smokehouse thief.

Xander said nothing, taking in the bloodied man from head to foot. The scars. The terrible iron collar with pronged horns that tore at the skin of his neck and shoulders. The leg iron that clinked loudly with every agonized move. An added humiliation was bells. Their music was anything but merry. The spectacle caused a fierce churning in Xander's gut.

"Stay here out of sight." He laid a heavy hand on Shay's shoulder. "Say nothing."

Laurent dismounted and strode down the dock ahead of his indentures, intent on the small shallop at wharf's end. Were they taking the African to James Towne for more punishment? Handing him over to the authorities and gaol? Now chary, Rose-n-Vale's own indentures paused in their loading of the wagons. McCaskey stared at Nurse Lineboro as she dismounted. The humid air ripened with hostility.

Xander stepped into the open, beyond the concealing shade. A murmur passed through the indentures. Laurent swung round, gaze sweeping the onlookers before settling on Xander. For the briefest second he seemed caught off guard. His hand went to his sword's hilt and stayed there.

Slowly, Xander walked toward the African, whose head was bowed as much as the iron prongs would let it be. "What charge do you bring against this man to have him bound so?"

"What cause have you to ask?" Laurent retraced his steps down the dock, past the African, to stand a stone's throw from Xander. "This is my lawful property to be used—or abused—as I please."

"The charge?"

Laurent's features tightened further. "All here know the punishment for a runaway slave is death. I intend to make him a public spectacle before all James Towne as a warning to future offenders."

"And I stand here and testify he did not run away but

returned to you after leading us to the Indian girl caged on your land," Xander replied, loud enough for all to hear. "If not for the African's aid, she may well have perished, bringing the Powhatans' wrath down on us all."

Cursing, eyes never leaving Xander, Laurent threw off his doublet. "You speak at your own peril, Renick, of matters you know not."

"I ken enough to defend a defenseless man. 'Tis you, Helion Laurent, who should wear the irons instead."

With a seamless sweep of his hand, Laurent drew his sword. "I am out of patience."

The ring of steel as it left the scabbard caused Xander to reach for his own weapon. *Forgive me, Selah. I did not mean for it to come to this.*

They began circling on open ground near shore as indentures fanned out in a wide arc around them. Laurent's weakness was his vanity. He would make a fine dance before so rapt an audience, displaying all the elegance of the art. But neither would he fight honorably. When his booted foot kicked sand in Xander's face, stinging and for a moment blinding him, Xander was prepared and escaped his quick thrust.

Lord, grant me a step and a mind sharp as steel.

The ground was unmercifully uneven. Still, they exchanged several thrusts, the rise and fall of Laurent's chest more pronounced as Xander lunged and sliced off his sleeve button. The rage in Laurent's gaze built with every parry and riposte, giving Xander a sliver of confidence.

An angry man was oft a losing man. And a dead one.

They were on the wharf now, men scrambling to get out of their way. A cry went up from the nurse as Xander lost his footing and Laurent aimed for his sword arm. The blow was glancing but drew blood, a warm, crimson swath against his shirt sleeve. Atop the wooden boards, the clash of their blades carried crisp over the water.

Laurent lunged and Xander parried, barely dodging the tip of his blade. They were now moving at a speed too fast for the eye, and Xander's head spun traitorously. He feinted, fooling Laurent, who stepped too close to the wharf's edge. Recovering, he found his balance and thrust again yet fell short. Strength ebbing, Xander struck him hard across his sword arm and put his point at Laurent's throat.

Xander forced one winded word through clenched teeth. "Yield."

"To the death!" Laurent spat as his sword lashed out, striking Xander's thigh.

They fought on, down the length of the wharf now cleared of all men. Color was leeching from Laurent's face. His wounded sword arm trailed blood. Still, his shoulders tensed and gave a warning, and he lunged again. Breathless, Xander leapt back, deflecting his blade. Next came a final, irreversible thrust, Xander's sword arm driving home. With a final cry of outrage, Laurent fell back into clear blue water with an ominous splash.

Xander stood at the wharf's end and looked down at him, chest so tight every breath was a battle. One of Laurent's indentures dove off the dock and swam to retrieve him.

In seconds, Shay was by Xander's side, hands full of linen. His eyes were wild with worry. "I've brought this from the warehouse to bind up your wounds, which I pray are not mortal."

"Not mortal, nay." Xander stood still as the lad began

bandaging him, gaze never leaving Laurent as he was heaved to shore.

A weighty silence ensued as the onlookers roused themselves out of their frozen stances and slowly surrounded the man lying on the sandy bank.

Xander bent his head. Waited for what he sensed was to come.

God forgive me.

"Stone-cold dead," someone shouted.

Xander turned toward the stunned group. Over the wails of the nurse he gave orders. "Take Laurent to James Towne for burial. Factor McCaskey and Nurse Lineboro shall accompany the body and explain to the governor and officials how things stood betwixt the three of them." He looked toward the man in irons, head still bent as if he was uncertain of his fate. "Leave the African to me. With keys."

Nary a murmur of dissent. One of Laurent's indentures came forward with the keys as others readied the shallop. Laurent's body was bound in a sheet from the warehouse. His sword and hat had been swallowed by the river.

Xander stood, breathing easier, till the shallop departed. As he took a step toward the waiting wagons with their load of hogsheads, his whirling head overtook him. He collapsed like a felled tree atop sandy soil.

46

Selah looked about the dining room table in the late September twilight. Her heart was so full she could barely speak. A husband on the mend. A child found. A brother and mother near at hand. Only one place remained empty at table, but Widow Brodie had set it just the same. Oceanus would come home in time, Lord willing.

A fortnight had passed since the duel, when Xander had returned to Rose-n-Vale in a wagon bed, frightening them all out of their senses. Selah looked to him now, hale and hearty and home from a day's trip to James Towne. And bringing news more fair than ill, she hoped.

"You look no worse for wear despite your journey." Candace smiled at her son-in-law as he carved a roast goose brimming with juices. "I suppose I should let you finish your supper before pestering you with questions."

Xander gave a mock glower as he finished carving.

Widow Brodie harrumphed, her gout making her testy. "Perhaps you can eat with haste."

To his left, Watseka smiled at him sweetly, her voice a

395

whisper. "Bring sweets?" She'd not forgotten that Ustis once filled her pockets.

He winked. "The shallop nearly sank from the surfeit."

She giggled, taking a bite of meat with a fork and eyeing Widow Brodie, who'd nearly given up reminding her to use utensils. Shay began passing dishes and reported on the fieldwork, the remaining barn to be rebuilt, and how Ruby and Jett had treed a bear cub near the mill.

Selah listened and savored her meal, thinking of her own busy hours stripping the geese of their feathers for quills and coverlets, then picking bayberries alongshore with Watseka ahead of candle dipping. But her every thought while at her tasks had been of Xander and how he fared in James Towne.

Once Izella served dessert, the barrage began. Xander pushed back his plate and opted for a pipe instead, giving his serving to Shay.

"You're no doubt wondering about McCaskey and Nurse Lineboro." He drew on his lit pipe for a few seconds, leaving them on tenterhooks. "They remain in gaol on charges of thieving and whatnot. The governor's council will decide their fate."

"What of the African?" Shay asked the question closest to Selah's heart. "Can he stay on here? He's a fine hand alongside your bound men."

"He's to remain at Rose-n-Vale, though I'll not enslave but indenture him."

"Praise be," Selah breathed, for that had been her very prayer.

"And Helion Laurent?" Widow Brodie remained the most vocal in her condemnation of the man and his misdeeds. "I suppose the miscreant's been given a proper burial."

"His casketed body is on a ship bound for France."

"Ah, his homeland. 'It is joy to the just to do judgment: but destruction shall be to the workers of iniquity,'" she quoted with no small satisfaction. "I suppose all Virginia is aflame with talk of his demise, though such tragedies are almost commonplace."

Selah didn't miss the shadow that settled over Xander's countenance. He'd told her of the duel in detail. How Laurent refused to yield at the last and live. But would her husband ever escape the harrowing memory? His sword he'd since hidden away.

"Let us talk of more pleasant matters," Selah said, summoning a smile. "A letter came from Cecily this very day—"

"Your tobacco bride?" Widow Brodie interrupted. "Goodwife Wentz?"

"The very same. She's expecting a child next spring and has asked we be godparents—"

A shout beyond the windows stopped Selah midsentence. All turned toward the sound. It rang out again, clear and joyous.

"Wingapo!"

Mouth open in wonder, Watseka jumped up from her chair. Her expectant gaze swung to Xander, who merely said, "Your kinsman comes."

Kinsman? Did he mean Meihtawk?

They all got up with a great clatter, Watseka leading as they made their way to the riverfront door and portico. Though only a scarlet ribbon of the brilliant sunset remained, Occanus's silhouette was unmistakable, Meihtawk by his side. Even in the gathering shadows, the new confidence and strength Oceanus exuded could not be overlooked. He was changed but still the beloved son they had so missed.

With a little cry, Watseka rushed toward them with such gladness that tears came to Selah's eyes. Xander soon stood beside Selah, his arm warm about her waist. Together they observed the long-awaited reunion, too overcome to speak.

Truly, joy cometh in the morning.

And the evening too.

Keep Reading for a Sneak Peek
of Another Captivating Novel by
LAURA FRANTZ!

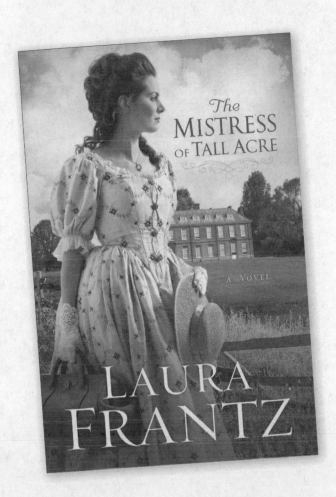

1

We mutually pledge to each other our Lives, our Fortunes, and our Sacred honor.

The Declaration of Independence

On this day, 8 August, 1778, a child was safely delivered . . .

Nay, not safely. Anything but safely.

. . . to Anne Howard Ogilvy and Seamus Michael Ogilvy of Tall Acre, Roan County, Virginia.

Dropping his quill pen, Seamus ran callused hands through hair bereft of a queue ribbon and watched a stray droplet of ink soak into the scarred desktop. Steadying his breathing, he picked up the pen and pressed on as if time was against him.

The infant's name is . . .

The heavy scratch of the nib against the family Bible's fragile page was halted by a knock on his study door. A servant to tell him he could finally see his firstborn? Or that his wife was dead? Or the both of them?

He called out with a shaky voice, but it was Doctor Spurlock who appeared, shutting the door soundly behind him. "A word with you, General Ogilvy, if I may." At Seamus's taut expression, Spurlock gave him a slight smile. "At ease, man, at ease. I'm not the undertaker."

Pulling himself to his feet, Seamus came out from behind the desk. "A word and a glass of Madeira are in order, at least." He went to a near cabinet and filled two crystal goblets as a newborn's wail rent the summer stillness, sharp and sweet as birdsong.

"'Tis about Anne," Spurlock said, a careful note to his tone.

Seamus passed him a glass. The doctor looked haggard after the lengthy ordeal, silver hair standing on end, spectacles askew, to say nothing of his waistcoat. Seamus was sure he looked equally unfit, having spent the night in his study.

"I don't need to tell you what a trial this birth has been. You've nearly worn a trail in the floor with your pacing." Spurlock regarded him with bleary, apologetic eyes. "Your wife is very weak. The baby, being so large, took a toll. Anne is a very narrow woman and continues to bleed heavily."

Blood. Wounds. Life and death. Seamus was used to such things. These were the staples of a soldier's life. Childbirth was, in a very real sense, battle. "I trust she'll recover in time."

Spurlock frowned. "Mistress Menzies, the midwife, nearly lost her at one point. If not for her presence of mind and the use of my forceps, we'd be having a very different conversation." He removed his spectacles and began cleaning them with a handkerchief. "On a brighter note, your wife's sister is coming from Williamsburg to help care for her, though I do worry about you returning to duty so soon."

"Orders," Seamus said through a stitch of guilt. "General Washington wants me at reveille come morning." As it was, he'd have to ride all night to reach camp by the appointed time.

"I speak not only out of concern for your wife but for you, General. I can tell from looking at you that your own health has been compromised."

Seamus squared his shoulders. "A malaise of war, little more."

"Spoken like a true soldier." Spurlock fixed his gaze on an open window. "Very well, I'll talk plain and fast. Your wife faces a long recovery. She's always been a bit fragile, a true gentlewoman. And though it will be hard for you to hear, I'm duty bound to tell you her very life will be in danger if there's a second birth. Mistress Menzies concurs."

A second birth—and she'd barely withstood the first. The words spun round Seamus's head but made no sense. Remembering his Madeira, he took a sip, listening as the doctor explained feminine things he didn't know. Didn't want to know. Things that made him itch under his uniform collar with a heat that had nothing to do with the humid Virginia afternoon.

"Of course, husbands have certain needs, certain rights, if you will . . ." The doctor's words were becoming more labored, nearly lost as the babe's cries reached a crescendo upstairs.

"Say no more," Seamus replied. Spurlock's warning was clear as a midsummer day. All marital intimacy was at an end. "As it stands, I'll be away for the duration of the war." His outward calm belied the storm breaking inside him. "I won't—I mean, there won't be occasion to—" He stared at his boots. "I understand."

Spurlock nodded and downed the rest of his Madeira. "I knew you'd take it like the officer and gentleman you are. Now, if you're ready, your wife would like to present you with your firstborn."

Firstborn. Final born. And a robust daughter at that.

The bedchamber seemed strange since Seamus had been away so long. Stepping inside the elegant green and gilt room brought about unwanted, ill-timed memories—a crush of passionate encounters beginning on their wedding night. It was the eve of the war when he'd wed the belle of Williamsburg, three years later when their daughter was conceived on a hasty visit. He hardly remembered either. War had driven such sentimental things from his head, replacing them with the stench of smoke and powder instead.

To reorient himself, he latched onto the open corner cupboard where medicines were kept, the two wing chairs and tea table before the cold hearth. His gaze finally settled on the bed dressed with crewel embroidery.

"Seamus." Anne lay back on the bank of downy pillows, looking exhausted but triumphant. "Come meet your new daughter."

Spurs scraped the heart-pine floor before he stepped onto a lush rug and took a seat on the edge of the four-poster bed as carefully as he could. In light of the doctor's unwelcome words, the ever-delicate Anne seemed made of spun glass. If she was broken, he was to blame, at sixteen stone and over six feet.

As she settled the newborn in his arms, the catch in his throat nearly stole all speech. One tiny hand peeked from the blanket, the plump face red and round as an orchard apple. He swallowed hard. "She's . . . beautiful."

Something wistful kindled in Anne's eyes. "You were hoping for a boy, though you never said so."

He gave a slight, dismissive shrug. "Soldiers always want sons."

"There'll be some, Lord willing. As soon as I'm well again . . ."

Her guileless words seared his heart. Spurlock hadn't told her then, but had left it up to him. Well, he wouldn't do it now. Let their dream of a large family be left intact a little longer.

Her lovely face turned entreating. "What shall we call her?"

The pride and expectancy in her eyes brought a wave of shame. He wouldn't confess he'd only entertained male names and had given little thought to a girl. Even his men had wagered on a boy, placing bold bets about the campfire till he'd ridden home to settle the matter himself.

"A name . . ." Lowering his head, he nuzzled the baby's ear, her downy neck and fuzz of dark hair. The decision came quick. He was used to thinking on his feet. As Washington's newly appointed major general, he could do little else. "Why not Lilias Catherine?"

"After my mother and yours?" Surprise shone in Anne's eyes. "Of course. 'Tis perfect."

He hesitated, looking into his daughter's face as if seeking answers. She seemed too little to merit such an onerous name. "We'll call her Lily Cate."

Nodding, Anne sank back on the pillows, her face so pale he could see the path of blue veins beneath. "I'm relieved. I didn't want you riding away without knowing."

He smiled. "Let me take her till you've slept for a few hours. Doctor Spurlock said she won't be hungry yet, and—" He took a breath, fighting the lurch of leaving. "I don't know when I'll be back." The casual phrasing was more lie. He didn't know *if* he'd be back.

Her hazel eyes held his. "How is it on the field?"

The question wrenched him. She rarely asked. Their brief times together were too precious to be squandered on melancholy things.

"'Tis a strange war. We drill. We wait. We fight and fall back." He wouldn't tell her the biggest battle of his life was imminent, or that American forces were weak—deprived and diseased—and no match for Clinton's redcoats. Leaning forward, careful of the warm weight in his arms, he kissed her gently on the cheek. "I'll go below and introduce Miss Lily Cate to the household."

Yawning, eyes already half closed, Anne gave a last, lingering look at the baby. Down the wide, curving stair he went to a staff on tenterhooks since dawn. The birth had been—what had Spurlock said?—brutal. His people deserved a look, at least. The midwife was in the foyer preparing to leave, her daughter with her.

"Mistress Menzies, I'll settle up with you before you go." He glanced from her to her daughter, both of them looking far less disheveled than the doctor.

"There's no fee, General, not for a hero of the Revolution." Pulling on her gloves, Mistress Menzies smiled in her genteel, unruffled way, reminding him that she was no ordinary midwife.

"I have you to thank for calling in Spurlock when the situation became . . . untenable," he told her.

"You can thank my daughter for that, General. She is fleet of foot and a midwife in the making."

He took in Sophie Menzies in a glance. Dark. Plain. Clad in a fine crimson cape like her mother's.

"Then I thank you too, Miss Menzies," he said.

She smiled up at him, blue gaze fastening on the baby in his arms. "Have you named her, General Ogilvy?"

"Aye, she's to be called Lily Cate."

The pleasure in her expression seemed confirmation. "Lovely and memorable," she said with her mother's poise and a hint of her father's Scots burr. "I bid you and your wee daughter good day."

They withdrew out the front door while he went out the back, which was flung open to the river and leading to Tall Acre's dependencies. At his appearance, the steamy kitchen at the end of a shaded colonnade came to a standstill.

"Why, General Ogilvy, looks like you mustered up a fine baby." Ruby, his longtime cook, hastily left the hearth as the other servants looked on. She leaned near, and one ebony finger caressed a petal-soft cheek. "She's got your blue eyes and black hair, but I see the mistress in her pert nose and mouth."

The maids and housekeeper gathered round next on the rear veranda, cooing and sighing like the dovecote's doves. Next he went to the stables, a fatherly pride swelling his chest. By the time he returned to his study, his daughter had slept through a brief meeting with his estate manager and a first look at a prize foal. Completely smitten, he crossed to a wing chair in his study, reluctant to let her go.

"You're only a few hours old and already you've worked your way into my heart." His voice was a ragged whisper. "But there are some things you need to know. I don't want to leave you. I'm willing to die for you . . . and if I don't come back, I want you to forgive me."

The choked words staunched none of the pain. His daughter opened wide indigo eyes and stared up at him, as if she understood every syllable. He pressed his damp, unshaven cheek to hers, savoring the feathering of her warm breath on his face. Her flawlessness turned him inside out.

"Till we meet again, Lily Cate Ogilvy of Tall Acre. Never forget your loving father's words."

Author Note

Readers often ask if I have a favorite book of the ones I've written. This is one of them. Though this story required more research than other novels, I've enjoyed the journey so much and have learned a great deal along the way. I even cried when I wrote "The End," something I don't always do.

From childhood I've been enthralled with Pocahontas's life and legend. But the Pocahontas I discovered while researching this novel was not the one taught to me in school. The most helpful sources came from Pocahontas's own people. Their unique perspective, oral tradition, and written history about her ring true and make her even more remarkable. I've attempted in a small way to honor her memory here.

John Rolfe's romantic letter about Pocahontas prior to their marriage is especially moving, and so I have included it in the novel:

> It is she to whom my heart and best thoughts are and have been a long time so entangled, and enthralled in so intricate a labyrinth that I could not unwind myself thereout.

Alexander Renick's character was inspired by John Rolfe, just as Mattachanna was inspired by Pocahontas herself.

When I was planning this novel, the NPS Historic Jamestowne website and Encyclopedia Virginia were of particular help to me in creating characters like the Hopewells. They were inspired by Captain William Peirce, his wife Joan, and their daughter, who married John Rolfe, the widower of Pocahontas. Sadly, John Rolfe disappears from the historical record around 1622, which makes me even more thankful to write fiction that offers hope and happily ever afters.

Historical purists will note that tobacco brides came to Virginia's shores earlier than the date of the novel. For the story's sake I chose 1634, as the colony was well past the starving time of earlier years and proved solid ground for the story to unfold. But it was still a highly volatile, dangerous period until the more settled eighteenth century. Place names like Mount Malady have been resurrected beyond their time in history to help in the telling of the story.

I had a great deal of fun with Widow Brodie's Old World insults and was only too happy to return to my love of etymology and discover that the phrase "do or die" originated in the fifteenth century, if not earlier.

The last time I visited Jamestown on a chilly spring day, few were there. It is a moving, beautiful place in any season and feels like hallowed historical ground. We'll never know all that happened during those early years, but one of the joys of historical fiction is breathing new life into people and events so that history and our American heritage are not forgotten.

Acknowledgments

Huzzah to Revell—my publishing home for twelve novels—for supporting my stepping back a century to write this book. They are exemplary in their commitment to bringing readers edifying fiction and nonfiction. It's an ongoing honor to carry their imprint.

And to my agent, Janet Grant, for always having a vision of what a story can be and cheering me on from start to finish. You make me a better wordsmith. Thank you.

None of this would be possible without readers, not fans but friends. So many of you have enriched my life, provided ongoing inspiration for my writing, and supported my books in countless ways. You are one of God's best gifts.

To those new to my novels or who want to stay connected, I'd love to send you my seasonal, free e-newsletter. To sign up, just visit my website: www.laurafrantz.net. I hope you'll visit my social media accounts on Instagram, Facebook, and Pinterest, where I post often about my novels and historical interests. Staying connected is a joy to me and I hope to you too.

I look forward to our next historical adventure!

Laura Frantz is a Christy Award winner and the ECPA best-selling author of twelve historical novels, including *The Frontiersman's Daughter*, *Courting Morrow Little*, *The Colonel's Lady*, and the Christy Award–winning *The Lacemaker*. When not reading and writing, she loves to garden, take long walks, listen to music, and travel. She is the proud mom of an American soldier and a career firefighter. When not at home in Kentucky, she and her husband live in Washington State. Learn more at www.laurafrantz.net.

THEIR STATIONS COULD NOT HAVE BEEN **MORE DIFFERENT** ...

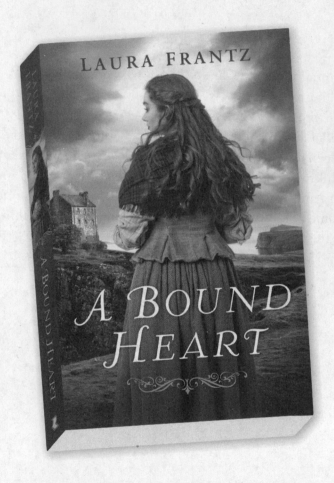

When a tragedy forces both a Scottish laird and a simple lass to colonial Virginia as indentured servants, can a love thwarted by tradition come to life in a new land?

Revell
a division of Baker Publishing Group
www.RevellBooks.com

Available wherever books and ebooks are sold.

IT IS THE EVE OF A NEW AGE
OF FREEDOM IN THE COLONIES.
BUT CAN A PROPER ENGLISH LADY DARE
HOPE FOR HER OWN INDEPENDENCE?

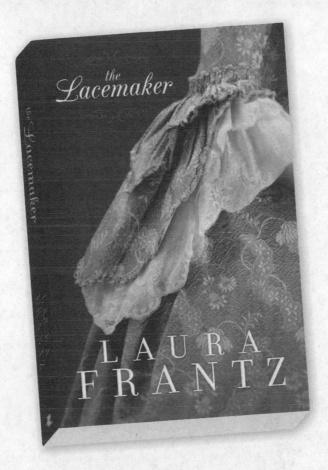

On the eve of her wedding, Lady Elisabeth Lawson's world is shattered
as surely as the fine glass windows of her colonial Williamsburg
home. In a town seething with Patriots ready for rebellion, her
protection comes from an unlikely source—if she could only protect
her heart.

Я Revell
a division of Baker Publishing Group
www.RevellBooks.com

Available wherever books and ebooks are sold.

MEET

LAURA FRANTZ

Visit LauraFrantz.net to read
Laura's blog and learn about her books!

f enter to win contests and learn about what
Laura is working on now

t tweet with Laura

P see what inspired the characters and stories